"What!" [...] own now. "Why [...]

"Hush, w[...] we don't want your father to hear how you're treating your guest, now do we?"

"Guest? You're no guest of mine."

Ty bit back a smile at her indignant tone. "I beg to differ. Your father and stepmother have invited me to join them for dinner. And since you're part of this household, that makes me *your* guest as well."

When Sassy made no reply, but merely kept her piercing lavender stare trained on him, Ty inched closer. "Listen, I'll make a deal with you. I'll accept your apology, if you give me something first."

He stopped only a hairsbreadth away. The scent of his shaving soap was stronger now, and she could feel the heat radiating from his body. In spite of her best efforts, she couldn't stop the trembling in her limbs, nor the frantic pounding of her heart from the overwhelming effect of his nearness. In a breathless whisper she said, "What do you want?"

"A kiss, Sassy. I want a kiss," he murmured. When she didn't move, he slowly lowered his head to her stunned face and grazed her lips with his.

A tingle of indescribable pleasure skittered up her spine. Carefully, he settled his mouth on hers, before pulling her into his arms. As he deepened the kiss, he tightened his embrace, holding her firmly against his muscular chest. His mouth teased and tantalized like nothing she had ever experienced.

WILD TEXAS BLOSSOM

ARLENE HOLLIDAY

ZEBRA BOOKS
KENSINGTON PUBLISHING CORP.

Wild Texas Blossom is dedicated to
my friend, my lover, my husband.
To Vern with all my love.

ZEBRA BOOKS are published by

Kensington Publishing Corp.
475 Park Avenue South
New York, NY 10016

First Printing: February, 1994

Printed in the United States of America

One

Ty Beaumont stilled his hand on the mare's neck.

"Aw, hell!" There was no mistaking the sound of a shell being racked into a rifle's chamber.

Having the business end of a gun trained on his back by an unknown adversary was not a familiar situation. Ty didn't like the feeling. He heaved an exasperated sigh, wishing he could give himself a good, swift kick for letting his normally sharp senses blow away with the stiff Texas breeze.

"Move away from my horse, mister. And keep your hands where I can see 'em, lessen you've got a real hankering to become a gelding."

Damn, a woman! He drew a deep, calming breath, an old saying popping into his head—something about an angry woman with a gun being as dangerous as standing bare-assed in a nest of rattlers. He might have smiled, if those words weren't such an apt comparison to his current predicament.

Moving slowly, Ty stepped away from the horse. "Take it easy, ma'am." He kept his voice calm, while gradually turning around. "I wasn't—" The words died in his throat when he saw the woman standing across the clearing.

5

As if he'd been kicked in the chest, his lungs struggled to fill with air. Although her clothes and posture were those of a man, the face and hair belonged to a female. Unless he missed his guess, a damn beautiful one.

As the young woman moved closer, the only sounds breaking the strained silence were the ruffling of the cottonwood trees, the light crunch of her boots on the ground, and the blood pounding in Ty's ears.

Rooted to the sandy earth, his gaze moved over the woman now standing no more than six feet away. Black as jet, her hair cascaded down her back in thick, shiny waves. Wisps of unruly curls framed an oval face. A dark neckerchief surrounded her slim neck, the ends brushing the front of her bibbed shirt. Although loose-fitting, the shirt didn't entirely conceal a hint of full bosom beneath the soft fabric. Skintight pants cinched in at a tiny waist did nothing to hide the flare of feminine hips or shapely thighs. Well-worn boots with large rowel spurs completed her attire.

In spite of his accurate prediction of her beauty, her eyes were like none he'd ever seen, holding him helplessly transfixed. Fringed with silky black lashes, they were the exact lavender blue of wild bluebonnets. Unfortunately, those beautiful eyes blazed with fire, shooting lavender flames in his direction. He could actually feel the heat of her scorching gaze.

While the man rudely looked her over from head to toe, she studied him as thoroughly. The color of his hair caught her attention—a combination of every shade of blond, some strands nearly silver, others the color of burnished gold—and caused her fingers to twitch on the rifle, itching to tangle themselves in the luxuriant locks grazing the collar of his shirt. With an extreme effort of will, she regained control of her traitorous hands and forced herself to look at his face. In contrast to his fair hair, the man's eyes were a deep chocolate brown, and set in ruggedly handsome features. *He sure is easy on the eyes.*

Normally unaffected by a man's looks, her admission came as a surprise and jerked her mind back to the reason she held a loaded Winchester pointed at him. Damn good thing she'd given up looking for the coyote that had been bothering their stock. If she hadn't returned to the creek when she had, he might have gotten clean away. Determined to finish her visual examination, she noted the breadth of his shoulders, his muscular chest, and narrow waist. Her gaze dropped lower, lingering on the generous bulge beneath the fly of his tight denim pants.

Realizing, too late, she was staring at *that* part of his anatomy, she commanded herself to get this over with. After glancing at his powerful-looking thighs and dusty boots, she lifted her head and met his gaze. One golden eyebrow arched knowingly, and his full lips curved into a smug smile. Mortified that he knew what she'd been staring at, she felt the heat of a blush warm her cheeks.

When he gave her a bold wink, her eyes widened with shock, and her flush deepened. Although she longed to scold him for his impudence, she found her usually sharp tongue stuck to the roof of her mouth. Then she remembered she'd caught him trying to steal her horse, and her anger flared back to life.

"Take off the gun belt," she managed to croak. "And toss it over here."

With the deadly Winchester pointed at his chest, Ty realized he had only one option. He carefully released the buckle, then eased the gun belt from his hips. Giving it a toss, it landed with a soft thump on the ground near her feet.

Easing the hammer back with her thumb, she uncocked the carbine. Never taking her gaze off him, she bent over to retrieve his side arm. In growing fascination, Ty watched the beguiling creature drape his gun belt over her shoulder, then pull a loop of rope off the waistband of her figure-hugging pants.

"Put your hands behind you," she ordered.

He fought back the urge to smile. There was no way she could tie his hands while holding the Winchester and balancing the weight of his gun belt on her shoulder. Rather than trying to wrestle the carbine away from her and risk having the gun discharge, he decided, for now, he'd play along.

When the man's hands were behind his back, she slowly circled him. Lowering the Winchester to the ground, butt first, she propped it against her left leg. She shifted the man's gun belt to a more comfortable position on her shoulder, then grasped one of his hands and slipped a loop of rope around his wrist.

He winced when she gave the rope a yank to snug it tight. "Hey, take it easy," he groused.

The man's husky whisper poured over her like warm honey, making her knees quiver. Wondering again at her unusual reaction to a man, she finished tying a knot and gave the rope another jerk.

Realizing the game had gone on long enough, Ty decided he'd better start talking. "So what's your name?" He cringed at the stupidity of the question. It didn't much matter what name she went by. Still, for some reason, he wanted to know.

She moved around in front of him, the carbine back in her hands. This time she aimed the Winchester at the ground between his boots. Ty resisted the strong instinct to move. It would be a simple matter of lifting the carbine's barrel to carry out her earlier threat. Her voice shook him out of his uneasy musing.

"I'm Sassy Mahoney. This is Mahoney land. And that," she nodded toward the mare, "is a Mahoney horse, the one you were trying to steal."

He gave a short bark of laughter. "You're not serious?" When the carbine shifted upward a few inches, his amusement fled. "Look, my name is Ty Beaumont, and I wasn't—"

"I know what I saw, Mr. Beaumont," she interrupted, hoping the intense pleasure she felt saying his name couldn't be detected in her voice. "Save your words for my father."

"Your father?" Squinting his eyes to glare at her, Ty's temper, so volatile these days, started to climb. "I think your little game has gone on long enough. If you'll untie me, I can explain."

She pointedly ignored him and moved to where her horse stood contentedly cropping grass. Keeping an eye on her prisoner, she pulled his gun belt from her shoulder and draped it over the horse's withers. "Why don't you just shut your yap and start walking in that direction?" She pointed to the south with the Winchester.

Ty's face burned with his growing anger; a muscle jumped in his cheek. *Damn! The little hellion isn't going to listen.* He tamped down any further argument, sighed with resignation, then turned, and started walking. He could only hope her father was more reasonable than the man's feisty-as-all-hell daughter.

Ty had taken two steps when he swung back around to his captor. "What about my horse?" He nodded toward a gray Appaloosa ground-tethered across the clearing.

Sassy never took her gaze off the no-account horse thief. "I'll bring your horse. You just start walking."

His jaw clenched in frustration, Ty nodded. Too bad she hadn't even glanced at Joker. She would have seen how the gelding put very little weight on his left foreleg. Cursing the stubborn woman under his breath, Ty did as he'd been told.

Following the creek bed that gave way to a well-worn path, Ty led the way. He stole an occasional glance over his shoulder. Each time she was a few feet behind him, astride her mare, the carbine still pointed at his back. At least she'd had the sense to retrieve his horse. But when he saw that the Appaloosa's limp had become more pronounced and the woman appeared not to notice, his frustration increased.

The sun nearly straight overhead, Ty wished he'd taken the time to drink from the creek. Anxious to approach the horse he'd come across, he'd forgotten about his thirst. Squinting up at the scorching sun, he wondered what else could go wrong. Ever since he'd started this trip, he'd been plagued with bad luck.

That morning it had gone from bad to worse. His horse went lame, and he'd been reduced to walking. Then he'd foolishly thought his luck had changed when he stopped at the clearing and found a horse he could borrow. *Yeah,* he snorted silently, *except it's Sassy Mahoney's horse!* It would be his misfortune to come across a horse with such a hardheaded owner. He couldn't afford another delay, but the fiery-tempered woman on the other end of the Winchester had a different idea in mind. Who knew what went on in Sassy Mahoney's beautiful head.

Sassy. He liked the sound of it, and what an appropriate name for such a spitfire of a woman. As his smoldering anger began to cool, his lips curved into a smile. *I wonder if her passion is as hot as her temper.* Catching

10

him off guard, his body hardened in response to such a stimulating thought.

The speed and intensity of his physical reaction to a woman he'd just met baffled him. Deciding his time would be better spent thinking about what to say in his defense, Ty forced his thoughts back to the present. While daydreaming about Sassy might be undeniably enjoyable, it wouldn't get him out of the latest mess he found himself in.

His musings ended when they crested a small knoll, and the spread of what he assumed was the Mahoney ranch stretched out before him. As he moved down the hill, he noted the number and well-kept condition of the outbuildings, the numerous corrals, and finally the ranch house. Built to resemble a Mexican hacienda, the large stone structure surrounded a courtyard visible through the open gate. He couldn't help being impressed.

As he started toward the house, a woman, heading for the largest of the barns, stopped and turned toward him. She pushed a strand of dark chestnut hair off her face, then used her hand to shield her eyes from the sun. She stood about Sassy's height, but her figure was somewhat fuller. When she lowered her hand, Ty studied her more closely. Her skin was smooth, though its golden hue said she spent time in the sun. Tiny lines radiated from the corners of her gray eyes, and deep smile lines bracketed her mouth. He guessed her to be in her mid-forties.

Quickly Sheena Mahoney took in the scene before her. She thought she'd seen all of her stepdaughter's antics, but this was a new one. Sassy was marching a stranger toward her at gunpoint! Sheena studied the man for a moment, noting his broad shoulders, narrow hips, and easy, graceful strides, then shifted her gaze to Sassy.

Based on the fierce glint in her stepdaughter's eyes and the stubborn tilt of her chin, Sassy was in a high temper.

When the man stopped a few feet from her, Sheena eyed him silently for several seconds, then said, "Good afternoon. I'm Sheena Mahoney." Noticing the rope dangling behind the man's back, she added, "It appears my stepdaughter has you at a disadvantage, or I'd offer my hand."

"Sheena!" Sassy snapped, throwing her right leg over the saddle horn and sliding to the ground in one easy motion. "He's a horse thief. I brought him here to see justice done, not for some fool social call."

"Horse thief?" Sheena looked sharply at Sassy.

"I'm not a horse thief, Mrs. Mahoney," Ty said. "As your stepdaughter so obviously believes."

"I caught him trying to steal Blarney," Sassy said through gritted teeth.

"I wasn't trying to steal your damn horse."

Sheena stepped between them, before the conversation turned into more than a shouting match. All too familiar with her stepdaughter's habit of leaping before looking, she said, "I think the man deserves a chance to tell his side of the story." She gave Ty a faint smile, then turned an accusing gaze on Sassy. "Something I'm sure you've neglected to let him do." The flush staining the younger woman's cheeks gave Sheena her answer.

Before Sassy recovered enough to speak, her attention was drawn to the barn behind her. Charlie Two Feathers, a mixed-blood Comanche who'd worked on the ranch for several years, led a yearling colt out into the yard. Holding the lead rope of a hackamore and murmuring softly, Charlie coaxed the colt forward.

Ty watched the dark-skinned man draw closer. Buckskins covered his whipcord lean frame, and a rawhide headband held his long hair away from his face. Ty's scowl changed to a grin.

Sassy's confusion at Ty's response to Charlie turned into shock, when the ranch hand looked up and saw the man beside her.

When his black gaze first swept over the stranger flanked by the Mahoney women, nothing registered on Charlie's face. Then a smile lit up his usually stoic features. "Ty Beaumont. What're you doing here?"

"Actually, Charlie," Ty said with a laugh, turning sideways to show his tied hands. "Miss Mahoney, here, is responsible for my presence."

Charlie shifted his piercing gaze to his employer's only daughter, and waited for her to explain.

"I caught him trying to steal Blarney," she retorted, turning to shove her carbine into the scabbard on her saddle with more force than necessary. Blarney tossed her head, sidling nervously at the rough treatment.

When Charlie laughed aloud at her statement, Sassy's earlier shock at Charlie and Ty knowing each other and her guilt at frightening her horse swiftly changed back to anger. "Dammit, Charlie, he *is* a horse thief," she spit out before she could stop the words.

"Sassy, that's enough." Sheena's tone warned Sassy not to repeat her outburst. "How do you know this man, Charlie?"

"We met a few years ago in Amarillo. Some men didn't like a *breed* in their saloon, so they hauled me into an alley to teach me a lesson. Ty stopped 'em before it was too late."

"Is that true, Mr. Beaumont?"

"Yes, ma'am. Those men scattered like chickens with a wolf in their pen, when I fired a warning shot over their heads."

13

Charlie took up the story. "I was in bad shape. Ty got me to a doctor, then stuck around 'til he was sure I'd pull through."

Sheena looked thoughtfully at the Dublin Star's ranch hand. Charlie had always been closemouthed about his past. Though just past twenty, there was something about his eyes . . . something that made him seem older. The story she'd just heard reminded her again of how much he must have suffered because of his mixed blood. She also knew Charlie was fiercely proud, and more importantly, he didn't lie.

"Sassy, untie Mr. Beaumont's hands. I'm sure we can trust him until we get to the bottom of this." She looked Ty squarely in the eyes. "We can trust you, can't we?"

Seeing the elder Mahoney had a bit of the fire Sassy had in such abundance, Ty quickly assured her he could be trusted. Having one woman catch him off guard was bad enough. He wasn't about to do anything to allow a second female to trounce on his already battered male pride.

"I thought so," Sheena replied, nodding with satisfaction. "Welcome to the Dublin Star, Mr. Beaumont. Come with me to the house where it's cooler, and we'll get this matter cleared up. It's hot enough out here to wither a fence post."

After watching her still simmering stepdaughter remove the rope from Ty's wrists, Sheena took several steps across the yard, then stopped, and turned around. "Sassy, see that Mr. Beaumont's horse gets some grain and a rubdown. Oh, and Charlie, be sure to check him over. He's pointing his left foreleg." She stared keenly at Sassy, gauging her reaction to the mention of the leg the Appaloosa had favored when crossing the yard.

Sassy's brows shot upward in surprise, followed by

another flush heating her face. An excellent horsewoman who dearly loved the beasts, Sassy was dismayed to learn she hadn't paid any attention to the horse she'd led from the creek. She should easily have noticed how the horse extended one foreleg, a sure sign of lameness. Yet, it never occurred to her that the man she'd found trying to steal Blarney might have had another reason for committing the crime, something other than simply wanting the blooded mare for his own herd. It pained her to realize her anger might have caused further injury to the animal. Rather than admit she'd made a mistake, she blurted, "That doesn't change anything. He was still trying to steal Blarney."

The emotions flickering across Sassy's face before she answered gave Sheena some insight to what was going on inside her stepdaughter's head. She added this bit of interesting information to the rest of her growing suspicion that Sassy was feeling more than anger towards Ty Beaumont. He had Sassy behaving in ways virtually unknown to the young woman. Sheena shoved such thoughts aside. "We'll see." Then, to the man rubbing his chafed wrists, she said, "Shall we, Mr. Beaumont?"

"If you don't mind, Mrs. Mahoney, I'd like to take care of Joker myself. I've put him through a lot lately."

"All right, I'll wait in the courtyard. Charlie, after the Appaloosa is settled, bring Mr. Beaumont to the house, please."

Charlie nodded, then said to Ty, "You bring the gray. I'll check his leg in the barn."

Ty moved to where Sassy stood clasping the reins to his horse. Holding out his hand, he met her defiant gaze with a cool stare. "May I?" he asked softly.

His words deepened the flush of her cheeks and set her heart to fluttering. Something hot and delicious ignited deep in her belly. Something she couldn't put a name to. It took every ounce of willpower she could summon not to pull her gaze from his hypnotic dark eyes. Her chin jutting forward with vexation, she held out the reins.

Ty took his time, moving his hand slowly, keeping his gaze riveted on her face. The instant his fingers brushed hers, he saw her eyes widen in response and the slight flaring of her delicate nostrils. His own heartbeat increased, sending a wild throbbing through his veins. Realizing he had somehow wandered into extremely dangerous waters and was on the verge of sinking, he snatched the reins from her hand, then turned away.

At that very moment he didn't know which was worse, being on the receiving end of Sassy's considerable temper, or having to tamp down the staggering desire he'd experienced ever since he crossed her path.

As he led his horse toward the barn behind Charlie and the young colt, Ty muttered, "Better watch your p's and q's, Beaumont. Or you'll be accused of being more than a horse thief."

Two

Sheena Mahoney waited until Charlie and Ty Beaumont disappeared inside the barn, then walked through the covered passageway. As she passed the kitchen, she called to the Dublin Star's housekeeper. "Rosa, find Mr. Mahoney, then bring some lemonade outside, please."

Sheena sat in the shade provided by the long, narrow porch, which ran along three sides of the inner courtyard. Deep in thought, she didn't hear her husband approach.

Rory Mahoney bent over to nuzzle his wife's neck. "What's going on?" he murmured next to her ear. "Rosa said you wanted to see me."

"It's Sassy," Sheena replied. As Rory stroked her cheek, she turned and brushed her lips over his knuckles. Glancing up at him, she studied the sun-darkened face, the crow's-feet at the corners of his green eyes, the black hair liberally sprinkled with gray. At fifty-one, he was still a handsome, virile man.

Rory took a seat next to her. "So what's that daughter of mine done this time?"

Sheena ignored his question and said, "I was just thinking about Tom Sanderson."

Rory's brows pulled together. "What made you think

17

of him? He hasn't been around here since—you know, I can't remember the last time he was on the Star."

Sheena smiled. "It was the Christmas we had the Sandersons over. After dinner Sassy and Tom took their horses out for a ride."

Rory chuckled. "I believe you're right. She brought him back hog-tied and draped over his saddle like a sack of grain."

"She sure did."

"What made her so angry that day, anyway? I can't recall."

"Actually, I don't think I ever told you the whole story. While they were out riding, Tom finally worked up the nerve to kiss Sassy. She might have put up with the kiss, but she didn't like being pawed." At Rory's quirked eyebrow, she explained, "When Tom leaned over to kiss her, his hand did a little exploring. Unfortunately for him, it was inside the shirtwaist of her dress."

"Why that randy young buck. If I'd known that, I'd have done more than hog-tie him."

Sheena laughed. "I see I was right in not telling you. Thinking back, it's a wonder Sassy didn't do more. She was furious when she told me what Tom had done." Sheena laughed again, recalling Tom's embarrassment while hanging over his horse's back. "Sassy brought him to the front of the house, then stomped off, leaving me with the task of untying the poor man."

She sighed heavily. "The worst part is, Sassy blamed the way she was dressed for Tom's behavior. That's why she refused to wear what she calls "those fool dresses" after that."

"As I recall, that's also when she refused to go back to school," Rory mused aloud. "She said the nuns at the academy weren't teaching her anything useful. Good thing the boys' new tutor didn't mind letting a willful girl wearing pants join his classes."

"True. At least Sassy got an education."

After a long silence, Rory said, "Listen, love, all this reminiscing is right nice. But I have work to do. What was it you wanted to see me about?"

"It's about the man Sassy brought to the ranch."

"Man? Did I miss something? I thought we just talked about Tom Sanderson."

Sheena turned to look at her husband, wanting to see his reaction to her next words. "No, the man isn't Tom Sanderson. I'm referring to the man Sassy brought in half an hour ago."

"Sassy? Bring a man to the ranch? Are you sure you haven't been out in the sun too long?"

Sheena chuckled. "No, I'm fine. Sassy really did bring a man to the ranch a little while ago."

Rory shook his head. "I'm still not sure we're talking about the same person. My daughter actually brought a man here?"

"Yes, only . . ." She paused, unsure how to tell him the rest. "Only, he didn't exactly come here willingly. Sassy made him walk at gunpoint, his hands tied behind his back."

Rory groaned. "Oh, sweet Jesus. Did he try something with her, too?"

"Not exactly. Sassy said this man tried to steal Blarney."

Rory straightened in his chair, his eyes blazing with fury. "A horse thief! Where's the son of a bitch?"

"Just stay put, Rory," Sheena said in a low voice, reaching over to grab his forearm when he started to get up. "He's in the horse barn. Charlie knows him, and I think Sassy may have jumped to conclusions again."

19

Slumping back in his chair, Rory turned his squinted gaze on the passageway leading to the yard. "We'll see. We'll just see."

Inside the large barn, Charlie showed Ty which stall to use, then took care of the colt. Ty removed Joker's saddle and bridle, then leaned over to check the leg the Appaloosa had been pointing.

"Were you trying to steal Blarney?" Charlie said, crouching down next to where Ty held Joker's left fore-leg.

Ty looked up, his gaze locking with Charlie's impassive, black one. "No. Joker pulled up lame this morning, and I planned to borrow the mare to find the closest ranch. Then Sassy showed up in the clearing."

Charlie grunted, then smiled. "Sassy's one fiery woman."

"I'll say," Ty grumbled, then moved aside so Charlie could examine Joker. "She dresses and acts more like a boy than a woman, though."

"It's not her fault." Charlie rubbed his hand down the Appaloosa's leg. "She was raised like a son."

"What do you mean, raised like a son?"

"Her mother died when Sassy was very young. Rory didn't know how to teach her to be a lady. So he raised her like another son."

"What about the stepmother?" Ty asked, watching Charlie test Joker's leg for injury.

"Sheena and Rory didn't marry until after Sassy was grown. By then she was too set in her ways to change much."

Ty remained silent while Charlie finished his exami-

20

nation. "The leg isn't serious," Charlie finally said. "Just a pulled tendon. He needs rest to heal."

"Yeah, he needs rest. Only what the hell am I supposed to do in the meantime?" Ty mumbled, standing up and giving Joker a pat on the neck.

"What'd you say?" Charlie asked, picking up a curry-comb and running it over Joker's coat.

"Nothing." Ty watched his horse's hide ripple with the movement of the comb. He had the sudden sensation of a similar feeling—only the cause was the caress of a hot-headed, lavender-eyed woman. Shaking off such thoughts, he said, "Well, I guess I'd best get up to the house, so I can get this straightened out. If Sassy has her way, they'll be throwing a rope over a tree branch. I hope her father has more patience."

Hanging the currycomb back on its peg, Charlie stroked Joker's nose, then moved out of the stall. "Rory Mahoney is a good man. He'll listen." After latching the stall door, he turned to Ty. "Come on. I'll take you to him."

Sheena watched the two men walk toward the house. She glanced at her husband. Rory sat stiffly erect in his chair, his gaze locked on the tall, blond man. She knew that look. Rory was sizing up the stranger, ready to draw the line of battle. She also knew that Rory was a fair man; he'd wait until he had all the information before making a judgment.

She turned her attention back to Ty. Observing the confident way he carried himself and the determination on his face, she knew that although her stepdaughter might have gotten the drop on this man once, Sassy wouldn't succeed a second time. Nor could she intimidate Ty

Beaumont. *Yes, indeed.* Sheena smiled to herself. *Sassy may have finally met her match.*

The afternoon was a real strain on Sassy's already frayed nerves. Time crawled by while she awaited the outcome of the meeting between her father, stepmother, and that blasted horse thief.

She hadn't even taken time to groom Blarney, a chore she enjoyed. Grooming her mare always relieved anything weighing on her mind—like the no-good varmint, Ty Beaumont. Instead, she'd turned the mare over to one of the ranch hands, so she wouldn't run the risk of seeing the man who caused her to feel a passel of new emotions.

She had spent the hours since cooped up in her room. After washing her face and changing into a clean shirt, she alternately paced and stared out the window. Deciding to put the time to good use, she picked up the lariat she was making. Five minutes later, she threw it aside in disgust. She'd have to unbraid the mess she'd made and start over. *There must be something I can concentrate on.* Looking around her room, she came up empty-handed.

Since she spent so little time in her bedroom—preferring to be outside with her brothers—the room was sparsely furnished. A bed with a trunk sitting at the foot, a dresser with a mirror on the wall above it, a nightstand, and a rocking chair were the only items in the room. The furniture was simple in style, which suited her fine.

The curtains and bedspread were another story. Sheena had decorated the room several years back, selecting a pale blue silk trimmed in off-white lace. If Sassy'd made the choice, she'd have picked something more serviceable, something plain as dirt—not this frilly, fussy stuff.

She didn't cotton to all the silly feminine geegaws. Still, she had to admit the softness of the silk was wonderful to touch. Staring outside, she idly rubbed the curtain between her fingers. *I wonder if a silk dress would feel this good brushing against my legs.* Shocked by her line of thinking, she jerked her hand away. *No need to wonder how a silk dress would feel. A gangly dolt like me ain't never gonna find out.*

Crossing the room, she sat down on the bed with a sigh. From beneath her pillow she withdrew a piece of satin ribbon. It was frayed and discolored, but Sassy didn't notice. The ribbon had belonged to her mother, worn in her hair the day she married Sassy's father. When she was feeling down, Sassy always found solace in holding the memento of the woman she barely remembered. Fingering the soft strip of satin, Sassy rose from the bed and moved to her dresser. She held the ribbon against her hair, and looked at her reflection in the mirror. "Papa says I look a lot like you, Mama," she whispered. "I wish I could have known you, then maybe I wouldn't be—" She halted the painful direction of her thoughts, and drew a deep, shaky breath. *What's done is done. I am what I am, and that's that.* Turning from the mirror, she tucked the ribbon back under her pillow and sat down in the rocking chair to wait.

The shadows had lengthened across her bedroom floor before she was summoned to her father's office. As she left her bedroom, her stomach rumbled loudly, reminding her dinner would soon be served.

Rory Mahoney told her both he and her stepmother were satisfied with Ty Beaumont's explanation. They were certain the man hadn't been trying to steal her horse.

When Sassy tried to protest, Rory quickly silenced her.

"I'm sure it must have looked like he was trying to steal Blarney, lass," he began softly, his Irish roots evident in his voice. "But he assured us he only planned to borrow your mare. He was heading toward San Antonio, when his horse pulled up lame. He started walking across what he knew was private land, hoping to find a way into town once he reached the closest ranch. He thought finding Blarney was a stroke of luck—until you stepped into the clearing and accused him of trying to steal her."

"You're awfully quick to take a stranger's word," Sassy said through a tight throat, "over your daughter's."

Rory's gaze roamed over the face of the stubborn nine-teen-year-old woman standing before him. Thinking again how much she looked like his first wife, his heart expanded with love. Sassy had the same shiny black hair as both he and her late mother, and her eyes had taken a bit of color from each of theirs—the result more lavender than the turquoise normally produced by mixing blue and green.

"I do believe you, Erin." Rory kept his voice firm yet tender.

Sassy cringed. Her father was the only one who used her given name, the only one who refused to honor her preference of the nickname she'd earned as a tot. When she'd talked back to one of the ranch hands, the man had laughed at her impudence and told her she was awful sassy for such a little mite. The name stuck. Since Rory had given his daughter the Gaelic name for the land of his birth, he persisted in calling her Erin.

"You thought he was stealing Blarney, and you reacted like anyone would have. But you know things aren't always as they appear. You heard Charlie's story of how Mr. Beaumont saved him from being beaten to death?"

At her nod, he said, "Well, there's something Charlie didn't mention. Ty Beaumont is a Texas Ranger."

"A Texas Ranger?" Sassy's eyes went wide with shock.

"Aye, lass. When Charlie brought him up to the house, he introduced him as Ranger Beaumont. I asked him about that, and he proved it by showing us his badge." He waited for his daughter to digest that bit of information, before adding, "I think you owe the man an apology, Erin."

Sassy rarely, if ever, gave up an argument, and doing so now was very difficult. She knew her father had the uncanny ability to quickly measure a man's worth and honesty. Apparently Ty Beaumont had passed muster. Being a Texas Ranger, plus Charlie's vouching for him, only added to his credibility. All serving to make her accusation appear less and less believable.

Knowing her father knew how hard it was for her to apologize, Sassy also realized he wouldn't have asked this of her unless he was certain it was the right action to take. Sassy slumped her shoulders in defeat, then nodded. "Okay, Papa, I'll apologize. But can I do it in private?" she whispered.

Rory saw the pleading in her eyes and pulled her into his arms for an understanding hug. He kissed her temple, then stepped back. "That's my lass. I knew I could count on you. I'll send Mr. Beaumont in here."

After her father left, Sassy stood staring out the office window into the purple beauty of the Texas evening. Through the opened window, she could hear one of the ranch hands singing to the horses as he settled them down for the night, and the soft rustle of the trees behind the house as a breath of wind swept over the Dublin Star.

As she waited, a strange feeling settled over her, a mixture of anticipation and uncertainty. Solving the mystery of her emotions proved even more unsettling. The source of those mixed-up feelings was the man she waited for.

A prickling along her neck told her she was no longer alone; Ty Beaumont was in the room. Dismayed to realize she was so far off kilter that she hadn't heard his entrance, she took a deep breath. Praying she would get through this meeting, she turned to face him.

"Jesus," Ty exclaimed beneath his breath. His gaze feasted on Sassy's glorious black hair, sparkling eyes, and slightly parted lips. A surge of desire flared inside him. It was a real test of wills to see which would win— his body or his mind. Finally, he managed to gain control of his wayward libido and forced his gaze to move away from her lush mouth.

Although she had changed into a clean shirt, she still wore the same indecent pants. In spite of her nonfeminine attire, Ty thought her strikingly beautiful. Even more appealing was her apparent lack of awareness of her beauty—not like other women he'd known who flaunted their good looks at every turn.

The tip of her tongue peeking out to moisten her lips pulled Ty's gaze upward. He bit back a groan. It took every ounce of his self-control not to grab her, taste her sweet mouth, and satisfy the hunger eating at his vitals. He closed his eyes, swallowed hard, and willed his feet to stay put.

Since their parting earlier when she'd stormed away in a snit, Ty had bathed and changed into a soft blue shirt and black pants that fit him like a second skin. Sassy's gaze hungrily appraised his still-damp hair, her nose twitching at the spicy scent of his shaving soap. She'd thought him breathtaking before, now he completely devastated her senses.

26

Again she felt drawn to him by his powerful male magnetism—a feeling she still couldn't name. With a wildly beating heart, her breathing quickened and a strange heat curled outward from the pit of her stomach. Unable to bear the unfamiliar sensations coursing through her body, she lowered her gaze. Nothing in her experience had made her feel this way. She trained her gaze on her feet, scuffing the toe of one boot on the floor in uncomfortable silence.

Remembering Ty was here for a reason, Sassy knew it was up to her to break the tense moment. She kept her gaze carefully averted from his penetrating dark eyes, then drew a deep, steadying breath. "I—" Her voice sounded more like a croak. Cheeks burning, she cleared her throat before trying again. "I want to apologize, Mr. Beaumont. My father tells me I accused you improperly, and I, uh . . . I'm sorry for the . . . uh . . . way I treated you."

When Ty didn't respond, Sassy forced herself to lift her head. Meeting his gaze, she tried to read his thoughts. She was unable to determine what went on behind those dark brown eyes.

His silence was like a match under the dry tinder of her temper.

"Well, do you accept my apology, or not?" She crossed her arms and tapped her toe impatiently on the plank floor.

In her agitation, she wasn't aware her arms had pushed her breasts up so far they threatened to pop the top button of her shirt. Ty noticed.

Desire again sizzled through his veins like liquid fire. He knew what he should do: the proper gentlemanly thing to do was accept her apology—though he suspected it was begrudgingly given—and get the hell out of the room. Yet, some perverse part of him made him tease her rapidly escalating ire.

The seconds ticked off as Sassy waited for his answer, her fury growing.

"No," he finally replied in a low voice.

"What!" she nearly screamed, her temper full-blown now. "Why you—"

"Hush, wildcat. We don't want your father to hear how you're treating your guest, now do we?"

"Guest? You're no damn guest of mine."

Ty bit back a smile at her indignant tone. "I beg to differ. Your father and stepmother have invited me to join them for dinner. And since you're part of this household, that makes me *your* guest as well."

When Sassy made no reply, but merely kept her piercing lavender stare trained on him, Ty inched closer. "Listen, I'll make a deal with you. I'll accept your apology, if you give me something first."

He stopped only a hairsbreadth away. The scent of his shaving soap was stronger now, and she could feel the heat radiating from his body. In spite of her best efforts, she couldn't stop the trembling in her limbs, nor the frantic pounding of her heart from the overwhelming effect of his nearness. In a breathless whisper, she said, "What do you want?"

"A kiss, Sassy. I want a kiss," he murmured. When she didn't move, he slowly lowered his head to her stunned face and grazed her lips with his.

A tingle of indescribable pleasure skittered up her spine. Carefully, he settled his mouth on hers before pulling her into his arms. As he deepened the kiss, he tightened his embrace, holding her firmly against his muscular chest. His mouth teased and tantalized like nothing she had ever experienced. Her head reeled dizzily. Not realizing what she was doing, she wrapped her arms around his neck and tangled her fingers in the thick silk of his hair.

Long before she was ready to stop this heady new experience, Ty pulled his lips from hers and stepped back. No longer supported by his embrace, she swayed drunkenly. His hands grasped her elbows to steady her.

In a voice made husky by his tightly reined passion, Ty whispered, "Apology accepted, Sassy." Releasing her, he spun on his heel and left the room, leaving a stunned Sassy in his wake.

Several long minutes passed before she could think, let alone move. When her senses returned, with them came her temper in all its scorching intensity.

"The nerve of that low-down snake," she muttered. Then she remembered her own response to his kiss. Her face burning with embarrassment, her anger slipped away.

After a few minutes passed, she realized she couldn't stay hidden in her father's office much longer. She was expected at the dinner table—Dinner, with Ty! She squeezed her eyes tightly closed for a second. *How can I face him again?* She took a deep breath and squared her shoulders with determination. *I'll just have to, that's all there is to it.*

Her composure somewhat restored, Sassy left her father's office. She crossed the courtyard and headed for the dining room, unable to shake the feeling she was heading to slaughter instead of dinner.

Three

Thanks to her stepmother, Sassy figured, she found herself sitting directly across the table from the man who made her feel a disturbing combination of emotions: embarrassment, guilt, and a third, foreign one she couldn't figure out.

Embarrassment was nothing new to Sassy, having suffered plenty of the degrading emotion four years earlier at the Ursuline Academy in San Antonio. A few months of the other girls constantly making her the butt of their jokes had convinced her she was the proverbial sow's ear. As for guilt, she hadn't felt more than a small twinge of it since she was ten years old and recklessly caused her horse to take a nasty fall.

Now, all in one afternoon, she'd experienced embarrassment, guilt, and, most confusing of all, that third unknown emotion.

Try as she might, she couldn't forget the kiss Ty had traded for her apology. After her first experience at kissing had ended on a sour note, she'd promised herself hell would freeze over before she'd want to try it again. She had the uneasy feeling she was heading toward reneging on that promise. Keeping her gaze carefully focused on her plate, she pushed the food around with her fork, trying to put a name to what Ty made her feel.

Finally, it hit her. The crazy swirling in her stomach, the ache deep in her belly, the wild thrumming of her heart, the inexplicable craving for some unknown end, had a name. Having been around her brothers and their friends when they'd discussed their physical relationships with their paramours, she'd heard their descriptions and comments about the sex act. When she put her brothers' talk and her symptoms together, the conclusion she drew made her want to retch. The name of her affliction was lust.

Giving the meat on her plate a particularly vicious stab, she cursed under her breath. She didn't want Ty Beaumont that way!

Did she?

Sassy's lack of appetite didn't go unnoticed. Sheena knew her stepdaughter usually ate with as much gusto as her brothers. She studied the dark head bowed over her untouched plate, and wondered what had caused Sassy's diminished hunger and high color. Since she didn't look ill, only one explanation made sense to Sheena: Ty Beaumont.

Looking over at her husband, Sheena met Rory's amused green eyes. His look told her he'd also noted Sassy's uncharacteristic behavior. When he lifted his shoulders in a small shrug, Sheena figured he hadn't guessed what ailed his daughter.

With an inaudible sigh, Sheena pushed thoughts of her headstrong stepdaughter aside and spoke to their guest. "Charlie tells us your horse's leg will heal with a few weeks' rest, Mr. Beaumont."

"Please, call me Ty. I'm glad the injury isn't more

31

serious. I watched Charlie work on Joker. He has a special touch with horses."

"Aye, that he does," Rory said. "It's his Comanche blood. Whether riding horses or stealing them, the Comanches are the best around."

Ty nodded in agreement. Raised in Comanche country, he knew firsthand how good they were with horses.

"Have you given any thought to where you'll be staying while Joker recovers?" Sheena asked, looking to her husband for approval. At Rory's nod, she continued, "We'd be pleased to have you stay on the Dublin Star. You can use our guest room."

When her stepmother's invitation registered, Sassy looked up from her contemplation of the congealed mess on her plate. *I don't want him around, constantly throwing my mistake in my face. Something I'm sure he'll do every chance he gets—and with a whole lot of enjoyment to boot!* She frowned. *But I don't want him to leave either.*

The last revelation caught Sassy by surprise. Never had she wanted a man around, unless there was a shooting or roping competition taking place. For some inexplicable reason, she felt an invisible pull toward Ty Beaumont. A pull that was stronger than her desire to be rid of him.

"That's a mighty kind offer, Mrs. Mahoney. I'm on an assignment, but I'd rather not go on without Joker."

Again Ty knew what he should do. He should vamoose out of there, even if it meant leaving his horse behind, before his whereabouts became known. On the other hand, the Dublin Star was a good distance from San Antonio, so he shouldn't draw any unwanted attention. Joker isn't the only one who needs a rest, he mused, surprised he was considering staying with the Mahoneys. *If I can borrow a horse to go into town, I guess there's no reason I can't stay.* His gaze shifted to Sassy. *Or maybe there is.*

Seeing the challenge flash in her lavender eyes, Ty made his decision. He turned to his hostess and said, "I'd be pleased to accept your hospitality, until Joker's fit to travel." His rapidly disintegrating conduct as a gentleman finally reasserted itself—or was it cowardice—and made him add, "But I'd be more at home in the bunkhouse." He stole another quick glance at Sassy. *At least in the bunkhouse, I'll be away from temptation.*

Catching the look Ty and Sassy exchanged, Sheena wondered if he wanted to stay in the bunkhouse to avoid staying under the same roof as her stepdaughter. She hid her amusement behind her napkin, as she dabbed at her mouth. "The bunkhouse it is then, but you must take your meals with us."

Realizing Sheena wasn't going to be swayed, Ty nodded his agreement, then changed the subject.

"I was wondering, Rory, about the bloodlines of your horses. I've never seen any like Blarney or the colt Charlie was working with earlier. Good-looking animals."

Rory smiled, pleased the man knew good horseflesh when he saw it. Always eager to talk about a subject dear to his heart, he said, "Both of those horses, plus most of the others on the ranch, are descendants of a pair of Connemaras I brought with me from Ireland almost thirty years ago. I started the Dublin Star by crossbreeding them with the wild mustangs here in Texas."

"Well, you've had some mighty fine results," Ty commented.

"Aye, we've got us some fine beasties here on the Star. You're welcome to ride one of our horses, while Joker heals. I don't mind telling you, that horse of yours

33

is one of the best looking Appaloosas I've seen. Don't see many with the gray-spotted blanket pattern."

Ty resisted the urge to sigh with relief, grateful Rory had spared him having to ask to use a horse. "Thanks, for both the offer of a horse and the compliment about Joker. He's the best horse I've ever owned. And yes, I reckon the pattern on his rump is a bit unusual in this part of the country."

The rest of the meal passed in a blur for Sassy, though she was keenly aware Ty Beaumont had captivated her family. She couldn't honestly fault them for accepting him; she felt a strong pull towards him as well. However, his ease with the Mahoney clan did surprise her. That was saying something, since her curious brothers constantly peppered him with questions between every mouthful of his meal.

While Ty maintained an outward appearance of complete absorption in answering the Mahoney brothers' inquisitions, a good portion of his mind lingered on the kiss he had unfairly demanded of Sassy in payment for accepting her apology.

Any other time, he would have readily accepted an apology from such a lovely young woman, even if she did dress like a man. For a reason he didn't completely understand, he hadn't been able to resist testing the waters of Sassy's volatile temper. Besides, once he stepped into her father's office and found her waiting for him, he couldn't think about anything except kissing those sweet lips.

Stealing another look at the woman filling his thoughts, Ty's pulse increased. Up close she was even more appealing than when he'd first seen her across the clearing at the creek. Her eyes were wide set and heavily lashed, her slender nose turned up slightly at the tip, and her mouth—ah, her mouth. Lips as sweet as a lump of brown sugar. His blood warmed from the tantalizing memory.

Another question directed at him pulled him from his musings. This one from Brodie who, at twenty-four, was the oldest of the Mahoney siblings.

Turning to the dark-haired young man, Ty met his curious blue gaze, then said, "I'm sorry, Brodie, what did you say?"

"Charlie said you're a Texas Ranger." He shoved a lock of wavy hair off his forehead. "Is that true?"

Ty hesitated before responding, "Yeah, it's true." *Well, technically it is. I still have my badge and papers identifying me as a Ranger.* He also knew that his superiors very likely no longer considered him a captain in their ranks, and wouldn't take kindly to his passing himself off as one. It pained him to tell a half-truth, as he'd had to do earlier when Rory asked him for his rebuttal to Sassy's charge of horse stealing. But dammit, for years he *had* been a Ranger, and a darn good one. Then two months ago his life had taken a very different turn. The Mahoneys wouldn't want him around if they knew the truth. He wouldn't be their dinner guest, if they knew he was on the run from the law.

"Did you know our brother, Sean? He was a Ranger." Lucas, the twenty-two-year-old middle son, joined in the conversation.

"No, can't say as I ever met him. You said he was a Ranger. What's he doing now?"

"He's . . ." Pain obvious in his turquoise eyes, Lucas glanced at his father, then said in a low voice, "He's dead."

Ty's throat tightened. The mention of a dead brother brought back the pain he thought he'd conquered long ago. He swallowed hard, wishing he could call back his thoughtless words. "I'm sorry. I had no idea."

"You couldn't have known, Ty. We lost Sean six years ago. He was killed trying to bring in a gang of cattle rustlers," Rory explained.

The room became unusually quiet, as painful memories of the family's loss flooded back. Only the clock ticking on the oak sideboard and the occasional clink of silverware broke the silence, until Rory shook himself out of his somber mood.

"So, tell us about your work, Ty."

"Yeah, tell us about all the outlaws you've caught." Trevor, youngest of the Mahoney boys, leaned forward in anticipation. The adventurous brother, he loved tales about anything having to do with danger. Even at twenty-one, he still liked spending an evening in the bunkhouse listening to the old-timers reminisce about cattle drives, shoot-outs, and fighting Indians.

Ty smiled at the young man's enthusiasm. All the Mahoney sons resembled their father—black hair, slight aquiline nose, square jaw, well muscled. Yet perhaps because Trevor had also inherited Rory's green eyes, Ty thought the youngest brother looked most like the Mahoney patriarch.

"Actually, Trevor, I do more investigating than catching outlaws." He paused, then with a twinkle in his eyes, he added, "There was this one time. I rounded up a gang of five bank robbers and hauled them off to jail." Certain he heard a snort of disbelief from Sassy's side of the table, he looked over at her bowed head, but couldn't be sure she'd made the sound.

When Ty said no more, Trevor prompted, "Sure would like to hear how you caught those desperadoes."

Ty chuckled. "Sure thing, Trevor, but some other time.

I don't want to bore everyone else—" He cast a pointed glance in Sassy's direction "—with the story of how I got the drop on those desperadoes. Fair enough?"

Trevor nodded, then smiled when Rosa entered the dining room carrying a large tray. When the housekeeper placed his dessert in front of him, Trevor whispered something in her ear, bringing an instant flush to the woman's round face. She gave him a playful swat, murmuring something about satisfying his sweet tooth, then served the others.

"I hope you'll forgive our curiosity," Sheena said after Rosa left the room. "It isn't often we have such an interesting guest at our table. Especially a Ranger like Sean." Although Sheena had never known the firstborn Mahoney son, she grieved with the rest of the family over his loss.

"There's nothing to forgive, Mrs. Mahoney. It's been awhile since I sat down to a family meal. I've really enjoyed it," Ty responded honestly.

"You're from a big family, then?" Rory asked.

"No, only one brother. My father was killed when I was a boy, and we lost my brother not long afterwards. So it's been just my mother and me." His voice was a harsh whisper when he added, "Although I haven't seen her much lately."

Lifting her head at the bitterness she detected in Ty's voice, Sassy thought she saw a flicker of pain in his dark eyes before he dropped his gaze. The strange, invisible pull, dragging her closer and closer, strengthened still more at his apparent misery. She wondered what could have caused that hurt. And what provoked the anger she sensed lurking just beneath his calm demeanor? She felt an overwhelming need to comfort him, to ease his suffering.

Questions about Ty's distress and her own reaction swirled in her mind. Why did she care what this man felt? More importantly, why did she feel the compulsion to become more than a passing acquaintance?

As her family finished dessert and lingered over another glass of sangria, Sassy surreptitiously watched their guest. Through the fan of her partially lowered lashes, she saw the easy smile Ty flashed her stepmother, the amusement dancing in his eyes at something one of her brothers said. A sudden pang of longing to be on the receiving end of those smiles and glances took her by surprise, tightening her throat as she took a sip of her drink.

Tears sprang to her eyes instantly. She fought to stop the intense pain brewing in her chest, holding her breath and pressing her lips together. It was no use.

A rush of air surged up her throat and burst through her lips, followed by a horrible choking sound and a deep rasping cough. When everyone looked in her direction, her ears burned with mortification. Before anyone else could react, Ty pushed his chair away from the table and started toward her.

"Is the wine punch too strong for ya, Sass?" Brodie asked, sending Lucas and Trevor a knowing look. His brothers responded with a hoot of laughter.

As he rounded the table, Ty caught the venomous stare Sassy shot her brothers above the hand she held clamped over her mouth. He wondered briefly what was behind Brodie's comment and his brothers' amusement, but he had more important things to think about—like their choking sister.

Using the palm of his hand, he gave her a firm whack between the shoulder blades, then another. Even touching her in a nonsexual way sent a stab of desire slicing through his body. He bent close to her flushed face and whispered in a husky voice, "Are you okay, Sassy? Can you breathe?"

Wishing she could blink her eyes and disappear, Sassy nodded, wiping furiously at her tearstained cheeks.

"Are you sure you're all right, lass?"

Swinging her blurry gaze to her father, Sassy managed to murmur, "I'm fine. I just swallowed down the wrong pipe, that's all."

Reluctant to leave Sassy's side, Ty slowly removed his hand form her back, then returned to his place at the table.

The look of concern on his face when he glanced over at her set Sassy's pulse to thumping wildly. When he offered her a small smile, she thought her heart would leap from her chest. She smiled weakly in reply. Then, feeling an unfamiliar shyness, she could not hold the stare of the intriguing man sitting across from her.

As the conversation resumed, Sassy picked up her wineglass, determined not to make a fool of herself again. The tightness in her throat finally eased, so she could swallow without the urge to cough and spew the sangria all over the tablecloth. Taking tiny sips, her mind continued to mull over her reaction to her family's dinner guest.

By the time Rory pushed away from the table, signalling the end of the meal, Sassy made another startling discovery. While she'd been furious with Ty when she thought he was stealing Blarney, she now knew she'd held onto her anger as a defense mechanism against her strong attraction to him.

Never having experienced such a powerful reaction to a man, it had been easier to continue stoking her temper rather than deal with the seed of a new emotion unfurling inside her. That realization led to another, more shocking one.

She wanted that seed to take root and grow. Yet, she didn't have the vaguest notion of how to go about it. Intuition told her to find a way to ease the anger and pain she detected in Ty. And being honest with herself, she also knew she had to find a way to get him to kiss her again.

Four

Two days later, Ty dismounted the blood bay horse—a gelding from the Dublin Star stuck with the ludicrous name Lover Boy—and looped the reins over the hitching post in front of the Gray Mule Saloon. He looked up Alamo Plaza in one direction, then the other, absently stroking the gelding's muzzle. Lover Boy nickered softly and nuzzled Ty's shoulder.

"Yeah, I know. It's late, and you wanna get back to your stall." Ty chuckled when the horse bobbed his head, as if in agreement. "This is the last place I'm gonna check, then we'll call it quits for the night."

Ty had arrived in town shortly after dark and spent the evening visiting one saloon after another, searching for information about Teddy. So far he'd learned nothing new about the gambler. He took a deep breath, then blew it out. Although he'd been in over twenty cantinas and saloons, that wasn't even half of the town's number of drinking establishments. The folks of San Antonio sure like to drink, he mused, pushing open the Gray Mule door and stepping inside.

Keeping his hat pulled low over his face, Ty approached the bar, taking a visual inventory of everyone present. The bartender was talking to two men at one end of the bar, two saloon girls kept a group of soldiers from nearby Fort Sam Houston company, three men sat at the faro table, and a poker game was in progress at the back of the room.

Ty ordered a beer, thankful he'd wisely decided to pass up drinking at the other saloons. Otherwise he wouldn't be able to see straight. He propped one boot heel over the foot rail, and leaned back against the bar. Sipping his beer, his gaze slowly moved from the men nearest him, to the satin-clad saloon girls and their uniformed companions, to the men playing faro, and finally to the poker players. The Gray Mule didn't look any more promising than the others.

He released a weary breath. Tomorrow night he'd search more saloons and gambling halls to see if he could learn something, anything, that would put him on the right trail to clearing his name and finding Teddy.

Beer mug in hand, Ty eased away from the bar and ambled over to the group of men at the back of the room. Maybe a hand or two of poker would take his mind off his search.

"You fellas mind if I sit in?"

"Hey, Ty, pull up a chair." The man pushed his hat back on his head and looked up with a grin.

Ty was surprised to find the invitation had been extended by Brodie Mahoney. "I didn't recognize you, Brodie," he responded, pulling up a chair and sitting down. Scanning the hat-shadowed faces of the rest of the men at the table, he picked out Trevor, but he didn't see Lucas.

Ty nodded to the other players as Brodie introduced them—Amos, Chet, and Grunt. Amos and Chet each said

"Howdy." The third man made some sort of noise Ty didn't understand—a sound similar to his name.

As Brodie shuffled the cards and dealt a hand of five-card stud, Ty studied the three men he'd just met. He was always on the alert when around strangers. The man called Grunt proved the most interesting. He was small-boned, but wiry-looking. A jacket hung loosely from his narrow shoulders, and tight leather gloves covered his slim hands. A floppy-brimmed hat, angled so the man's entire face was hidden in shadows, prevented Ty from making out any of Grunt's features. Strange name, Ty thought, then shrugged. A man's got a right to go by whatever handle he wants. There's no law against it.

"So where's Lucas tonight?" Ty asked, picking up his cards and arranging them in his hand.

Trevor met his brother's amused gaze, then answered Ty's question. "Lucas is . . . uh . . . busy. He had a promise tonight." The rest of the men laughed knowingly.

Guessing the reason for their laughter, Ty's mouth pulled into a grin. "A promise, huh? Well, he couldn't disappoint the lady, now could he?"

Everyone laughed again, although Ty couldn't be certain if Grunt joined them.

"No, Lucas won't disappoint Della none. All the Gray Mule's *ladies*," Amos smiled, revealing a gap between his front teeth. "like him to take 'em upstairs."

"Yeah, ol' Lucas'll give Della one hell of a ride," Chet agreed.

"It's a wonder we can't hear the bed a squeakin' all the way down here." Brodie looked up at the ceiling, then back at his cards. "'Course, he's been up there quite awhile already, so maybe they're catchin' their breath."

"Or maybe they ain't on the bed," Amos offered, flashing his toothy grin again. "Lucas told me 'bout this one

43

time when he took Della upstairs. She was hotter'n prairie fire. They barely got inside the door 'fore she was all over him like stink on shit. He said he just hiked up her skirt and took her right there agin the wall."

"Stop that kinda talk, Amos," Chet complained. "I'm hard as a gun barrel from just hearing 'bout all the ways the two o' them could be doin' it." He shifted in his chair, trying to ease the tightness of his pants.

"Maybe you should find yerself a hot-to-trot woman and have her take care of that *gun barrel* of yorn," Amos suggested.

"Naw, maybe later. Whose bet is it, anyways?"

When the bidding started, Ty decided Grunt was well named. Whenever it was his bet, he merely grunted his response. Ty couldn't differentiate the sounds the man made, although everyone else at the table had no trouble understanding.

The game proved to be a needed diversion for Ty, his search temporarily forgotten. His companions were a lighthearted, fun-loving group, who didn't take their gambling very seriously, and spent as much time talking as playing cards.

At the end of one hand, Chet threw his cards down, pushed his chair away from the table, and rose. "Be right back, y'all. I gotta take a piss."

"Hey, Chet, if ya shake it more than once, yer playin' with it," Amos called after him.

Ty found himself laughing as loudly as the rest of the men at Amos's kidding. When he glanced over at Grunt, the laughter died in his throat. The man's shoulders shook so hard with silent laughter, his hat had slipped sideways. For a fraction of a second, Ty caught a glimpse of finely arched, black eyebrows over the beautiful lavender eyes always hovering in his mind.

Feeling the intensity of someone's gaze, Sassy turned to meet Ty's amazed stare. She quickly looked away, straightening her hat so her face was again hidden by the wide brim.

Ty's reaction at finding out Grunt was not a man at all, but Sassy Mahoney, momentarily tongued-tied him. Recalling the earlier off-color banter, a hot flush crept up his neck and cheeks, making his ears burn. Raised to be respectful of the fairer sex, Ty knew men shouldn't talk the way these men had been doing in front of ladies. Well, maybe Sassy wasn't a lady, he amended. She was a half-wild tomboy, whose social graces left a lot to be desired. But she damn sure wasn't a saloon girl either.

His eyes narrowing with suspicion, Ty swung his gaze to Sassy's brothers. They have to be in on this, he decided, suddenly furious with Brodie, Trevor and the absent Lucas for bringing their sister to a saloon, let alone allowing her to play poker, drink beer, and hear their raw talk.

Neither of the Mahoney boys were aware of Ty's glowering gaze, nor his awareness of the deceptive game they were playing. Watching Amos, then Chet when he returned from his trip outside, Ty couldn't determine if these two also knew Grunt's true identity. He forced himself to stay calm, while he tried to decide what to do about what he'd just learned.

Inspiration came quickly.

Scraping back his chair, he said casually, "Think I'll get me a cigar."

When he returned to the table, Ty held out his hand. "Here, I got one for each of us," he said around the long, black cheroot clamped between his teeth. Each man took a cigar, until only one remained. Ty moved his hand closer to the only player at the table without a smoke. Grunt.

Sassy vehemently shook her head, praying her hat wouldn't fly off and reveal her tightly braided and pinned hair.

"Come on, Grunt," Ty coaxed. "Be a man and join us in smokin' a fine cigar."

Brodie and Trevor exchanged an anxious glance, but kept silent. Their sister had always been able to take care of herself.

Ty's words had exactly the desired effect. Sassy couldn't turn down a challenge, and Ty dangled one right in front of her nose.

Snatching the cigar from his outstretched hand, Sassy bit off the end and stuck the vile tasting cheroot in her mouth. When Ty handed her a match, she scratched the sulphur tip along the edge of the table and held the flame to the cigar. This wasn't the first time she'd smoked; there wasn't much her brothers did that she hadn't tried. But unlike some of their other pastimes, smoking cigars wasn't one she enjoyed.

She tentatively drew in a puff of smoke and exhaled slowly, praying there wouldn't be a repeat of the reaction she'd had to her first cigar several years ago. Her stomach knotted, then roiled violently, bringing bile to her throat. She swallowed once, twice. It didn't help.

The card game forgotten, the air above the table filled with a heavy, blue fog of smoke. The men's peaceful silence suddenly ended when Grunt leaped from his chair and bolted for the door.

Ty's hand clamped down on Brodie's shoulder when the younger man started to rise. "Stay put. I'll see to her."

Brodie sucked in a surprised breath and eased back

46

down. He met Ty's dark gaze almost fearfully. "We were just havin' some fun, Ty. She loves poker, and it didn't do no harm to let her come here with us."

"She! Who y'all talkin' 'bout?" Chet demanded.

Ignoring Chet, Ty said to Brodie, "Has she come here with you before?"

Brodie considered lying, but the forbidding look on Ty's face changed his mind. "Yeah, a couple of times. It got to be a game, to see if she could fool folks with her disguise."

"Disguise? Just what the hell's goin' on?" Amos looked from Ty to Brodie, but neither appeared to have heard him.

"It was just a harmless game, Ty," Brodie finished in a lame voice.

"Well, Brodie, the game's over," Ty replied softly. Grabbing the whiskey bottle on the table, he rose and turned toward the door.

Ty found Sassy around the corner of the saloon, at the rear of a narrow alley. One hip leaning against the adobe wall, she was doubled over, arms crossed tightly across her stomach. The sound of her retching was loud in the quiet alley. For an instant, Ty felt remorse for goading her into smoking the cigar. But then, she needed to be taught a lesson. Still, the gagging sounds of her stomach emptying itself sent a surge of concern and tenderness through him.

Setting the whiskey bottle down next to him, Ty wrapped his arms around Sassy from behind. He held her firmly against his chest, crooning softly when she tried to evade his grip. When her sickness passed, he turned her in his arms. Her body was limp and pliable, like a rag doll. Retrieving the whiskey bottle, he ushered her back toward the street.

47

He stopped in the shadows near the entrance of the alley and removed her hat. "Here, take a swig of this," he told her, handing her the whiskey bottle.

She did as he instructed, uncharacteristically biddable, her hand visibly shaking as she tipped the bottle to her mouth. When the fiery liquid started down her throat, she fought the urge to cough and forced herself to swallow. Holding her breath, she waited for the whiskey to hit bottom. When her stomach didn't rebel, she released a ragged sigh. Grateful for the sudden warmth the whiskey sent rushing through her, she took another draught from the bottle.

As her tongue peeked out to claim the last drop of whiskey from her lush mouth, Ty was struck with an intense longing to lap the moisture from her lips, to again taste her sweetness. Pushing such untimely thoughts aside, he reminded himself of what he'd caught her doing. He should turn her over his knee, not kiss her senseless as he longed to do. Her weakened, light-headed state prevented him from seriously considering either action. Instead he cradled her against him, her head resting on his chest.

"Damn, fool woman. What were you trying to prove?" Before she could form a reply, Ty continued, "Dressed like a man, playing poker and drinking beer for Christ's sake! And the things those men were saying! I can't believe your brothers let you hear such crude talk."

"I've heard worse," she mumbled against his chest, her breath fanning the thatch of golden hair curling out of the opened neck of his shirt.

Ty closed his eyes and dropped his head back against the wall of the saloon, praying for control over his easily stirred desire. For some reason, he just couldn't keep his body from reacting to Sassy whenever she was near.

Again he forced his mind back to the matter at hand. Lowering his head until his chin rested on top of Sassy's dark hair, he sighed heavily. "Why do your brothers let you go with them to saloons?"

"I go everywhere with them," she answered softly, then quickly added, "Well, not everywhere. Not upstairs at the Gray Mule." Her throat was raw from the cigar smoke going down and the contents of her stomach coming up, yet her husky voice sent another ripple of desire leapfrogging up Ty's spine.

Dammit, Beaumont, she just emptied her stomach. How can you want her now? he berated himself, irritated that even after she'd been ill, she could still affect him so strongly. He took a deep, cleansing breath.

"Don't you ever go to any of the places women like? The theater, dances, church socials?"

Sassy made a rude sound in her throat. "That kinda stuff is for prinking ninnies. I'd rather play poker and drink beer, even smoke cigars, than stand around talking about ladies' stupid hats and drinking lily-livered tea."

Ty had to bite his lip hard to keep from laughing aloud. Clearing his throat, he pushed Sassy away from him. "You're a woman, a beautiful woman, and you should be talking about ladies' hats and drinking tea."

Sassy's heart swelled at Ty's words. He'd called her beautiful! No one but her father had ever mentioned her looks in a favorable way. But Rory's opinion didn't count; all fathers called their daughters beautiful. The girls at school had called her bean pole or worse, and her brothers started calling her Grunt because of her attempts to sound masculine when she'd first started going to saloons with them. Neither did much for her self-esteem.

Well, her figure had filled out since her aborted school days, so she was no longer a bean pole. But Sassy didn't

49

think she could be described as beautiful either. Searching Ty's face, she tried to read his expression. The poor light in the alley made seeing his features impossible.

"I'm not beautiful," she finally said in a flat voice.

"Oh, indeed you are, Sassy. You're a true beauty. A man would have to be a fool not to see it, in spite of the clothes you wear. Put you in a dress, and I guarantee you'd turn every male head in San Antonio."

Her heart leaped in her chest. Could his words be true? Not likely, she thought, the embarrassment and hurt of her past failure at becoming a lady snuffing out the spark of hope. Yet, hearing the honesty in Ty's voice, she believed him when he said *he* thought she was beautiful—and that's all that mattered.

Her mind racing on what she would do with that knowledge, she jammed her hat back on her head. "I've gotta get my brothers and head for home. You coming with us?"

"Sure, lead the way." Ty followed her out of the alley and around to the front of the saloon.

Instead of going inside, she curled her lips and whistled shrilly. Brodie, Trevor, and a hastily summoned Lucas came through the doors a few minutes later. Sassy smiled at her second-oldest brother. "I didn't catch you at a bad time, did I, Lucas?"

"Nope. I already finished scratching my itch." He grinned, then added, "Several times, in fact."

Brodie and Trevor laughed halfheartedly, keeping their gazes carefully away from Ty. Only Sassy dared glance in his direction. The light through the saloon's front window revealed a blush staining his clenched jaw. Finding Ty's embarrassment at her exchange with Lucas immensely amusing, she clamped her mouth tightly shut.

50

She wisely kept any comment she would have liked to make to herself, unwilling to risk rousing his anger.

On the way back to the Dublin Star, Ty pondered whether he should tell Rory Mahoney where his daughter had spent the evening. Surely Rory didn't know about Sassy's visits to saloons, or he would've put a stop to them. Then again, like Charlie said, she'd been raised like one of her brothers, so perhaps Rory did know what kept his daughter occupied. The problem disturbed him a great deal, but he finally decided it was none of his business. And since he was a guest of the Mahoney family, he'd best keep his opinions to himself.

As she rode along next to Ty, Sassy wondered what he was thinking—did he wish he could take back his words about calling her beautiful? She hoped not. Her own tumbling thoughts soon overrode figuring out what had Ty so preoccupied.

Although she had repressed any feminine feelings that had tried to make themselves known over the past four years, Sassy could no longer deny them. She wanted very much to act like her true sex, to be a woman men would find attractive. Stealing a glance at the man to her right, the realization struck again that Ty Beaumont was responsible for the strange feelings whirling inside her. She also realized something else. There was no telling how long he would be staying on the Dublin Star.

The idea of Ty leaving filled her with panic. She had to do something. Fast.

Five

Sheena found Sassy slouched in a chair in the *sala* the next afternoon. Seeing the woebegone look on the younger woman's face, her brow furrowed with concern. "Sassy, are you feeling poorly?" She entered the room and laid her hand on her stepdaughter's forehead.

Sassy sighed heavily. "I'm fine. I just had some thinking to do, that's all."

Taking a seat on the sofa, Sheena studied Sassy's face. Perhaps she wasn't physically ill, but something was bothering her. Sheena hoped she was reading Sassy's expression and her behavior since Ty Beaumont joined their household correctly, when she said, "I've been doing some thinking, too. I've decided we should make dinner a formal occasion." At Sassy's confused look, she continued, "You know, the men in coats and ties. You and I in pretty dresses."

Sassy made a disgusted sound, then said, "Why would we want to do that?"

"Because we have a guest. I should have thought of it sooner, but we can still do it for the rest of Ty's stay." When Sassy didn't respond, she added, "Besides, nothing catches a man's eye quicker than a woman in a pretty dress."

Sassy's head snapped up at that. Her eyes squinting skeptically, she said, "Are you saying, I have to get all gussied up to make—I mean—to eat dinner?" She cleared her throat. "You know I don't like wearing a dress. It's like being weighted down, all that fool material around my legs. Besides, I don't have any dresses."

Sheena rose from the sofa and moved across the room. At the doorway, she turned back to look at her step-daughter. Sassy's chin was tilted in familiar defiance, but Sheena saw something more. "Yes, I know how you feel. Pants are more comfortable for some things. But wearing a dress has its advantages, too. If you change your mind, we have time to alter one of my dresses for you."

Sassy glanced at the clock on her bedside table, then back to the mirror. Ty's words to her at the Gray Mule the night before, about wearing a dress, kept going through her mind. She studied her reflection, then scowled.

Why had she accepted Sheena's offer? She glanced down at the dress her stepmother had hastily altered. The smoke gray cotton had always looked good on Sheena—not that Sassy considered herself an authority on women's fashion. But surely Sheena hadn't felt this uncomfortable. The lace edging of the high collar itched her neck, and the cuffs of the full sleeves were most annoying. Thank God she hadn't given in to Sheena's efforts to convince her to put on one of those awful corsets. When her stepmother told her corsets were part of every lady's attire, she announced she did not intend to have the stuffing squeezed out of her just because she'd agreed to wear a dress. She hated to think what she would have done had Sheena not relented. This compulsion to attract Ty's attention was making her behave in ways she didn't completely understand.

Doubt nearly made her take off the dress and throw it across the room. Then she remembered what Sheena had told her. Running the brush through her hair, she murmured, "I sure hope she knows what she's talking about."

Finding a way to get Ty alone was proving to be more difficult than she'd envisioned. She'd been unable to snatch more than a minute of privacy with him. Not enough time to begin helping him forget whatever caused the pain she'd seen in his eyes, or start easing the bitterness she heard in his voice. Or maneuver him into giving her another kiss.

Now, here she stood, wearing a dad-blamed dress. *Humph, I must be outta my mind!* Taking one last look at herself in the mirror, she took a deep breath, then turned to leave her bedroom.

The high-heeled shoes pinched her toes, and getting the hang of keeping her balance took some practice. Walking from her bedroom to the *sala* took longer than usual, since she had to take tiny steps to keep from tripping and falling on her face. Standing just outside the room, she heard the voices of her family chatting over a drink before going in to dinner.

Taking another deep breath, she carefully stepped into the *sala*. Several seconds passed before anyone noticed her arrival.

Ty was the first to acknowledge her presence. He turned toward where she stood nervously just inside the door. As he looked at the woman who possessed a rare mixture of childish uncertainty and feminine sophistication, his heartbeat quickened. Not only did she look lovely, even in clothes she obviously felt uncomfortable wearing, but the doubt swirling in her lavender gaze touched him even more. He started toward her, a compliment on his lips, but Lucas's voice stopped him.

"Well, would ya look at that," Lucas announced in a loud voice.

The others turned toward the source of his comment. Two splotches of bright color appeared on Sassy's cheeks.

"Sassy, is that really you?" Trevor asked. "We haven't seen you wearing a dress in a month of Sundays."

"I think it's more like a year of Sundays," Brodie added with a laugh.

"Maybe she's playing dress up," Lucas offered, earning a glare from his sister.

"Naw," Brodie drawled after a long silence, rubbing his chin thoughtfully. "I think it's something else. If ya ask me, I think—" He glanced over to where Ty stood near the fireplace with Rory, then lowered his voice so it wouldn't carry across the room. "I think our little sister's got her eyes on a man." At his brothers' surprised looks, he added, louder this time, "And, we all know what happened last time she wore a dress."

Sassy's gasp of outrage was masked by the collective hoots of laughter from the Mahoney brothers.

Seeing her face darken with a deep flush, Ty's eyebrows pulled together. What was going on? Again he started across the room. This time her voice stopped him.

"Well, I didn't ask what you think, Brodie Mahoney, so you can just put a sock in it." Changing the target of her fire-filled gaze to Lucas and Trevor, she added, "I didn't ask what any of you fools think."

Her anger nearly choking her, she tried to swallow the lump in her throat before making her final statement. "You three can go take a flying frig, for all I care." Leaving a gape-mouthed Ty and her suddenly solemn brothers, she spun around and stormed from the room.

Ty stared at the empty doorway. Taking a sip from his glass of whiskey, he thought about Sassy's surprising vulnerability. He never thought he'd see her cut and run. Apparently she had an Achilles' heel, and her brothers knew just where to prod to get a reaction. Recalling the pain on her face before she fled from the room, he felt a sudden surge of anger. The Mahoney brothers had no right to treat her like that. Excusing himself, he left Rory and headed across the room.

Stopping in front of the young men, he kept his voice low when he said, "If I wasn't a guest of your family, I'd take you three outside and knock your heads together."

At Lucas's startled look, Ty said, "Has it ever occurred to you that maybe your sister doesn't deserve the way you treat her?"

"Sass? Naw, she doesn't care—" Brodie cut his reply short when he saw the look on Ty's face.

"Hey, we were just having some fun," Trevor said.

Ty turned to the youngest brother. "Maybe you should ask Sassy what it's like to be on the receiving end of your fun."

Giving them each a pointed glare, he turned and rejoined Rory by the fireplace.

Barely inside her bedroom, Sassy kicked off the painful shoes while pulling and jerking on the hated dress. When the row of black buttons running down the front of the bodice wouldn't cooperate, she gave the fabric a vicious yank, sending the pieces of jet bouncing across the floor. The tight cuffs proved just as difficult. More buttons scattered. She finally managed to get her arms out of the sleeves, then shoved the dress down over her hips, letting it fall into a mangled mess at her feet.

Stepping out of the circle of gray cotton, she gave it a kick, then started pulling off the rest of the paraphernalia she'd had to don. Several petticoats, a camisole, garters, and silk stockings soon joined the dress on the floor.

Sassy'd just stuffed her shirt into her denim pants when there was a knock on the door. "Sassy? Are you all right?"

Closing her eyes for a moment to garner her strength, Sassy said, "I'm fine, Sheena."

"Can I come in for a minute?"

Sassy heaved an exasperated sigh. *Sure, why not. And while you're at it, why don't you bring those three jerks I have for brothers with you?* Aloud she said, "Come on in."

Sheena stepped into Sassy's room. Though one brow lifted at the pile of clothes on the floor, she didn't comment. "You do realize your brothers were only teasing, don't you?"

Sassy whirled to face her stepmother, her eyes glittering with fury. "What's that supposed to mean? The things they said shouldn't hurt, just because they were teasing?" More softly she added, "I should never have let you talk me into wearing that damn dress."

She glanced down at the pile of clothes. Her cheeks warming, she said, "I'm sorry, Sheena. I think I ruined your dress."

Waving off the younger woman's apology, Sheena said, "I meant what I told you earlier. Nothing catches a man's eye quicker than a woman in a pretty dress. Ty noticed you tonight, and he agreed your brothers' comments were uncalled-for."

Sassy's head snapped up. "What?"

"After you left the *sala,* Ty had a talk with them. I didn't hear the conversation, but the three looked pretty shamefaced afterward."

When Sassy said no more, Sheena left her alone to brood.

When the family made their way into the dining room a few minutes later, Sassy joined them, this time wearing her usual shirt and tight pants. She stiffened when she saw her brothers hang back to wait for her, and tried to brush past them. Brodie's hand on her arm brought her to a halt.

"Wait a minute, Sass, we've got something to say to you."

She glanced at each of her brothers. Though each wore a look of penance, it did nothing to cool her still simmering temper. "What is it?" she finally snapped.

"We . . . um," Lucas swallowed, then plunged ahead. "We want to tell you we're sorry for the things we said. We never thought our jokes hurt you, until Ty—"

"That's right, Lucas Mahoney," she interrupted, her cheeks burning with a blush of both embarrassment and fury. "And that also goes for you two." She turned her gaze onto Brodie, then Trevor. "None of you ever thinks about anything except what's in your pants." With that she lifted her chin and strode past her stunned brothers.

She barely spoke during the meal, flashing her brothers fuming looks, and avoiding Ty's gaze whenever possible.

* * *

After a few more days of Ty steering clear of her any time she was within six feet of him, Sassy suspected he was purposely avoiding her. She felt sick at heart. He obviously believed—like everyone else—that she was a failure as a woman.

Ty was avoiding Sassy, although not because she lacked anything as a woman, but for the exact opposite reason. Her unorthodox style of dress and often outlandish behavior appealed to him too much!

When he'd first accepted the Mahoney hospitality, he made the decision to stay away from Sassy. To get involved with her would only complicate his life even more. Still, he didn't miss her attempts at using her obviously undeveloped feminine wiles to lure him into a private liaison. The radiant smiles and smoldering looks she sent him while trying to corner him in the barn, or in the courtyard after everyone else had retired, while flattering, were about as subtle as a kick in the shins. He saw the desire flare in the depths of her beautiful eyes each time their gazes met. And after she'd gone so far as putting on a dress, he realized he would have to work harder to stay out of her line of fire. Although her efforts at flirtation were awkward and unschooled, they still had an instantaneous effect on him.

The little minx doesn't know what she's doing to me, or my self-control, he groused silently one afternoon, while making his way toward one of the corrals.

Sassy stepped through the courtyard gate and spotted Ty by the corral of yearling colts. She smiled. Perhaps her luck was about to change. Her father and Sheena had gone into San Antonio, Brodie and Lucas were out on the range with most of the other ranch hands, and Trevor

59

was seeing to a recently foaled colt in the foaling barn on the other side of the yard. That meant she and Ty were alone, and she intended to take full advantage of the opportunity.

Enjoying the quiet, Ty tipped his face up to the hot sun, thankful he'd decided to stay at the ranch. The Mahoney clan was a lively, seldom calm group. While he was glad to have some time alone, the solitude also disturbed him. His thoughts kept straying from what he should be thinking about—his plans for leaving the Dublin Star—to Sassy.

Ah, Sassy. What an enigma she was, all wrapped up in such an intriguing female bundle. What made her even more appealing was her total lack of awareness of her attractiveness. Beautiful or not, Sassy had been raised like another son, just as Charlie told him. Her unusual skills proved that.

The day she'd found him at the creek, pointed her Winchester at him, and threatened to shoot if he didn't follow her orders, that hadn't been a bluff. She was a crack shot. He'd seen proof of her abilities firsthand during a friendly competition between the Mahoney siblings. Her skills with a rifle were equal to many men, better than some.

Ty had no doubt that if he'd made one wrong move when she thought he was stealing Blarney, he wouldn't be having thoughts of her today. Especially sexual ones, he told himself, recalling her audacious threat to geld him. In spite of the seriousness of that prospect, his lips curved into a smile.

Propping one boot on the bottom rail of the corral fence and folding his arms across the top rail, he focused his attention on the yearling colts frolicking in the warm

Texas sun. While the young horses filled his vision, Sassy filled his mind.

His smile broadened. She'd looked so lovely in a dress several nights past, although she'd obviously been uneasy with her appearance. Then her brothers had to ruin it for her.

Remembering the hurt reflected on Sassy's face before she'd bolted from the room, Ty's heart cramped with sympathy. It was plain she'd been trying her best to be more feminine—no doubt for his benefit—but thanks to her brothers, she fled, believing she'd failed miserably. Ty knew better. Whatever she wore, he instinctively knew no woman could ever affect him the way Sassy did.

He sighed. The feeling was apparently mutual, since Sassy wasn't bashful about her intentions. While that knowledge flattered his male ego—and he would have liked nothing better than to fall under Sassy Mahoney's spell—he didn't trust himself to get too close. She was a temptation he had to resist.

It had been a long time since he'd been with a woman. Not since the last time with— Ty stopped the direction of his thoughts, his mouth tightening into a harsh line. He had to concentrate on the nightmare of the past few months, even if it did swamp him with bitterness. On the verge of losing everything that mattered to him, he had to clear his name.

"Dammit, Teddy, I'll find you," he snarled, a muscle twitching spasmodically in his clenched jaw. Recalling the person who was the reason he'd been forced to start his quest to see justice carried out, Ty realized this was most definitely not the time to get involved with a woman.

"There may never be a right time," he muttered savagely, the familiar helpless fury roiling inside him.

61

The more his thoughts dwelled on the ironic twist of fate that had forced him to run from the law he had made his life's work, the angrier he became. Then thoughts of Sassy shoved their way into his mind. His anger slipped away like smoke in the wind.

While he tried to convince himself that getting involved with Sassy was the worst thing he could do, his body told him a different tale. Closing his eyes, he allowed his thoughts to dwell on their kiss. He remembered the taste of her sweet lips, the untapped passion he sensed waiting to burst free beneath her tomboyish facade. While she was obviously inexperienced in kissing, her response to him had a more profound effect than any of the practiced women he had known. Taking a deep breath, he tried to push those thoughts aside, but they refused to fade. Instead, they became more intense. He could even smell the fresh scent that was uniquely Sassy.

Oh God, I can even feel her hand on my arm.

With a jolt he realized it wasn't his overactive imagination. Willing his heart to slow to normal, Ty opened his eyes and turned to face the woman standing beside him.

The pain mirrored in the depths of Ty's dark eyes shocked Sassy. Her heart filled with tenderness at his obvious distress, and she wondered again at the cause.

Seeing the sympathy on Sassy's face, Ty jerked his gaze from hers, embarrassed to have her see him with his emotions bared. An expert at hiding his true feelings, he quickly masked his tortuous thoughts.

His look changed so drastically that for a minute Sassy wasn't sure she'd actually witnessed his suffering. The tightness around his mouth, the hard set of his jaw, and the bunched muscles of his arm beneath her hand, told her she hadn't imagined the pain he now refused to let her see.

Sassy longed to reach out to him, to comfort him. However, she was wise enough to realize such actions wouldn't be welcomed, not until he was ready to share his hurt. Then she would help heal the wounds she knew he had deep inside. She would make this man shrug off his past and show him how to begin enjoying life again.

Ty Beaumont was a very special man, and the man she wanted. After the first day, when Sassy had discovered the feelings he stirred in her, she had done a lot of soul-searching. She always reached the same conclusion. Ty was meant for her—the man she'd tried to impress by wearing a dress and opening herself up to more ridicule. She believed they were meant to be together as strongly as she believed some unknown force had caused his anger and bitterness—a force she intended to help him conquer.

A sudden stab of fear made her question her decision. Her recent attempt at trying to be a lady had ended in failure, just like it had four years ago. In truth she wasn't sure she could be anything other than what she was—a woman who preferred pants and cussing to more sedate clothes and refined language—though she would like it to be different. Now Ty made her want desperately to be a real woman. His woman.

Pushing her doubts aside, she smiled brightly and hoped her voice didn't betray her inner turbulence. "I'm taking Blarney out for a ride. Would you like to come along?"

Although he wanted to say no—knew he should say no—Ty heard himself agree before he could stop the words. He followed her to the barn, unable to keep his eyes off her swaying hips. Even wearing an old cotton shirt, scuffed boots, and well-worn denim pants, he had never seen a more desirable woman. Silently cursing himself, he wished he'd found the strength to refuse her invitation.

Once out on the range, their horses stretched out in a run, Ty felt the tension drain from his body. He knew the woman next to him, more than the exhilarating ride, was responsible for lifting his spirits. As they raced across the Texas countryside, he glanced at Sassy's profile. The picture she presented was pure enchantment. Dark hair flying around her shoulders like a silken cape, her sensuous lips pressed together in deep concentration, her expressive eyes sparkling with excitement. She was so alive, so wild and free. He hoped nothing would ever crush her indomitable spirit.

When their mounts began to tire, they eased the horses back to a trot, and finally to a walk. Unaware of the direction they had taken, Ty looked at the scenery around him. They were at the creek where he'd first seen Sassy.

A little bell went off in his head, warning him to leave this place with all haste. He couldn't make himself heed the warning. Instead, he swung down from Lover Boy and looped the reins over a tree branch.

When Ty made no move toward her, Sassy decided she'd have to take matters into her own hands. While she considered how to phrase what she wanted to say, her heart pounding madly against her ribs, she chewed on her bottom lip.

She'd always been brave—game to try anything her brothers did—but she'd never done anything like this. A coil of doubt formed in her chest, her insides twisting with fear. Was she going to make a fool of herself again, like the time she'd attended her first dance at the Ursuline Academy?

Her cheeks warmed with a blush at the memory of that night. How was she to know wearing riding boots with a dress was wrong? She'd never even heard of the flimsy, little dance slippers the rest of the girls wore. When one of them noticed her scuffed boots peeking from beneath the hem of her dress, word quickly spread among the rest of the guests. Sassy knew she was the topic of conversation, and tried to ignore the snickering and pointing. Then she heard someone call her a country bumpkin with two left feet. Unfortunately, she couldn't let it lie. Approaching the loudest of the name-callers, she politely told the girl to "go piss up a rope." Head held high, she marched from the room, not caring that "foul-mouthed boor" was added to the already long list of names the other students had for her.

Sassy's throat tightened at the painful memory, a memory she'd never shared with anyone. Swallowing hard, she quickly shoved the hurt from her past failing aside. *No use crying in your beer,* she scolded herself. *This isn't one of the silly girls from the Academy, this is Ty. He's all you need to be thinking about.*

Straightening her spine, she moved across the clearing. When she stood next to him, she cleared her throat, then opened her mouth to do what her father said was the best way to handle something weighing on your mind— just say it straight out.

Sassy's voice pulled Ty from his silent contemplation of their surroundings. He swung around to look at her, his eyes wide with surprise. "I beg your pardon?"

Six

"I said, I want you to kiss me again." Sassy's voice sounded less certain this time. When Ty remained silent, her apprehension grew. "Are you sorry you kissed me, is that why you've been avoiding me?"

Ty blinked once, then stared at Sassy, unable to grasp what was happening. Never had a woman voiced such a request, not outside a bawdy house anyway. Sassy's frankness caught him off guard. On second thought, it shouldn't have. She wasn't a typical woman, not by a long shot.

Shaking himself out of his stupor, he said, "Listen, Sassy, respectable ladies don't make requests like that."

Her heart sank. Had she acted rashly again by not considering the consequences? She already regretted going to the Gray Mule with her brothers. Having done everything with them since she could walk, it never crossed her mind that Ty might show up at the saloon, or worse, he'd find out Grunt's true identity. "Is that why you won't kiss me, because I'm not a respectable lady?" she whispered, staring at her worn boots.

The anguish in her voice touched a tender spot in Ty, a spot he thought had callused over. "I didn't say that."

With thumb and forefinger he lifted her chin. When she met his gaze, he gave her a smile of encouragement.

Sassy saw the truth in his dark eyes. Her hopes soared until he spoke again.

"It's just that I don't think—" Her fingers pressed to his lips interrupted him.

"Please, Ty," she whispered, moving closer.

Her gaze remained locked with his. Against his will, he sank deeper and deeper into those twin lavender pools. Her natural woman's scent surrounded him, her moist lips parted in invitation. Ty knew all was lost.

With a soft growl, he pulled her into his arms and captured her mouth with his. Not a gentle kiss, it was hard and demanding, but Sassy responded in kind. His tongue delved between her opened lips into the velvet warmth beyond. Feeling her stiffen at this intrusion, her inexperience hit home once more. Still, he couldn't bring himself to stop. He softened the pressure until she relaxed in his arms. Slowly, he explored the sweet cavern beyond her lips, coaxing her tongue into his mouth.

Eagerly, she mimicked the movements he had used, thrilling at the taste and texture of him. Gasping with both surprise and pleasure when he gently suckled her tongue, she squirmed restlessly in his embrace, feeling a tugging sensation in a place far removed from her mouth.

This was nothing like their first kiss. This was better, much better! Her mind spinning, she leaned closer to his muscular body. At last he pulled his mouth from hers, his breath rasping harshly in her ear. At her whimper of protest, he rubbed his hands in soothing circles on her back. Whispering words of reassurance, he pressed his lips to her eyelids, her temple, her exposed throat. He gently nibbled the tender spot behind her ear, before slanting his mouth over hers once more.

Just as he was ready to lay her down in the grass and make her his completely, reality pushed through Ty's passion-clouded brain. He lifted his head and drew a deep breath through his clenched teeth. Trying to clear his reeling senses, he looked down into Sassy's upturned face. Her eyelids fluttered open, revealing eyes darkened to the color of purple pansies. Her flushed face and kiss-swollen lips made him want nothing more than to make long, leisurely love to this wonderfully responsive woman. He forced himself to remember that she was untouched, the daughter of his host, and to continue down this path would only complicate his life even further. Those truths extinguished the last of the desire racing through him.

"We'd better get back, Sassy," he murmured in a thick voice.

She could only nod, unable to speak because of the blood pounding in her ears and the throbbing low in her belly. In a daze, she followed him to where their horses were tethered. She allowed him to help her mount Blarney, although she had never needed or wanted assistance before, then watched through eyes still glazed with the residue of passion as he swung onto Lover Boy's back.

Turning toward home, Sassy kicked Blarney into a trot. She looked over her shoulder at the man who made her want to investigate the world of sexual delights—territory she'd never contemplated exploring. What would happen the next time they were alone? A shiver of expectation raced up her back. She couldn't wait. Recalling Ty's words at the Gray Mule about women liking the theater, dances, and socials, she decided to visit her friend, Greta Bergstrom, as soon as possible. Greta would teach her about all that feminine stuff.

Ty recognized the anticipation and longing on Sassy's face. He gritted his teeth in frustration. She wanted more than he was willing to give. Pulling his gaze from the woman who affected him like a drug, he prayed there wouldn't be a next time. Next time he might not be able to stop himself from making love to this beautiful wild Texas blossom.

Sassy's decision to visit Greta at the earliest opportunity went unfulfilled. A string of mustangs brought in to be broken and three new foals kept her too busy to ride over to the Bergstrom ranch. The delay made her cross. And to make matters worse, Ty hadn't been spending much time around the ranch, making her irritability even more pronounced.

When Sheena asked if she'd like to go to town three days later, Sassy jumped at the chance. Accustomed to her perfunctory invitations being refused, Sheena was momentarily taken aback. Fully aware Sassy hated making the weekly shopping trip, she chose to make no comment. However, when Sassy agreed to ride in the buggy rather than riding Blarney, Sheena could no longer hold her tongue. "Are you okay, Sassy?"

"Couldn't be better," she replied, refusing to meet her stepmother's gaze. "Why wouldn't I be?"

"You've never accepted my invitations to go to town, for one thing. And you just agreed to ride in the buggy. You have to admit, either of those things alone would make me suspicious."

"Yes, well . . ." Sassy began, feeling the blood rush to her cheeks. She lifted one shoulder in a shrug. "I just thought it would be . . . um . . . a nice . . . change," she finished lamely.

Sheena gave Sassy a long, measured look. Not sure whether to believe her stepdaughter, she finally nodded, then stepped up into the buggy.

"I want to see about getting a length of fabric," Sheena told Sassy during their ride to San Antonio. "The Bergstroms are giving a party—"

Party! The word clanged around in Sassy's mind, making her sit up straighter on the buggy seat.

"—on the twentieth, and I want to make a new dress." Glancing at the young woman next to her, Sheena saw the flicker of interest on Sassy's face. "We can get you a dress length, too, if you like."

Sassy started at her stepmother's words, wanting to shout yes. However, since she knew showing enthusiasm for something she had previously abhorred would only bring questions she didn't want to answer, she stilled the response. On the other hand, refusing the offer didn't sit well either. "I'll think about it," she said at last.

Sheena guided the buggy down Commerce Street and stopped several doors from the mercantile. Sassy had just stepped from the buggy when a high peal of female giggles drifted to her, followed by a man's deep rumble of laughter. Farther down the street, a man and woman stood next to each other on the sidewalk, laughing at some shared amusement.

Sassy stiffened. Her eyes squinted with fury, she stared at the couple. *What the hell is Greta doing talking to Ty?*

Ty's smile died when he turned and saw the two women approaching. As his gaze roamed over Sassy, the rosy beauty of the pale blond woman next to him paled. While Greta Bergstrom had been a delight to talk to, even after he'd nearly toppled her over in his preoccupied

70

stupor, she couldn't compare with Sassy. Though the look on Sassy's face told him she'd never believe that.

"Mrs. Mahoney. Sassy," Ty said, touching his fingers to the brim of his hat.

"Mr. Beaumont," Sheena responded. "I see you've met Sassy's friend, Greta."

Sassy's friend? Ty hoped his surprise didn't show. After finding Sassy in a saloon, drinking beer and playing poker, he never figured she would have any female friends. Shifting his gaze from the delicate blonde to the fiery-eyed Sassy, he had to stifle a laugh. *No wonder she looks ready to skin me alive. She's actually jealous because she thinks Greta is horning in on what she sees as her territory.* In a sudden decision to see how far he could push her, he said, "Yes, Miss Bergstrom—" he turned to Greta and gave her a smile and a courtly nod. "—and I just happened to bump into each other."

Greta smothered another giggle behind her hand, her eyes dancing with delight. "That's right. Mr. Beaumont just saved me from taking a nasty fall." She batted her eyelashes at him playfully. "He's such a gentleman."

Gentleman, my ass, Sassy thought crossly, fighting the urge to throttle both her friend and *gentleman* Ty Beaumont. "Yeah, well, Sheena and I have some shopping to do, so if you'll excuse us?"

"I have to be going, too," Ty replied. "It's been a pleasure. I hope to see you again, Miss Bergstrom." He lifted one of Greta's small hands and pressed a kiss to her fingertips. A sound from Sassy's direction brought a smile to his lips. He couldn't tell if the noise she'd made indicated repulsion or envy.

"Oh, I'm sure we'll be seeing each other again very soon." Greta flashed Ty another smile. "Mama and Papa

71

are having a party a week from Saturday. They won't mind if I invite you. Please, say you'll come."

"If I'm still around, I'd be honored." Again, he touched his lips to Greta's fingertips.

In spite of her irritation, Sassy watched Greta's behavior and Ty's reaction with intense interest. His remark about his eventual leaving made her realize she had to act quickly. "Bye, Greta. I'll be over to see you tomorrow morning," Sassy said, moving to walk between Ty and her friend.

Ty took a step back when it appeared Sassy meant to walk right through him. But he wasn't quick enough. As she tried to move past him, her shoulder brushed against his chest. An instant fire of wanting roared through his veins. Watching Sassy and Sheena disappear inside the mercantile, he rubbed his chest absently in an attempt to ease the heat Sassy's touch had caused.

"What's gotten into her?" Greta asked, her brow puckered in a frown.

Ty had a theory, but kept it to himself. Aloud, he said, "Beats me. She's been prickly as a cactus all week."

Sassy trailed behind Sheena through the mercantile, her mind still on the way Ty had behaved with Greta. Maybe wearing a dress and batting her eyelashes at him like a witless ninny was the way to get his attention. She cringed at the thought.

When Sheena headed for the back of the store where the piece goods were displayed, Sassy took a detour to the gun case. Normally the collection of rifles and shotguns on display held her interest. Even when the salesclerk pointed out a new Winchester, she merely nodded, his words barely registering. Her mind was preoccupied with the advice Lucas had given her on attracting a man.

The day after her brothers had humiliated her at dinner, Lucas made a point of approaching her again to apologize. He swore they were only teasing and meant no harm. After convincing her to accept his apology, he went on to say that if she was serious about Ty, she'd probably have to wear a dress again—since pants and a shirt weren't what a man expected to see on a lady.

When she said why should she do that, only to have the three of them make her the butt of more of their jokes, Lucas quickly promised her there would be no more teasing. She hadn't taken his advice seriously . . . until now. Would Ty be more receptive to her advances, if she dressed like Sheena and Greta?

Turning on her heel, she headed for the rear of the store.

Sassy approached her stepmother, then stood quietly next to her. She idly fingered a bolt of fabric, unsure of what to say.

Sensing Sassy's presence, Sheena glanced up from the bolts of various fabrics she'd selected. "Which do you like, Sassy?"

Glancing at the material laid out on the counter, she shrugged. "They're all nice."

"I can't decide between the primrose bouclé and the pink moire silk."

"The yellow would look good with your hair," Sassy offered tentatively.

Sheena looked up sharply at her stepdaughter, her eyes wide with surprise. "Why, I believe you're right, Sassy. The primrose it is." Seeing the way the younger woman's gaze kept straying to a bolt of lavender silk with a delicate, cream-colored floral pattern, she added, "Are you sure we can't get you some material for a new dress, while we're here?"

"You don't have time to make two dresses before the Bergstrom party."

"Nonsense. If I can't get them both finished, Rosa will help. So, do you see something you like?"

Sassy's hand immediately settled on the bolt of fabric she'd been eyeing. Pulling it off the counter, she said, "I like this one."

Sheena unrolled several yards and held it up to Sassy's face. "It's lovely. The lavender nearly matches your eyes. You have a real knack for this, Sassy. We'll need to select a dress pattern. And how about some lace to trim the sleeves and neckline, something in cream to match the flowers?"

When they left the mercantile a few minutes later, Sassy was amazed at the realization that she'd actually enjoyed her first experience at feminine shopping. Stepping up into the buggy, she decided that accepting Sheena's offer to make her a dress for the party had been a good idea—definitely a step in the right direction to turning Ty's head.

The next morning, Sassy paced uneasily in the Bergstrom parlor, while Mrs. Bergstrom summoned her daughter. Greta was Sassy's one and only female friend, the only student at the Ursuline Academy who hadn't made fun of her or treated her like a leper. In the few months Sassy attended the school, the two had forged the beginnings of a strong friendship. And in the following years, they had remained close, although Greta was the complete opposite of Sassy.

Just about ready to break into Franz Bergstrom's liquor

supply to steady her nerves, Sassy sighed with relief when Greta swept into the room.

"Sassy, I'm so glad you came." Her full skirts rustling softly, the petite woman crossed the room to hug her friend.

In contrast to Sassy's darkness, Greta was fair from the top of her pale blond head down to her tiny feet. Watching Greta take a seat on one end of the sofa and arrange her skirts around her, Sassy felt like a saddle tramp in dusty pants and shirt.

Greta folded her hands in her lap and raised a questioning gaze to Sassy. "Should I have some tea brought in?" At Sassy's sour look Greta smiled. "Sorry, I forgot you think tea is for—What is it you call us tea drinkers?"

"Prinking ninnies," Sassy replied in a low voice, recalling she'd said those exact words to Ty. Her cheeks burned with a blush. Remembering her vow to have Greta teach her how to be a lady, she realized she might have to eat crow regarding her opinion of drinking tea.

"Can I offer you something else? Coffee?" Greta said, wondering at her friend's discomfort. "Or maybe some of Papa's whiskey?" she added in a loud whisper.

"Pipe down, Greta. You know I wouldn't touch your father's liquor." Realizing she'd considered doing exactly that just moments before, Sassy's cheeks burned even more. She hastily turned away from Greta's piercing blue gaze to stare out the parlor window.

After a few moments, Sassy spoke, her voice slightly tremulous. "Greta, I want you to teach me how to be a lady."

Greta's mouth fell open, and her eyes widened in surprise. Nothing her friend said could have shocked her more.

When Greta didn't respond, Sassy swung away from

the window. Feet widespread, hands fisted on her hips, Sassy's chin came up in silent challenge. "Don't just sit there gawking. Will you teach me or not?"

Snapping her mouth closed, Greta blinked once, then said, "Of course, I'll teach you, Sassy. I didn't mean to stare. You took me by surprise, that's all." She sat back on the sofa, studying her friend for a moment. "What brought about this sudden decision? After you left the academy, you swore you'd—what was it you said?" Greta's brow furrowed for a moment, then cleared. "Oh yes, you swore you'd rather be dragged through a patch of prickly pear than behave like a lady."

Sassy wanted to kick herself for not foreseeing Greta's reaction. After all, Greta knew her better than anyone, and would naturally wonder at her request. Although she had shared nearly everything with Greta in the past, this time she intended to keep quiet. If she made a fool of herself with Ty, no one else would know. "I'm planning on coming to your parents' party, and I just decided I should try being a lady. Is that so hard to believe?" Would Greta accept her explanation? she wondered. *I can hardly believe it myself.*

Laying a finger against her cheek, Greta stared thoughtfully at her friend. She could think of only one possibility for a tomboy like Sassy to not only plan to attend a party, but also decide she wanted to be a lady. That couldn't be. Sassy couldn't be interested in a man! The thought made Greta bite the inside of her lip to stifle a giggle. Whatever the reason, the look on Sassy's face told Greta she was dead serious.

"No, I guess not," she said at last. "Now, the first thing we need to do is get you some decent clothes. Then you can get rid of those." She wrinkled her nose and waved her hand toward Sassy's pants.

"Clothes can wait. Teach me about the stuff ladies should know about, and how they're supposed to act."

"You mean social graces?"

"If that's what you call it, then, yeah, I guess so."

Greta smiled at the taller woman standing across the room. "When do you want to start?"

"I don't have much time, so I want to start right away. Today. Now, if possible."

"What do you mean, you don't have much time?"

Sassy silently chastised her loose tongue. "I . . .uh . . . I just meant the party is a week from Saturday. That gives me just nine days to learn what I need to know." She couldn't bring herself to meet Greta's gaze.

Greta contemplated Sassy's response. As bizarre as it sounded, she couldn't help thinking there had to be a man behind this. Finally, she said, "Okay, Sassy, we'll start right now. Let's begin with deportment lessons."

"Deportment? What the hell is that?"

"Deportment is the proper way to conduct oneself. And ladies *do not* curse. Swearing offends politeness and good breeding."

Another blush suffusing her cheeks, Sassy nodded contritely.

"Let's begin with how a lady should walk." Rising from the sofa, she moved to the opposite end of the parlor. "Now, walk toward me."

Sassy sighed, then did as Greta directed, her boots clumping on the wooden floor.

"No, no, no!" Greta took a deep breath, then said, "Don't take such long strides, and don't slouch. The gait of a woman should be neither fast nor slow. She should walk erectly and with ease, not stiff and slovenly. Try it again."

Sassy walked across the parlor again, trying to take smaller steps, her back straight, her head high.

"Shorten your strides a little more, and don't swing your arms. Remember, today's slim skirts won't allow you to take such long steps. Try again."

"My neck's getting stiff," Sassy groused, rubbing her shoulders and rolling her head from side to side to ease the tightness.

"You have to learn to relax, while holding your head regally erect. It just takes practice. Come on, walk for me again."

Turning, Sassy walked across the room once more, her face pinched in concentration.

"That's better. Now try again."

Presenting her back to her friend, Sassy clenched her fists in irritation, a silent snarl on her lips. *God help me to get through this without snatching every blond hair from Greta's head.*

Finally satisfied with Sassy's progress, Greta said, "That's enough walking. Be sure to practice every chance you can, and it would be a good idea to wear a skirt and high-heeled shoes when you do." Seeing the strange look flash across her friend's face, she asked, "You do intend to wear a dress and proper shoes to my parents' party, don't you?"

"Yes. I picked out fabric for a dress yesterday. Sheena offered to make it for me, and I already have a pair of shoes."

Greta's eyebrows shot up. "You picked out the fabric? That's wonderful." Noticing Sassy's embarrassment, she changed the subject. "Now, let's move on to how you should sit." Waving to the sofa, she said, "Take a seat."

Conscious of Greta watching her every move, Sassy lowered herself carefully onto the sofa and crossed one

78

ankle over the opposite knee. When her friend made no comment, she hid a relieved smile. Then she saw the look on Greta's face. "What's the matter? I didn't flop down like I usually do."

Greta moved to sit next to her. "Ladies don't cross their legs. Such behavior is accepted in men, but is ill-bred and disgustful in women."

Sassy dropped the crossed foot to the floor. "Just how the he—uh, heck am I supposed to sit?"

"Sit with your back straight, feet on the floor, knees together, hands folded in your lap. You must appear modest and dignified."

Sassy followed Greta's instructions, earning praise from her friend. "That's perfect." Seeing the mutinous look on Sassy's face, she added, "It's not uncomfortable once you get used to it, I promise."

When Sassy made no comment, but simply flashed her a doubtful look, Greta said, "Okay, the last thing we'll work on today is how a lady should speak."

"You already said they shouldn't curse."

"Yes, well there's a little more to it than that. A lady should never speak too loudly, since a loud voice sounds like scolding, and scolding is the strongest indication of low breeding. It is also bad taste for a lady to be a babbler, a real nuisance to society. Her manner of speaking should be both sweet and charming."

Sweet and charming, ugh! Sassy thought, momentarily wishing she hadn't asked Greta to be her teacher. How in the world would she ever remember all of this in time for the party? Exhaling a weary breath, she gave Greta a weak smile. "I've got to get home, but I'll be back tomorrow."

* * *

Over the next few days, Sassy arrived at the Bergstrom ranch each morning to continue her lessons. Greta relentlessly drilled her in the art of being a lady, making Sassy repeat the exercises time and again, until she was ready to scream. Yet surprisingly, she seldom complained. Instead, she used the time to ask Greta carefully worded questions about men. What they liked in women, how to get a man's attention—questions Sassy hoped sounded innocent enough, sort of a natural progression from her lessons. Yet, the questions Sassy asked weren't just idle conversation or simple curiosity.

She had a very important reason for wanting the answers—putting them to practical use with Ty Beaumont.

Seven

The blue roan mare took the bit between her teeth, dropped her head, and sunfished her sleek body in another attempt to buck Ty off her back. All four hooves hit the ground at once, sending a bone-jarring jolt from the top of Ty's head to the tips of his boot-clad toes.

Nearly a week had passed since he'd run into Sheena and Sassy in San Antonio—nearly a week of doing anything he could to avoid Sassy, and the reason he found himself on top of a bucking horse.

The animal was putting up quite a fight, amazing Ty with the strength she showed in trying to dislodge him from her back. The fence rail was crowded with the Star's ranch hands and the Mahoney brothers, all avidly watching Ty's attempts to tame the horse. As her bucking motions took him close to the fence, he heard one of the men yell to the others, "That roan could buck a man's whiskers clean off his face."

Ty couldn't agree more with the man's observation, and would have laughed with the rest of them, if he hadn't been so busy hanging on for dear life. His entire body aching from the pounding inflicted on him, he cursed his own stupidity for swinging into the saddle in the first place.

The Mahoney boys had been spending the day helping the ranch hands break a new string of mustangs. When they asked Ty if he wanted to help, he had foolishly agreed, forgetting the kind of punishment a bucking horse could inflict.

And he couldn't remember ever trying to break a horse as stubborn and determined not to bend to his will, as this contrary mare. Recalling the conversation he'd had the first night with Rory about the Mahoney horses, he knew mustangs were important to the ranch for crossbreeding with the horses having Connemara blood. He also knew, as Rory had pointed out, mustangs were known for their obstinate natures. That's why he'd selected this particular mare, thinking she wouldn't have the strength to put up much of a fight. Boy, had he been wrong! *Hell, this female's as hardheaded as Sassy,* he thought with a snort. Somehow he managed to smile at his comparison of Sassy and the uncooperative horse beneath him.

At last the roan's movements slowed to a few half-hearted crow hops around the corral. With heaving sides, the mare finally stopped, her head down, her entire body quivering with exhaustion. Ty spoke to her in low soothing tones, and patted her foam-flecked neck until her trembling stopped. She lifted her proud head and nickered softly.

Isn't that just like a female. He grinned at the thought. *A few softly spoken words and a gentle caress, and they settle down nice as you please.* Congratulating himself on a job well done, Ty pushed his hat back on his head and wiped the sweat from his face with his sleeve. He straightened gingerly in the saddle, trying to work the kinks out of his back.

Before he realized what was happening, or could do anything to prevent it, the supposedly now docile mare suddenly dipped her head. With one mighty buck, she neatly flipped Ty into the dirt.

Dazed from his sudden contact with the ground, he sat there for several seconds, willing his head to clear and trying to figure out if he'd broken anything. Deciding only his pride had been bruised, he rose carefully and turned to face the once again passive mare. When she shook her head and blinked her intelligent dark eyes at him, he could have sworn the horse wore a smug smile.

"Think you're pretty smart, do you, hellcat?" Ty said, dusting off his hands. Grabbing the reins, he stepped into the stirrup and swung onto her back again. "Hellcat. I think that's a good name for you. What do you think?" he asked, touching his heels to the mare's sides and sending her forward at a walk. Ty stiffened in the saddle and gripped the reins tightly, in preparation for a second round of bucking. This time the horse offered no protest to the burden on her back and quickly became a model student to Ty's role as teacher.

He couldn't help wondering if the mare's gentleness was only because it suited her not to fight him right then. It was never his intention to break her feisty spirit. He knew it was still intact—slightly bent maybe—but not broken. Again visions of another hellcat, the lavender-eyed Sassy, intruded into his mind. *I never want to see her spirit broken either.* Shaking off his wayward thoughts, he turned his attention back to the horse, now behaving beautifully under his guidance.

After putting Hellcat through a few more minutes of instruction to make sure she knew he was the boss, Ty dismounted. He unsaddled her, then spent a great deal of time rubbing down her blue-gray coat, to accustom her to his touch and scent. He talked continually in a low, soothing voice, until the mare dozed peacefully. As he finished grooming Hellcat, he decided to ask Rory if he could buy the mare. She would produce some terrific colts. He'd already bought a stallion to begin the line of horses he wanted to breed on his ranch. Putting the stud to Hellcat would be one of his first priorities when he got back to the Circle B.

Thoughts of his ranch brought reality crashing down around him. He might not get a chance to see Hellcat foal. If he didn't get his name cleared of murder, he wouldn't be able to devote his time to the ranch he'd been neglecting for too many years. He made a mental note to talk to Charlie Two Feathers about Joker. He'd already dallied on the Dublin Star too long.

Giving the roan one last pat, Ty headed for the ranch house, where he quickly gathered up a towel, soap, and a change of clothes. He was covered with a layer of sweat, and thanks to Hellcat's stubbornness, plastered with a layer of dirt as well. His body hurt everywhere, making him feel every one of his twenty-seven years. He made his way to the creek, whistling at the prospect of a bath and a long soak in the cool water.

Reaching the bathing pond, Ty quickly stripped off his filthy clothes and walked into the clear water. He eased his body down onto a large rock, sighing with pleasure. With quick efficient movements, he washed and then rinsed himself. Tossing the soap to shore, he leaned back on his elbows and let the soothing water ease his aching muscles.

As soon as he closed his eyes, Sassy's face appeared in his mind, as it did all too frequently. For a few minutes he allowed his imagination free rein. In those fanciful musings, Sassy joined him in his bath. Since he wouldn't allow it to happen in reality, he gave in to his urge to taste her passion and let himself become the aggressor in his daydreams.

Picturing Sassy approaching the creek bank, a smile touched his lips. The rustle of the bushes near the edge of the water brought his eyes open slowly. His smile broadened. *Damn, I can see Sassy so clearly, it's like she's here.* His eyes drifted shut again, the fantasy continuing behind his closed lids.

Somewhere overhead a bird gave a loud squawk, shaking Ty out of his daydreams and bringing his eyes open again with a start. He searched the area in confusion. Then his gaze settled on Sassy, a very naked Sassy, moving toward him in the pond. His mouth gaped open in surprise. "Jesus, I wasn't daydreaming. She really is here," he whispered.

Forgetting about his own state of undress, Ty jumped to his feet. "You . . . you shouldn't be here." His voice sounded strained even to his own ears.

Sassy couldn't reply; she could barely breathe. Having cut her lesson short with Greta, she'd arrived home just as Ty swung onto the mustang's back. Watching him ride the blue roan, then give the mare a rubdown, had aroused her senses to a fever pitch. She felt his hands run over the mare's shiny coat as if he were caressing *her* skin. Ablaze with the desire Ty unknowingly sparked, she had followed him to the creek.

Finding Ty sitting in the bathing pond, naked as a jaybird, she decided it must be fate. This was her chance to find out if her brothers' talk about pleasures of the flesh was correct. Since they often forgot about her true gender, no subject was avoided in her presence. She'd listened to them discuss their sexual conquests with great interest, but never considered trying what they praised so highly—until now. Without weighing the consequences of her actions, Sassy stripped off her clothes and stepped into the water.

Her heart pounding in her ears, she stared at Ty, fascinated with the water cascading through the thick golden hair covering his bare chest and down over the flat, ridged, muscular plane of his stomach. For an instant her gaze settled on that most masculine part of him. Recalling the first time she'd seen him, she realized her first impression had been correct. He was big there. Raising eyes dilated with both excitement and desire to meet his, she saw an answering desire flash in their dark brown depths. Smiling timidly, she continued closing the distance between them.

Mesmerized by the beautiful water nymph moving toward him, Ty couldn't move, though he knew he should at least cover himself for modesty's sake. But his body refused to cooperate. He remained standing straight and tall, while her hungry eyes traveled over him. Never one to be conceited about his looks or worry what others thought of his physical appearance, Ty was nonetheless extremely pleased with her reaction to his nakedness.

He, too, was pleased with the naked curves exposed for his visual inspection. He'd always known Sassy would be beautiful in this most natural state. Still, reality proved far better than his imagination. Her legs were long, her calves and thighs firmly muscled. His gaze moved upward to linger briefly on the curly dark triangle at the apex of her thighs. A stab of staggering desire sizzled through him. He forced his gaze away from that tantalizing spot, moving up over her concave stomach, narrow waist, and finally her breasts. She wasn't overly endowed, but the firm mounds were high and round. He had the sudden urge to taste the rosy tips with his tongue.

When he met her gaze again, Ty accepted defeat. He held out his arms, and she stepped into the circle of his embrace. He pulled her against his chest, then captured her lips with his. Sassy pressed her naked flesh wantonly against the length of his body, moaning deep in her throat when his kiss grew more urgent. His body on fire from her nearness, Ty thought surely the water surrounding them would soon boil, then turn to steam.

Acting purely on instinct, Ty lifted Sassy into his arms and strode to the creek bank with her held tightly against his chest. He eased her down onto the soft bed of grass beneath a large cottonwood tree, then stretched out next to her. His hands explored the hills and valleys of her silken body, his mouth claiming hers in another heated kiss. When he pulled away, Sassy's breathing was as labored as his.

Ty lowered his head and closed his mouth over one of the pert nipples he longed to taste. He groaned with pleasure. His tongue laved the tip until it stood up in a tight rosette. Greedily, he suckled the tasty morsel.

Sassy had never experienced such pleasure. She was amazed to feel the stimulation of his lips on her breast much lower on her body, in that secret place between her thighs. Wanting more of the wonderful sensations he created, she arched her back to press closer, to ease the ache deep in her belly.

For a few minutes, Ty lost all contact with reality, completely forgetting his vow not to touch this woman again. When her hand raked through the mat of hair furring his chest, then moved lower to brush against his throbbing manhood, reason returned in a rush. He pulled his mouth from its assault of her bosom. Rolling away from her, he forced his quaking legs to support his weight as he got to his feet.

Lying so temptingly at his feet, Sassy looked up at him, questions lurking in her eyes. His heart contracting with tenderness, he wished he could take her in his arms again. But he couldn't.

"Get dressed," he ordered, his voice more fierce than he intended. When his words registered, he watched the desire burning in her eyes flicker, then die. He longed to kiss away the pain. Stifling the urge, he moved to where he'd left his clothes and started pulling on his pants.

From out of nowhere, a fist-swinging, cursing wildcat came flying at him. Grunting from the impact, he took a step backward, then another. Unable to maintain his balance, he went down hard, the air *whooshing* from his lungs. Lying on his back, he opened his eyes to find a very angry Sassy straddling his belly.

"Damn you, Tyler Beaumont," she spit out. "Why did you stop?"

As he tried to fend off her fists, he realized that even like this—a fiery-eyed tigress, crouching buck-naked over him—Sassy appealed to him more than ever. Her hair flying in wild disarray around her shoulders, her eyes, still darkened to purple with the residue of passion he'd stoked, pierced him with an icy glare. In spite of his position, he struggled to keep a smile off his face.

Tyler. Only his mother called him that, and then only when very displeased with him. Obviously Sassy was cut from the same bolt of cloth, only he couldn't quite picture his mother sitting naked on a man's chest while taking him to task.

"Take it easy, wildcat," he shouted, flinching when one of her fists caught his left cheek with a glancing blow.

He finally managed to stop her attempts to pummel him by grasping her wrists and pulling her forward, until he held her hands immobile over his head.

Unable to continue venting her frustration with her fists, the fight went out of Sassy as quickly as it had begun. Her body went limp, her head falling forward in defeat against her extended arms. "Why?" The word came out in a pain-filled whisper.

Ty couldn't think, much less answer intelligently—not with a very desirable, naked Sassy poised over him, her chest now directly above his face. Pulling his gaze away from her heaving breasts, jiggling enticingly near his mouth, he managed to find his voice. "Get dressed, Sassy. Then we'll talk." He slowly released his grip on her wrists.

Realizing he wouldn't answer until she obeyed him, Sassy rose and quickly pulled on her clothes. When she turned to face him, her entire body felt flushed and throbbed with unfulfilled need. Still miffed over his rebuff of her advances, her anger began to fade when she saw the pain on his face.

"I'm sorry, Sassy," he began softly. "I lost my head when you approached me nak . . . uh . . . like you did. And I should never have started what I had no intention of finishing. I won't be here much longer, and I can't allow myself to get involved with you. There's no future for us," he concluded.

The bitterness of his last words erased the last remnants of Sassy's anger. "Whatever it is, I can help you, Ty," she pleaded gently.

Shocked by her perception, he berated himself silently for allowing her to see his hurt. "I don't need your help," he ground out between clenched teeth. The pain in her

89

expressive eyes made him regret his harsh words, yet he didn't call them back.

Bracing himself for another volley of her temper, Sassy surprised him by calmly accepting defeat and walking away. Stunned that she didn't retaliate after his brusque words, he stood rooted to the spot, dumbly watching her stiff-backed exit from the glade. Again she had thrown him off balance with her unpredictable behavior. And again he felt his attraction to her grow.

Ty entered the dining room that evening unsure which Sassy he would encounter, a spitting wildcat, a timid kitten, or some other kind of feline. He held his breath while taking his usual seat across the table from her. Exhaling slowly to bolster his courage, he raised his gaze to meet hers. When she greeted him with a dazzling smile, he nearly fell out of his chair. Desire sprang to life so powerfully, he had to force himself not to leap from the table, scoop her into his arms, and spirit her away to finish what they had started at the creek.

He shifted his gaze from her glowing face, a myriad of questions tumbling through his mind. Would he ever understand the constantly changing Sassy: one minute exhibiting a wild sensuality, the next a blazing fit of temper, and now, calm, gracious sophistication? Could he resist her advances should she corner him again? And more importantly, did he want to?

Before he'd looked away, Sassy glimpsed the confusion reflected in his eyes. Her insides cramped with the need to erase the troubled expression on his face. As she continued putting on a very convincing smiling facade, her mind spun with a multitude of questions. What is causing Ty so much torment? What can I do to help him?

How do I get him to share his pain with me? And remembering the way her body burned with desire as they lay entwined beneath the cottonwood tree at the creek, will he resist me if I try to seduce him again?

In spite of the uncertainties, Sassy refused to give up. Forcing herself to swallow her doubts, her determination to get her questions answered reasserted itself. Confident once more, she squared her shoulders and sent another smile to the object of her thoughts.

She would get Ty right where she wanted him one way or another. He just didn't know it yet.

Eight

Alone in the Dublin Star office, Ty sat with a glass of Irish whiskey to pass the time until the Mahoneys were ready to leave for the Bergstrom party. He'd poured himself the liquor to shore up his strength for the evening ahead, yet he doubted it would help—nothing could shore up his strength when it came to Sassy. Although he'd tried not to want her, she affected him more than any woman he'd ever known.

Taking a sip of the potent whiskey, he realized he'd made the right decision. He planned to leave in the morning, even though he would be taking a chance riding Joker, when the gelding's leg wasn't a hundred percent healed. But he had to take the risk. He just couldn't hang around any longer.

He'd made the announcement to the Mahoneys several nights earlier, the day after he nearly lost control of his physical hunger for Sassy at the creek. The episode at the bathing pond had shaken him badly—his attraction to Sassy was entirely too strong, and even worse, it continued to grow stronger. As painful as the thought was, it was best to get the hell off the Dublin Star, far from lavender eyes flashing with desire and silky skin begging for his touch.

The sounds of the Mahoneys gathering in the court-yard interrupted Ty's thoughts. Swallowing the last of his drink in one fiery gulp, he left the office to join them. Rory and Sheena greeted him, followed by Brodie, Lucas, and Trevor. There was no sign of Sassy.

He wondered if she refused to attend the party because of her abhorrence for any of the activities women were expected to enjoy. "Where's Sassy?" Then another thought hit him. "She isn't ill, is she?"

"No, Sassy's fine," Sheena replied. "She went over to the Bergstroms this morning, to help them get ready for tonight."

Nodding absently, he followed the Mahoneys through the passageway to the carriage waiting at the gate. Knowing Sassy would be at the party proved just as disturbing as thinking she'd taken ill. The paralyzing fear he'd felt at that possibility changed into nervous tension.

During the ride to the Bergstrom's party, Ty wished for the hundredth time he'd begged off. But Greta's parents had made a point of adding their invitation to hers, so he couldn't very well insult them by not attending. He knew his reluctance to go stemmed from Sassy's brazen behavior at the bathing pond. Who could blame him? Especially when his gut instinct told him she hadn't given up trying to get him to seduce her. *Seduce her, hell. She's trying to seduce me!* He smiled in spite of his gloomy mood.

His efforts to avoid her after the near disaster at the creek had paid off. But the party would change that. Sassy would be close by, her nearness teasing his already overwrought senses. The evening would be a real trial, especially since he wasn't sure he could remain immune to her advances much longer.

Yes, it was definitely best for him to move on. As much as he hated the thought of never seeing Sassy Mahoney again—at least not as long as he was on the run from the law—he knew that if he stayed around, he'd end up doing something he'd regret.

Sassy studied her reflection in the mirror over Greta's dressing table. Her eyes glowed with anticipation, and a little fear as well; her cheeks were rosy with a flush of excitement. She couldn't wait for the Bergstrom party to begin.

Having decided not to reveal her new feminine skills until she made her entrance tonight, Sassy had spent the day at the Bergstrom ranch. After a long bath, Greta had given her a manicure, clucking at the horrible state of her nails, then helped her dress and arrange her hair.

Turning from the mirror, Sassy said, "Greta, are you sure I look all right?"

Greta looked at her friend and smiled. "Sassy, for the tenth time, you look wonderful. Your hair is perfect, your dress is perfect. And your dancing will be perfect."

Sassy giggled in spite of the nervous fluttering of her stomach. "Well, maybe, but Wilhelm's feet will never be the same."

Greta laughed, recalling how she'd coerced her younger brother to partner Sassy in dance lessons, then sworn him to silence. "Don't worry, he'll survive. And you'll do just fine, so stop fretting."

Stop fretting. Sassy repeated the words several times in her head, hoping to calm her nerves. She'd spent all her free time practicing the things Greta taught her, determined to make a favorable impression at the Bergstrom party. Now that the evening had arrived, Sassy found waiting—especially for Ty's arrival—nearly unbearable. Even though he had successfully avoided her for the past several days, she was determined he wouldn't avoid her tonight.

When she thought about how her time was about to run out, pain clutched at her heart. On the evening following her aborted attempt to advance their relationship, Ty had announced he would be leaving on Sunday. Somehow she'd managed to hide her shock at his announcement. Though she knew he planned to leave eventually, hearing him say the words threw her into a near panic. He couldn't leave—not yet, not before she got the chance to show him they were meant for each other. She'd wanted to box his ears, but by sheer willpower had been careful not to let any of the emotions tumbling inside her show.

Certain he'd made the decision as a result of her boldness, her suspicions were confirmed when she spoke with Charlie Two Feathers about the condition of Ty's horse. Joker was much better, she'd been told, but not completely healed. From what Charlie said, she deduced that Ty had pressed him about the horse's ability to travel on the morning after her failed seduction at the creek.

Greta's voice pulled Sassy from her musings. "I'm going downstairs to help Mama. Shall I call you when your family arrives?"

Sassy nodded, praying Sheena would make sure the Mahoneys were on time. Time dragged by, one interminable minute at a time, until Greta finally called her.

"Well, Sassy, me girl, this is it," she told her reflection, using the Irish accent her father lapsed into on occasion. She studied the dress she and Sheena had selected as her coming-out attire for the party. Although the neckline revealed more than a hint of cleavage, she knew they'd made the right choice.

She smoothed an errant curl, made sure the pearl-studded combs in her hair were firmly in place, then took a deep, calming breath to slow her racing heart. Recalling her plans for the evening, an impish smile played about her lips.

The party had just begun when the Mahoney carriage arrived. Lanterns in the mesquite trees surrounding the patio at the back of the house created a gay atmosphere for the people gathered there. Tables overflowed with food under the protection of a vine-covered arbor, while another table held a punch bowl and other assorted drinks. A group of men had gathered around the latter, each with a drink in hand and laughing at something one of them said.

An area at the edge of the patio had been cleared for dancing, and the sounds of musicians tuning their instruments could be heard above the chatter of the guests.

Ty was the last to step from the carriage. He remained at the patio gate, watching the Mahoneys head in different directions: Sheena and Rory went in search of their hosts, Brodie headed for Ellen McDaniel, the daughter of another neighbor and the girl he was courting, and Lucas and Trevor joined a group of young men. Spotting his destination, Ty headed straight for the drink table.

Sassy stepped through the veranda doors and stopped. The patio was filled with guests. Remaining in the shadows, she searched the crowd until she found her father

96

and Sheena talking to the Bergstroms. Her gaze continued moving over the guests, until she located each of her brothers. Her forehead wrinkled with confusion. Where was Ty? A momentary panic gripped her. Searching the crowd again, she finally caught sight of him by the refreshment tables. Who was he standing next to? No, not Greta!

Viewing her friend's small stature, heavy bosom, and flashing, light blue eyes, Sassy felt a stab of jealousy. She couldn't help wondering if Ty preferred her friend's looks to her own. She'd never considered her friend's beauty a threat before. Now Sassy saw it as competition. The painful image of Ty in the arms of someone other than herself was so staggering, that for a moment she couldn't do anything but stand in frozen terror.

"Sassy! Is that really you?" Lucas's voice broke through her trance.

Seeing the startled look on her brother's face, her good humor returned. "No, I'm a fairy princess," she said, giving him a mischievous smile.

Lucas laughed, then stepped back to take a better look at her. He whistled softly. "I see you took my advice about needing to wear a dress, if you want to attract a man. When Ty gets an eyeful of you, he won't know what hit him."

"I don't know what you're talking about," she replied, grateful the pale light cast by the lanterns didn't reveal the blush creeping up her neck.

"Okay, Sass, have it your way. Your secret's safe with me." He gave her a conspiratorial wink, then turned to leave. "See you later, little sister."

Sassy watched her brother weave his way through the crowd. In spite of the embarrassment his words had caused, his compliment also restored her self-confidence.

Smiling brightly, she stepped onto the patio. She'd circulate among the guests, letting the excitement build. Then she'd make her move to get Ty exactly where she wanted him—which was most definitely *not* in Greta Bergstrom's arms.

As the evening progressed, Sassy didn't approach Ty. But he was never out of her sight. Each time her gaze chanced to meet his, she sent him teasing flirtatious glances, meant to set his blood on fire. It wasn't in her nature to act coy, but Greta had insisted that men thought they should be the ones doing the chasing. However, Greta had also said a woman could help her cause, by flirting with a man to get his attention and prompt him to make the first move. Not entirely certain she could pull it off successfully, Sassy decided to try what sounded more like a game of cat and mouse than a tactic to maneuver a man into thinking it was his idea to take chase.

So far, batting her lashes and sending Ty secretive smiles hadn't brought him any closer to her than when the evening had begun. Sassy wondered if she was playing the coquette all wrong.

When the dancing started, Sassy couldn't squelch the hope that her come-hither looks would produce the desired results. Her hope of Ty's falling victim to her heated glances was quickly dashed. He remained firmly entrenched near the refreshment table, making no move to join the dancing couples.

Swallowing her disappointment, she accepted a dance with one of the local men, hoping to stir Ty's jealousy and prompt him to act.

The action that followed wasn't what she had in mind. She watched helplessly over the shoulder of her dance partner as Ty put his drink down and moved toward the group of women gathered across the patio. She nearly choked with pain when he turned back to the dance floor, a smiling Greta hanging on his arm. When Ty smiled in return, Sassy missed a step and brought the heel of her shoe down hard on the foot of her dance partner. The man's grunt of pain brought her back to reality. She quickly mumbled an apology, trying not to look at the attractive couple across the dance floor. Yet in spite of her resolve not to, her gaze continually strayed to the pair of blond heads, Ty's dark gold one bent close to Greta's much fairer curls.

Somehow Sassy managed to get through that dance and the next two, although she had no idea who she had danced with. She was aware of only one thing. Ty had danced all those dances with Greta, and now they were standing together on the far side of the dance floor. *Well, that's about to end,* she fumed silently. She marched toward her longtime friend and the man she was determined to have.

As she approached the couple, Sassy tried to relax her tight facial muscles so her smile would appear natural. Controling the wild pounding of her heart proved more difficult.

"Excuse me, Greta," she said in what she hoped passed for a pleasant tone. "But could I have a word with you?"

"Certainly, Sassy," Greta responded, then turned back to Ty. "Would you mind getting us some punch?"

Ty recognized the look on Sassy's face and knew it forebode trouble. Thankful for any reason to get away from the woman with the blazing eyes before the fireworks started, he quickly nodded his agreement and headed for the punch bowl. He'd been aware all evening of every sizzling glance Sassy had directed at him from across the patio. Even with his back turned, he'd felt the heat of her gaze scorching through his clothes, keeping his desire at the point of ignition.

Now, having seen her up close . . . He took a deep breath, then blew it out slowly. *Damn, this isn't getting any easier.* His first sight of her earlier in the evening had been a complete shock. He thought he'd at least begun being immune to her beauty. He was dead wrong. Seeing her in a fashionable dress, her hair arranged in a cluster of curls cascading down her back, her eyes alight with excitement—a true epitome of femininity—had nearly knocked him to his knees. Then, having her stand next to him, even briefly, allowing him to notice how the tight-fitting bodice of her dress exposed the upper swell of her breasts, had sent his self-control even closer to the breaking point.

What was behind her wearing a new dress and her flirtatious behavior? She was up to something, he just knew it. He was equally certain he'd be smack-dab in the middle of whatever mischief she had in mind.

Watching Sassy and Greta while waiting his turn at the refreshment table, Ty wondered what Sassy was saying to her friend. He had only asked Greta to dance as a courtesy, since she was the daughter of his hosts and the one who'd originally asked him to the party. Finding Greta easy to talk to, he hadn't thought it improper to extend the invitation to the next two dances.

Now he wished he'd stayed with the men, since it looked like Greta was receiving the brunt of Sassy's temper. And from his vantage point across the patio, he had the uncomfortable suspicion he was to blame.

"I want you to leave Ty Beaumont alone," Sassy whispered fiercely, as soon as Ty was out of ear shot.

"What do you mean, leave him alone? We were only talking," Greta replied. *So, I was right! A man is respon-*

sible for Sassy wanting to be a lady. Deciding to play dumb, she added, "Besides, he's a very nice man, and I enjoyed dancing with him." Seeing the sparks leap into Sassy's eyes, Greta couldn't resist one last remark. "And he's sooo handsome, don't you think?"

"He's *mine,* dammit," Sassy said through clenched teeth. "I'm warning you, Greta, leave him alone."

Although Greta didn't condone Sassy's affinity for swearing, and had warned her countless times during their lessons about cursing, at least she no longer flinched each time her friend used an off-color word. She'd heard nearly Sassy's entire repertoire during the last few days. "Yours? You've never been interested in a man in your life, Sassy Mahoney. How was I to know Ty Beaumont carried your brand? He didn't act like he was spoken-for," Greta answered innocently.

Realizing the truth of Greta's words, the starch went out of Sassy. "You're right." She sighed heavily. "You had no way of knowing I'm interested in Ty, and I know it looks like there's nothing between us. But there's going to be," she finished, her voice again firm.

Seeing Ty approach them, Greta gave her friend a quick hug as she whispered, "I understand, Sassy, and I won't interfere. I promise."

When he rejoined the young women, Ty eyed one then the other, trying to determine their mood. "Here's your punch, ladies." He studied the two more closely, relieved to see Sassy's anger hadn't progressed beyond a few heated words.

As Sassy accepted the glass of punch, his fingers brushed hers. A powerful current leaped between their hands. Ty lifted his gaze past her moist lips and slightly flared nostrils, until he looked into her smoldering lavender eyes. Again he knew she was responsible for the strange quivering of his insides. Her eyes held him captive, making him long to snatch her into his arms and kiss her senseless.

Even though Greta was lovely, and he'd enjoyed talking to her, no woman could hold a candle to Sassy. From the first moment he'd seen her, he knew he wanted her. He now realized with sudden clarity that she was the only woman he'd ever want.

Aware he was contributing to his own demise, Ty couldn't stop himself from asking Sassy to dance. He wanted to be near her and smell her sweet scent. He especially wanted to touch her. Escorting her to the dance floor, he had eyes only for the woman on his arm. He was silently grateful the song the musicians struck up was a waltz, so he could hold Sassy close, rather than a fast-paced reel where he would have to relinquish her from his embrace.

He nearly groaned aloud when Sassy stepped into his arms. The urge to pull her body tightly against his almost overpowered him. Using every bit of willpower he possessed, he mastered the need and held her the proprietary distance away.

While they danced in silence, oblivious to their surroundings, Ty tried to control his increasing ardor by forcing himself to remember the conversation he'd had with Sheena Mahoney that morning. She'd invited him to join her for coffee after Sassy had left the house. Once they were seated on the porch, she came straight to the point.

"Ty, I think you should know something about Sassy. I'm sure you're aware she's a very complex young woman. You know firsthand about her temper and her tendency to act rashly," she said with a smile.

At Ty's answering grin to her understatement, Sheena

continued the speech she had prepared. "I want you to know how Sassy came to be the way she is, so perhaps you'll understand her better. Rory was born and raised in Ireland, a very poor country where the quality of living is very different from here in Texas. His family constantly struggled to put enough food on the table and keep a roof over their heads. They had nothing that wasn't absolutely necessary, and not always that.

"When Rory had a chance to come to America to start a new life, he jumped at the opportunity. He started this ranch and swore his children would never suffer the hardships he had endured. He taught all of them how to defend themselves and to fight for what they wanted. He encouraged them to be independent thinkers. They were also taught never to give up on something that's really important to them. I'm afraid Sassy may have learned that lesson a little too well." She smiled again, almost apologetically. "But I also want you to know she doesn't have a selfish bone in her body, and has the kind, gentle heart of her Irish ancestors. Her volatile temper and strong will make her a worthy adversary, or a fierce ally."

Sheena paused to let Ty absorb everything she'd said. "What I'm trying to say, Ty, is this. Don't underestimate my stepdaughter's abilities or her determination. She'll keep fighting for something she believes in until her last breath. I truly believe that, and you should, too."

Sheena excused herself, leaving Ty to mull over her words. Her explanation of her stepdaughter's upbringing did help him better understand Sassy's behavior. It also worried him. Would Sassy actually go to whatever lengths were necessary to get what she wanted?

His thoughts returned to the present when Sassy leaned closer, her breasts brushing against his chest. Looking down at the lovely bundle of complicated womanhood filling both his arms and his thoughts, his breath caught in his throat. She met his gaze, her eyes smoldering with desire. Having her look at him like a starving dog staring at a meaty bone, completely unnerved him.

Waiting for the music to end, her pulse increased. When Ty asked her to dance, she'd recognized his invitation as the opportunity she'd been hoping for. And since she likely wouldn't get a second chance, she knew she had to act quickly. As soon as the music stopped, while the other guests were busy claiming partners for the next dance, she'd make her move.

When the last strains of the waltz faded away, Sassy drew a deep, calming breath to settle her jangling nerves. Calling on all her inner strength, she set into motion the plan she knew would change her life forever.

Nine

Sassy led Ty away from the party, the sounds of music and laughter growing fainter and fainter. Surprised he hadn't objected when she looped her arm through his and steered him away from the dance floor, she wasn't about to ask why. She was just thankful he'd allowed her to tow him toward the barn without a word of protest.

She quickened their pace, not wanting a scene in the middle of the yard. If Ty decided to balk at her scheme, she wanted to be safely inside her destination, away from prying eyes and ears. The Bergstrom barn wasn't very imaginative, but with so many people around, she'd had little choice. Since she didn't consider herself a romantic, the setting didn't matter. Not as long as it made Ty realize they were meant for each other. She was confident that once they made love—which she was determined would happen—he'd see they belonged together. Then when he left the Mahoney ranch, he'd want her to go with him.

As she passed through the arched doorway into the dark interior of the stone barn, the scents of hay, leather, and horse droppings assailed her. The familiar combination of odors eased her apprehension.

She moved toward the hayloft ladder, her hand clasped

tightly over Ty's. When she put her foot on the first rung and started to climb, he hesitated.

His voice a raspy whisper, he said, "Sassy, I don't—"

"Shh, it's okay. Come on," she whispered back. She held a nervous breath until he started up the ladder instead of protesting further.

Thinking his brain must have turned to mush, Ty followed Sassy up to the loft. He wanted to say the words, knew he should say the words, to halt whatever she had planned. Yet, his insight about her being the only woman he wanted stilled his tongue. When they reached the hay-filled loft and Sassy wrapped her arms around his neck and pressed her mouth to his, he completely forgot about the reservations he should be voicing. Instead, he concentrated on returning her kiss.

He kissed her long and deep, his tongue dueling with hers. He finally had to pull away to draw a cleansing breath, and slow his quickly escalating desire.

"Make love to me," Sassy implored, her voice husky with need.

Looking into her face, barely visible in the weak light from the window high in the loft's peak, Ty knew he had lost the inner battle he'd been waging. Sassy was obviously determined to get him to make love to her, and he no longer had the strength to continue fighting either her or the desire she stirred in him. His need for Sassy went far beyond the fact that he hadn't been with a woman in months. The truth was he wanted, needed Sassy much more than just to satisfy his physical hunger.

He wished things could be different. If only he didn't have to leave. If only he didn't have to clear his name. But he was wanted by the law, and had to get back to his search for Teddy. That left just tonight to create a memory to take with him, a memory that would have to

106

last him a lifetime. Still, he felt compelled to give her one last chance to back down.

"Are you sure, Sassy? Absolutely sure?" he asked, his voice as husky as hers.

Moving her hands to his shirtfront, Sassy began slipping the buttons through their holes. "You're leaving tomorrow, so this is our last night together," she replied, pushing the shirt from his wide shoulders. When she touched his bare flesh, a groan deep in his chest rumbled beneath her hands, making her shiver with pleasure. Thrilling at her newfound power, she explored the heavy muscles of his chest, running her fingers through the covering of soft hair, then down over the ridges of his ribs and on to his hard, flat stomach. Her hands moved to the waistband of his pants, impatiently struggling to free the button.

"Jesus, wildcat, take it easy. Here, let me help you," he said, pushing her fingers away. He took a step back, sat down in the straw, and tugged off his boots. His pants quickly followed. When he looked up from his task, his breath caught in his throat at the vision Sassy presented. Her clothes in a pile near her feet, she turned to face him. Naked.

Spreading his shirt out next to him, Ty held out one hand. "Come here, darlin'. Let me love you."

Her body quivered with excitement at his endearment, and a little fear at what was about to happen—even though she wanted it more than anything. Sassy moved to where Ty sat in the hay and knelt beside him.

Raising up on his knees, he pulled her against his chest, then closed the distance between their lips. As his mouth settled on hers, she groaned his name, fanning his already blazing desire.

Her breasts crushed against his hair-roughened chest,

her thighs pressed against the muscles of his legs, she could feel his manhood throb against her belly. She had never known such overwhelming pleasure, and tried to press even closer. A heat continued to build deep inside her, centering on the spot in the nest of curls shielding her womanhood and quickly becoming as hot as a prairie fire.

Unconsciously she shifted her body to straddle one of his rock-hard thighs. With a rhythm she was unaware she knew, she rubbed against him in an effort to ease the pulsing ache continuing to build between her legs.

As Sassy moved erotically against him, Ty felt the heat radiating from her secret woman's place. The wetness of her need on his flesh filled him with momentary panic. He suddenly feared he would lose control, spilling himself against the silky skin of her belly, not deep inside her where he longed to be. Drawing away from her, he whispered hoarsely for her to lie down.

The hay was scratchy where Ty's shirt didn't protect her, but the discomfort was soon forgotten in the wake of the craving his kisses and caresses created.

Sassy boldly explored Ty's body, her fingers skimmed over him, taking delight in the texture of his skin. The shudder rippling over him, and the groan she elicited from deep in his chest when her hand brushed his engorged hardness, increased her own excitement to a fever pitch.

When she wrapped her fingers around him and started moving awkwardly, he grabbed her hand and pulled it away. What would normally have been welcome attention was too much for him now. His control already hung by a thread, and he had to stop her before it snapped. Rolling her onto her back, Ty turned his attention to reciprocating the pleasure she had given him.

He began with her breasts, capturing one peak with his lips and pulling it into his mouth. His tongue circled its tip until it stood up hard and erect, bringing a gasp of delight to Sassy's lips. While his mouth continued ministering to each of her creamy breasts, he lowered one hand to the patch of curls between her thighs.

She jerked with both shock and pleasure when his fingers came in contact with her damp flesh. Quickly growing accustomed to his intimate touch, she let her thighs fall open in invitation. When he grazed the sensitive bud nestled in the folds of her femininity, a moan tore from her throat, her hips lifting to meet his hand.

"Sassy, I can't wait any longer," Ty managed to say. Moving between her opened thighs, he lowered himself onto her quivering body.

The hair on his chest rubbed erotically against the tightened tips of her breasts, heightening her already stimulated senses. Then his male hardness brushed her inner thigh, probing for entrance.

Through her muddled brain came the chilling realization that his sex was much bigger, more intimidating, with his full arousal. Suddenly overcome with panic, she began struggling to push him away.

It took him a minute to realize she no longer writhed with passion beneath him, but was trying to get free of him. His ardor cooling at her sudden reluctance, he ceased his attempt to join their bodies. Bracing himself on his elbows, he cupped her face in his hands to halt her thrashing.

"Sassy, it's okay. You can stop fighting me," he whispered, brushing damp curls away from her face.

She went still at his words. Opening her eyes, she fearfully met his gaze. She expected him to be angry—after all this was her idea—and she braced herself for his censure. Instead she saw only concern mixed with desire mirrored on his face.

"I'm sorry," she managed to croak.

"What is it, Sassy? I thought you wanted this. Why are you so frightened?" he asked in a gentle voice, the backs of his knuckles rubbing her cheek in a soft caress.

Sure her face flamed dark scarlet, she was glad of the poor light in the barn. She swallowed hard, then began speaking in a small voice. "I did, I mean, I do want to make love. But you're—" She swallowed again, then finally blurted out, "You're so big, and I thought you would . . . that I'd be . . ." her voice trailed off, unable to finish her painful confession.

If Sassy hadn't been so serious, or so obviously scared of what she believed would happen to her, Ty would have laughed aloud at her being afraid of anything. Instead he cleared his throat to erase the last vestiges of amusement. His fingers traced her arched eyebrows, high cheekbones, and kiss-swollen lips. "Don't be afraid of my size, darlin'. Your body can accommodate me. Trust me."

Other women he had known expressed eagerness after seeing his engorged, fully aroused member. Of course, none of them had been as inexperienced as Sassy when it came to such knowledge. Protesting the delay, the part of his body under discussion throbbed painfully with the need to finish what he'd started.

Watching her face closely, he saw she wasn't yet reassured and decided on a different tact. Shifting his body to support his weight on one forearm, he grasped Sassy's hand and lowered it between their bodies. With his hand firmly cupped over hers, he forced her fingers to brush past the dark curls and touch herself where he wanted desperately to be.

"Feel how ready you are for me, Sassy. So slick and

110

wet. That's your body's way of preparing for me," he murmured, releasing her hand.

She could feel the dewy moisture on her fingertips, and even though she should have been mortified at what he'd made her do, strangely, she wasn't. Although she had been embarrassed to admit her reluctance to consummate their fevered lovemaking—after shamelessly offering herself—she now trusted Ty's insistence that he wouldn't hurt her. She no longer felt any hesitation, when she whispered, "Make me yours, Ty."

His burning need returning in a full-fledged rush, he growled with pleasure. Lifting her legs up around his hips, he pushed into her. As her exquisite tightness began to surround his shaft, luring him deeper with rippling contractions, he prayed for control. His teeth gritted with determination, he forced himself to ignore the urge to drive into her with one thrust.

At last, he carefully eased forward, allowing her to grow accustomed to his presence. When he felt resistance, he stopped and whispered in a voice thick with tightly reined desire. "There will be a moment of pain, Sassy. But then pleasure, only pleasure, I promise you."

Once he had begun the deed that would make her a woman, his woman, her desire returned, fierce and demanding, and more potent than before. The threat of pain did nothing to cool it. "Please, Ty," she murmured. "Please."

Ty's tightly held restraint snapped with her plea. He gave one quick thrust forward, then held perfectly still. Vaguely he heard Sassy's sharp intake of breath at the breach of her maidenhead. Then he could only hear the pounding of his heart in his ears, the rasping of their mixed breaths. The muscles deep inside her gripped his manhood, contracting in a milking motion that nearly

111

sent him over the edge. He struggled to gain some measure of control over his rapidly escalating urge for completion.

Wrapping her long legs more tightly around his waist, he groaned when the position drove him even deeper into her pulsing center. Unable to wait any longer, his hips began moving. Slowly at first, then faster and faster he pushed forward, then pulled back, teasing her inflamed nerve endings with his shaft. When he found the movement that brought a gasp from Sassy and caused her hips to arch up with his every thrust, he concentrated on continuing that motion.

Although he knew she was very near her climax, his own release began before he could guide her to hers. He knew it was rare for a woman to reach the pinnacle of sexual pleasure the first time she made love, yet, he was disappointed Sassy would be denied because of his inability to curb his own need.

Just before the world began to spin crazily and his manhood throbbed its release against her womb, he promised himself to see to her pleasure as soon as he recovered from the most satisfying lovemaking he had ever known.

Somewhere in the barn a horse stomped restlessly, and another whinnied softly. Outside a coyote howled for its mate, and in the hayloft only the sounds of breathing in deep heavy pants could be heard. Sassy shifted restlessly beneath Ty's sweat-dampened body. Somehow he managed to summon the strength to move, rolling off her and onto his side.

"Just give me a minute, and I'll take care of you," he murmured.

"Take care of me?" She turned to look at him, her brow furrowed. "I don't understand, I'm fine."

Raising up onto one elbow, Ty looked down into her flushed face. "I want to see to your pleasure."

"But I did have pleasure. It was wonderful," she told him honestly.

Chuckling lightly, Ty placed the heel of his hand on the hair-covered mound at the base of her stomach, and teased her still sensitive flesh with his fingers.

She gasped, her hips lifting at his touch, her body instantly aflame with renewed need. When he leaned over to kiss her, she eagerly met his lips.

Raising his head, he murmured against her mouth, "You haven't experienced a woman's true pleasure, darlin'. A man should always see to his woman's pleasure, and that's what I aim to do."

Thrilling at Ty calling her *his* woman, Sassy let herself be swept away by his fingers rubbing the distended kernel of flesh between her thighs. Her hips started rocking in response to his rhythm. Somewhere in her passion-clouded brain, she knew the truth of his words. Her earlier enjoyment was a mere shadow of the intense pleasure she now experienced. Her blood surged like liquid fire through her veins, settling in the spot beneath Ty's hand. Her hips bucked against his knowing fingers, the hot fullness he stoked spreading outward until she thought she would lose her mind if she didn't find relief soon.

Just when she thought she couldn't stand any more of his delicious torment, her body stiffened. Responding to Ty's words of encouragement whispered against her ear, she gave herself over to the spasms of ecstasy racking her body. When a cry started to erupt from her throat, Ty quickly lowered his mouth to absorb the sound with his kiss.

When Sassy's senses finally returned, she lifted eyelids

made heavy by the incredible pleasure she had just experienced to look up at Ty.

She reached up with a hand still trembling with the aftermath of her powerful climax and stroked his cheek. The look of wonder on her face brought a grin to his lips.

"So, now do you understand?" he teased.

Not trusting her voice just yet, she could only nod in reply.

Long minutes passed while they lay together in the sweet-smelling hay, allowing their heart rates to return to normal and their breathing to slow. Running her fingers through the thick hair growing in such profusion across Ty's chest, Sassy traced lazy circles over his muscular torso, while she tried to find a way to ask him the question uppermost in her mind.

Not being able to voice her thoughts was new to Sassy, and the direct result of the man whose naked body she was pressed against. Ty made her do and feel things she had never done or felt before, and she found the realization very unsettling. She didn't want to change for a man; that was why she'd never had a beau. No man had been willing to put up with her sharp tongue and easily ignited temper, which had been just fine with her. Now there was Ty Beaumont.

Aside from the fact that she couldn't make him jump through hoops, he was a very special man. That he hadn't tried to change her, plus the feelings he stirred in her, made Sassy realize just how special. Most unsettling—yet, also pleasing—was an even more startling realization: she'd fallen in love with him.

All those thoughts strengthened her resolve to ask her question, even if doing so shattered his languid mood.

"Ty, can I go with you tomorrow?"

At first, Sassy thought he hadn't heard her softly spoken words. But when his body stiffened next to hers, she knew he had indeed heard. Raising up onto one elbow, she peered into his face to gauge his reaction. The earlier desire had been replaced with simmering anger.

"So that's what this was all about. You throw yourself at me like a two-bit whore, then after I take what's offered, you figured I'd feel honor-bound to marry you, in case you're with child. And, of course, when I leave, I'd feel compelled to take my wife with me."

She dropped back onto the hay next to him, so he wouldn't see the truth reflected on her face. He'd seen through at least part of her plan, but he had the reason for taking her with him all wrong.

In case you're with child. The words rang in her head. She'd been so caught up in the excitement of wanting to be with Ty, the idea hadn't occurred to her. By making love, Sassy had hoped he would see they were meant for each other, not play on his sense of honor.

You dunderhead, she thought peevishly. *Can't you see what's as plain as the nose on your face?* She longed to say the words aloud, but instead said, "No, that wasn't what this was about. And how dare you call me a whore! You know damn well I never did this before." Struggling to control her growing anger, she sat up and began yanking pieces of hay from her hair.

Seeing he had insulted her when he never meant to, Ty wished he could take back his words. His heart ached for the woman whose wild-as-the-wind nature had captivated him from the start, and he knew he deserved her reprimand. His comment was totally uncalled-for. *Damn, how could I be such a cad? First I make love to her, when I knew I shouldn't have, then I make it worse by calling her names.*

Heaving an exasperated sigh, he said, "You're right, I had no call to say that, and I'm sorry." His voice hardened when he added, "But I still can't take you with me."

Realizing again some unknown force drove Ty to say the things he said, her anger died. Something ate at his insides, and so far she'd been unsuccessful in getting him to share whatever it was. Rising from the loft floor, she snatched up her clothes and began dressing in silence.

Ty quickly followed suit. After pulling on his boots, he turned to find Sassy struggling to get into her dress. The idea of Sassy in a dress was still hard to get used to. He cleared his throat to hide an amused chuckle.

Unable to resist the woman who touched his heart like no other ever had, he carefully lifted the lavender silk and dropped it over her head. Smoothing her wildly curling hair, he bent and gently kissed the tip of her nose.

Sassy dropped her head to keep him from seeing her smile. He wasn't as immune to her as he wanted her to believe. And even though he'd spoken to her angrily, she knew his anger was born from the pain he felt, not directed at her.

Although she longed to rant and rave at him about needing her help to solve whatever problems he faced, she swallowed the words and followed him down the loft ladder. He still planned to leave tomorrow, and she was determined not to spend their last hours together locked in combat.

When she reached the barn floor, Ty grabbed her arm. "Wait a minute. There's still hay in your hair." He removed several pieces from her curls, then brushed more from her dress. "Come on, we'd best get back to the party, before we're missed."

"You're not going anywhere," a voice called from the doorway.

Ty stiffened. Glancing over his shoulder, he saw Rory Mahoney, and just behind him stood Lucas and a woman he didn't recognize. Ty turned an accusing glare on Sassy. "I should have known there was more to your plan," he snarled in a low voice. "After coaxing me into the hayloft, you arranged to have your father find us."

Her eyes wide with shock, she shook her head. "No! I didn't—" The look on Ty's face silenced her protest.

Rory took in his daughter's disheveled appearance and the mutinous look on Ty's face. "I think you and I better have a talk, Beaumont."

Ten

Sassy marched from the barn, her hands clenched in fists at her sides. She didn't know who she was angrier with—Ty for thinking she'd planned for her father to find them in the barn, or Lucas for ratting on her. She longed to smash her fists into both their faces.

Seeing the furious glare his sister shot at him, Lucas moved closer. "When I said you might have to wear a dress to get his attention, I didn't mean you should let him haul you off to a hayloft."

Sassy gave him a withering glance. "And just what were you planning on doing in the barn—" She nodded to the woman walking next to him. "With her? If you hadn't gone there yourself, you wouldn't have found me."

A muscle jumped in his jaw. "That's different."

"No, it isn't."

"It sure as hell *is*."

Sassy stopped and whirled to face her brother. "But why?"

"Because it is, dammit, so leave it at that." Lucas gave her a shove toward the Bergstrom house, then quickened his pace to catch up with his father and Ty.

* * *

After a hasty goodbye to the Bergstroms, the Mahoneys headed for the Dublin Star. The ride home was painfully quiet. When the carriage rolled to a halt at the ranch house, Rory jumped down and turned to help Sheena.

"I expect to see you in my office in ten minutes," he said to Ty. "And as for you." He looked at Sassy. "Stay in your room until I call you."

Sassy was summoned to her father's office half an hour later. When she stepped into the room, Ty stood ramrod stiff in front of her father's desk. Her father sat just as stiffly behind it.

"Sassy, Ty and I have discussed the situation. He has accepted responsibility for his actions and has agreed to do the proper thing. You'll be married as soon as we can get a priest out here."

For a moment, her brain didn't register what she'd just heard. Then when her father's words sank in, she glanced first at Ty, who hadn't even looked at her since her entrance into the room, then back at her father.

"Wait a minute. Don't I have something to say about this? And what do you mean Ty has accepted responsibility for his actions? He didn't force himself on me, if that's what you think. Going into the Bergstrom barn was my—"

"That's enough, lass," Rory interrupted. "You don't have any say. I've always told you and your brothers to be prepared to take responsibility for your actions. Which means, sometimes you have to pay the consequences." He glanced up at Ty, then back to his daughter. "You'll marry him, lass."

"I don't know what you're so all-fired het-up about. Brodie, Lucas, and Trevor have all had plenty of women.

You ain't never told one of them they had to get married. Besides, didn't you always tell them, 'why marry the cow when the milk's free?' So why—"

"Enough!" Rory snapped, his face a dull red. "What's good for my sons doesn't necessarily hold true for my daughter."

"Why doesn't it?"

"Because it's different for girls."

"Different? That's what Lucas said. I don't understand why—"

"It's just different, that's all."

"But why is it different?" she insisted. "I've always done everything my brothers do. Why should losing my virginity be any different? I waited a lot longer than any of them, that's the only difference."

Rory's flush deepened, completely at a loss on how to deal with his daughter's logic. He finally cleared his throat and said, "Perhaps I'm to blame for allowing you to think you can do anything your brothers do. However, that doesn't change the fact that your reputation will be ruined if word gets out about what happened tonight. So, you'll accept Ty's offer of marriage."

Sassy started to protest, then bit her lip. *I love Ty, so why am I fighting this?* Because he doesn't love you, came the answer. Glancing at Ty from the corners of her eyes, she knew he might not love her now—but he would. He obviously desired her, and with time she was confident he would return her love.

"Okay, Papa, I'll marry him."

At Sassy's words, the stiffness left Ty's shoulders. Although he might have been able to convince Rory Mahoney that Sassy's reputation could be salvaged, he knew her virginity could not. So, was that why he'd agreed to marry her? Even more confusing was his relief when

120

she'd accepted. He pushed such thoughts aside; he had to concentrate on getting back to his search. He couldn't let his impending marriage—no matter how desirable he found his bride-to-be—interfere with his mission. He had to get Teddy to tell the authorities the truth, so the charge against him would be dropped. Unfortunately, finding Teddy was the problem.

The wedding was set for eleven the next morning. Since Rory was a generous donor to his church, the priest summoned from San Antonio had no problem dispensing with the banns when he learned of the circumstances and the need for haste.

At ten forty-five Sassy stood in the center of her bedroom, alone. After Sheena helped her with the dress she'd stayed up half the night altering, her stepmother left to get herself ready for the upcoming ceremony.

Sassy moved to stand in front of the mirror. The dress she wore had been Sheena's wedding gown, taken in to fit Sassy's more slender frame. The dress really was lovely, and just as her stepmother predicted, its cream color perfectly complimented her golden complexion and dark hair. Sassy touched the brocade satin skirt tentatively, then ran her fingers over the lace edging the high, round neckline, before lifting a hand to the ribbon in her hair. Her mother's ribbon. For a moment her throat clogged with emotion.

Sheena had been so kind: offering the dress she'd worn when she married Sassy's father, helping with the numerous buttons on the tight-fitting bodice, arranging Sassy's hair in a cluster of curls with the frayed ribbon she'd kept all those years. Yet Sheena hadn't said one

word about the suddenness of what was about to take place.

Sassy knew her stepmother probably wanted to condemn her for her actions. Thankfully Sheena had kept such talk to herself, saving Sassy from having to say she wasn't sorry for what she had done. She loved Ty and was about to become his wife. A knock on the door pulled her from her thoughts.

"It's time, lass." Rory's voice came clearly through the door, but lacked its usual warmth.

Sassy took a deep breath, then turned, and walked across the room. Lifting her chin, she opened the door. Rory stood rigidly on the other side. Glancing up at him, she saw the hard glint in his eyes. His posture softened somewhat when she took his offered arm.

As they walked to the *sala,* Sassy longed to beg him to forgive her, but she said nothing. Her father's coldness cut her deeply, but she refused to let it show. Her head held high, she entered the room where she would soon become a married woman. When her gaze found Ty, standing stiff and unyielding in front of the priest, her unruffled facade nearly cracked.

Digging deeper for more inner strength, she took her place next to him. As the priest began the wedding mass, she snuck a quick peek at Ty's face. He stared straight ahead; a muscle jumped in his clenched jaw. She wanted to grab him and shake him. *Can't you see we belong together, you numskull?* Somehow she managed to remain still, her lips tightly sealed.

She tried to pay attention, but the low drone of the priest's voice reciting the Latin she'd never mastered soon allowed her mind to wander. What was Ty thinking? And how would he treat her after the ceremony? Would he—

She was jerked back to the present with a start. It wasn't the priest's voice she heard. It was Ty's.

He spoke his vows in a strong voice, though the expression on his face remained closed and inscrutable. Then it was Sassy's turn.

She swallowed, praying none of the quaking she felt inside would be reflected in her speech. Her voice was clear, though unusually husky as she repeated the words that would bind her to Ty for all time. Though she longed to turn and look Ty full in the face to better gauge his thoughts, she didn't give in to the urge.

At last the ceremony ended, the priest pronouncing them man and wife. Sassy turned slowly toward Ty, afraid of what she'd read in his expression. When he made no move to seal their union with a kiss, pain at his refusal clutched at her insides. Then his shoulders lost some of their stiffness, and he bent down to press his lips gently against hers.

Though the kiss was far from passionate, Sassy was consoled that at least he hadn't refused. And for an instant she'd felt his lips soften slightly against her mouth. When he lifted his head, she opened her eyes to gaze up at him. Though he kept his thoughts hidden from her, she sensed a change. The harshness had left his face; he appeared almost relaxed. Perhaps he *did* feel something for her. She prayed it was true.

Sassy had been Mrs. Tyler Beaumont for less than an hour when her new husband pulled her aside.

"I'll be leaving as soon as I get my things together."

"Leaving?" She searched his face for some sign of teasing. "But we just got married. Sheena had Rosa fix a spe-

cial dinner for us. And what about tonight, we haven't—"
Her face flamed at what she'd started to say.

"I'm afraid I'll have to miss the dinner." He smiled
faintly. "And, as for the other . . ." He cleared his throat,
reluctant to let her know how much he'd miss their wedding night. "I have a very important investigation to get
back to, and I have to leave."

Grasping his forearms, Sassy gave him a pleading
look. "Then take me with you, Ty. A wife belongs with
her husband."

"Maybe some wives do." He removed her hands from
his arms, then added in a fierce voice, "I don't even
want a wife." Keeping his gaze from hers, he turned and
left the room.

Ignoring his cruel words, Sassy ran outside after him.
"Then, why did you marry me?"

Crossing the yard, Ty never broke stride when he replied, "In case you've forgotten, your father had a thing
or two to say about it."

"You could have refused."

Ty gave a bark of laughter. "Right. Then we'd have
been married with a gun aimed at my back."

"Papa wouldn't have done that."

Ty stopped abruptly and turned to face her. Sassy
looked so beautiful in the cream-colored dress. He
longed to touch her, to run his fingertips down the silky
length of her neck. "Let's just drop it, okay?"

"I want to go with you, Ty," she pleaded softly.

"And I said you can't."

Seeing the hard set of his jaw, Sassy changed tactics.
"Then, stay until morning. It's already past noon. Aren't
you hungry?"

He didn't miss the flare of fire in her eyes, or the
obvious double meaning of her words. "I have to—"

She placed one hand over his lips to silence his protest. "Please stay tonight. You can leave first thing tomorrow."

Ty knew that if he agreed, he'd end up spending the night in Sassy's bed—right where he wanted to be, but also right where he shouldn't be. Yet he couldn't form the words to deny her request.

The afternoon and evening droned on forever, and Sassy had long since lost the thread of conversation. After the marvelous dinner Rosa had served in honor of the newlyweds, the bride wanted nothing more than to excuse herself and retire to her bedroom with her husband. Yet, even she knew that wouldn't be acceptable behavior. Now that darkness had nearly fallen, her anxiety grew with each passing minute.

When Rory and Sheena finally rose and said their good nights, it was all Sassy could do not to jump to her feet and scream her relief.

Ty had watched Sassy squirm and fidget through the long hours since their discussion about his leaving. He also felt the thrill of anticipation he knew she was experiencing. After the others left the *sala,* Ty took a deep breath and approached his wife. "Shall we?" he said in a soft whisper, holding out his hand.

Her smile caused his heart to do a strange flip-flop. Thinking it was only his physical hunger for a taste of her passion, he discounted any other reason and escorted Sassy to her room.

Inside her bedroom, she found herself at a loss over what to do. Did she just grab Ty and throw him onto the bed as she longed to do, or must she wait for him to make the first move? Before she could decide on her course of action, his voice broke into her thoughts.

"I'll go out for a smoke, while you get ready for bed."

Before she could say anything, he stepped through the door and closed it softly behind him. Resisting the urge to rip her clothes off for fear of ruining Sheena's gown, she slowly undressed, then poured water into the basin on the washstand. She wished she could soak in a tub of warm water, but tonight such a luxury wasn't possible. A quick sponge bath would have to do.

Turning down the lamp on her bedside table, she slipped between the cool sheets to await her husband's return.

Five minutes passed, then ten. How long did it take him to smoke a cigarette? she wondered in growing frustration. Every sound made her heart pound with anticipation. And each time the sound didn't bring Ty's return, her anxiety increased. In spite of her best efforts to stay awake, her eyes dropped closed, her breathing slowing to the steady cadence of sleep.

That was how Ty found her, hair spread out on the pillow like a dark cloud, one hand curled next to her face, lips parted softly in her peaceful slumber. For a minute Ty considered leaving before she awakened. One glance at the curves outlined beneath the single sheet covering her, chased such thoughts from his mind.

Removing his clothes with fingers made clumsy with impatience, he slid into bed beside her and leaned over to kiss her sweet mouth. Slowly her eyelids fluttered open. The twin lavender pools blinked with confusion, then as recognition dawned, their color darkened.

"You're back," she whispered, raising one hand to stroke his cheek.

"Yes, I'm back. I can't seem to . . ." His words trailed off as he captured her lips in another ravishing kiss. He wished he could resist her. But when faced with Sassy's lips parting beneath his to accept his probing tongue, and her body writhing against him in blatant invitation, he couldn't control himself.

When he finally broke the kiss, Ty propped himself up on one arm to look at the naked beauty curled next to him. "I don't want to rush this time, Sassy," he murmured. "I want to make love to you all night."

Sassy nodded her head eagerly at the picture his statement painted, then put her arms around his neck, and pulled him down next to her.

As his lips grazed hers, he heard her murmur, "Yes, all night."

Ty fulfilled the promise of his words and made slow, leisurely love to his wife. His lips tasted and teased, his hands caressed and aroused, until she became mindless with the need to gain her release. At last, he rolled atop her and joined their bodies. She gasped almost immediately, as wave after wave of her climax crashed over her. He waited until the last of her spasms passed, then began moving again. At first he stroked slowly, then more quickly, establishing a rhythm that brought her to the brink again. This time they soared over the edge together, their groans of delight blending in perfect harmony just as their bodies were doing.

After dozing for a few minutes to regain his strength, he began another slow, purposeful journey to ecstasy. Finally, he followed Sassy into an exhausted sleep, replete at last.

Just before dawn, Sassy floated up out of her deep slumber to find Ty moving over her. She was shocked her body had responded to him even while she slept. Shock quickly turned into red-hot desire, as he artfully brought her to passion's peak. Then suddenly she went cascading over the top and sailing on the heaven-reaching wings of sexual release. Ty shuddered atop her, then groaned against her ear. She had never known such contentment.

His strength all but gone, Ty relieved Sassy of his weight and rolled onto his side, gathering her into his arms.

When the magic spell of their loving began to recede, she whispered, "Ty, please take me with you." She felt his body stiffen.

He'd been daydreaming about spending every day with Sassy, tasting her passion every night. Her untimely question jerked him out of his reverie. "Is that why you insisted I stay the night? So you could work your feminine wiles on me, and get me to change my mind? Or was this just part of your plan to trap me into marriage?"

She pushed away from him and sat up, her eyes flashing with displeasure. "That's not true. I admit, I wanted to see if fornicating was as good as my brothers claim. As for trapping you into marrying me, that is *not* true." She lifted her chin defiantly. "But since we are, I want to go with you."

Already flushed with anger, Ty felt his face burn even more at Sassy's frankness. Looking into her eyes, he knew she spoke the truth. Yet, he refused to acknowledge it aloud. "Like I told you yesterday, I can't take you with me. I have to get to Austin as soon as possible, then head north to catch a train to El Paso."

"Why can't I go?"

"Dammit, because I don't want a woman tagging along!" He hated being so harsh, but that's the way it had to be. She would stay on the Dublin Star, and he would go on alone—maybe to be alone for the rest of his life—or if he didn't get his name cleared, he might end up getting his neck stretched.

Sassy's voice dropped to a whisper. "Even if the woman's your wife?"

Hardening himself against the pain in her voice, Ty said, "Yes, even if she's my wife. I don't need you getting in my way."

He was sorry as soon as the words were out of his mouth. The pain in Sassy's eyes hit him like a physical blow. Rolling from the bed, he reached for his pants. *It's better if she feels anger toward me.* He dressed in silence, prepared to receive the full force of her temper. Again she surprised him by not turning on him like a screaming shrew and calling him every foul name she could think of.

Sassy's temper stirred at Ty's harsh words, but she held her tongue. She'd seen the look of despair on his face before he'd gotten out of bed. She knew in spite of his hurtful words, his anger wasn't directed at her, but at whoever or whatever continued to cause his pain. Touching his arm lightly, she said, "Ty, please. I—"

"It could be very dangerous, Sassy," he interrupted, before she could finish what he assumed to be another plea to change his mind. "And I just couldn't risk your safety."

Using the possibility of danger as an excuse told Sassy he might be willing to take her, if circumstances were different. She had to try one last time. "If it's as dangerous as you say, what about you? Won't you be in danger, too? Let me go with you to help. You've seen how I handle a gun."

Her fear for his safety tugged at his heart, making him long to pull her close and kiss those luscious lips. Instead he smiled at her tenderly, amazed again at the delightful package Sassy presented. The unusual combination of traits she possessed—fierce yet gentle, outrageous yet

129

engaging, temperamental yet passionate—were most definitely not typical of the women of his acquaintance. And he knew in his heart he wouldn't want her any other way.

"No, Sassy, I won't be in any danger. I'm a lawman, remember, trained to handle those kinds of situations."

Although she knew his words to be true, she still wasn't convinced he wouldn't be in danger. Not wanting him to think she thought him incapable of handling the situation, she tactfully dropped the subject.

When she didn't continue arguing, Ty sighed with relief. He wished he could tell her he'd be back, wished he could promise her more nights like the one they'd just spent together, but the uncertainty of his life forbade it.

Though he might never see her again, he'd have the memory of their one night of incredible passion. Sassy had been a wildcat; his back bore scratch marks to prove it. The discomfort was worth it, since it kept his mind off another, more intense pain: the bone-deep ache he felt at having to leave her.

Ty had to swallow the lump in his throat before he could speak. "I've got to go." He found he couldn't leave without tasting her mouth one last time. As their lips parted, he whispered, "Goodbye, darlin'."

Sassy was sure Ty didn't realize he'd used the endearment, yet her heart sang with joy just the same. She watched him slip from her room, then flopped back on the bed. Her brow creased in thought, she stared at the ceiling.

She had to think of a way to reunite them. Not only did she want to be with Ty because she loved him, but she also wanted to help erase whatever plagued him. When she decided on a plan of action, she smiled with satisfaction.

Closing her eyes, she fell into an exhausted sleep.

* * *

"Have you lost your mind?" Greta stared in disbelief, hands planted on her hips.

Sassy smiled at her friend's outrage. "No, I haven't lost my mind. I meant what I said; I'm going after Ty."

Greta knew the stubborn set to Sassy's jaw only too well. Once she set out to do something, no amount of talking could change her mind. Yet, she felt obligated to try. "El Paso is a long ways, Sassy. A lot could happen between here and there."

"Oh, Greta, you're such a worrywart. I'll be fine."

Wishing she had more of Sassy's optimism, she replied, "Who's going with you? Oh dear, don't tell me you planned on asking *me* to be your chaperon."

Sassy laughed. "Married women don't need chaperons."

"Married?" Greta's eyes widened. "You're not say— You're married? You and Ty?" At Sassy's nod, she said, "When?"

"A week ago last Sunday."

Greta's brow furrowed. "That would make it the day after my parents' party." She looked at Sassy suspiciously. "Something happened here that night, didn't it?"

The splotches of color staining Sassy's cheeks answered her question. "Oh, Sassy, how horrible for you, being forced into marriage."

Sassy's chin came up. "No, it wasn't horrible. I . . . I love . . ." She cleared her throat, then murmured, "I love him."

Greta studied her friend for a moment, then whispered, "Truly?"

"Yes, truly."

Greta clapped her hands with delight. "Now, I see why

131

you're so anxious to join Ty. He must love you a lot, to ask you to meet him in El Paso. He'll be thrilled when he sees you."

Sassy nodded absently, the corners of her mouth lifting in a thin smile. How could she tell Greta, who thought all this terribly romantic, that Ty hadn't asked her to meet him? Nor could she admit thrilled was the least likely reaction she expected from Ty.

Leaving the Bergstrom ranch a few minutes later, she decided it didn't matter that Ty didn't want her with him, or what his reaction would be. She planned to leave first thing in the morning, and nothing anyone said would change her mind.

Eleven

Sassy stood in the shadows cast by the depot roof, anxiously awaiting the departure of the nine-fifteen train to El Paso.

She'd arrived in Fort Worth late the afternoon before, only to learn she'd have to wait until morning to continue her trip. Resisting the urge to don her Grunt clothes and visit a saloon to pass the time, she'd spent the evening holed up in a hotel room near the train station.

Ten days had passed since her new husband's departure. *Damn you, Ty Beaumont!* she grumbled silently. *I felt like a newborn calf whose mama won't accept him, having to explain how come you left me high and dry the day after our wedding.* His demand that she stay on the Dublin Star still rankled. The possibility that she lacked some feminine skill to keep a man, hurt more than she wanted to admit.

We should be together, she thought, grimacing from the constant pain of her new shoes. *This trip would be a whole lot more comfortable, if I didn't have to wear these miserable toe-pinchers. They're turning me into a cripple!*

The whinny of a horse pulled her thoughts from what

she'd like to do to her offending footwear. "That sounded like Blarney," she murmured, suddenly fearful she'd made a mistake in bringing the mare. Yet, since she'd told her father and Sheena she was meeting Ty in Austin before heading to her new home on his ranch, it was natural to take her horse.

She started toward the stock car where Blarney had been loaded, then stopped abruptly. Sucking in a surprised breath, she stared at a man waiting to board one of the passenger cars.

Ty Beaumont stood not thirty feet from her.

Sassy took a step back, hoping the deeper shadows would hide her presence. She devoured him with her gaze, her heart thumping heavily in her chest. Although she wouldn't have admitted her relief aloud, she'd been secretly concerned about finding him. He'd told her his destination was El Paso, yet she'd worried he would change his plans. Thankfully, he hadn't.

Longing to run to him, she held her ground. He'd likely send her home, if she approached him now. She decided to wait until the train was well on its way to El Paso, before she made her presence known.

At the conductor's call for final boarding, Sassy stayed put, reluctant to leave the protection of the roof's shadows. Watching the passenger car Ty had entered, she inched forward, ready to retreat to cover if he reappeared in the doorway.

"Hey, lady, are ya gettin' on this train or not?" The conductor's exasperated words jerked her to attention.

Flashing the man an annoyed look, she snapped, "Don't get your drawers in an uproar. I'm coming."

A deep rumble of laughter came from behind her. Glancing over her shoulder, Sassy saw a man dressed entirely in black, walking toward the train. She scowled in his direction, then hurried to a passenger car several ahead of the one Ty had boarded.

In her haste, she caught her heel on the hem of her skirt and tripped up the last step. She went down on her knees hard. "Damn fool dresses," she muttered, struggling to get her feet untangled from the yards of fabric in her dress. "This lady shit really gripes my ass."

Another burst of laughter brought her head up with a snap. The man dressed in black put one hand under her arm and helped her up. When she'd regained her balance, he said, "Is that any way for a lady to talk, Miss?"

Sassy glanced up at him, straining to see his face. The brim of his hat kept all but the lower half of his face hidden. She thought she could see a scar running down one side of his stubble-covered jaw, but she couldn't be certain. Shaking off his hand, she lifted her chin proudly. "It isn't Miss, it's Mrs. Mrs. Tyler Beaumont."

The man's mouth fell open. When he didn't speak, Sassy said, "Excuse me, I have to find my seat." She moved past him and swept through the railcar door.

Gaping after her, Kit Dancer snapped his mouth shut. "Well, I'll be damned, Mrs. Ty Beaumont," he murmured, before entering the passenger car on the opposite side of the platform.

Ty chose a seat in the back of the railcar, and tried to get comfortable for the long, boring train ride to El Paso. He wasn't looking forward to having nothing but his glum thoughts to keep him occupied while making the trip.

Fort Worth had been a waste of time, just like all the other tips he'd followed over the last few months. His prey wasn't in Fort Worth, and no one had any new information. El Paso was the only lead left to check out. Although not sure the long trip would pay off, he had nothing else to go on. Disappointed by his previous efforts, he tried not to let his expectations get too high this time.

The rocking of the train soothed his overwrought nerves, making him drowsy. He hadn't slept much lately, and it was finally taking its toll. Wiggling until he was halfway comfortable, he stretched his legs out in front of him as far as he could, tipped his head back against the seat, and let the rhythm of the train lull him to sleep.

Only in his dreams did the memory of Sassy return. During the day he forced away thoughts of the woman who fired his blood like no other. He couldn't afford to think about her; the pain was too great. So she invaded his mind when he had no control over his thoughts. In his dreams he couldn't stop her lovely image from filling his head, nor did he want to.

Since leaving the Dublin Star, his nights had been so filled with the passionate Sassy and their heated lovemaking, that he awoke every morning painfully aroused, a sheen of perspiration covering his body. Several times he'd given serious thought to seeking relief from his constant torment, by visiting a saloon employing women who did more than push drinks and dance with the customers.

But he didn't. He told himself he couldn't risk being seen, in case someone could describe him later. Deep down he knew the truth; no woman but Sassy could appease his burning hunger. And since he couldn't have her, he didn't want anyone else. Besides, like it or not, he was married to the chit—vows he was shocked to realize he had taken seriously.

That day his dreams didn't disappoint him. Sassy was

there behind his closed eyes, pressing her lips to his, inviting his heated response.

After traveling for several hours with nothing to occupy her time but her disconcerting thoughts, Sassy decided it was time to face Ty. She rose from her seat and—fighting the swaying of the train and her ungainly skirts—headed toward the back of the train.

Gingerly, she made her way from one car to the next, taking care on the platforms between them not to lose her balance. Reaching the car she believed Ty had entered, she stood outside the door and peered through the small window. She smiled triumphantly. He was in the back of the railcar, his head resting against the back of the seat, eyes closed and jaw slack with sleep.

She entered the car and closed the door carefully behind her. Grateful the other passengers paid no attention to her entrance, she tiptoed down the aisle. Reaching the seat where Ty sat slumped against the window, she stood quietly for a minute, content to just look at him.

His golden hair was much longer than she recalled; the lines of worry she remembered creasing his forehead, were eased by his sleep. Her gaze traveled eagerly over his thick eyebrows and the darker gold eyelashes resting against his sun-darkened cheeks, then on to something new, the beginnings of a mustache. She contemplated the addition to his appearance, deciding she liked the silky blond hair curling above his full mouth.

Those lips beckoned her. Taking great care, she knelt on the seat next to him, braced her arms on either side of his head, and tentatively touched her lips to his.

At first his immediate response to the pressure of her mouth surprised her. Then a thrill of excitement shot through her veins, and she deepened the kiss. It felt like ten months rather than ten days since she'd tasted his mouth. The nearness of him and his intoxicating male scent turned her insides to jelly.

Sassy leaned closer until her breasts brushed his hard chest. Instantly their tips tightened in response to the contact; heat started to build between her thighs. A moan from deep in her throat escaped before she could stop it.

Ty hungrily returned her kisses. "Oh Sassy, Sassy," he groaned in his sleep. *"I've missed you something awful."* Like water given to a man dying of thirst, he drank deeply of the life-sustaining nectar of her lips. His loins filled with a rush of desire. He longed to join their bodies and find relief in the pleasure of her hot feminine center.

While all his dreams of her were sensual, this one was different. It was still erotic, but it was so real, as if she were actually with him, actually drugging him with her kisses.

A second throaty groan brought his eyes open with a start. He blinked several times, certain he was seeing an image created by the last dregs of his dream-filled sleep. When the image didn't disappear, he wrenched his mouth away from hers. Grasping her arms, he pushed her away until she sat crouched on her knees next to him.

Slowly Sassy opened her eyes. When her deep purple gaze met his, Ty nearly lost control. Ignoring the strong urge to kiss her again and let the flames of her fiery passion consume him, he forced himself to remember the more urgent matter he had to deal with—Sassy's presence.

His emotions went through an abrupt but complete transformation: Intense, burning desire became barely controlled rage.

He tightened his hands on her arms and gave her a hard shake, nearly rattling the teeth out of her head. For an instant, his rough treatment made Sassy almost regret her actions.

"Just what the hell are you doing here?" he snarled.

Sassy had been prepared for his being less than pleased to see her, even extremely upset at her sudden appearance. She hadn't expected his reaction to be the fierce anger etched on his face, or the viselike grip of his hands on her arms.

Loaded to the muzzle with rage. Her stepmother's saying described Ty perfectly, she decided, nearly choking on a giggle threatening to erupt.

She kept her gaze downcast, hoping her posture appeared contrite. If he saw her amusement, all hell would break loose.

"Well?" he ground out, giving her another shake.

His continued rough handling was the catalyst to arouse her temper. Lifting her face, she boldly met his dark turbulent gaze.

In a chillingly haughty voice, she announced, "Take your hands off me, you son of a bi—"

"Don't say it, Sassy," he warned. He jerked his hands from her arms, as if touching her was suddenly repellent.

He released her so quickly, that she lost her balance and had to grab the back of the seat to steady herself. Rubbing her arms where his fingers had bit into her flesh, she shot him a nasty look. To give herself time to regain her composure, she kept her gaze averted while shifting around to sit on the seat, then carefully smoothing the wrinkles from her skirt. She stole a glance at him from beneath her lowered lashes, trying to gauge the strength of his anger.

Although obviously still more than a little put out with

her, his nostrils no longer flared, the muscle in his clenched jaw no longer jumped—signs his temper had cooled.

She hoped.

Ty took a deep breath and exhaled slowly, then slumped back in the seat. He took several more cleansing breaths, trying to erase what remained of his hot-blooded reaction to seeing the last person he'd expected to find on the train—the very woman who'd been haunting his dreams. His wife. Forcing thoughts of his marriage to retreat to their hiding place in his mind, he turned his gaze on her.

"Okay, Sassy, what are you doing here?" Although he had to ask, he wasn't sure he wanted to hear her answer. He wasn't going to like it; he just knew it.

Meeting his penetrating stare, Sassy looked him straight in the eye when she replied, "I'm here because I want to be with you, Ty. After you left the Star, I couldn't stand it. You said you were heading for El Paso, so I decided to join you there."

When his eyes narrowed with suspicion, she gave him a weak smile and added, "I just happened to catch up with you before you got there."

"Oh, God," Ty groaned. He closed his eyes to block out her beautiful face, saying a silent prayer. *God, save me from independent, unpredictable women!*

"What we had before you left was special," she continued softly, when he said no more. "And I . . . I didn't want to risk losing it, or you."

His eyes opened, revealing unmistakable longing hidden in their depths. She saw pain there as well. The same pain she'd noticed and wondered about before.

"Come on, Sassy. I know you well enough to know

you don't believe in such drivel. Tell me the real reason you did such a foolish thing."

Sassy's back stiffened. "It wasn't foolish, dammit!" At his warning glance, she swallowed hard. "All right, I followed you because I love you," she blurted, glancing around to make sure no one had heard her admission.

Ty threw back his head and laughed. "What do you know about love? Just because I was the first one to get into your britches, you think that's love? Well, let me tell you some—"

"No, that's not what I think," she interrupted, her face flushed with anger. Deciding to plunge ahead, she kept her voice low when she said, "I started falling in love with you the first time I saw you. At the time, I was too angry to realize it."

Ty laughed even harder. When he regained his composure, he wiped his eyes, then flashed her a crooked grin. "That's a good one. Sassy Mahoney believes in love at first sight."

Sassy's hackles rose at his statement, but she held her tongue. Turning away from him, she settled for giving him what-for in her mind. *It's Sassy Beaumont now, you idiot! And yes, it's true!* She vowed silently not to say the words again—not until he said them first. Hands clasped in her lap, she sat rigidly in the seat, staring straight ahead. Ty said something, but she ignored him, the pain of his laughing at her confession too fresh.

"Sassy!" He touched her hand to get her attention. "I said, what did you tell your family?"

"I told them you'd left because you had important business in Austin, that we'd made plans to meet there, and then we were going on to your ranch near Waco."

Ty jerked upright. "How did you know my ranch is near Waco?"

141

She shrugged, then said, "I asked Charlie Two Feathers. He said your ranch, the Circle B, is on the Brazos not far from Waco."

The tenseness left his shoulders. "I see. Well, following me was still a harebrained idea. Don't you realize you could have been hurt, or worse? What if you'd caught the eye of some lowlife and . . ." Ty shuddered, unable to list the misfortunes that could have befallen Sassy. His anger came flooding back, his fear for her safety making him realize the chance she'd taken by chasing after him.

When Ty's tone turned cross again, Sassy had the sudden urge to kick him in the shins. But when he called her idea harebrained, she took on the demeanor of an angry kitten: back hunched, claws bared, spitting and hissing its displeasure. Before she could find her tongue to give vent to her agitation, she noticed his gaze remained fixed on her mouth.

Her pique forgotten, a hint of a smile teased her lips. His unconscious actions gave her some needed answers: how to cool his temper once and for all, and more importantly, how to gain his acceptance of her traveling with him.

Turning on the seat, she leaned toward Ty. As she came closer, his eyes widened in surprise. When he opened his mouth to speak, she pressed her fingers to his lips.

"Shh, I'm here and I'm staying," she whispered, replacing her fingers with her mouth.

He tried again to stop whatever she had in mind. But her tongue slipped between his parted lips before he could utter a sound. Instead of protesting her tactics, he groaned in response, wrapped his arms around her, and pulled her close.

Never letting her lips break contact with his, Sassy ran a hand over his hard-muscled chest, down over his ribs, then lower to settle on the front of his trousers. Her fingers found and massaged his throbbing flesh. His manhood jerked in immediate response to her touch, snapping Ty out of the passionate stupor he'd fallen into.

"Sassy!" His voice sounded more like a croak, clearly revealing his shock.

"Ty, I want you," she murmured in response, her fingers searching for the buttons of his fly.

"Sassy, stop," he pleaded, gripping her hand and shoving it from his lap. Although he longed to hike up her skirt and ease his painful arousal, he didn't. "We're not alone."

She whimpered in protest, but pushed away from him and collapsed against the seat. "Dammit!" she murmured softly, bringing a chuckle from Ty.

"I wholeheartedly agree, darlin'. But I don't want to get put off this train because we, uh—" He ran a forefinger lightly down her cheek. "Well, let's just say, because we behaved inappropriately."

She smiled in return, deciding to take advantage of his light mood. "Ty, I meant what I said. I want to be with you." She prayed she didn't sound like a whiny child.

"And I meant what I said. You can't go with me."

As he watched the stubborn look he knew only too well settle on her flushed face, he knew there was only one way to get her to understand. Although loath to do what must be done, he had no other choice.

"Look at me, darlin'," he ordered softly.

The trust, and another emotion he didn't dare name, shining in her eyes, nearly made him shout *to hell with it*. But he couldn't do it. She had to be told the truth.

Hardening his heart with a purpose he didn't entirely feel, he tried to keep his voice level when he spoke.

"Sassy, I can't take you with me because . . ." he swallowed hard. *Damn, this isn't going to be easy, not with her looking at me with those passion-filled purple eyes.*

Taking a deep breath and keeping his gaze riveted to hers so she'd see he was dead serious, he said the words before he lost his nerve. "You can't go with me, because I'm wanted for murder."

Twelve

Murder!

The word rattled around in her head like a pebble in an empty bucket. Of all the reasons Sassy could possibly imagine for Ty's refusal to let her accompany him, his being wanted for murder was not one of them.

Ty, guilty of murder? Her mind shifted through what she knew about the man she'd married. It wasn't much, she realized with a sinking heart. For a moment doubt assailed her. Could he have murdered someone?

"Murder? But you're a Texas Ranger. Aren't you?"

Ty saw the uncertainty cloud Sassy's face, heard it in the slight quiver of her voice. He turned to look out the window, unable to stand the pain of her lack of confidence. It's for the best, he told himself.

No! Sassy's mind screamed, her reason returning. She refused to believe the man she loved capable of such a crime. Realizing the suspicion in her words had caused him to turn away, she cupped his face with her hands and forced him to look at her. As his anguish-filled gaze met hers, she felt a squeezing in her chest for allowing him to see her brief attack of doubt.

"I don't believe you're a murderer, Ty," she declared softly.

Searching her face, he looked for some clue she wasn't being honest. He found only the truth of her words; she believed in him! His heart soared skyward. For the umpteenth time since meeting Sassy, he wished things were different. Wishing won't change anything, he reminded himself.

Grasping her hands, he pulled them from his face and gave them a gentle squeeze. He didn't release her fingers, but kept them intertwined with his, and began speaking in a quiet voice.

"Yes, I'm a Texas Ranger. I was within a few months of turning in my badge and retiring to my ranch, when this nightmare started. I didn't murder anyone, but I'm wanted for the crime just the same. That's why you can't go with me, Sassy. I'm wanted by the law, and I don't want you dragged into it."

"Tell me what happened," she prompted.

At first she thought he wasn't going to answer. He just sat next to her, silently staring at their clasped hands. Then, as if the dam holding everything inside him burst, the story poured forth.

In a voice devoid of emotion, he outlined the events leading to his being wanted for murder. He told her how Benjamin Slater, an employee of the New York and Texas Land Company, had badgered Ty's mother for months to sell the Circle B. Since his job as a Ranger kept him from home a great deal, he was unaware of this until he stopped by the ranch for a few days, and found a letter from Slater.

Maggie Beaumont confessed that the land speculator had been pressuring her to sell out to the land syndicate. She hadn't mentioned it, because she didn't want to bother her son. Ty saw red. Learning Slater was still in Waco, he went looking for him. He found the man playing cards in a hotel saloon.

"He was so arrogant, so smooth and unruffled. When I told him we didn't want to sell, and to leave us alone, he tried to brush me off like a pesky fly," Ty recalled. "Then he made some nasty remarks about my mother. I lost my temper, and told him he'd regret it if he ever set foot on the Circle B again."

Sassy's sudden indrawn breath brought his gaze up to meet hers, the pain of reliving that scene filling his eyes. "I was angry, I admit that. But I didn't kill Slater, I swear it!"

"I know you didn't, Ty," Sassy assured him gently. "What happened then?"

Taking a deep breath and exhaling it slowly, Ty forced himself to recount the rest of the night that had changed his life so drastically. He told her how he'd gone back to Slater's hotel after he'd cooled down, to apologize for his rash words. "When I left him, he was alive. The next thing I know, the man's dead, and I'm accused of murder."

"Holy shit!" Sassy whispered under her breath.

In spite of his painful recollections, Ty's lips curved into a smile. Sassy might have changed to look like a lady on the outside, he mused to himself, but some habits die hard.

Wiping all trace of amusement from his face, he finally replied, "Exactly."

She mulled over what he'd told her. "What about the murder weapon?" she finally asked.

"Ah, yes, the murder weapon," Ty snorted. "Slater was stabbed, a wound like a bowie knife would make. And as chance would have it, I just happen to carry a bowie

147

knife. All Rangers do." He released her hands and turned to stare stonily out the window, a deep scowl marring his face.

Sassy absently chewed her lip, picturing in her mind the scene his words painted.

"But there wasn't blood on your knife," she stated triumphantly, thinking she'd hit on something useful.

"Very good," he said, turning back to meet her gaze, admiration shining in his eyes. "You're right, my knife was clean. When I pointed that out to the Waco Sheriff, he said there were bloodstains on the bedding that indicate the murder weapon had been wiped off.

"Just my luck, running into a tidy killer." He gave a halfhearted laugh, then quickly turned serious again. "Anyway, a clean knife proves nothing."

The conductor announced the next stop. The train stopped, took on passengers, and lurched forward in its westward journey. Sassy and Ty were too embroiled in their individual thoughts to notice.

Many miles passed before Sassy's voice finally broke the silence. "Why weren't you arrested, if the sheriff thought you killed Slater?"

"I was," he answered gruffly, remembering the humiliation he'd felt. "The sheriff came out to the ranch, told me I was under arrest for killing Slater, then took me back to town in handcuffs. An old friend of mine, a U.S. Marshal, was in Waco on official business, and was at the jail when we got there. I was never so glad to see anybody in my life.

"Josh was shocked to learn I'd been arrested for murder. He tried to tell the sheriff I was a Ranger and wouldn't kill anyone in cold blood. The sheriff wouldn't listen, and said my being a Texas Ranger didn't mean squat, not when he had an eyewitness who said I killed

Slater. Josh tried to convince him to leave us alone for a few minutes. He didn't want to, but he finally gave in to Josh's authority as a U.S. Marshal.

"After Josh heard what happened, he agreed it looked real bad for me. I told him whoever accused me had lied, and I'd probably need help getting my name cleared."

"How could a U.S. Marshal—who's sworn to uphold the law—help you?"

"Josh Madison and I have been close friends, like brothers, for years," Ty explained. "We met about five years ago, when Josh was with the Rangers. He believed me when I said I didn't kill Slater. Even so, I didn't think, friend or not, he'd let me go. Like you said, upholding the law is real important to Josh. And he said as much when I brought it up. But he said if the sheriff returned and found him out cold, he wouldn't be held responsible for my escape. The silly grin on Josh's face should have tipped me off that he was up to something." Ty chuckled lightly.

"Before I took him up on his offer to let me slug him, Josh told me he'd do everything he could from his office in Austin to help me. I was concerned he'd get himself in a jam—a high-ranking officer of the law helping a wanted man—but he insisted he'd keep his investigation secret. I was still hesitant to do it, until I realized I'd do the same for him, if the situation was reversed. So I told him I'd appreciate his finding out the identity of the eyewitness the sheriff mentioned. I planned to stop by the ranch to let my mother know what was happening, then lay low. Josh said he'd find out the person's name, then meet me the next evening." Ty fell silent, caught up in his thoughts.

"So did you hit Josh to get away?"

"Sure did." Ty grinned. "I knew I'd have to hit him

real hard to knock him out—Josh is one helluva tough fighter—so I gave him my best punch. He crumpled to the floor like a rag doll. My hand hurt like the devil for a week, but it was worth it to keep from being locked up. After getting my gun and knife out of the desk, I took off."

He frowned, then shifted his gaze back outside. It pained him to be on the run from the same law he'd taken immense pride in upholding for the seven years he'd been a Texas Ranger. Unfortunately, he'd been left with no other choice.

"So that's the important investigation you told me about before you left the Star," she murmured.

"Yeah," came his terse reply.

"Well, tell me about him," she said, tugging on his arm to get his attention.

"Him?"

"The man you're trying to find. The one who accused you of murder. Do you know him?"

"Yeah, I know Teddy," he answered carefully, not liking the direction the conversation had taken.

"Is he supposed to be in El Paso? Is that why you're going there?"

"I'm going to El Paso because the town has a lot of gambling halls."

"Gambling halls? Is that how Teddy makes his living, as a gambler?"

He nodded, then said, "Professional gamblers move around a lot, and El Paso is a favorite hangout. So far, I haven't found Teddy." A fierce glint came into his eyes. "But I will, even if it takes the rest of my life."

Sassy shivered at the savageness she saw on his face and heard in his voice. Ty would be a formidable opponent, she realized, certain she didn't want to be in his accuser's shoes when Ty finally cornered him. She knew Rangers were trained to use quick thinking rather than force to get their man. Her brother Sean had said he'd learned that philosophy when he joined their ranks. She also knew Rangers adopted the practices of the men they sought. They learned the horsemanship and tracking skills of Indians, and became experts with the weapons they carried: rifle, six-shooter, and bowie knife.

Although seeing this frightening, feral side of Ty for the first time, she knew he had a gentle side, too. The side she had fallen in love with. Now she knew the reason for the pain she'd often seen in his dark eyes: the pain of being accused of a crime he didn't commit, the pain of running from a life's work he obviously loved, and the pain of not knowing what the future held. Now that she knew the truth, so many of the things he'd said and done made sense.

"When did this happen?"

"January," he answered curtly, suddenly weary of talking.

January! Today's the first of April, Sassy thought in amazement. Compassion filled her heart for Ty's miserable circumstance. For months he'd been forced by an unfortunate string of events to maintain a solitary existence.

Then another terrifying thought came to mind. He could be recognized and arrested, while on this search. When she vocalized her fears, he gave her a reassuring smile.

"That concerned me, too, until I happened to see my wanted poster back in Fort Worth. I don't know if I have Josh to thank for giving a poor description of me, or if the artist the Waco sheriff hired was just plain bad. At any rate, the drawing doesn't look much like me."

"But you're a Ranger. People around Texas must know you," she quizzed, still not convinced.

"Most of my work as a Ranger has been secret assignments, so my identity isn't well known. 'Course, I guess it's possible one of the few who know me will see my name on the wanted poster, and whether the drawing looks like me or not, decide to turn me in if they get the chance. I'm hoping those posters weren't widely distributed. But even if they were, I think I have pretty fair odds of not being recognized. I'm more concerned someone will remember Joker, because I had to bring him with me."

"I hope he likes riding a train more than Blarney does," she mused aloud.

Ty's eyes widened. "Let me guess. You brought Blarney with you." At her nod, he shook his head with disbelief. Recalling her impulsive nature, he shouldn't have been surprised.

"Joker's as accustomed to riding a train as I am, since I seldom go anywhere without him." He chuckled dryly, then instantly sobered. "I couldn't leave him in Fort Worth. I figured the law would be able to trace my leaving town, as soon as they found my horse and started asking questions. Anyway, sometimes a horse sticks in a person's mind more than the man on its back. I'm counting on Joker not being the only gray-spotted blanket Appaloosa people have ever seen. Otherwise his appearance could run up a red flag in someone's memory. Regardless, I've got to take the risk of either myself or Joker being recognized."

Sassy digested the information carefully, reaching the same conclusion. Chances were good Ty wouldn't be recognized. Even if the odds weren't in his favor, she knew he'd still be on this personal crusade to see justice carried out. She just wished Joker's coat was a little less unusual. She also wished she could see Ty's wanted poster, to assure herself it was as poor a likeness of him as he claimed. His voice pulled her from her thoughts.

"And as if I don't have enough to deal with, ever since I left Austin, I've had the feeling I'm being followed."

"Followed? Do you have any idea who it is? Your friend the marshal, maybe?"

"No, Josh's job as marshal wouldn't allow him to follow me, unless his superiors knew about it. And he swore he'd keep his helping me a secret. If he'd changed his mind about my guilt and planned to arrest me, he wouldn't be playing hide-and-seek. He'd just come right up to me and haul my ass to jail." He smiled sheepishly at his choice of words.

"Besides, I stopped in Austin long enough to see him. I had to wait until nightfall before I could risk revealing myself. When I told him I'd come up empty again, he said he had some news. He'd located a friend of Teddy, another professional gambler, who said Teddy was in Fort Worth. Since I'd planned on going to El Paso, and would be going through Fort Worth anyway, I took the time to check it out.

"Josh told me he'd keep doing what he could, and I believe him. So like I said, he isn't the one following me. Whoever he is, he's good at sneaking around and staying out of sight."

Sassy sat quietly, her mind absorbing everything Ty had told her.

"I take it you didn't find Teddy in Fort Worth, or hear anything new about him," she said after a long silence.

"Nope, didn't find hide nor hair. Every lead I've had has sent me chasing from one end of Texas to the other. With the tip about Fort Worth turning out to be another wild-goose chase, I'm hoping the man in San Antonio who told me Teddy was heading for El Paso wasn't feeding me a line. The information is weeks old, but I have nothing else to go on."

"So, what do you plan to do in El Paso?"

"Since Teddy is a professional gambler, I've decided I should be a part of that calling, and spend a lot of time in gambling halls and saloons," he explained.

"Is that the reason for the mustache and longer tresses?" she teased, giving the blond hair brushing his collar a gentle tug.

Ty turned his head and placed a kiss on her palm. Flashing her a smile, he answered, "Since I'll be spending most of my time in public places, I wanted to do whatever I could to reduce my chances of being recognized.

"Plus," he chuckled, "I want to fit in, and most gamblers sport more hair. I also bought some fancy duds in Fort Worth." He pointed to a black frock coat and a floral print satin vest thrown over the seat in front of them.

"Buying the clothes is one of the reasons I was delayed leaving Fort Worth, and had to catch a later train," he told her pointedly.

As it turned out, Ty was glad he had left later than he'd originally planned, although he wouldn't admit it to Sassy. If he hadn't stuck around Fort Worth for a few extra days, she wouldn't have caught up with him. If he'd left sooner, or not headed for El Paso at all, she would be traveling alone. And Lord knows what kind of trouble she could have gotten into. Just thinking about all that could have befallen her, made a fear like he'd never known settle around his heart.

Sassy saw his jaw clench, and understood that his not-so-subtle hint meant he hadn't forgotten her rash behavior. Purposely ignoring his reference to their earlier argument, she turned her thoughts to his plans for El Paso. The excitement began to build inside her—excitement about the upcoming adventure she and Ty would be making.

"El Paso can't be much farther," she remarked. "Don't you think we should start making our plans?"

One eyebrow arching with surprise, Ty looked at her incredulously. He couldn't believe she actually thought she would be staying with him, after everything he'd just told her. *Doesn't she realize how dangerous this trip could be?* Obviously not, he told himself, struggling to keep a clear head concerning Sassy's stubbornness.

Tamping down the urge to turn her over his knee and paddle her soundly, he finally managed to speak in a voice lower than the roar threatening to erupt.

"We?"

Thirteen

Caught up in her thoughts about their arrival in El Paso, Sassy paid no heed to the look on Ty's face or the disbelief in his voice.

The prospect of moving within a circle of people she had never thought to know, aroused her adventurous spirit. Although she'd visited the Gray Mule Saloon in San Antonio countless times, by necessity she'd never become acquainted with the other customers or the people who worked there. The challenge of playing a part—this time as a woman rather than Grunt—in the kinds of places she loved, intrigued her. There was something intrinsically thrilling about the world of gamblers and games of chance, inside businesses catering to the thirsty, fun-seeking male.

Just thinking about what lay ahead sent a shiver of exhilaration up her spine. There was undoubtedly danger, too, the logical part of her brain reminded her. She refused to let the gunfights that often erupted where men, liquor, and gambling met, dampen her excitement.

Ty's voice brought her back to the present. "Did you say we?"

"What? Oh, yes, I said we'd better start making plans for—"

His fingers grasped her chin, cutting off her words. With thumb and forefinger he turned her face toward him. Meeting her gaze, his agitation died. He tried to recapture his fiery anger, but found it impossible to feed the flame when he saw the trust shining in Sassy's eyes.

"I can't let you stay with me, Sassy," he murmured softly.

"I'm staying, Ty," she replied firmly. "I can help you, and I—"

"Now listen to me, Erin Mahoney," he ordered in a voice devoid of its previous softness, now harsh and demanding.

The use of her given name got her attention like nothing else could have. She jerked away from his touch, as if his fingers burned her flesh.

"Don't call me that," she snapped, peeved he remembered the name she'd been forced to use when they exchanged their vows. "And, it's Beaumont now," she added quietly.

"Listen to me, Sassy, this is no carefree lark. Something I know you've had your share of," he couldn't resist throwing in. "I told you Josh is helping me. He's all the help I need. I won't drag a woman around with me; the whole idea is ridiculous. Have you forgotten this could be very dangerous? I don't want you exposed to the sort of people I'll be associating with. When we get to El Paso, I'll arrange for you to return to San Antonio."

Her eyes flashing with fury, she glared at him. "Okay, I listened to you, you overgrown bully. Now you listen to me, Tyler Beaumont. You need me—"

At his snort of disbelief, she rushed on, "Don't you see? The law is looking for a man traveling alone, not a man *and* a woman, so you won't draw the attention of the authorities with me along! And another thing, you won't be dragging me around, I'm going with you willingly," she declared hotly, chin jutting forward in defiance. "And besides, I'll be an extra set of eyes and ears. That could make a very big difference in your search."

Seeing the determination on her face, Ty clamped his mouth shut. After brooding over her words, he realized he couldn't fault her reasoning. *Damn her hide, she has a point.*

There *was* a good chance he wouldn't be recognized with Sassy at his side. *Who am I kidding, I won't get a second glance, if this beauty is within ten feet of me.* A ghost of a smile teased his mouth. After a fruitless search for the past several months, he could use someone else looking and listening for clues.

Except Sassy doesn't know the whole truth, he thought, shifting uneasily on the seat.

That settled it! He just couldn't involve Sassy in his plan. In spite of her obvious eagerness to help him, he was sure she had no inkling what she'd volunteered to do.

"I can't ask you to do that, Sassy," he replied at last, making her jump at the fierceness of his voice. "Do you have any idea what people will think of you, if you go to saloons? They'll think you're a . . . a fallen woman," he answered his own question, before she could reply. "A woman fine, upstanding citizens will shun. I can't—I won't—allow that to happen."

"I don't know anybody in El Paso, so it doesn't matter what the townspeople think of me. And even if I did, I don't give a rat's as—" Seeing his eyebrows pull together in a warning frown, she amended, "Uh . . . behind *what* they think. Not as long as I'm helping you."

"Maybe you don't know anyone in El Paso, but what about the next town we visit, or the next? Sooner or later, you're going to run into someone who knows you or your family," he persisted.

Sassy's heart quickened at his words. He spoke as if he'd already decided she could continue this trip. Realizing his resolve to send her home had weakened, she smelled victory.

"Perhaps eventually I will see someone I know, but it's doubtful, since I've never been to west Texas. And even if we go to a town where I know everyone, I won't change my mind. Helping you is more important than what other people think of me." She wished she could say something else to convince him, but the words remained unsaid. Still smarting from his laughter at her declaration of love, she refused to use her feelings for him in her arguments.

His throat filling with emotion, Ty longed to wrap her in his arms and hold her close. Instead, he kept his hands to himself and nodded in reply.

At that moment, he despised himself for his attraction to her, and his inability to stick to his original plan to send her home. He swore he would do everything possible to protect her, while they hunted down his accuser.

His accuser. Recalling how Teddy had turned his life into such a horrible muddle brought a vile taste to his mouth. Again his anger stirred. His normally hard-to-rouse temper continually simmered beneath his calm exterior these days, just waiting to be unleashed at the smallest provocation. He'd managed to keep it pretty much in check with Sassy, but thinking about the person who'd charged him with murder sent it rocketing skyward.

Dammit, Teddy, you'll pay for this, he vowed silently,

his body rigid with tension, his hands balled into tight fists on his thighs.

"Ty?"

Somehow the concern in her voice penetrated the depths of his anger-fogged brain. Glancing down, he saw one of her hands lightly touching his sleeve. When he met her concerned gaze, the tight knot in his stomach began to unravel. He sighed in defeat.

"All right, Sassy, you win. You can go with me. But if I decide it's too dangerous, I'll send you home so fast it'll make your head spin. And I don't want any argument about it."

Any elation she might have felt, or rebuttal she might have made about her abilities to take care of herself, died at the hard edge of his voice.

Before she could respond, he continued "You know we'll be sharing a bed, while we're on this trip, don't you?" he asked bluntly, his gaze pinning her with its fierceness, daring her to disagree. "Well, don't expect any commitments from me. There's no future for us."

Sassy blinked once, unable to comprehend what he was telling her. "But, we're married," she replied.

"A situation I hope to rectify as soon as possible."

"What do you mean?"

"Neither of us wanted this marriage, so I'll file for divorce." He ignored her sharp indrawn breath, and added quietly, "You shouldn't be shackled to a wanted man."

Divorce! Sassy's heart lurched at the word. "Are you saying, if you clear your name, we'll stay married?"

"No, I'm not saying that. Even if I *can* clear my name, you'd still have to bear the stigma of being married to a man who was once arrested for murder. That's a hard taint to erase."

160

"It doesn't mat—"

He held up his hand to halt her protest. "I think, under the circumstances, it would be better if we got a divorce."

Tears sprang to the backs of her eyes, but she refused to let Ty see how deeply he'd hurt her. She knew in her heart he didn't mean to cause her so much pain. His bitterness and frustration made him lash out at her. Still, his determination to divorce her left her speechless.

"I'll protect you with my life, if necessary, but as for our marriage, it will be over soon."

Swallowing hard, Sassy pushed aside the urge to throttle him and finally found her voice. "I'll willingly share your bed, Ty. Don't worry, I expect nothing in return. And I accept your offer of protection. I'll do the same for you."

Ty flinched inwardly at having his words thrown back at him. *How could I have been so callous with her, when she only wants to help me?* An apology sprang to the tip of his tongue, but he forced his lips to remain tightly sealed.

It's better this way. Better to give her no hope, than fill her head with promises I may not be able to keep.

"Fine," he said curtly, then turned away. He couldn't bear to look at her. He was already a first-class bastard, and seeing the hurt reflected in her eyes would only make him feel worse. "I'm glad we understand each other."

Right then, what Sassy understood was her desire to give Ty a swift kick in the seat of his pants. She wanted to scream her displeasure, but settled for silently giving him a piece of her mind. *You dolt! You're just putting on this jackass routine, 'cause you're feeling so angry and helpless. Well, I'm going to help you get your name cleared, Mr. Ty Beaumont. And you'd better get used to havin' me around, 'cause once this mess is straightened out, I intend to do everything possible to make sure we're*

161

together forever. So there, you hardheaded, ungrateful wretch!

She felt better for having had her say, although she never opened her mouth. Voicing the words aloud would have risked the withdrawal of his agreement to let her stay. And as for his talk of divorce, she never could resist a challenge. There was no point in telling him she had accepted the gauntlet he'd thrown down. To do so would only start another round of arguing. She shot him an aggravated look, but said nothing.

Ty could tell Sassy purposely maintained her silence to save more argument. He'd never met a more determined, hardheaded woman. He hid the smile her stubborn nature caused, by wiping a hand over his jaw. *Sassy may be determined, but so am I.* He fully intended to make good his threat and send her home at the first hint of trouble. He knew he couldn't live with himself, if something happened to her.

Giving another sidelong glance to the woman sitting next to him, he wondered what went on in her head. The mutinous set of her chin told him it wasn't good. When his gaze rose to linger on her soft mouth, his thoughts changed direction, his body responding instantly to his visual perusal. He shifted in the seat to ease his discomfort.

Sassy had seen the desire flare in the depths of his eyes, and figured his squirming was an attempt to hide the physical evidence of his response. Dropping her gaze, she bit her lip to halt the giggle bubbling in her chest. Calling on her newfound woman's wiles, she feigned a yawn, then slowly stretched her arms over her head, while lazily arching her back.

Her full breasts pushing against the bodice of her dress, drew Ty's eyes like a magnet. As he fought to control his growing passion, he forgot the reasons he didn't want her along on this trip, as well as the reasons he shouldn't be reacting to her. All he could think about was getting to El Paso, and finding a hotel room where he could bury his throbbing flesh in the hot depths of Sassy's sweet body.

After a few more minutes of silent enticement by seductively moving her body this way and that, Sassy knew her ploy had worked. While the burning in his eyes had originally sprung from anger, its nourishment now came from desire. She silently congratulated herself on a successful performance.

Keeping her expression carefully blank, she turned to face him. "Now, tell me what you plan to do when we get to El Paso."

Ty jerked his gaze from her tantalizing bosom, a dull flush warming his cheeks. He closed his eyes for a moment, to halt his rapidly escalating need. When he spoke, his voice still bore a slightly raspy tinge. "Okay, here's my plan."

The engine belched one last plume of smoke, the brakes screeched, the wheels slowed, and finally the train pulled into the Texas and Pacific depot, just northeast of downtown El Paso.

Sassy and Ty stepped down onto the boarding platform, the last passengers to leave the train. By delaying their exit, the depot was as Ty had hoped, nearly deserted. Most of the other passengers and the people waiting for them had already departed. Glancing around, he nodded with satisfaction. Their arrival would draw no unwanted attention.

Kit Dancer nonchalantly watched his fellow passengers get off the train from the position he'd taken next

163

to the depot. When the last two made their exit, he snapped to attention. What should have been an easy job had become complicated by the unexpected, and unwelcome, arrival of a woman, claiming to be Ty Beaumont's wife. "Now what the hell do I do?" he grumbled, watching the couple supervise the unloading of their horses from one of the stock cars.

Deciding he had no choice except to bide his time, Kit ambled away from the train station. He passed close enough behind where the Beaumonts waited for their luggage to be loaded into a carriage, to hear Ty give the driver their destination.

Kit hurried away, realizing he'd have to be more careful about staying out of sight, since Mrs. Beaumont might remember him from Fort Worth.

On the ride to their hotel, Ty contemplated the plan he'd outlined for Sassy. The enthusiasm she'd shown had snared him as well. He'd never looked forward to an assignment with such excitement—excitement directly attributable to his wife.

His *wife*. He still found his marriage to the most beautiful, most desirable woman he'd ever known hard to believe. Recognizing where his introspection was leading, he put a halt to his thoughts. It was easier to deal with his desire for Sassy—pure physical lust—rather than delving deeper into his emotions, and discovering something he'd be better off not knowing.

For now, they'd carry out their ruse as a professional gambler and his wife. And like he told her, eventually, he'd file for divorce, ending not only their marriage, but his feelings for her as well.

At least, he prayed it would.

Fourteen

"The dealer takes two," Sassy said, then nimbly slipped two cards off the deck.

"I'll bet ten dollars." Ty smiled at the surprised arch of her eyebrows.

Pulling her mouth into a pucker of concentration, she studied her hand again, then looked at the growing pot in the center of the bed.

After renting a suite of rooms in the St. Charles Lodging House, Ty had been anxious to begin the role he'd created for himself. Then he realized his debut as a professional gambler would have to wait. Sassy needed more appropriate clothing, something women who frequented saloons wore, before she could go with him. He refused to entertain the idea of beginning without her. God only knew what mischief she could get into, if left to her own devices.

He'd located a seamstress and immediately ordered several dresses. Unfortunately, the silk creations would take a few days to complete, creating an unavoidable delay. With time on his hands, Ty decided to teach Sassy some of the casino games she'd soon see firsthand. As a supposed frequent visitor of saloons, she'd be expected to be familiar with the various games of chance.

After exhausting his knowledge of faro, craps, roulette, and several other games she was likely to see, tonight he had opted to play a game she already knew. Having played poker with her brothers since she was old enough to hold the cards, there wasn't much he could teach her.

Normally they played cards at the table in the sitting room of their suite. Tonight, Sassy decided the bed would be more comfortable.

"Okay, Mr. Cardsharp, I'll see your bet," she said, tossing the poker chips into the pot. "And I call."

Chuckling lightly, Ty spread his cards on the bed in front of him, "Two pair, ladies and treys."

"Very good," she said seriously, studying the queens and threes in what he assumed to be the winning hand.

When Ty reached out to scoop up his winnings, Sassy's voice stopped him. "But not good enough, I'm afraid," she said smugly, laying her cards on the bed.

Ty looked at the full house, kings over fives, and shook his head. "Lucky," he grumbled, gathering the cards back into the deck.

Concentrating on shuffling the cards, his hands suddenly stilled, his sharply indrawn breath lodged in his throat. He glanced down to see Sassy's hand move up the inside of his thigh. Raising his gaze to meet hers, he knew the poker game had ended.

Never breaking contact with her smoldering eyes, he tossed the cards aside and held out his arms.

"Come here, wildcat," he growled softly.

When she giggled in delight and tried to scoot away, he rose up on his knees and, unmindful of the poker chips on the bed, lunged toward her. He caught her around the waist and flipped her onto her back in one fluid motion. Pressing his body down on top of hers, his weight held her pinned to the bed. With a screech of fake terror, Sassy tried to break his hold, but couldn't against his greater strength.

"Please, sir, I must protest your familiarity," she pleaded in her best Southern drawl, her eyes wide and beseeching.

The whole bed shook with the deep rumble of Ty's laughter. "What an imp you are," he murmured, before lowering his mouth to capture her lips.

This time she offered no protest. Slipping her arms around his shoulders, she tunneled her fingers into the thick hair at his nape. She moaned with delight, moving provocatively beneath him. Ty made quick work of removing their clothing, then knelt between her opened thighs. He took no time for further preliminaries. There was no need. Sassy was ready and eager for the blending of their flesh. In one smooth stroke, he slid inside her.

As he pushed deeper and deeper, Sassy held a pent-up breath. When he filled her completely, she exhaled a sigh of ecstasy. The fire of her desire grew even hotter. A fire he continued to stoke with his mouth, his hands, the slow movements of his hips. The flames continued to lick higher and higher, taking her on a delicious mind-boggling journey, her need bursting into a raging inferno only Ty could extinguish.

With a high keening wail, she arrived at her destination. As the enormous breakers of her powerful climax repeatedly broke over her, she bucked wildly beneath him, her inner muscles tightening around his engorged manhood.

Hearing and feeling her reach her peak, Ty finally allowed himself to attain his own release. As he spilled himself deep within her, he groaned his pleasure against her damp neck, then collapsed atop her.

Their explosive lovemaking had completely sapped his strength, making it impossible to move. She shifted restlessly beneath him.

"What's the matter?" he mumbled, his voice little more than a croak.

"Something's poking me," she answered, trying to wiggle out from under him.

Summoning enough strength to lift himself up onto his elbows, he peered down into her face. "Darlin', you wound me to the quick. *I'm* poking you," he whispered, giving her a devilish grin.

In spite of the blush his words sent racing up her cheeks, she shot him a nasty look, then shoved ineffectually against his heavily muscled shoulders. "I meant there's something on the bed jabbing me in my backside," she responded tartly.

"Well then, let's just see what it is, hmm?" he replied, rolling onto his side next to her.

She sat up, slipped her feet over the side of the bed, and stood up on wobbly legs. At Ty's sudden burst of laughter, she whirled around to glare at him through narrowed eyes. "What's so funny?"

"You must believe in keeping your winnings close to your . . . I was going to say, close to your vest. But—" His gaze slid down to her pert breasts. "You aren't wearing one." At her perplexed look, he controlled his amusement long enough to say, "You have the spoils from the last pot stuck to your lovely derriere." He collapsed on the bed, howling with laughter.

Looking over her shoulder into the mirror, she saw what Ty found so hysterical: a half-dozen poker chips stuck to her bottom. Peeling them off and tossing them across the room, she stomped to the washstand and grabbed a washcloth. Dipping it in the basin of water, she washed off her sweat- and sex-dampened body with jerky motions. When she finished, she turned to face the bed.

"Would you like to be rinsed off?" she asked sweetly.

Looking at her through tears of laughter, he missed the mischief dancing in her eyes, and nodded in reply.

Before he realized her intent, or could react to her sudden movement across the room, the contents of the wash basin sloshed over him.

"What the hell," he sputtered, gasping with shock at the tepid water hitting his heated flesh.

"I thought you wanted to be rinsed off," she said, looking at him innocently, her voice dripping with sugar.

"You know damn well what I meant," he snarled, giving her a piercing glare. Then he noticed the sparkle in her eyes, and the twitching of her mouth.

"Okay, I deserved that," he said in a much gentler tone, willing to be the target of her joke. "Now, give me a towel. Please, wildcat."

Her sudden pique at his laughing at her vanished with his softly spoken words.

She brought a towel to him, but insisted on drying him herself, even rubbing places the water hadn't touched. Her tender ministrations soon led to another romp in the now-wet bed. Neither felt any discomfort, the heat of their bodies quickly drying the damp sheets.

It was a very long time before either of them slept that night.

The next day, Ty announced that he planned to go to one of the saloons that evening, to begin making his presence known around town. His plans took Sassy by surprise, since her evening gowns still weren't ready. She started to speak, then snapped her mouth shut. Since he'd made it clear he wouldn't let her accompany him without the proper clothes, there was no point in asking.

Startled by her quiet acceptance of his plans, Ty hoped her acquiescence signaled she'd finally started giving up her argumentative, impulsive ways. He kissed her long and hard before leaving for the evening. With a wicked smile, he told her to keep the bed warm for him.

Sassy truly intended to stay in their suite all evening. She knew he was right to make her wait until she could join him appropriately attired. But as the hours ticked by and he still hadn't returned, her impatience began to wear thin. She could only play so many games of solitaire, before she began to get fidgety. Feeling the walls start to close in, she couldn't stand being cooped up any longer, and decided to go out for some air.

Giving no thought to the possible consequences, she rushed down the stairs of the lodging house and out into the warm evening. Once she stood on El Paso Street—one of the town's busiest with its abundant saloons—Sassy's good intentions slipped away. The sounds of lively music and gay laughter drew her feet down the street. Before she could talk herself out of it, she made her way toward Sam and Charley's Saloon, Ty's destination for the evening.

She passed the Chief Saloon, then the Ranch, where she stopped to listen to the sounds coming from inside. Someone pounded on a piano, forcing it to emit what passed for a spirited song. Through the doors Sassy could see snatches of bright colors whirl past—the colorful dresses of the dance hall girls being swung around by their enthusiastic partners.

Humming the catchy tune, she continued toward the main intersection of town. She passed a crowded, but relatively quiet Gem Saloon in the next block, then crossed the street. The Red Garter Saloon, immediately opposite the Gem, was also crowded, but more boisterous. When she started to walk past Lane and White's Parlor Saloon, the doors crashed open, and a man came sailing through the open portal.

Stepping back with a gasp, Sassy was certain whoever had tossed the man out the door would soon follow. She stood pressed to the front of the building, her heart pounding with both surprise and excitement. Eyes wide with wonder, she watched the man pick himself up off the boardwalk, straighten his jacket, then with a whoop of laughter, head back inside.

In spite of her desire to hurry, she couldn't resist a quick look inside, as she carefully eased past the open doors. Shaking her head in amazement at the scene she'd just witnessed, she continued down El Paso Street, until she reached Sam and Charley's Saloon near the intersection of San Francisco Street.

Arriving at her destination, she stopped to gather her thoughts. *I won't go in. I'll just peek in the window.*

Ty was having a decent night at cards. While he hadn't won a large pot, he had claimed several smaller ones. So far he was content with staying even, or slightly ahead for the evening—an acceptable position. The game he'd joined wasn't for high stakes—not the kind to interest Teddy—so he doubted any of these men knew the gambler. Still, he spent the time getting to know his opponents, since one of them could lead him to other, more expensive, games.

Through carefully worded questions, he'd learned the Red Garter Saloon was the most likely spot for a professional gambler to find a rich poker game. Sitting back in his chair, he absently watched the man to his left shuffle the cards for the next hand.

From the corner of his eye, something caught his attention across the room. Turning toward the two large windows facing the street, he scanned the panes of glass. Someone stood outside, face pressed against the grimy window, peering into the saloon with wide, curious eyes. Staring at the face, distorted by the rippled glass, Ty's mildly interested expression changed abruptly. His brows pulling down in a scowl, his lips thinned into a severe line. *Dammit, that's Sassy!*

Picking up the cash laying in front of him with hands shaking with rage, he scraped back his chair. "You'll have to excuse me, gentlemen. I have some business that needs my immediate attention. Perhaps we can play again."

With a round of good nights from the other men, Ty strode purposefully to the door, his fury growing with each step.

Standing on the boardwalk, he took a deep breath before turning toward Sassy. Deep in concentration, her nose remained pressed to the saloon window. She obviously hadn't noticed his departure. Taking care to walk silently, Ty moved to stand behind her.

"What's going on in there?" he asked in a deceptively silky voice.

Sassy gave a yelp of surprise, bumping her nose against the glass. To make matters worse, there was no mistaking who had frightened her.

Oh shit, how did I miss hearing him sneak up on me?

172

Rubbing her nose, she slowly turned around. She met his furious gaze steadily, refusing to buckle under.

Before she could utter a word in her defense, she was grabbed by the arm and nearly dragged down the street. Although she had long legs, she had to do an awkward half-skip half-run to keep up.

"Ty, slow down, I—"

"Don't say a word, Sassy, not a goddamn word," he ground out, slowing his brisk pace so she could better match his strides.

As they retraced Sassy's steps up El Paso Street, she was grateful he said no more. She knew she had really angered him this time. His fury was so tangible, she could feel its presence swirling around her like a living, breathing being. Catching her toe on a loose board, she felt herself pitch forward, but managed to regain her balance. The image of her falling and Ty never breaking stride, but hanging onto her arm and hauling her behind him like a sack of grain, popped into her head.

If the situation hadn't been so serious, she would have laughed at the picture her imagination had painted. She kept silent, turning her thoughts to how best to defend herself.

When they were back in their rooms, Sassy was immediately contrite, having decided throwing herself at his mercy was her safest course of action.

"I'm sorry, Ty," she said, pulling off her shoes and tossing them across the room. "I know I shouldn't have gone out. But I was so bored, I was ready to climb the walls. I just *had* to get out of these rooms. This waiting is driving me mad," she finished lamely. Standing with drooped shoulders and bowed head, she waited for his tirade to begin.

Although still seething at her latest stunt, Ty knew exactly how she felt. Wasn't that why *he'd* decided to go out tonight, to ease his own impatience? Wasn't she entitled to feel the same chafing at the bit that he'd been experiencing? The answers to those questions soothed his anger, reducing it to merely annoyance.

"Sassy, look at me," he ordered in a soft whisper.

She raised her head cautiously, not sure what to expect from such a softly spoken voice, when moments ago he was ready to wring her neck. She was surprised to find his temper had unexpectedly cooled, the angry glint in his eyes replaced with compassion.

"I understand why you went out tonight."

"You do?" she asked, unable to hide her shock.

"Yes, darlin', I do. I shouldn't have gone out without you," he said, giving her lips a quick kiss. "That doesn't mean I'm not mad as hell. I should spank that lovely bottom of yours, for risking your safety to relieve your boredom." He grasped her shoulders, holding her at arm's length so she could see the seriousness of his words reflected on his face.

Sassy searched his features to gauge the state of his temper. Had his anger really melted so quickly? She saw gravity etched in his furrowed brow, but his eyes were clear of their earlier ire.

"Do your worst," she dared saucily, holding her breath and hoping she hadn't misread him.

With a growl of playfulness, he swept her up into his arms and carried her to their bed. "My worst, huh? I think I'd rather give you my best," he murmured, moving his mouth to sample the tender flesh behind her ear.

His hot breath and moist lips sending shivers of delight up and down her spine, she stirred restlessly in his arms.

"Anxious, darlin'?" he crooned, lowering her to the bed, then easing down beside her. "No need to rush. We have all night." Moving his lips to hers, he captured her eager mouth in a steamy kiss that made her toes curl.

As Ty began making slow and thorough love to Sassy, he promised himself to visit the seamstress he'd hired first thing in the morning. He'd pay whatever it took to get one of Sassy's dresses immediately. Neither of them could take much more of the inactivity they'd been forced to endure. Although, he definitely couldn't complain about how they spent their nights.

This particular night, Ty plied Sassy with every stimulating caress, every passionate kiss, every murmur of encouragement he could, to bring her to the ultimate pinnacle of pleasure. And he did so, time and again, purposely denying himself his own release, until he was positive she was completely satisfied. Then and only then, did he allow himself the luxury of seeking his own gratification.

Pleasantly exhausted, he rolled to his back, pulling Sassy close. It astounded him to realize that by delaying the culmination of his own desire to concentrate on Sassy's fulfillment, he had increased his own pleasure immensely. It had never been that way with—

Stop it! Don't think about her. He turned his thoughts back to the woman snuggled in his arms. Sassy, Sassy, his mind chanted over and over. *You're making me see and feel things I never knew about, before you came barreling into my life.*

Easy, Beaumont, he cautioned himself. *Remember what happened last time you let a woman get close. You thought she could be trusted, then* wham, *she showed her true colors.* Although he was married to Sassy and had nothing concrete to go on, Ty wasn't convinced he could trust her. *What if she's in cahoots with whoever's following me?* The thought didn't sit well. Yet, there was one fact he couldn't deny: he hadn't noticed anyone following him until *after* he'd left the Dublin Star.

Sighing heavily, he pulled the sheet over them and let himself slip into the arms of sleep, where neither his doubts about Sassy nor the uncertainty of his future disturbed him.

Fifteen

The noise in the Red Garter Saloon was unbelievable, a roaring din making it impossible to carry on a conversation below a shout. A blue gray cloud of smoke hung heavily in the air, smarting the eyes and irritating the nose. The barroom was crowded with every sort of man: cowhand, businessman, local drunk, and stranger passing through.

Sassy loved the place on sight.

Earlier that day Ty received word that Sassy's dresses were finished, allowing them to begin what they'd come to town to do. They had just stepped through the bat wing doors of the Red Garter, and already Sassy was wide-eyed with barely controlled excitement.

Watching her reaction, Ty smiled. "Sassy, you're staring," he said in a low whisper.

Her gaze snapped to his face, her curiosity momentarily suspended by his admonishing words.

Ever since the night he'd caught her window peeking, he'd been an ornery cuss. From then on, he refused to leave her alone, not wanting to risk a repeat performance. His failure to cajole the seamstress into finishing Sassy's dresses ahead of schedule had added to his ill temper.

Forced to cool his heels a while longer, Ty found fault easily. And since they were together constantly, she became the unfortunate target for the brunt of his displeasure. Only at night, when their passion ignited, did he become the gentle, caring man she knew him to be.

Searching his face for some sign she'd unknowingly stirred his temper yet again, she was relieved to find only amusement dancing in his eyes.

Sensing her uncertainty, he gave her a warm smile, then whispered against her ear, "It's okay, darlin'. Just try not to stare. You're supposed to be familiar with the inside of a saloon, remember? And don't forget what we talked about earlier. I'm using the name James Beauregard."

She gave him a withering look. "I won't."

He chuckled again, then tucked her arm through his, and gave it an encouraging squeeze. "Good girl."

As Ty stepped farther into the room, Sassy clutched his arm, trying to be less obvious in her scrutiny of one of the biggest and fanciest saloons in El Paso.

Much larger and definitely more interesting than the Gray Mule, the Red Garter had Sassy nearly bubbling over with anticipation.

Smiling and nodding while trying not to miss anything, she let Ty escort her through the throng of men gathered in the barroom. They passed the massive, elaborately designed mahogany bar with its white aproned bartenders, then headed for the gambling room.

Ty paused a moment beneath the arched doorway, to take in the other people assembled there. Slowly all heads turned toward the doorway. The men quickly took his measure, then switched their attention to Sassy.

Self-consciously she touched the black velvet ribbon circling her throat, then nervously adjusted the ruffled, short sleeves of her black silk gown. She wondered if something about the Spanish-styled dress with its full, layered skirt was inappropriate. A good portion of her bosom was exposed by the tight bodice and off-the-shoulder neckline, and for a moment she worried the dress revealed too much.

Sensing her unease, Ty murmured, "The dress is perfect, and you look beautiful."

She flashed him a relieved look, then, lifting her chin, she glanced around the room at the men openly staring at her. If she hadn't already been flushed with excitement, their bold inspection would have flooded her face with hot color. Her fingers tightened on Ty's arm. Never having been the center of such blatant male interest, she wasn't sure if she should be flattered or furious.

"Easy, tiger," he said in a low voice, keeping a smile pasted on his face. "Let them look their fill."

When she relaxed her grip, he gave her hand a squeeze of approval, then whispered, "Shall we?"

Tilting her chin a notch higher, a smile frozen on her lips, she glided into the room on his arm. After circling the room to find a promising game, he approached one of the poker tables.

Stopping behind an empty chair, he said, "Mind if I join you, gentlemen?" Ty smiled at the three men seated at the table.

One of the men, a middle-aged Mexican with shiny black hair and a swarthy complexion, leveled his obsidian gaze at him and shrugged his shoulders. *"Sí,* if you wish. Your name, *Señor?"*

"Beauregard. James Beauregard." Ty took a seat and listened carefully as one of the men recited the rules.

Sassy silently watched Ty play draw poker from her position next to his chair, one hand resting on his shoulder.

179

Between hands, Ty slipped an arm around her hips and ran his fingers over the silk of her dress in a possessive caress. From the interest he saw reflected on the faces of the other men, establishing his claim on Sassy was imperative.

Although Sassy was his wife—and he'd made sure the others knew it—some of these men might have no qualms about going after a married woman, even right under her husband's nose. Though Ty planned to end his marriage, in the meantime he wasn't about to share his wife. And if he'd been totally honest with himself, he would have extended his refusal to share her to a lifetime.

The card game soon began to bore Sassy's adventurous nature. Shifting restlessly, she finally told Ty she was going to walk around. Surprised she'd stayed next to him for as long as she had, he gave her a don't-get-into-trouble look, but didn't stop her.

She explored the gambling room first, stopping to watch the action at a craps table, then at a faro table, where she had trouble following the fast and furious game. Shaking her head with wonder, she moved on. She particularly liked the roulette wheel. Apparently others did as well, since a large crowd had gathered to watch the wheel spin and the ball rattle from one number to another before coming to a rest. Mixed groans of defeat and cheers of victory rang in her ears, as she continued her wandering.

Passing the blackjack, monte, and keno tables, she was glad Ty had taken the time to explain each of those games. If not for his instruction, she wouldn't have recognized them. Instead of feeling like a greenhorn, she moved through the crowded casino like she'd done it a hundred times before.

Having explored all areas of the gambling room, she

went into the barroom. The sound of music, just barely audible above the clamor of the crowd, caught her attention. It came from the theater room on the opposite side of the barroom.

Drawn to the music, Sassy tried to cross the room, squeezing between dusty cowboys and fashionably dressed businessmen. Everyone graciously stepped aside, until she reached two men, more than slightly drunk, who refused to let her pass.

When one of them made a vulgar remark about what he'd like to do to her, she brought the high heel of one of her slippers down heavily on his foot. As he jumped around on one leg, yowling in pain, she smiled sweetly and offered a sugar-coated apology. Sober enough to know she'd done it on purpose and admiring her grit, the men offered no further resistance and allowed her to slip past.

After dodging a waiter girl with a tray full of drinks, she broke through the last of the crowd. Slightly out of breath, she arrived at the door of the theater room, where a capacity crowd cheered the evening show with wild enthusiasm.

While Sassy thought all the performances very entertaining, the dancers were her favorite.

When the announcer stepped onto the stage to introduce the finale, she could feel the excitement ripple through the audience. "Gentlemen, the cancan," the man shouted above the roar of the crowd. As the piano player struck up a lively tune, the dancers returned.

Sassy stared in fascination. Dressed in costumes of red satin with short, ruffled skirts trimmed in black, tight-fitting, low-cut bodices and matching red satin headpieces trimmed with ostrich feathers, the five women began a dance like none she had ever seen.

Standing in a line, they began their dance by picking up their skirts and strutting around the stage. Their hiked-up skirts revealed black net stockings and a scandalous two inches of bare flesh above ruffled red garters.

The men in the audience jumped to their feet, clapping and yelling their encouragement. Sassy gaped in wonder.

When the music slowed, signaling the dance was about to end, the dancers turned their backs to the audience. With a flurry of satin, they bent over and flipped their skirts up over their backs, presenting ruffled batiste bloomers to the whistles and catcalls filling the air.

As the red velvet curtain closed, Sassy sighed, wishing the show hadn't ended. Turning to leave the theater, she gave a cry of surprise when she bumped into someone standing immediately behind her.

Slowly lifting her gaze from the man's floral vest to his dark brown eyes, she sighed with relief. "I didn't know you were there, Ty. You scared the daylights out of me." Before he could respond, she added in a breathless rush of words, "Did you see the cancan dancers?"

He immediately recognized the sparkle in her eyes, the unmistakable glow he was beginning to know so well. Grasping her shoulders firmly, he looked her straight in the eye. "Yes, I saw them, but it's *James,* remember? And don't even think about it."

"Sorry. I forgot." Her brow furrowed at his last statement. "Don't think about what?"

"You know what I'm talking about. I know what goes on in that head of yours. You were wondering what it would be like to dance the cancan. And when you wonder about something, you usually come up with a scheme to find out."

He released her arms and turned her toward the door.

"But not this time," he added, putting an arm around her waist and escorting her from the room.

Sassy didn't deny his words. How could she, when they were true? Even his warning didn't stop an idea from forming. *At least I can talk to the women and ask them what it's like to go on stage.* Ty said don't think about being a dancer; he didn't say anything about talking to them.

Over the next several days, Sassy carried out her plans to talk to the dancers at the Red Garter. The five girls, all young and pretty, answered her questions readily. Although they were all friendly, she particularly liked the leader of the troupe, a strawberry blond known as Kitty La Rue.

Since Sassy and Ty had begun spending their evenings at the Red Garter—often not getting back to their boardinghouse until early in the morning—they didn't rise until nearly noon. With her afternoons free until she joined Ty for a late supper before going to the saloon, Sassy found herself spending more and more time with Kitty.

In spite of having little in common, Sassy and Kitty hit it off immediately, chatting like the closest of friends or even sisters from the start. It was as if they'd known each other for years, rather than days.

Sassy learned Kitty's real name was Katherine Wilson. Although her nickname had always been Kitty, she'd changed her last name to La Rue to go with her specialty, the French originated cancan.

"One word outta my mouth, though, and everybody knows I ain't French," she had told Sassy with a giggle.

The two often stayed in Kitty's small suite of rooms

above the Red Garter, when they didn't go out. Today they visited while Kitty put a hem in a dress she'd made.

"Where'd you learn to sew like that, Kitty?" Sassy asked, watching her new friend's pouty mouth pucker in concentration over each tiny stitch.

"I've been sewing long's I can remember. My Ma showed me how to cut patterns and sew 'em together, when I was a youngun," she responded in a soft drawl.

"I wouldn't know what ta do with myself, if I couldn't keep my hands busy sewing. Sometimes, I wish . . ." her voice trailed off. Deftly tying a knot, she carefully cut the thread, then held up the dress. "Well, what do ya think?"

Wondering at the wistful look she'd seen on Kitty's face, Sassy looked at the dress Kitty had fashioned.

"It's beautiful, Kitty," she exclaimed, amazed at the woman's skill with a needle and thread. "Is it for you?"

"No, it's for one of the ladies I sew for. 'Bout a dozen women in town come to me for their dresses. 'Course they don't tell nobody my name. Wouldn't want the taint of a saloon girl ta mar their lily-white reputations, if their friends found out I was making their clothes."

The bitterness in Kitty's voice changed to mirth. "Funny thing is, not one of 'em knows me—an uneducated bar dancer—also sews for all their snobby friends."

Sympathy welled up inside Sassy for the life Kitty led, and other women who'd been forced to take up an unrespected profession. A woman working in a saloon was viewed as little better than trash to most people. Sassy knew firsthand how it felt to be shunned by those passing judgment. Such biased opinions were so unfair and so sad. Especially when Sassy knew Kitty was as good, probably better, than some of those who condemned her.

Although she knew some dance hall girls had the morals of an alley cat and earned the scorn they received, Kitty wasn't one of them. Sassy remembered vividly the conversation they'd had about being a saloon dancer.

"My folks got a small ranch, where they grow cotton," Kitty began in response to Sassy's question about how she'd ended up dancing at the Red Garter. "They worked that piece of land from sunup ta sunset, but all they ever managed ta make was more babies. I'm the oldest of eight, maybe more now, and I don't remember anything about my childhood, 'cept taking care of my brothers and sisters and working in the cotton fields.

"I loved my family, but I couldn't take the back-breaking work no more. I vowed I'd find a way ta get away from the ranch and make a living, so's I could send money back home. When I heard 'bout the handbills posted in town advertising for saloon dancers for a town in west Texas, I saw it as my golden opportunity. When I met the man who'd put out the handbills, he promised me big wages and a train ticket west. So I agreed ta go with him and signed the paper—my contract, he called it—that he shoved at me."

"Is that when you came to El Paso?" Sassy asked.

"Yeah, that was five years ago," she replied sadly.

"Didn't he keep his promises?"

"Oh, the money was good, I admit. And I was able ta send most of it home, but, I . . ." She cleared her throat to stop the trembling in her voice. "I couldn't read much, and I thought the paper I signed was an agreement ta work for him for three years. After we got here, he told me it was time ta start the other part of our deal. When I told him I didn't know what he was talking 'bout, he got mad and shoved me onta his bed. He tore my clothes off, telling me I'd agreed ta warm his bed whenever he wanted. And he wanted it right then, so he—" She swallowed hard. "He forced himself on me."

Sucking in a sharp breath, Sassy whispered, "Oh, my God."

Kitty turned tear-filled eyes to stare out the window. She blew her nose, then went on. "Afterward, he told me ta stop crying or he'd beat me. I was young and naive, and I couldn't read my contract, even if he'd let me see it, ta find out if he was telling the truth. So I had no choice but ta believe him. I became his whore," she said bitterly.

"Oh, Kitty, no," Sassy said, kneeling in front of her and grasping her hands. "You didn't know what you'd agreed to when you signed that contract, so you weren't a whore."

Kitty turned to look at her and smiled faintly. "I know that now, but back then I thought I was his personal whore, ta be used whenever he wanted me. Anyway, during our . . . uh . . . relationship, I had one of the other dancers teach me ta read. It took me a long time ta find where he'd hid my contract, but I found it. And ya know what it said?

"The bastard lied ta me," she spit out venomously before Sassy could reply. "I'd signed three years of my life over ta that man all right, but as a dancer in his saloon, not as his damn whore!"

"What'd you do then?"

"There was one part of my contract he'd never mentioned: the part about paying him back for my train ticket ta El Paso, plus my room and board. The amount I owed him was staggering. I'm sure he thought I could never come up with that much money, since I sent most of my wages home. He didn't know I'd been taking in sewing

186

almost from the first day I got here, and had saved nearly every penny."

Kitty smiled brightly. "I wish you coulda seen the look on his face, when I told him I'd read my contract and I refused ta share his bed ever again. When he threw the debt in my face, I calmly told him I intended ta pay back every cent. He just smiled and said I'd be back in his bed within a month. He never touched me again," she stated proudly.

"It took me almost a year, working every free minute I had. But I did it. He was furious when I handed him the money, but there was nothing he could do. I moved outta his saloon that night, and came here ta the Red Garter. That was over two years ago. I swore then I'd never take another man inta my bed again—like some girls do ta make extra money—unless I loved him," she'd finished with conviction.

Kitty's soft giggle brought Sassy back to the present. "Sassy, what ya thinking 'bout? Y'all must be a million miles away."

Sassy smiled good-naturedly, then said, "Kitty, have you ever thought about leaving El Paso and going back home?"

"All the time," she replied. "I've been saving my money ta open a dress shop. 'Course, it can't be here, 'cause then it would get out that the wives of some of the fine men in town have been buying their dresses from a saloon girl. Soon as I have enough money, I intend ta leave El Paso and go ta some town where nobody knows 'bout my past."

"Don't you want to see your parents?"

"Yeah, I want ta see 'em. I will someday, but I can't face 'em yet. Not after what I've done."

"Kitty, that's ridiculous. Your parents don't know what happened to you when you first got to El Paso, do they?"

"No, I couldn't bear ta send 'em a letter telling 'em what happened," Kitty whispered in a tortured voice.

"Then they don't have to know. Besides, even if they did find out, you're their daughter. Their love for you is more important than anything in your past. They won't blame you, Kitty, I know they won't," Sassy said gently.

Kitty brightened, hope shining on her face. "Maybe y'all're right, Sassy."

"I know I'm right. Then, after you open your dress shop, you'll probably sweep some handsome man off his feet. And he'll ask you to marry—"

Sassy's words came to a halt, when she saw her friend's stricken look. "What is it, Kitty?"

"Y'all may be right about my parents accepting what I've done. But no decent man will ever want me for his wife."

"Don't be silly. There's a man out there just waiting for you to step into his life. And he'll understand about your past."

At Kitty's doubtful look, Sassy continued. "Have you ever been in love, Kitty? Have you ever given your heart to a man? Or made love to a man with your mind as well as your body?"

Kitty shook her head to each question.

"You see, you still have a lot to offer a man. And he won't care what happened before he met you, not as long as you return his love. Do you understand what I'm saying?"

Although Kitty was older than Sassy by three years, in many ways she felt younger. When she left the protection of her family, she'd been forced to grow up fast, living a life that wasn't easy and often exposed her to some harsh realities. Yet, in many ways, she was still an innocent girl.

"Yes, I understand, Sassy. I just hope y'all're right about finding a man who won't care about my past," Kitty responded gravely.

"I know I am. Now come on, let's go down to Mrs. Reed's Millinery Shop. She got a new shipment in yesterday." Though she thought the frilly pieces of netting and feathers a waste of money, Sassy knew Kitty dearly loved hats.

Kitty's good spirits restored, they walked the few blocks to the millinery shop on San Antonio Street, then window-shopped on the way back to the Red Garter. As they strolled along, Sassy made a decision.

"Kitty, there's something I need to talk to you about. But you have to promise not to tell anyone."

" 'Course I promise, Sassy. What is it?"

"Do you know a professional gambler named Teddy?"

"No, I don't rightly recall a Teddy. Gamblers are a dime a dozen around here, and there's plenty of other saloons in town. Besides, even if he did come inta the Red Garter, I might not hear his name. Why are ya interested in him? I thought James was your man."

My man, Sassy thought dreamily. *He's more than my man, he's my husband! And I want him to remain my husband for the rest of our days. That's why we have to find Teddy.*

Teddy! The name brought Sassy back to reality with a jolt. Not wanting to reveal the entire truth about their presence in El Paso, she knew she'd have to tell Kitty at least part of it. "I . . . uh . . . have a confession to make. James isn't my husband's real name. It's Ty." At Kitty's quizzical look, she explained. "He's using a fake name, because he has a personal score to settle with Teddy. If he found out we're looking for him, he might hole up somewhere, and Ty doesn't want to risk that happening. So if you hear anything, will you let me know right away?"

" 'Course I will," Kitty promised, squeezing Sassy's hand. "We're friends ain't—I mean, aren't we?"

"Absolutely," she responded. "Make sure you use the name James when we're around other people. Oh, and don't say anything about Teddy in front of Ty."

Kitty's brows drew together. "I thought you said Ty has a score to settle with him."

"Yes, he does," Sassy replied, trying to come up with a plausible explanation. "It's just that Ty wants to handle this himself, and he doesn't want me in any danger. If he knew I asked you about Teddy, he'd be a little put out." Sassy crossed her fingers, praying she never got the chance to find out if her description of Ty's reaction was as much an understatement as she thought.

Sixteen

"Hi, Sassy. How're y'all tonight?" Clad in only corset, stockings, and garters, Kitty smiled and waved Sassy into the dressing room.

"I'm fine, Kitty," Sassy responded, taking a seat near Kitty's dressing table.

Watching the dancers outline their eyes, darken their eyelashes, and apply lip paint was Sassy's favorite part of their routine.

After finishing her makeup, Kitty stepped into the emerald green costume for the first dance number and pulled it up over her hips.

"Will y'all fasten me?" Kitty asked, turning and presenting her back.

"Sure." Sassy quickly fastened the row of hooks and eyes on the tight bodice, then helped secure the headpiece of matching brilliant green feathers in Kitty's upswept hair.

Picking up one of her high-heeled dance slippers, Kitty spit into one before slipping it on her foot.

Sassy shook her head, then smiled. "Let me guess, spitting in your shoe is for good luck, like having someone pick up your scissors when you drop them, or the piece of bread you carry in your purse?"

Kitty glanced up from tying her shoes. "If I didn't spit in my shoe—" She visibly shuddered, gooseflesh rising on her arms. "Well, I hate ta think what might happen."

Sassy wanted to tell her all that silliness was pure poppycock, but she didn't. She'd come to realize that Kitty's superstitions were as much a part of her personality as her own penchant for cursing. *Hell—uh—heck if Kitty thinks such nonsense brings good luck, I'm not gonna upset the apple cart by telling her what I think.*

Smiling indulgently, Sassy moved to the dressing room door. "I'd best get back, before Ty comes looking for me."

"Is he still sore as a frog on a hot skillet?"

Laughing at Kitty's reference to Ty's surly mood of late, she nodded. "I think it's because he's got a lot on his mind."

"That man he's looking for—Teddy?"

"Yes, we still haven't heard anything about him."

"I've asked some of the girls at the other saloons ta let me know if they hear anything," Kitty said, standing and fluffing the skirt of her costume.

"Thanks, Kitty. I appreciate it. Hearing something about Teddy would help sweeten Ty's disposition. Until then, I've decided to take matters into my own hands to improve his mood—at least for tonight."

Seeing Sassy's grin and the sparkle of mischief in her eyes, Kitty cocked her head to one side. "What have ya done?"

Leaning close to Kitty so the other girls wouldn't hear, she whispered her plan.

Kitty gasped. "Sassy, ya didn't!" When her friend nodded, she burst out laughing. "That should take Ty's mind off his troubles," she stated when her laughter died.

* * *

Sitting at the keno table, the spot he'd chosen for the night's action, Ty couldn't keep his mind on the game. After Sassy had returned from visiting Kitty, she'd come into the gambling room, but didn't take up her usual place next to him. Tonight, for some reason, she stayed just out of reach.

He wouldn't have thought much about it, except for the heated glances she kept sending across the room at him. Feeling the heat of her gaze again, he looked up from his cards to see her run the tip of her tongue slowly over her painted lips in an obviously provocative gesture. He nearly leaped out of his chair, desire surging through him like a river swollen with spring rain. It was only through extreme self-control that he stayed put.

Watching her work her way through the crowd, he wondered if she had an ulterior motive for her actions. Sassy never ceased to amaze him, one of the reasons he found her so fascinating. He scowled. That's a dangerous line of thinking, he warned himself.

After an hour of her silent flirting, she stopped by his chair and allowed him to put his arm around her hip. When he ran his hand over the silk of her dress, he froze. Something was different.

Tentatively moving his fingers, he realized what that *something* was. Jerking his hand away, his gaze snapped to her face in disbelief.

Her sly smile confirmed what he had discovered. She wasn't wearing anything under her dress. The enticing thought brought an instant arousal.

Seeing the flare of desire in his eyes and the rapidly throbbing pulse in the side of his neck, Sassy gave him a smoldering look. She walked away, biting her lip to hold in a giggle, satisfied with his reaction.

When she reached the opposite side of the room, she

looked over her shoulder and blew him a kiss. Another giggle threatened. The look on his face was priceless. *This flirting is more fun than I figured.*

Thoughts of finishing the game of keno—a game he had never mentally been in anyway—faded into oblivion. Watching the twitching of Sassy's perfectly shaped bottom, he had only one purpose in mind. The sudden realization that he might not be the only man who noticed Sassy's state of dress, propelled him to his feet.

Cashing in his chips and stuffing the money haphazardly into his pocket, he moved away from the keno table, nearly upsetting his chair in the process. Shoving through the crowd, he caught up with Sassy at the roulette wheel.

Grasping her arm firmly, he silently escorted her through the barroom and toward the front door. As soon as they were outside, Ty pulled her into the shadows. Without saying a word, his mouth claimed hers in a kiss that spoke loudly of his desire.

When he finally lifted his head, his breathing was ragged. "Come on," he gasped, grabbing her hand and heading for the St. Charles Lodging House.

Inside their suite, he locked the door behind them, then approached Sassy with measured steps. "Okay, wildcat, you've been asking for this all evening." He shrugged out of his jacket, then loosened his tie with one fierce tug. "And now you're gonna get it."

The gleam in his eyes and his obvious arousal kept her from panicking at the harshness of his voice. Never taking her gaze from his, she pulled the pins from her hair, then shook the heavy tresses free. For each piece of clothing he removed, she matched with one of her own.

Watching her strip had him frantic to join their bodies

in the song of love. Unable to continue their titillating game, Ty scooped her into his arms and carried her to the bedroom. He lowered himself onto the mattress, Sassy still nestled in his embrace. Pushing her to her back, he rose on his knees between her parted thighs.

He settled over her, slipped into her welcoming warmth, and pushed forward. When firmly seated within her, a throaty growl of pleasure came from deep in his chest. He didn't move, praying for his desire to ebb before he continued. But there was no slowing his need, he was well beyond the point of control.

Aware but not caring that Sassy hadn't removed her stockings and garters and he still wore his shirt, he made love to her with a wildness he'd never known. He kissed and caressed, thrusting into her slowly, then more quickly, until he could hold back no longer. With a shout of joy, he thrust into her one last time in a climax that started at his toes. Still experiencing the tremors of his release, he realized she hadn't joined him. Shifting so he could get one hand between their bodies, he sought her heated center.

When his fingers found her, she gasped, digging her heels into the mattress. He rubbed her slick flesh, teasing the hardened bud, until she cried out. Tossing her head from side to side, her hips bucking beneath him, she followed him into the world of satiated bliss.

Of all the times they'd made love, Ty knew they had never shared such wantonness, such urgency. This time their loving had bordered on an almost savage need for each other.

As he relieved her of his weight and rolled to his side, the mental burden he'd been carrying around lifted as well. How this firebrand of a woman and her outrageous scheme to charm the pants off him—literally—could pull him out of his sour mood with so little effort, befuddled him. Yet, she'd done it.

For the first time in days, he actually felt carefree. He didn't dare let his lightened mood carry over into thinking about how important Sassy had become to him, or how she knew him so well she could easily reverse his churlishness. Thoughts along those lines would only make him analyze what he felt for her, and he couldn't let himself do that.

Finding Teddy was what he should think about. His jaw hardened. *Dammit Teddy. This has gone on long enough. It isn't Sassy's fault I haven't found you, and she sure as hell doesn't deserve the way I've been treating her.* He heaved a weary sigh. If only he could find Teddy and get his name cleared, then he wouldn't have to divorce Sassy. Hope surged through him, but he quickly put a stranglehold on it. *Don't get ahead of yourself, Beaumont. Just take it one day at a time.*

Pulling Sassy into his arms, he kissed the top of her head. He made a silent promise to do his best to keep his frustrations to himself.

Sassy stirred next to him, throwing one leg over his thighs and draping an arm across his chest.

"Sassy?"

"Hmm?"

"Thanks."

She smiled into the thick hair covering his chest, then murmured in a sleepy voice, "Someone had to brave the lion's fury and remove the thorn."

"What?"

"Nothing. 'Night."

Mulling over her strange words, Ty gave up trying to figure out what she meant, then pulled her tighter against him.

196

"Oh, damn, damn, double damn." Kitty was definitely not her usual gentle, sweet-natured self as Sassy breezed into the living room of the dancer's suite above the Red Garter.

Laughing gaily at Kitty's cursing, Sassy took a seat on the sofa. "Come, sit," she urged, patting the cushion next to her. "What has you so upset?"

Catching Sassy's light mood, Kitty smiled, her displeasure fading. She sat down on the sofa and laid her head against its high back.

"It's Jewel," Kitty said with a sigh.

"What about her?" Sassy asked, wondering how one of the other girls in the dance troupe had caused Kitty's agitation.

"She got her monthlies today and can't dance tonight. Wouldn't ya know, her time would havta come when I gave Tina and Marta some time off. That leaves only Rosalie and me for tonight's show."

"Can't you ask Tina or Marta to work tonight?"

"I wish I could. They went ta see Marta's family up in Las Cruces, and won't be back 'til tomorrow afternoon."

Sassy sat quietly, tapping one finger against her pursed lips thoughtfully. At last she said, "I have a solution to your problem."

One of Kitty's eyebrows raised in question. "Ya do?"

"Yes. Listen, Jewel and me are about the same size, aren't we?"

"I'd say so. But—"

"I'll take her place tonight. We have all afternoon for you to teach me the dance routines. Let's start now," Sassy said, jumping to her feet. Forgotten was Ty's warning. The prospect of slipping into a frilly costume, stepping in front of an audience to strut and kick her way across the stage, was too exciting to pass up. After the first night in the saloon, she'd accepted the other men ogling her. Although their stares were often downright rude, her long dormant desire for men to admire her as a woman overrode her initial discomfort.

There was also another benefit, every gaze she drew was one less that might recognize Ty. And while the dance costumes would reveal more of her to ogle, she wasn't concerned. She knew the theatre hired bouncers to keep overzealous customers off the stage. "Well, come on. Are you going to teach me, or not?"

Kitty looked at her dubiously. "Are ya sure y'all want ta do this? I don't think Ty would be none too pleased ta find out—"

"He won't find out, Kitty. He spends the entire evening at the gambling tables, you know that." Grabbing Kitty's hands, she pulled the blonde to her feet. "Show me the cancan first."

Kitty stared thoughtfully at her friend. "Well, I do have a blond wig you could wear. That oughta help."

"Perfect. Now teach me the dances we'll be doing tonight."

Catching her friend's bubbling excitement, Kitty broke into a fit of giggles. "Okay, Sassy, here goes."

By the time Sassy left Kitty's rooms several hours later, she had to run to the St. Charles. It was late, and she wanted to bathe before Ty got back from an afternoon of poker at the Gem Saloon.

Over supper Ty related a story he'd heard about a gunfight the previous night at the Gem.

198

Staring at the dish of ice cream the waiter placed before her, Sassy silently thanked the fates for diverting Ty's attention. She heard him say something about a gunfight, but her mind wandered off after that.

Spooning the frozen dessert into her mouth, she didn't savor the wonderful treat as she normally did. Her thoughts kept straying to her hurried dance lesson. *God, I hope I remember the steps.* Smiling vacantly at Ty, she wondered if Kitty had finished the minor alterations of Jewel's costumes. *Hell's bells! I can't keep my mind off—*

Sassy's musings ended abruptly with the realization that Ty had stopped speaking. Raising her gaze, she took in his furrowed brow and questioning eyes uneasily. *Was he still talking about that gunfight? Or did he ask me a question? Dear God, what was it?*

Finally, she swallowed all pretense of pretending to know what he'd said. "I'm sorry, Ty. My mind was miles away. What did you say?"

Giving her a strange look, he wondered at her preoccupation, but reserved comment. "I said, are you ready to go?"

Taking a deep breath, Sassy nodded, then dropped the spoon she'd been absently twirling in the now-melted ice cream.

Arriving at the Red Garter, she was thankful she'd established the routine of stopping in to see Kitty before the show, so she wouldn't have to come up with an explanation. She accepted Ty's kiss on her cheek and offered him a weak smile. After he walked away, she was struck with a case of stage fright. Shaking off her nervousness, she hurried to the dressing rooms.

Rolling the black net stockings up her legs and securing them at mid-thigh with fancy red garters—the well-known trademark of the saloon's dancers—Sassy's jitters eased.

Kitty helped her with the blond wig, showed her how to apply her makeup, and had just finished fastening the hooks on the back of her costume, when a commotion at the door drew Sassy's attention.

In spite of Rosalie's protests, the door burst open, and the person causing the ruckus barged into the dressing room.

Finding herself standing face-to-face with Ty, Sassy's mouth went dry. "What . . . What are you doing here?"

Ty blinked several times, his mind slow to grasp what his eyes told him. The woman beneath the blond wig and heavy makeup was Sassy.

Snapping out of his shock, he said, "I was worried about you. You were preoccupied during supper, and I thought maybe you'd taken ill. Apparently, I was wrong." He raked his gaze over her, his eyebrows pulling together at the amount of skin her costume revealed. *Holy Christ, there isn't enough material in that getup to dust a fiddle.* He lifted his gaze to her face. "I think the question is, what are *you* doing here?"

He stared at her, a myriad of emotions skittering through him: relief she wasn't ill as he'd feared, surprise at finding her in a skimpy dance costume, overpowering jealousy that if he hadn't showed up, Sassy would be parading around on stage revealing her shapely body to an all-male audience, and finally, livid fury that she had disobeyed him. Again!

Sassy gulped convulsively, belatedly realizing the folly of her actions. Vaguely, she heard Kitty and Rosalie slip from the room, leaving her alone with Ty and his towering anger.

Ty took a deep breath, then another, hoping he could

get through this without bloodshed. "I know I'll undoubtedly regret asking, but what's your explanation for this?"

Sassy swallowed again before answering in a timid voice, "Two of Kitty's girls are out of town and Jewel's in bed with her . . . uh, she's indisposed. So, I offered to take her place."

When her response didn't soften the hard lines of his face, she rushed on, "Kitty is my friend, and I wanted to help. It's only for one night, Tina and Marta will be back . . ." Her words trailed off when his expression hardened even more. He continued to stare at her with a dark, icy glare, making her shiver, as if a cold draft had touched her exposed skin.

Sassy straightened her back with determination. Although she knew she couldn't talk her way out of this, she refused to be cowed.

Deciding her best defense was to face the bull head-on, she blurted, "Guess I'm in deep shit, huh?"

In spite of his choking anger, Ty's mouth twitched at her bold-as-brass statement. Yes, she was, as Sassy had so succinctly put it, in deep shit. Forcing his lips to remain in a severe line, he moved closer to the woman who managed to keep his life in a constant uproar.

"If you step one foot on that stage tonight, or any other night," he added for good measure, "I'll send you home so fast you won't know what hit you."

Realizing there was no point in arguing any further, since she had absolutely no doubt he would make good his threat, Sassy had the common sense to give in.

"Okay, I won't go on stage." Her voice was dull with resignation. Then her good humor returned, and she flashed him a smile. "Since I'm already wearing the costume, can I show you the dances Kitty taught me?"

Ty's icy stare melted like a block of ice in the desert

sun, quickly climbing the opposite scale, until his eyes blazed with the heat of a forest fire.

He wasn't sure if he'd answered her, since he couldn't hear anything over the pounding of his heart in his ears. But he must have given an affirmative response, because she proceeded to demonstrate her dancing skills.

Ty's desire for the scantily clad Sassy soon overrode his need to sit in a smoke-filled room playing poker all evening. Wrapping her in a coat, he spirited her back to their lodging house, forfeiting another night at the gambling tables.

Seventeen

"Kitty, what is it?" Sassy was instantly alert to Kitty's obvious excitement.

"Let me catch my breath," she wheezed, fluttering a hankie in front of her face.

Sassy waited anxiously, wondering what brought Kitty to the St. Charles Lodging House. Kitty had always insisted they meet at her place, since she didn't think the proprietress would welcome a saloon dancer at the St. Charles. Sassy knew it had to be important for Kitty to risk Mrs. Moore's scorn.

Her breathing finally returning to normal, Kitty explained. "I went ta see Lydia, a friend of mine who works at the Ranch Saloon, and she told me about a high-stakes poker game set for next week at the Ranch. She said a whole bunch of gamblers from all over Texas were invited. And I found out one of the players who was supposed ta be in that game is named Teddy."

"Really? Oh, Kitty, that's wonderful. Teddy is coming here." Sassy was ecstatic, sorry Ty wasn't there to share the news.

"No, he ain't coming here."

"But, I thought you said—"

203

"I said, he was *supposed* ta come here," Kitty interrupted. "The game got cancelled, when some of the other men couldn't make it."

"Damn, another dead-end." Sassy sighed, sagging wearily onto the sofa.

"Maybe not," Kitty said. "Teddy's telegram said he couldn't make it to El Paso, but he'd see everyone in Laredo."

"Laredo? Are you sure? Laredo is hundreds of miles from—" Sassy stopped mid-sentence to give Kitty a wide-eyed stare. "How do you know Teddy sent a telegram?"

"I snuck inta the saloon office, while Lydia stood guard in the hall. I found the telegram in a pile of papers on the desk. It said, 'Can't make El Paso. Plan ta be in Laredo on the fifteenth,' and it was signed 'Teddy.' "

Surprised at the effort Kitty put into finding out information about Teddy, Sassy's heart swelled with love for the friend she'd had for such a short time.

"So, what do you think Ty will do?" Kitty asked when Sassy remained silent.

"Go after him, I suppose," Sassy replied, on her feet and pacing the sitting room. "I've got to find him and tell him Teddy is headed for Laredo."

Kitty nodded, then cleared her throat nervously. "Sassy, I have a favor ta ask."

Hearing the tremor in Kitty's voice, Sassy stopped her pacing. "What is it, Kitty?"

Swallowing the urge to call back her words, she plunged forward. "I'd like ta go with ya, when y'all leave town. I reckon you're right that Ty'll want ta head for Laredo. And I want ta go, too. Will ya ask Ty, if I can go with ya?"

Kitty's request caught Sassy off guard. Although they

had discussed Kitty leaving El Paso and starting over somewhere, Sassy never got the impression that Kitty planned on starting a new life quite so soon. Deciding Kitty's reason for her change in plans was none of her business, she said, "Of course, I'll ask him." She hoped Ty would be in such a good mood after finally hearing something about Teddy, that he'd consent to letting Kitty travel with them.

"I'll find him right away and tell him. And then I'll ask about taking you with us."

Seeing the relief wash over Kitty's face, she wondered again at her friend's strange behavior, but didn't want to pry. She had to find Ty.

Sassy gave Kitty a quick hug, grabbed her purse, and headed for the door. "Come on, I'll walk you to the Red Garter. After I talk to Ty, I'll let you know what he said."

When Sassy charged into the Gem Saloon, interrupting his afternoon poker game, Ty's eyes narrowed. *Now what's she up to?*

The urgency of her whispered request to see him outside told him this was not another of her half-baked schemes. Whatever brought her to the Gem was serious.

Excusing himself, Ty followed her outside, a frown creasing his forehead.

"Laredo?" he responded to her rush of words. "Kitty's sure Teddy's going to Laredo?"

"Absolutely sure, she saw the telegram herself," Sassy answered proudly.

"Not 'til the fifteenth, huh? That's three weeks away, plenty of time to get to Laredo and get settled," Ty theorized aloud.

"Come on." He grabbed her by the hand, pulling her

down the boardwalk. "Let's find a streetcar. I want to go to the depot and check the train schedule."

The next few hours were so busy—making arrangements to go to Laredo, sending a telegram to Josh Madison about their plans, and beginning their packing, although they wouldn't be leaving for two days—that Sassy didn't broach the subject of Kitty's request until they were getting ready to go out that night.

"She asked you *what?*" Ty turned toward Sassy, his face partially covered with shaving soap, the razor he held poised in mid-stroke.

"She asked to go with us when we leave," she repeated, not sure she liked Ty's initial reaction.

"Absolutely not," he declared, turning back to the mirror and applying the blade to his lathered face.

"But, Ty—"

"There's no way I'll agree to take her with us," he interrupted. "You know how I feel about having *one* woman along on this trip, so you should know I'd never agree to having two of you. Just drop it, Sassy."

Damn, she thought peevishly. *Now, what am I supposed to do? Kitty was depending on me.*

"I'm sorry, Kitty. Ty said no." Sassy had expected Kitty's disappointment, but she hadn't expected to see terror replace the hope on her face.

"What's wrong, Kitty? You're shaking."

"I . . . I didn't tell ya everything about my visit ta the Ranch Saloon," she began in a low voice. "The owner is Lloyd Peters, my former boss."

Although Kitty had told Sassy the story of her arrival in El Paso, she hadn't revealed the name of the man who had tricked her. The risk Kitty had taken to get the information Ty needed became apparent.

"Oh, Kitty. I never intended for you to go there, of all places, when I asked you about Teddy."

"Going there ta see Lydia was nothing, and even getting in Lloyd's office was easy. It was what I saw in his office that's the problem. After I found the telegram from Teddy, I found a couple of invoices for some new gambling equipment. I was curious, so I read 'em. Then I heard Lydia warning me Lloyd was on his way. I got out of there as quick as I could, but I'm sure he saw me come out of his office."

"So, what's the problem? Will he be angry, because you were in his office?"

"I wouldn't care if that's the only reason he got angry. The thing is, I didn't get a chance ta put those invoices back. As soon as he looked at his desk, he'd know I saw 'em."

When Sassy continued looking at her expectantly, Kitty explained. "The invoices were from the Will and Finck Company." When Sassy didn't react, she said, "They make dishonest gambling equipment. Those invoices were for rigged faro-dealing boxes, crooked dice, a fixed roulette wheel, and who knows what else."

"I've never heard of the company," Sassy ventured. "Maybe he'll think you haven't either."

Kitty shook her head sadly. "He told me about the company himself. But he swore his games were honest, and that he'd never buy anything from 'em. I shoulda known he'd lie 'bout that, too."

"So, what do you think he'll do?" Sassy asked, an uneasy prickling running up her neck.

"I can only guess. When I told him I refused ta play his whore and intended ta pay off my contract, he was fit ta be tied. I reckon that's still eating at him. After seeing me at his saloon the other day, he's probably been thinking 'bout that and getting himself all worked up inta a real tizzy." She swallowed, clasping her hands tightly in her lap. "There's a man, Oliver, who works as a bouncer and bodyguard for Lloyd, and sometimes he does other things—like keep Lloyd's employees in line, if they give him any trouble."

Kitty didn't have to explain her last remark, Sassy understood it loud and clear. She shuddered at the thought. "Do you think Lloyd would really send that man after you?"

"He'll give me a chance ta keep my mouth shut. But if I refuse ta do what he says, then I'm sure he'll threaten me with a visit from Oliver. Lloyd always said I was the best he'd ever . . ." Her face flushed a dull red. "Well, you know. Anyway, I'm sure he'll try ta get me back inta his bed, by threatening ta sic Oliver on me. I won't do it, Sassy. I swore he'd never use me again, and I ain't changing my mind. That's why I hafta leave town. If I stay here . . ." her voice trailed off, unable to talk about her bleak future in El Paso.

"I'll talk to Ty again. This time I'll make him understand you *have* to go with us! That means I'll have to tell him about you and Peters," Sassy warned. At Kitty's nod, she went on. "We aren't leaving for two days. Will you be all right?"

"Yeah, I think so. I don't expect Lloyd ta do anything for a day or two. He's like a cat toying with a mouse— hurting it so it can't get away, but refusing to put the poor thing out of its misery until he gets tired of the game. Lloyd always said using a person's fear, then making 'em wait was the best way to get what he wanted. He's planning on me being so afraid of what he'll do, that I'll agree to whatever he wants. He'll give me some time to stew about it, then move in for the kill. So I'll be fine for a couple days."

"I'll do everything I can to help you, Kitty, I promise. I want you to be extra careful until we can get out of town—all three of us."

Sassy waited until after she and Ty made love that night, before bringing up the subject of Kitty going with them. Although ashamed of herself for using their love-making for another purpose, she had to. Kitty's safety depended on it. While relaxed and sated, she intended to use Ty's tranquil mood to her advantage.

Snuggled close to him, her head on his shoulder, Sassy traced lazy circles on his chest with her fingertips.

"Ty?"

"Hmm?"

"Won't you please let Kitty go with us? She's—"

Ty's exasperated sigh cut off her words. "We've already discussed this, Sassy."

Rising up onto one elbow, she looked at him with imploring eyes.

"But I didn't know Kitty was in danger then. You've got to let her go with us, Ty. You've just *got* to!"

Drawing his eyebrows together in a frown, he searched her face for some sign of duplicity. "What do you mean, she's in danger?" he demanded softly.

She quickly told him Kitty's story: how she came to El Paso, how the man who'd brought her west used her, and finally how she'd recently come under his wrath.

She concluded by adding, "Kitty is sure Peters will seek revenge. Knowing his games are rigged puts her in danger, and she wants to leave town before he tries anything. We have to help her."

Ty stared at Sassy's flushed face and kiss-swollen lips, thinking over what she'd said. In spite of the seriousness of their conversation, her sensuality kept one part of his mind focused on how much he wanted her, bringing a new stirring of desire in his groin. Forcing his greedy body to behave, he finally said, "Does Kitty honestly believe Peters would have Oliver hurt her?"

"Yes. She told me about a woman who worked for Lloyd as a monte dealer a couple years ago. He thought she was skimming from the house winnings, so he had Oliver pay her a visit. Kitty found her the next day. Both her hands had been broken.

"Kitty tried to get her to go to the sheriff, but she refused. She'd been threatened with more than broken bones, if she opened her mouth. Kitty knew who was behind it, but she couldn't convince the woman to swear out a complaint. Kitty has no doubt Lloyd will send Oliver, if she doesn't do what he wants."

Ty's gut wrenched at hearing of such vile treatment. "The bastard," he grumbled under his breath. Sassy had told him Kitty planned to open a dress shop—an occupation requiring the use of her hands—so he could well imagine her fear of suffering a similar fate. "The man should be horsewhipped."

A man who ordered one of his thugs to subject a woman to such cruelties was the lowest sort of coward in Ty's estimation, and roused his chivalrous nature. He could never be callous enough to overlook behavior that pitted a man's strength against a weaker female opponent.

Still, he didn't like the idea of someone else traveling with him. He already had his hands full with Sassy, and all the trouble she got herself into. And besides, he wasn't sure he could trust Kitty—hell, he wasn't sure he could trust Sassy. And what about the man following him? He hadn't solved that mystery, still feeling the man's presence nearly everywhere he went.

Seeing Ty wasn't going to be easily convinced, Sassy said, "Kitty doesn't know why you're looking for Teddy. I won't tell her, I swear. She won't cause any trouble." When his eyebrows shot up, she quickly added, "I won't cause any more trouble, either."

"Humph."

Sticking her chin out, she gave him a mulish glare. "Well, I won't. I promise. Please, Ty, I'm asking you to let Kitty go with us."

The pleading in her eyes and the fact that she'd asked—rather than demanded—made him forget his objections. He dismissed her promise to behave. He didn't think Sassy could remain out of trouble for very long, no matter how hard she tried. Clearing his throat to halt his musings, he pulled her down next to him. "Okay, darlin', Kitty goes with us. I don't like it, but I won't leave her here to face scum like Peters and that henchman of his."

"Oh, Ty, thank you," Sassy squealed, hugging him fiercely and pressing her lips to his neck.

"Listen to me, Sassy," he began, trying to ignore the ripple of pleasure her touch sent rushing over his body. "This will be a hard trip. You heard the railroad agent say the only way to get to Laredo by train is to go to San Antonio first, then switch trains."

Sassy had, indeed, heard the man tell Ty the Southern Pacific didn't go any farther south than a spur line to Eagle Pass. To get to Laredo by train, they'd have to go miles out of their way, or go to Eagle Pass, then make the rest of the trip on horseback. After hearing their choices, she was afraid Ty would choose the train and leave her in San Antonio.

Feeling her stiffen in his arms and understanding the reason, Ty bit back a smile. Let her chew on that for a while, he thought selfishly, then decided he couldn't keep up the charade.

"Don't worry, I won't drop you off in San Antonio. I've decided to put Joker and Blarney to work. It'll take longer than the train, but we have plenty of time to reach Laredo ahead of Teddy. Plus, I don't want to risk having one of us recognized in San Antone."

He didn't tell her he had never seriously considered leaving her in San Antonio, even if he'd chosen that route. Although he still intended to file for divorce, he wasn't ready to give her up, not until he had absolutely no other alternative.

Sassy's lips nibbling on his earlobe halted his wandering thoughts. He quelled a groan, another surge of desire shooting through him. Swallowing with some difficulty, he forced his mind back to what he'd been saying.

"You'd better make sure Kitty can sit a horse, and is willing to spend some long days in the saddle, before she agrees to make this trip." His voice sounded strained, his breathing becoming labored.

Continuing her assault with mouth and tongue, she whispered, "I'm sure she will."

Ty didn't respond. He couldn't. Not only was Sassy's mouth working its magic, but one hand had trailed down his chest over his belly, to coax his half-interested manhood into total throbbing attentiveness.

Before surrendering to his escalating need, his last coherent thought was that Sassy had done it again. *She had me by the short hairs, and I gave up with barely a quibble. And I thought I was in charge.*

Sassy's swift shifting of her position ended his silent complaints. When her mouth replaced her hand on his hardened length, his hips lifted off the mattress of their own volition. Though he had loved her in this most intimate way, he'd never expected her to reciprocate. When she suckled on him, he couldn't hold back a yell of pleasure. "Oh, my God. Sassy!" He wasn't sure he could survive the hot velvet of her mouth surrounding him.

Then all thought processes stopped. He could only feel, every nerve ending in his body screaming in carnal joy.

Eighteen

"Oooh, honey," the redhead purred. "You're a randy one, ain't ya?" She gave him a knowing smile, her gaze admiring the obvious arousal beneath his gun belt.

Locking the door behind him, Kit Dancer only grunted in reply. He scanned the room thoroughly, not wanting any surprises during his stay.

Satisfied, he swung his gaze back to the stunning woman with the flaming hair. He'd never fancied redheads, but this one whose eyes threatened to devour him, was an exception.

Already stripped down to her corset, she raised her hands to his black silk shirtfront. "Here, let me help ya," she offered, her voice sultry with promise.

"Douse the lamp," he ordered softly, brushing her fingers away from his chest, where they worked to free the buttons.

"What? But I wanted to undress all of that big body of yours," she murmured, her painted lips puckered in a pout.

"Not tonight, Red. Now, turn out the lamp, then come here."

The room went dark. Only a tiny flickering of light came through the drawn curtains at the single window.

Now certain she couldn't see his face, Kit removed his hat and tossed it aside.

He didn't often make use of prostitutes. Controlling his lust had never been a problem, having pretty much eliminated sexual needs from his life. To feel passion only reminded him of what could have been, if not for his own stupidity. Lately though, following the Beaumonts, seeing the looks passing between them and imagining what went on behind their lodging room door, Kit found he could no longer hold his own desire in check.

There was no getting around it. He needed a woman—bad!

Deciding he could leave his nightly vigil of watching Ty Beaumont's movements long enough to satisfy his lust, he'd gone to El Paso's tenderloin district. There he'd spotted the gorgeous redhead at Gypsie Davenport's place on Utah Street. Her name was Faye, though he preferred Red, and she apparently hadn't worked at her trade very long. She still looked young and vibrant—not the tired, old-before-their-time women often found in places like Gypsie's.

Having arranged for an hour of Red's time, Kit was eager to sample her charms in the darkness of her bedroom. He'd barely stepped out of his pants, when she was all over him. "Hey, take it easy, Red," he said, grasping her shoulders and holding her at arm's length.

"We only have an hour," she groused, shrugging off his hands and shimmying out of her corset.

The milky white of her skin made her face a pale oval in the dimness of the room, her pouting lips a dark smudge.

Kit chuckled lightly, gave her lush mouth a quick kiss, then spun her around. Smacking her bare bottom playfully, he murmured, "We have plenty of time. Now get into bed."

His now-husky voice sent a dusting of gooseflesh over her skin. Faye recognized what the change in timbre signaled. Flashing him a bright smile, she slipped between the satin sheets and opened her arms to her mysterious customer. His wish to keep his identity a secret became an aphrodisiac to her own growing desire. She couldn't remember ever reacting so strongly to one of the men who paid for her time. But this man, dressed entirely in black and wearing his gun low on his hip, had inflamed her from the moment he'd touched her arm to escort her upstairs.

An hour later, Kit left an exhausted, sleeping Faye curled on her bed, and slipped from her room. Recalling her concern about only having an hour, a grin creased his face.

Faye had been a wildcat, he mused on his way downstairs, absently rubbing his shoulder where she'd sunk her teeth into him at an especially frenzied moment. Her eagerness to please and the obvious enjoyment he gave her had driven him to heights he hadn't experienced in a very long time. He shook his head in wonder. As incredible as it seemed, she'd given him three heart-stopping climaxes during their romp in her bed.

Kit stopped to see the brothel's madame at the front door. Handing the woman several bills, he said, "See that Red isn't disturbed. She's earned the rest of the night off."

Laughing merrily, the woman tucked the money between her enormous breasts. "Y'all come back and see Faye again, ya hear?"

As he stepped through the front door, Kit nodded his agreement, though he knew he'd not likely see Red again.

He headed back to the Red Garter, hoping nothing had happened while he'd seen to his physical needs. *Maybe now I can keep my mind on business.* Feeling more relaxed than he would have thought possible, he turned his thoughts to Ty Beaumont.

If he only knew what part the woman—whose name he'd learned was Sassy—played in Ty's life. Was she really Beaumont's wife, as she'd claimed? Or was that a ruse to throw him off the scent of Ty's trail? Another confusing issue was Ty going by the name James Beauregard. If he changed his name to avoid the law, why would he stay in the public's eye? Kit wished he had the answers, then he could wrap this up. He got antsy if he had to spend too long on one job—especially like his current one. Dredging up feelings and memories he thought he'd buried long ago, made him wish he'd never seen Ty Beaumont's wanted poster—poor likeness that it was—or spotted the man in Austin.

Entering the Red Garter, Kit tried to remain as unobtrusive as possible. He took a seat in the barroom, where he could see into the gambling room. He breathed a little easier when he spotted Ty, still at the same keno table. Glancing around the room, he didn't see Sassy. She had to be in the saloon somewhere, since Kit knew she came there each night with Ty.

When Kit first arrived in El Paso, he'd taken extra care not to get too close to the Beaumonts. Although he had met Captain Beaumont once five years earlier, it was doubtful Ty would remember him, especially with the change in his looks. It was Sassy who Kit had been more concerned about. Relieved when she hadn't paid him any attention, he'd been able to move his post of vigilance closer. Although not ready to make his presence known, at least he could sit in the same room with some measure of comfort.

Rubbing a hand over his face, he traced the scar on his right cheek with a fingertip, while he studied Ty. The mustache, longer hair, and fancy gambler clothes bore little resemblance to the Texas Ranger Kit remembered. Pondering the change in appearance, he wondered why Ty had remained in Texas rather than fleeing the state. Changing his looks was obviously part of a plan, but to what end? And there was the woman to consider. Was she part of whatever scheme Ty had concocted? Kit didn't have the answers, but he intended to get them before he made a move.

Ordering a beer from a passing waiter girl, Kit settled back in his chair, content to keep watch until Ty and Sassy left for the night.

Two days after Ty had given his approval to let Kitty go with them, the Southern Pacific train pulled out of the El Paso depot. Ty sat in stony silence across from Sassy and Kitty.

"I just knew y'all'd let me go with ya," Kitty whispered to Sassy.

"How did you know?"

"The bottom of my foot started itching something fierce the day after I told ya 'bout Teddy's telegram. That's a sure sign I'd be walking in strange places," she explained.

Sassy laughed at hearing another of Kitty's superstitions. "I wish you'd told me," she whispered back. "It would have saved me a lot of time and energy, trying to convince Ty you had to go with us."

Recalling exactly how she'd expended her time and

energy the night Ty agreed to let Kitty accompany them, Sassy's face grew hot. She knew Kitty gave her a confused look, but she ignored it, refusing to elaborate.

Though Ty shared the women's excitement over leaving town, he only half-listened to their chatter. He stroked his full mustache thoughtfully, struck with the notion he'd made a terrible mistake.

Allowing Kitty to travel with them wasn't one of his brightest decisions. It was more like a true lack of sound judgment, he decided with self-disgust.

Realizing he now had the responsibility of keeping two woman safe, in addition to finding Teddy and keeping himself from getting arrested, his mood turned sour. *Why did I allow my solitary search to turn into a group effort?*

Determined not to lose control of his mission, he spoke sharply, interrupting Sassy's and Kitty's conversation. "I want you two to know this is not a holiday. This is a business trip—a very serious business trip."

As the pair of startled expressions turned to look at him, he continued, "I want both of you to promise you'll do exactly as I tell you. And with no back talk." The last added for Sassy's benefit, he turned his gaze on her. He held his breath, afraid he'd given her a demand she couldn't resist thwarting.

Kitty quickly agreed to follow his instructions to the letter. The stubborn tilt of Sassy's chin told him he wouldn't wrest a promise from her so easily.

Then she proved yet again that he could never second-guess the workings of her mind.

Her willful expression cleared; her pursed lips curved into a smile. In a sugary voice, Sassy said, "Of course, I promise to listen to you, Ty."

Staring at her guileless expression, his eyes narrowed. *That was too easy.* Holding his breath, he waited for the other shoe to drop. When she remained silent, he decided not to press his luck.

Seeing Ty wasn't going to question her, Sassy hid a smile. Obviously, it hadn't occurred to him that she'd promised to *listen* to him. She'd promised nothing about *doing* what he said.

The excitement of the train trip soon wore off, and Kitty's exhaustion of the past several days overtook her. When Sassy noticed her friend's head nodding, she said, "I'll move over next to Ty, then you can lie down for a while."

Kitty smiled her thanks and curled up on the seat. With a contented sigh, she fell into a deep sleep.

Sassy snuggled next to Ty, his arm draped around her shoulders. After a long silence, she said, "I've been wondering about something."

Rousing from a doze, he nuzzled her hair, inhaling the scent of her shampoo—a spicy mixture of wildflowers he would always associate with Sassy. He swallowed hard, his throat clogged by the realization he might be left with only memories of her some day. The insight that he'd begun thinking of Sassy as a permanent part of his life, momentarily shocked him. Finally, he said, "What's that?"

"Why would Teddy name you as Slater's killer?"

Ty sighed heavily, his thoughts still lingering on his discovery. "Who knows what motivated Teddy to lie to the sheriff? I sure can't figure out why she did it."

For a moment, Sassy didn't reply. Then, in one swift movement, she pushed away from him and sat upright. "She?"

Closing his eyes to the suspicious look on her face, Ty sighed again. "Yeah, she. Teddy is a woman."

Staring at him incredulously, Sassy gave him an aggravated punch. "Why didn't you tell me?"

"Hey, that hurts," he replied, rubbing his arm. "And keep your voice down." He nodded toward Kitty.

"Dammit, Ty, why didn't you tell me the truth?" Sassy persisted in an angry whisper.

"I . . . uh . . . didn't think it was important."

"Important!" she nearly yelled. At his warning look, she added in a lower tone, "Of course, it's important. How many women gamblers are there? Not many, I'd venture to say. We might have found her before now, if I'd known who we were *really* looking for." She shot him a pained look. "Dammit, Ty, I trusted you."

Ty wished he could say the words back to her, but he no longer trusted anyone. "Look, Sassy, I'm sorry I didn't tell you the truth. Don't you see how it would look, if I'd admitted a woman accused me of murder, a woman I've been trying to find for months?" He jabbed a finger at his chest. "Ty Beaumont, trained tracker, can't find one damn woman."

Sassy looked at him long and hard, trying to understand his anger. "I reckon that is embarrassing—a woman accuses a Texas Ranger of murder, then gives him the slip."

His eyes narrowed. "Are you making fun of me?"

"No. I was just saying, I understand how you feel."

His jaw tightened. "How would you know what I feel?"

Sassy started at his abrupt demand. "Well, I . . . I guess I don't know, exactly."

"You're damn right, you don't!"

Unsure whether to test his volatile mood, Sassy

couldn't just let the subject rest. "How long have you known Teddy?"

After a long silence, Ty said, "We met in New Orleans three or four years ago. She was there visiting friends, and I was on an assignment. After that, I saw her a couple times a year in different towns around Texas. Even then she never stayed in one place very long."

Although Sassy knew she might regret hearing Ty's answer, she had to know. "How well do you know her?"

"We were close friends." Ty gave her a quick sidelong glance. Determined to have it all out in the open, he added, "Very close."

"You . . . you were lovers?"

"Yeah."

A loud buzzing in her ears drowned out all other sound. She knew there were women in Ty's past, but as long as they remained nameless, she could deal with it. Now that she knew he had been intimately involved with Teddy, jealousy twisted her insides. Unsure why she continued to pursue such a painful subject, she said, "Tell me about her."

Ty didn't immediately answer, looking out the window in an unblinking stare. After a few moments, he said, "Teddy is a very unusual woman. She spends her evenings in gambling halls and saloons, and yet I've never known a more refined woman." He chuckled dryly. "She said she's a direct descendent of English royalty." He shrugged. "Can't say if that's true, but she sure looks like she has royal blood. Besides being a real beauty, she's well educated, sophisticated, charming."

Ty's words pricked Sassy's skin like a knife, each new declaration of Teddy's attributes pushing the blade a little deeper. She stoically withstood the agony of his painting Teddy as a paragon of womanhood, until she could stand

222

no more. "You make her sound like she's your frigging ladylove, instead of the one who——"

The cool glare he turned on her halted her words. "Teddy's the most important person in my life."

Sassy stared back, her eyes wide with shock. The buzzing in her ears returned. An intense pain ripped through her heart, nearly doubling her over. She might have swooned had she not thought the practice another of the fool rituals women did to appear featherheaded and fragile. Refusing with her usual determination to give into the pain, she held her breath until it eased. When the buzzing faded, Ty's voice drifted back to her.

"Teddy likes having the best: expensive jewelry, gowns in the latest fashion, the fanciest hotel suites. That's why she chose the life of a gambler, so she could afford to keep herself in the style she wants."

Somehow Sassy summoned the strength to ask, "She's never been married?"

Ty smiled. "Teddy? Married? She always said she'd never considered marriage, until she met me."

Sassy gave him a startled look. "She wanted to marry you?"

"She actually proposed; I told you she's unusual. But I knew she wasn't serious. She likes her freedom too much. I told her that when I turned her down."

Sassy wasn't so sure Ty's assessment was correct, but withheld comment. Instead, she said, "Is Teddy really her name?"

"Her real name is Theodora, Theodora Fitzsimmons. She's always hated her given name. When she took up gambling, she started using the name Teddy."

Theodora Fitzsimmons, Sassy silently repeated. The name fit the woman Ty had described *She's nothing like plain old me.* Glancing down at her simple dress, she felt like a frump again. Swamped with her old doubts, her heartache increased. *The man I'm married to wants another woman, the kinda woman I'll never be. I'll never be refined, sophisticated or charming, so why do I bother trying?* An immediate answer didn't come to mind. Even so Sassy wasn't about to pull up stakes and leave her claim without a whimper. No sir, she'd never given up on a fight, and she sure as hell wasn't going to start now. Determined to find a way to get Ty to switch his affections to her, she inhaled a deep quivering breath, then slowly exhaled.

Her shuddering sigh chased memories of Teddy from Ty's mind. Shifting his gaze to Sassy's face, her expression puzzled him. *Why's she acting like her feelings are hurt? I only told her—Oh, shit!* Realizing his careless words had caused her pain, he wasn't sure what to do about it. What he'd told her was true—except she'd obviously interpreted his words differently. For reasons he didn't want to delve into, he wanted to comfort her. Wrapping an arm around her, he tried to pull her close. At first, she resisted. Then the stiffness left her spine and she slumped against him, her head dropping onto his shoulder.

Stroking her hair in a gentle caress, he considered what he should do. He lifted a lock of wavy black hair to his nose. The scent of wildflowers surrounded him, and sent his heart racing. His lips curved in a wry smile. One thing for certain, he might not know what to say to Sassy, but his body never had trouble knowing what to do to her.

His smile faded. That didn't solve his current dilemma. Though he knew he should be grateful for any breach between them, he wasn't. In truth, he wanted the smiling, cussing wildcat with him, not alienated and perhaps thinking about returning home. When the time came—if it came—to give her up, he'd have to live with it. For now, he'd treat her with extra kindness, pay more attention to her, in the hope she wouldn't decide to cut her losses and run. *So, do I try to explain about Teddy?*

After considering the issue, he finally decided it was best to leave well enough alone. *I've already told her I plan to file for divorce, so letting her think Teddy is the woman I want will make it easier for her to accept.* He squeezed his eyes closed for a moment. *But will it make it easier for me?*

Nineteen

When they arrived at Eagle Pass, the terminus of the Southern Pacific Railroad, after traveling several days, Ty explained his plans for continuing their trip. He'd already bought what supplies he could from a general store in Langtry, where they'd spent the previous night. In Eagle Pass, he planned to buy a horse for Kitty and a couple of packhorses.

"I'll see to the horses and the rest of our gear, as soon as I get you two settled," he told Sassy and Kitty after departing the train. He glanced toward the west, where dusk had turned the sky a deep purple. "We'll stay here tonight, then leave at first light. It's over a hundred miles to Laredo. And although we have time to spare, we'll still have to make good time each day. Get yourselves some comfortable clothes and boots. And wear hats." He rattled off his instruction in a clipped voice.

Ty knew he was being overly harsh. Even if they made less than twenty miles a day—a good pace with packhorses—they'd arrive in Laredo in about a week. He just didn't want any misunderstandings from the outset of this leg of their journey.

At the eager nods of the two women, Ty took the lead and headed toward the main section of town.

When they left Eagle Pass the next morning, Ty noted the split riding skirts, boots, and hats both Sassy and Kitty wore. Pleased they had taken his words to heart, he nodded his approval, then turned Joker to the south.

The sun hung low on the horizon, before Ty finally called it a day.

Although an expert rider, Sassy's recent absence from the saddle and the long hours Ty kept them riding made her stiff and sore. Easing off Blarney's back, she eyed the nearby creek with longing, absently rubbing her aching backside.

Ty's voice next to her ear startled her. "Can I do that for you, darlin'?" he whispered.

Darting a quick glance to Kitty, Sassy shook her head. Ty understood her warning, but also read the disappointment in her eyes. He brushed a quick kiss across her mouth, then said, "Guess giving you a bath is out, too, huh?"

She pushed on his chest, forcing him to take a step backward. When she drew her arm back, he ducked sideways to avoid her punch. He chuckled as her fist glanced harmlessly off his shoulder. "Okay, how about you giving me a bath?" His grin erased her momentary pique.

"Go get some fire wood," she ordered in a prim voice, hard-pressed to keep from bursting into laughter. "I'll unpack what we need for the night."

Whistling to himself, Ty unsaddled and hobbled the horses, then went to look for dry wood.

Sassy watched him work from across the clearing. She still wasn't sure what to make of his behavior of late. Ever since he'd told her about Teddy, he'd been especially attentive. Though she basked in the tenderness he displayed, she couldn't figure out the reason for the sudden change. Not that he'd ever been mean to her—but now he treated her almost as if he were happy they were married. As much as she wanted to believe he'd had a change of heart, or maybe was beginning to love her, his threat to divorce her remained in her thoughts.

Shaking off her confusion, she pulled out the supplies for supper, then shook out their bedrolls.

He'd just set down his plate and poured himself another cup of coffee, when a noise at the edge of camp drew Ty's attention. He could make out something moving just beyond the circle of light cast by the campfire.

"What is it, Ty?" Sassy asked, having heard the same noise.

"An animal of some kind, I reckon. It isn't dangerous though, otherwise the horses would be acting up." Putting down his cup, he rose and moved toward the brush.

When he returned to the fire a few minutes later, he held a nearly grown, skinny, black and white dog. Setting the pup down, Ty chuckled when it lifted its nose to sniff his plate.

"The poor thing's starved," Kitty remarked, reaching out to stroke a speckled ear.

The dog immediately cowered and tried to scoot closer to Ty.

"Ya poor baby. Somebody's mistreated ya, ain't they?" Kitty's voice broke with emotion, remembering her own fear when someone she didn't trust reached for her.

Crooning softly, Ty moved his hand to stroke the quivering pup. Although wary, the dog accepted his touch. The shaking stopped, and the black eyes closed when Ty found a particularly sensitive spot behind one ear.

"He sure likes you," Sassy observed.

"She," Ty corrected, smiling when the dog lazily turned her head and licked his hand.

"Maybe *she* would like what's left of supper. She sure could use it." Sassy moved the frying pan closer.

Though tentative at first, the dog accepted the food from Ty's hand, then finally ate directly from the pan. When she finished, she curled up at Ty's feet and promptly fell asleep.

"Would ya look at that," Kitty murmured. "Ain't she something?"

"She sure is," Sassy agreed.

"Yeah," was all Ty said. He hoped by morning the dog would be gone—he didn't need anyone else to look after.

No such luck.

Ty awoke at the first blush of dawn to find the pup stretched out next to him on his bedroll. In spite of trying to remain immune to the dog, he couldn't resist rubbing the curly hair on her head. When she tried to wiggle even closer, he smiled. "What am I gonna do with you, Domino?" he whispered, using the name he'd already chosen for her black and white markings.

An animal lover from the time he was a toddler, Ty could never stand to see one abused. While he could be ruthless in his treatment of his fellow man—especially the criminals he'd hunted down—he'd never hurt an animal. Domino's ill treatment at someone's hands made his heart ache for what she'd endured. Against his will, his concern and protectiveness for the fluffy ball of curly black and white fur increased.

Rising, he stared at the dog still snuggled in his bedroll, determined to leave her behind when they broke camp.

As he helped repack the gear and saddle the horses, Ty was disgruntled to see Domino nearby. Head resting on her front paws, her black eyes watched his every move.

When everything was secured on the packhorses, he stepped into the stirrup and swung onto Joker's back, keeping his gaze from the dog. Turning his horse toward the road, he winced at the plaintive whine behind him. When he glanced over his shoulder, he was immediately sorry. The forlorn look on Domino's face, and her sad eyes begging him not to leave her, made him curse his soft heart.

He dismounted and crouched next to the dog. "What am I gonna do with you?" he asked again, smiling when Domino licked his face then rolled over, presenting her belly for him to scratch.

"Just what I need," he grumbled, "another female to take care of."

A few minutes later, Sassy, Kitty, and Ty left the clearing, Domino safely tucked into a sling fashioned from a gunnysack and secured to Ty's saddle horn.

Seeing the look Sassy and Kitty exchanged, Ty said, "Domino's too young and weak to make the trip on foot."

When Sassy only smiled knowingly in reply, he harrumphed and said, "Well, she is." With that he clamped his mouth shut, and urged Joker into a lope.

In the following days, the trio had to stop more than Ty would have liked. As Domino grew stronger, she required more time to romp and expend some of what Kitty called, her excess "piss and vinegar."

While Ty fussed about the extra stops, he watched the young dog chase her tail or roll in the dirt with the ball Kitty had fashioned from an old woolen sock, like an indulgent, proud parent.

Sassy saw the expression on Ty's face and felt a pang of longing. One day she hoped to see him looking at their child that same way. The turn of her thoughts surprised her. Where had the sudden desire for motherhood come from? Until she'd met Ty, she hadn't had the nerve to act like her true gender. And now she was thinking about becoming a mother! She shook her head with wonder, finding the changes she'd undergone hard to believe.

Glancing over at him, she knew she couldn't voice her thoughts aloud. To announce she wanted his child would have devastating results. He'd probably refuse to touch her for fear he'd get her with child—a possibility he apparently hadn't considered—or worse, file for divorce on the spot! A possible child from their union increased her determination to avoid a divorce and filled Sassy's thoughts, helping to pass the time.

They spent six days sitting in unforgivably rigid saddles from dawn till dusk, cooking their meals over a campfire and sleeping on the hard-packed ground in thin bedrolls.

As the outline of Laredo became visible on the afternoon of the sixth day, a bone-weary Ty glanced over at equally tired Sassy and Kitty. He couldn't help admiring the stamina the two women had displayed, while making the trek from Eagle Pass. Not once had he heard either of them complain about having to rough it for a week, or about the lack of conveniences—like a bathtub filled with warm, scented water, the softness of a mattress covered with a feather tick, or meals served on china dishes and a linen tablecloth. Nor had he heard a complaint about the lack of privacy.

For Ty, the latter had been the worse to endure. Since he and Sassy had grown used to satisfying their physical hunger for each other whenever the mood struck, not being able to spend time alone was particularly frustrating. The forced closeness of traveling and sharing a combination living-eating-sleeping quarters each night with a third person, ended their intimate relationship with unequivocal certainty.

When Ty made the plans to travel from Eagle Pass to Laredo on horseback, the ramifications of Kitty traveling with them never occurred to him. By the time the unforeseen complication became apparent, they were well into their journey. Knowing the situation was temporary, he tried to take the celibacy which befell him in stride. Still, being in such proximity to Sassy and seeing the flare of desire in her eyes each time their gazes met, the strain got to him quicker than he would have imagined.

As they pushed farther south, the growing heat and the long days astride their horses had them all as tight as overwound watch springs. And as their frustrations grew, so did their tempers. Sassy and Ty found fault with one another over the smallest transgressions, or snapped at each other for no reason at all.

Kitty watched Sassy and Ty tiptoe around each other with a mixture of guilt and amusement. She knew they wanted to seek solace in each other's arms at night, but held back because of her presence. While she hated to be the cause of the sharp words they exchanged, she couldn't make herself disappear in a puff of smoke. And since Ty had warned both her and Sassy not to wander far from their campsites, she'd had no alterative except being the spoilsport.

In spite of wishing she could grant them time alone, she watched them try to steer clear of each other and exchange singeing glances that spoke of desire, not anger, with silent mirth.

As the three entered the heavily Spanish-influenced

town on a very quiet and deserted Santa Maria Street, only Domino was oblivious to the tension surrounding their group.

"Where is everyone?" Sassy asked. Two lazy hounds whose halfhearted barks caught Domino's attention, and several old men dozing in the shade, were the only visible inhabitants.

Looking down the side streets for signs of life, Ty shrugged. "Taking a *siesta,* I guess."

"Siesta?"

When he turned to meet Sassy's sparkling gaze, he easily read her excitement. The silent communication passing between them lightened his weariness.

"I think that's just what we need," Sassy announced. "A nice, long *siesta.* What do you think, Kitty? Could you use a nap in a comfortable bed?"

Kitty tried to keep a smile off her face. "Yeah, after a good scrub in a bathtub." Nudging her horse up next to Joker, she reached for Domino. "Here, let me take her with me." Silently adding, *Y'all don't want a playful dog in your room, while your attending ta more pressing matters.*

After settling into their rooms in the Rio Grande Hotel, baths became the first priority. Sassy, totally naked and clean for the first time in days, fell onto the bed and stretched languorously on the cool sheets. Ty had just returned from his turn in the bathing room down the hall, and was attempting to get out of his clothes as quickly as possible.

"Damn," he muttered under his breath, hopping around on one foot. Still damp from his bath, he struggled to strip off his uncooperative pants.

Slipping off the mattress, Sassy pushed him to a sitting position at the foot of the bed, then knelt in front of him.

"Here, let me help you before you hurt yourself," she said, a smile teasing her lips.

Looking down at the top of her dark head and watching her work his pants down over his thighs and then his calves, Ty's temperature started to climb. Her gentle touch did crazy things to his insides, let alone what it did to his outside. He grew increasingly impatient to be as naked as she.

When she finally finished her chore and tossed the offending garment across the room, she remained kneeling between his legs. Lifting her head to meet his gaze, she found the same passion surging through her veins reflected in his eyes. A bolt of lightning flashed between them, igniting their already smoldering desire.

In an instant, Ty melded his mouth to Sassy's, his body clasped against hers in a tight embrace. Falling back onto the bed, the cool sheets soon burned as hot as the sunbaked streets outside.

Sassy found their way of spending a *siesta* much more enjoyable than sleeping. Much more!

Kit Dancer pushed away from the adobe building he'd been leaning against, and pressed his fists into his lower back. Having stood in one position too long, he stretched sideways to ease his cramped muscles and stomped his feet to restore the circulation.

With legs widespread and thumbs hooked in his gun belt, he looked across the street to the Rio Grande Hotel. Ty, Sassy, and a second woman—whose name he'd learned from the hotel desk clerk was Kitty—had taken rooms in the establishment, when they'd arrived in town earlier.

By a stroke of luck, Kit had overheard Ty tell the

owner of a general store in Langtry about his plans to travel by horse, once he reached Eagle Pass. If he hadn't heard that conversation, Kit might have lost valuable time, ending up halfway to San Antonio before he realized his error. He shook his head. *If I can be so damn lucky as a bounty hunter, how come it didn't carry over into my personal life?* He clenched his teeth, angry at himself for letting his thoughts drift.

The ride from Eagle Pass had been enjoyable for Kit. He preferred the solitary life—responsible for no one but himself, not answering to anyone but Kit Dancer—that's why he'd chosen his current profession. Bounty hunting required being good with a gun, the job paid well, and most enticing to Kit, it was solitary work.

Able to make better time traveling alone, he'd reached Laredo early that morning. Staking out the road where Ty would enter town, he'd followed the trio to the Rio Grande Hotel. Allowing them time to get to their rooms, he slipped inside to speak with the desk clerk.

Leaning one shoulder back against the wall, he decided to keep watch a little longer, then find his own bed. After another hour and no sign of the Beaumonts, he mumbled, "They obviously had other plans." Thoughts of how Sassy and Ty were spending the evening made him think of Red.

As he headed toward the room he'd rented, the memory of his lusty romp in her bed brought a lazy smile to his lips. It wasn't often a man found a soiled dove who was such an inventive and passionate lover. His smile broadened. He'd sure picked a winner.

Kit hadn't wanted a woman in his life for a long time, but he found himself thinking about Red a lot lately. He also thought a lot about the promise he made before she fell asleep.

She'd asked him to come back to El Paso, and he promised he would. His smile faded, the corners of his mouth turning down in annoyance. He hadn't promised anybody anything in years. The last promise he made ended up costing him everything he loved.

Gritting his teeth, he forced his thoughts back to Red. Well, hell, why not, he thought. *El Paso is as good a place as any, especially with a women like Red waiting for me. I'll head there as soon as I deposit Ty Beaumont into the hands of the Waco sheriff.*

Twenty

Sassy strolled down Santa Maria Street, a happy Domino prancing along beside her. Normally, Ty took the dog out for her morning walk to enjoy the coolest part of the day. Today, Sassy elected to take over the duty. A week had passed since their arrival in Laredo, and with the day of the high-stakes poker game fast approaching, Ty had begun suffering from insomnia. Not wanting to awaken him when Domino started scratching at the door, Sassy decided to let Ty sleep and took the dog out herself.

Stopping to untangle Domino from a piece of string she'd picked up, the sound of feet pounding on the boardwalk drew Sassy's attention from the dog. She looked up just in time to see a young boy come barreling toward her. Hitting her with a glancing blow, the boy bounced off her shoulder with a rolling motion. Before he could spin away, she grabbed one of his arms.

"Hold on there, half-pint. What's the big rush?"

Lifting his head, the boy warily met Sassy's gaze. Although he stuck his chin out in mute defiance, he shifted uncomfortably.

"I must go, *Señorita, por favor.*"

Though he tried to sound brave, Sassy detected a

237

flicker of fear in his black eyes. Studying the rest of his face, she had the distinct impression he was hiding something. She kept one hand on his arm and rose from her crouched position. Glancing down at her gaping handbag, the reason for his discomfort became apparent.

"It's *Señora,* you little devil," she said, not unkindly. "Now hand it over."

"Señora?"

"You know what I'm talking about. Give me my coin purse, or I'll have to turn you over to the authorities."

His dark brows pulling together with confusion, he cocked his head to one side. "Au . . . thor . . . ities, *Señora?"* His voice quivered slightly as he stuttered over the unfamiliar word.

Sassy struggled to keep a grin off her face.

"Yes, the authorities. You know, the sheriff, the marshal. Whoever is at the jail." Like many Texans, she knew passable Spanish, and repeated her last sentence to be sure he understood.

The stark terror appearing on his face sobered Sassy's amusement. She had never seriously considered turning the boy over to the law; she just wanted to scare him. Apparently, she'd been successful.

His hand shook as he reached inside his tattered shirt and withdrew her coin purse.

"Take it, *Señora,"* he said, shoving the purse toward her with grubby fingers. "I no want to go to *el cárcel.*"

She tucked the coin purse back inside her handbag with one hand, keeping the other wrapped firmly around his arm. For the first time, she noticed how thin he was— like he hadn't had a decent meal in months—and how his clothes were little more than rags, and like him, could use a good washing.

"What's your name?" she asked gently.

The boy eyed her suspiciously, uncertain why she treated him kindly after she'd caught him filching her coin purse. *"Me llamo Juan,"* he murmured softly.

"Well, Juan," she said, making a sudden decision. "How would you like to come to my hotel and have breakfast with my husband and me?"

He searched her face, looking for some sign of trickery. Finding only sincerity in the woman's features, he finally nodded.

Releasing his arm, Sassy extended her hand. "My name is Sassy Beaumont, Juan. I'm pleased to meet you."

Tentatively, he put his small hand in hers. "Pleased to meet you, *Señora* Beaumont," he repeated carefully.

Ruffling his dark hair playfully, Sassy smiled. "Call me Sassy. Now come on, breakfast's waiting."

For the first time, Juan noticed Domino, who had been sitting quietly nearby. When he bent to pet the little dog, Domino yipped with excitement, her tail thumping wildly on the boardwalk.

"El perrito, it is yours, *Señora* Sassy?" He ran his hand over Domino's head, giggling when she licked his fingers.

"Domino is my husband's dog." Seeing the longing on his face while he petted Domino, she added, "I think she would like a playmate who is more her size. Do you know of someone who might want to play with her?"

Pulling himself up to his full height, Juan thumped his thin chest with one hand. *"Sí, Señora* Sassy, I could play with her. I am the right size, no?"

"Sí, Half-pint," she said with a chuckle. "You're just the right size."

Not understanding the name Sassy called him again, Juan didn't ask its meaning. Her tone of voice told him it wasn't bad. Whatever it meant, he would carry the name proudly. It had been a very long time since anyone had shown him kindness.

Entering the hotel lobby, Sassy escorted Juan up the stairs. "We'll wash up in our room, and then Ty and I will take you to breakfast, okay, Half-pint?" Juan nodded eagerly, looking around him with wide-eyed wonder.

When Sassy stepped inside the sitting room of their suite, she found Ty reading a newspaper. Blocking his view of the door, she moved toward him.

Flashing her a smile, he said, "Morning, darlin'."

She returned his smile, relieved to see him looking rested and relaxed. "Good morning," she whispered, before brushing a kiss across his mouth.

"Did you and Domino enjoy your walk?"

"Yes, very much."

"Where is she anyway?" Ty asked, trying to look around Sassy's skirt. "She usually comes running in here hell-bent-for-leather after her walk."

"She's with our new friend."

Ty gave her a quizzical look. "New friend?"

Sassy stepped aside, allowing Ty a clear view of the doorway, where Juan stood holding Domino's leash. "Ty, I'd like you to meet Juan." Turning toward the door, she said, "Juan, this is my husband, Ty Beaumont."

Juan walked into the room. *"Señor* Beaumont," he said, stopping in front of Ty and offering his hand. "Pleased to meet you." He cast a quick glance at Sassy, and smiled when she nodded her approval.

For a moment Ty said nothing, his lips pressed into a thin line. Finally, he shook the boy's hand and said, "Juan."

The abruptness in Ty's response shocked Sassy, but

she didn't comment. Instead she said, "I've invited Juan to have breakfast with us."

Although he gave her a disapproving look, he mumbled, "Fine," then folded the newspaper and rose from his chair.

Embarrassed by Ty's cool reception to Juan, Sassy turned to the boy. "Come on, I'll help you get cleaned up, then we'll go eat."

Sending a wary glance at her angry-looking husband, he whispered, *"Sí, Señora* Sassy."

"I told you, you can drop the *señora.* Just call me Sassy."

Juan nodded and followed her into the bedroom of their suite. After he scrubbed his face and hands in the wash bowl, Sassy took a comb to his hair, then pronounced him ready for the dining room.

Already sitting at their usual table, Kitty's eyes lit up when Sassy introduced Juan. Immediately taken with the youngster, she found his flashing black eyes and bright smile totally engaging. "Tell me, Juan, where are your mama and papa?"

"I never knew *mi padre,"* he replied between bites of his meal. *"Mi madre,* she died last year." Dropping his gaze, his thin throat worked as he swallowed hard.

"Oh, ya poor dear," Kitty whispered. "Then, who do you live with, an aunt or your grandmama?"

Raising his head, he stuck his chin out. *"Nadie,"* he declared. "I live with no one. I take care of myself."

Kitty sucked in a surprised breath, meeting Sassy's compassionate gaze across the table.

Hoping to lighten the sorrowful mood, Sassy changed the subject and soon had Juan giggling and digging into his food with renewed relish.

Ty remained quiet. He answered when Sassy or Kitty

spoke directly to him, otherwise he said very little. His gaze continually strayed to Juan. Each time he looked at the boy's straight black hair, equally dark eyes, and reddish brown skin, his scowl deepened.

Sassy wondered at Ty's reaction to Juan, thankful the boy was too busy shoving food down to notice.

Full at last, Juan sighed and pushed his plate away. Sitting back in his chair, he yawned, his eyelids heavy with sleep.

"Come on, Juan, how 'bout you taking a little nap in my room?" Kitty asked.

He stifled another yawn, then nodded. *"Gracias, Señorita* Kitty," he murmured, slipping off his chair. He lifted pleading eyes to Sassy. "Can Domino come, too?"

Glancing at Ty, who only shrugged indifferently, she said, "Sure, Half-pint. Kitty can get her out of our room."

As Kitty and Juan headed for the stairs, Ty and Sassy went outside for some air. For a few minutes, they walked without speaking, Ty maintaining his stony silence and Sassy unsure what to say. Occasionally, she would glance up at him, each time still unable to read his mood.

Finally, when she could stand the tension no longer, she stopped and turned to face him. "Okay, Ty, you've been chewing on something ever since I introduced you to Juan. Are you going to tell me why you're as ornery as owl shit, or not?"

Ty's head jerked around to look at her, his eyes wide with surprise. "I don't know what you're talking about."

"Don't give me that crap." She brushed his hand away when he tried to take her elbow and resume their walk. "I know you, and I know when something's eating at you."

When he refused to answer, she said, "It has to do with Juan, doesn't it? You never even met the boy before

242

I brought him to our room, so I know he couldn't have done anything to make you angry. Don't you like him, is that—"

Ty swung around to face her again, his eyes squinted with fury. "He's a damn Indian, for God's sake. The way you carry on, you'd think he was your own flesh-and-blood, not the bastard of some Comanche."

Too shocked to respond to Ty's tirade, Sassy stared at him in mute horror. When she found her voice, she said, "So what if he's part-Indian? And how do you know he's Comanche? There *are* other Indian tribes in Texas. You have no right to judge Juan."

"I have every right," he snarled. "The damned Comanches destroyed my family. They killed my father, burned our ranch, and took my brother."

"What?"

Ty swallowed hard, trying to regain his composure. "I was six, and my brother, Dayne, was eight. Dad had taken Dayne into town, and I was at the ranch with our mother. A raiding party of Comanches swooped onto our ranch one afternoon with no warning. They ransacked the house and barns, ran off our livestock and horses, then set everything on fire. If Mom and I hadn't hidden in the storm cellar, they would have found us. Dad and Dayne came home while they were still whooping and hollering around the burning house." He swallowed the bile rising in his throat. "Later, we found Dad in the yard, dead. Dayne was missing. Some men from town followed the raiding party's trail. They thought that if they could find their camp, the Comanches might accept a ransom for my brother."

"Did they get him back?"

He shook his head. "Several parties of men tried again later, but they never found any sign of Dayne. They figured the bloodthirsty savages who took him must have tortured him to death, then dumped his body somewhere."

"Oh, Ty, I'm sorry. When you told my family you'd lost your father and brother, I had no idea it was in an Indian raid."

"Yeah, I know. I don't talk about it much."

She looped her arm through his. "Come on, let's walk for a while."

After a few minutes, Sassy cleared her throat nervously. "Ty," she began, not sure how he would react to her words. "At the Star, you didn't treat Charlie Two Feathers any differently than you treated me or my family, and he's part Comanche."

"Charlie's different."

"Why is he different?"

"Because, Charlie's mother was taken captive by the Comanche during a raid on her family's ranch the same year the Circle B was hit. Carol's family lived up the Brazos, not far from us. When she fought the braves who'd captured her, she was whipped into submission. They tore off her clothes, then took turns with her."

Sassy blinked back tears. She'd heard of Comanche cruelty, but never from a person who knew one of those who had been brutalized.

"Carol gave birth to Charlie nine months later, never knowing which brave had fathered him. She stayed with the Comanche as a slave, until she escaped with Charlie and his younger sister a few years later. She came back to Waco, but her family wouldn't have anything to do with her. They didn't want her and her half-breed bastards within fifty feet of them, so they sent her packing. Carol settled in town and tried to provide for her children. From the time her family shut her out, she died a little each day. When Charlie was eleven, Carol's suffering ended.

"Left with no one who cared whether they lived or died, Charlie took his sister and headed back to the Comanche. At least they accepted them. He stayed with the tribe until several years after the government forced them onto a reservation, then set out on his own. I'd heard the story about his mother when I was growing up, but I didn't meet Charlie until the time he told you about in Amarillo. He couldn't have been more than seventeen, but he would have fought the men who'd dragged him into the alley until his last breath, if I hadn't come along.

"We ran into each other a time or two after that, then I lost track of him. Must be when he started working for your father," he added as an afterthought.

Sassy thought about what Ty had told her, then said, "Juan obviously is also a mixed blood, so how is he different from Charlie?"

Ty blew out an exasperated breath. "I don't know, he just is."

She longed to box his ears for letting his hatred blind him. Instead she said, "Let me tell you what Juan told me, then you decide if he deserves to be treated with such hostility."

Ty gazed at her with hooded eyes, then nodded.

"Juan said he lived with his mother in a small house in the Mexican section of town until last year. An epidemic of yellow fever swept through here, and his mother died. The house they lived in was rented, so after his mother's death, he lost his home, too."

When Sassy paused, Ty took the hint. "Okay, where does he live now?"

"He has a room in the back of the livery. The owner

was a friend of his mother, and lets Juan stay there in exchange for working in the stable."

"Working?" In spite of his aversion to the boy, Sassy's statement took him by surprise. "He can't be more than five or six."

"Six," Sassy confirmed. "That's not the worst of what he told me. He also works at one of the saloons whenever the manager needs extra help. He sweeps floors and empties spittoons, so he can buy food. When he can't find work, he . . ." Sassy hesitated, a lump forming in her throat.

"He what?" Ty prompted.

"He . . . um . . . picks pockets."

Ty swung his disbelieving gaze on Sassy. "Is that how you met him? He tried to steal from you?"

"Yes. He came a hella-ca-tooting down the street, and purposely ran into me so he could slip his hand into my handbag. He would have gotten away with my coin purse, if I hadn't grabbed him to make sure he wasn't hurt. Then I saw my handbag hanging open, and realized he wasn't just an energetic boy who'd accidentally bumped into me."

Having reached the San Augustin Plaza in the center of town, Ty sank down on a bench.

"Poor Juan has had a miserable life for one so young," Sassy said, joining Ty on the bench. "He needs a home with a family, a real bed, and three meals a day."

"Yeah," Ty agreed, his thoughts turning to his own family. Thinking about losing his father and brother at the hands of the Comanche, Ty's hatred sputtered to life. "He's still a damn thieving Indian."

Sassy turned to him, her eyes blazing. "Listen to me, Ty. I realize you have every reason to hate Indians, especially the Comanche, for what they did to your family.

246

But not every Indian you run into should have to suffer your wrath. This is 1885, there hasn't been trouble with the Indians in years. It's time to put your hate behind you."

When Ty remained silent, she continued, "Just like Charlie, Juan didn't chose to be born with Indian blood, any more than you or I chose to be born the way we are. You can't hold Juan's mixed blood against him. He's only a boy. What if you found out he was related to you, would you hate him then?"

Ty rubbed a hand over his face, then stroked his mustache, his thoughts dwelling on Sassy's last words. Could he actually hate a member of his family because of the blood running through his veins? Closing his eyes against the raw pain surging through him, he hoped he'd be more tolerant than Charlie's family. Yet, having such fierce hatred burning inside him for so long, he just couldn't be sure.

Opening his eyes, he said, "I know you're right. Still, I can't stop how I feel. Every time I see an Indian, I remember the day the Comanche raided our ranch, my father lying in a pool of blood in the dirt. It's like there's a festering sore in my gut that won't heal."

Sassy grasped his hands and pulled them into her lap. "You have to let go of your hatred. Hanging onto it will only eat at you until there's nothing left."

Ty lifted their clasped hands and kissed her fingers. "I know, Sassy. Only, I'm not sure I can erase twenty years of painful memories just like that." He met her beseeching gaze. "I'm not making any promises, but I'll try."

Sassy knew how hard it was to change—she still didn't have the hang of all the little idiosyncrasies of being a lady. So Ty's agreeing to try to rid himself of the hatred he'd harbored all those years was a big step. She just wished she could get him to return her love. With Teddy still in the picture and his plans to file for divorce, she wasn't sure she'd be successful.

Twenty-one

"So, what are we going to do about Juan?"

Sassy's question pulled Ty out of his musings. He gave her a quizzical look, then said, "Why do we have to do anything?"

"He's six years old," she declared. "He has no family. He lives in a stable, works in a saloon, and steals to eat. We have to do something to improve his life." When Ty didn't reply, she continued, "I was thinking, maybe he could work for us."

"Work? I thought we agreed he's too young to work."

"Yes, he is too young. The alternative is charity. And I'm sure Juan would never accept a handout. He may be only six years old, but he has the pride of a sixty-year-old man. I thought we could offer him a job helping with Joker and Blarney. He likes animals, and he already knows about taking care of horses from the livery. We wouldn't give him any hard work, only a few easy chores to make him think he's earning his own way."

Ty nodded. "How about if we tell him room and board are part of his pay." His voice turned sharp. "And he'll have to give up picking pockets."

Sassy listened to Ty's enthusiastic warming to her idea,

her love for him growing even more. Keeping the promise she'd made to herself, she didn't voice her feelings. She wondered if she'd ever be able to tell Ty she loved him. If he never said the words first . . . She pushed such depressing thoughts aside. Juan needed their help, and she must think about him.

"That's a wonderful idea. I couldn't bear having him return to the life he's led for the past year." Just thinking about another pickpocket victim catching Juan and not being as kindhearted as she'd been, sent gooseflesh across her skin.

"Do you think Kitty would mind letting Juan sleep in her room?" he asked. "I could have a cot sent up for him."

"I don't think she'd mind in the least. You saw how fast she took to him at breakfast, clucking over him like a mother hen," Sassy answered with a laugh.

Her spirits restored, she jumped to her feet and tugged on Ty's arm. "Come on, let's give Joker and Blarney some exercise, then we can go back to the hotel and talk to Kitty."

Catching her light mood, Ty rose from the bench and turned to leave the plaza. Without saying a word he started back to their hotel at a brisk walk, leaving Sassy staring after him. As he walked along, whistling softly, a streak of blue sped past him. When recognition dawned, he stopped short, too shocked to move. The flash of blue was Sassy, the full skirt of her dress hiked up to her knees, so she could run without tripping.

The words she yelled drifted back to him in snatches, "Race you . . . stable. Last one . . . saddle . . . horses."

Ty threw back his head and roared with laughter. Accepting her challenge, he took off at a run. His longer strides soon had him breathing down Sassy's neck, then he pulled up dead even. Neither of them cared about the strange looks people on the street cast their way. They were content to race through town like carefree children.

Face flushed and hair in wild disarray, Sassy slid to a stop inside the livery just a few seconds after Ty.

"Drat, I almost had you," she sputtered between deep breaths. "If it wasn't for these heavy skirts and these damn shoes, I could've beaten you."

Before she could move out of his way, she found herself pressed against Ty's chest, her legs dangling as he swung her around in a circle.

"You're something, you know that, wildcat," he choked out, more breathless from laughter than from their race.

Halting the twirling motion, he relaxed his grip, letting her slide down his body. When her feet touched the livery floor, he lowered his head to capture her lips with his. After a very long, very thorough kiss, Ty heard a noise behind them and reluctantly relinquished her mouth.

"You folks here to get your horses, or just get some kissin' in?" the owner of the livery asked with an amused grin.

Smiling sheepishly, Ty released Sassy and responded, "A little of both, I reckon." Stepping away from her, he murmured, "We'll finish this later." Then louder, so the other man could hear, "We'll take care of getting our horses, you don't have to bother." He headed for the tack room to fetch their bridles and saddles.

"Wait a minute," Sassy said. "I lost. I should be . . ." Her words ended abruptly, when she saw the livery owner look at her quizzically.

No need to tell the man about her sudden inspiration to challenge Ty to a footrace. Apparently Ty wasn't sticking to her definition of the forfeit required of the loser, so there was no point in enlightening anyone else. Instead, she attempted to smooth her hair and straighten her skirts. Feeling the livery owner's gaze while waiting for Ty to saddle their horses, she hoped she gave the appearance of a demure lady.

Finally, the man lost interest and went back to his work at the rear of the stable.

On the way back to the hotel after their ride, Sassy and Ty stopped at a mercantile to buy Juan some new clothes. When they arrived at Kitty's room, they found him happily playing with Domino on the floor, his boyish giggles filling the air.

While Ty took Juan down the hall for a bath—over his protests that he'd already washed his face and hands once that day—Sassy sat down to talk to Kitty.

"So Ty and I were hoping you'd be willing to share your room with Juan," Sassy concluded, after telling Kitty what she'd told Ty about Juan and their plans to offer the boy a job.

" 'Course, I will. That little sprout needs some attention, besides a clean bed and three squares a day. I'd be happy ta have him stay with me. I'm sure y'all wouldn't want him in your room at night," she added with a wink, bringing a dark flush to Sassy's face. "Sorry, I couldn't resist saying that."

"It's okay, Kitty. I didn't take offense. We bought Juan some new clothes," Sassy said, changing the subject before her face grew any hotter under Kitty's amused gaze. She opened the package and dumped its contents onto the bed.

"I'll have him change inta his new duds, 'fore we go down for dinner." Eyeing the new shoes, she added thoughtfully, "Hope he don't put up a fuss 'bout those. His feet ain't gonna like 'em much. I recall going barefoot all summer back home, then having ta put on shoes come fall. My feet would holler something awful."

A much different-appearing Juan sat down with them for supper that evening. Noting the pinched look of pain on his face after he'd taken his seat next to her, Sassy remembered Kitty's words. Sending Kitty a questioning look and mouthing "the shoes," she received a nod in reply.

Juan's feet obviously hurt from their sudden restriction inside the stiff leather of the new shoes, yet he hadn't said a word. That he hadn't complained about the discomfort made Sassy's heart swell with love.

Leaning over to him, she whispered against his ear. "It would be okay, if you took off your shoes, Juan. I think you've had them on long enough for the first time. Wear them a little longer each day, until they're broken in, then they won't hurt your feet."

The look of relief on his face made Sassy's already soft heart melt even more. Again she was struck by the closeness she felt toward Juan. She'd never been around children much, so her unusual reaction surprised her. Again she was reminded of her recent revelation regarding motherhood. Giving her head a shake to clear her mind of such thoughts, she smiled when he slipped the shoes to the floor and wiggled his toes with pleasure.

During the meal, Sassy made their proposal to Juan. His eyes widened with surprise, then turned to look first at Kitty then at Ty. Each gave him an encouraging nod before he looked back at Sassy.

She could see his throat muscles work while he contemplated the offer. Glancing down at his new clothes, then at the abundance of food on the table, he nodded his head in agreement.

"*Sí, Señora* Sassy. I will work for you and *Señor* Ty."

"And you promise to give up being a pickpocket," Ty pressed.

"*Sí,* no pick pockets again, *te prometo,*" he said solemnly, holding one hand over his heart.

The mood over supper turned jovial, a celebration of Juan's new position. Sassy ordered cake and ice cream, and had to bite her lip not to laugh aloud at his look of pure pleasure over his first taste of ice cream.

While she, Ty, and Kitty lingered over a cup of coffee, Juan finished his second bowl of ice cream, then suddenly piped, "*Mi abuelo* was a great war chief."

Sassy shot Ty a quick glance, then said, "How do you know about your grandfather, Half-pint?"

"*Mi madre,* she told me about him. His name was Horse Back."

Ty stiffened in instant recognition. Horse Back, also known as Champion Rider, was the longtime leader of the Comanche. Ty's hand tightened on his coffee mug, and a muscle jumped in his jaw.

Seeing Ty's reaction and knowing he struggled to control his hatred, Sassy hoped she wouldn't make the situation worse by saying, "What else did your mother tell you about him?"

Oblivious to the tension around the table, Juan thought for a minute, then said, "She say he was very brave and very nice to *mi abuela*. He took her back to *Méjico* when she say she miss her family. *Mi madre* also say I should not be embar—I forget the word."

"Embarrassed?" Sassy suggested.

"*Sí,* embarrassed about *mi abuelo* being Indian. She

say she proud to carry his blood, and I should be, too."
He straightened in his chair, thrusting his chin forward.

Sassy looked across the table at Ty. She could tell
Juan's innocent words had affected him. The flash of hatred she'd seen flicker across his face had changed to
unbidden shame.

"Your mother was right. We should all carry our ancestors' blood proudly, Half-pint." From the corner of her
eye, she saw Ty's hand grip his coffee mug tighter, then
relax. She exhaled a sigh of relief.

Over the next several days, Sassy watched Juan's face
lose its pinched look, and his body fill out from the
hearty meals he put away. He had blossomed under the
shared care of herself, Kitty, and even Ty. Though her
husband hadn't taken an active part in Juan's transformation, Sassy knew Ty was beginning to care for the
boy. After they'd learned that his grandmother had been
taken by Horse Back during a raid into Mexico, and had
given birth to Juan's mother while the war chief's captive—making the boy one-quarter Comanche—Ty had
treated him kindly. He'd even started taking him along
for Domino's morning walk.

Ty's attitude toward Juan began to undergo a subtle
change. The boy was a quick learner, eager to please,
and a natural with the horses. Whatever Ty asked him to
do, he never complained, performing each task with enthusiasm and every day earning a little more of Ty's re-
spect.

On one of their morning walks, Ty's feelings for Juan
underwent an even more drastic change. Near San
Augustin Plaza a group of boys had stopped on their way
to school to play mumblety-peg.

As Ty and Juan walked past where they were crouched on the ground, one of the older boys nudged his companions. "Hey, looky there, the stinkin' Injun's wearing shoes."

Juan stiffened at the slur, but said nothing, keeping his gaze straight ahead, his head proudly high.

"What's the matter, Injun, cat got your tongue?" one of the others called with a snigger.

Ty stopped abruptly, his lips pressed together in silent anger. Something tugging on his sleeve pulled his gaze down to Juan.

In a low voice, the boy said, "Don't worry *Señor* Ty. They do not bother me."

An enormous lump formed in Ty's throat at the brave front Juan displayed. How many times had Juan heard such remarks? The boy might be too small to stick up for himself, but Ty sure as hell wasn't going to let it slide. Handing Juan Domino's leash and murmuring for him to stay put, he approached the group of boys.

"I think you owe Juan an apology," he told them in a cool but commanding voice.

"I ain't apologizing to no Injun," the biggest of the boys declared.

He longed to grab them and knock their heads together. Instead, he bent down to pick up the jackknife they were using in their game. Straightening, he tested with blade with his thumb. "I don't believe I heard you right."

Their gazes glued to the man's hands and his deft handling of the knife, one of them said, "Okay, Mister, we apologize."

"I'm not the one you need to say it to."

One by one the boys repeated the words loud enough for Juan to hear.

Closing the jackknife, Ty handed it to the boy nearest him. "If I hear any of you call Juan anything other than his name, I'll personally demonstrate ways to use that knife that you couldn't possibly imagine. Do I make myself clear?"

Their Adam's apples bobbing, they nodded in unison.

"Good. Now I suggest you get yourselves off to school."

Grabbing their lunch pails, they took off without looking back.

When he returned to Juan's side, the boy flashed him a bright smile. *"Gracías, Señor* Ty."

The admiration shining in the boy's eyes made him extremely uncomfortable. It shamed him to realize the other boys' taunts were no worse than his own might have been, had the target for their jeers not been Juan. "It was nothing," he finally said.

Over the next few days, the incident in the plaza kept returning to Ty's thoughts. He also thought about what Sassy had told him about his attitude toward Indians. Finally, after a great deal of soul-searching, he realized he was wrong to condemn everyone with Indian blood.

Although his hatred for the Comanche hadn't died completely, he now recognized a distinct difference between the innocent by-products of Indian raids and rape, and those who were true Comanche. The first, he'd come to realize, should be accepted without prejudice. The second, he continued to despise.

While Ty's hatred of Indians began to diminish, his impatience over finding Teddy continued to increase.

All too aware of Ty's mood, Sassy was careful to stay out of his way, calculating every move and contemplating every word before she did or said something that might rile him further.

257

Taking Juan up to get him ready for bed, Sassy shook her head with wonder. She had never before moderated her actions for anyone. Her love for Ty had her behaving in ways she would have never imagined.

Love certainly works in strange ways, she thought. She'd heard that expression for years, but never thought it would apply to her. There was no denying that love had changed her life. The problem was the man she loved. *Why did I have to fall in love with a man I want to whack over the head one minute, then make love to the next?*

Juan's voice pulled her from her thoughts.

"Will you tell me another story, *Señora* Sassy?"

Sassy nodded. He still refused to drop the *señora,* and she'd stopped asking him to. Since the first night he'd spent with them, when she told him a story about one of the exploits of her and her brothers, a nightly story had become a ritual.

After Kitty tucked him between the sheets of his cot, she took a seat on her bed and Sassy sat on a chair between them.

"Well, let's see. Did I tell you about the time one of my brothers snuck a plug of tobacco out of the bunkhouse, so we could try it?"

At his wide-eyed stare and the shake of his head, she began the story.

"I must have been about your age. That would make my oldest brother thirteen. Anyway, the five of us decided to have a tobacco-spitting contest."

Juan giggled and she laughed with him. "Not too smart, huh? We would try anything once, and believe me, chewing tobacco *once* was enough. We went out behind the horse barns, and each bit off a piece of tobacco.

"By the time we'd chewed it long enough to work up

258

some juice, Lucas had already gotten sick. Brodie and Trevor turned green and fought not to empty their stomachs, too. That left just Sean and me."

"Sean—he's the one who is *muerto?*"

"Yes, Half-pint, Sean was killed six years ago." She swallowed the pain welling up in her throat.

"Who won, *Señora* Sassy?" he asked softly.

Ruffling his hair, she smiled. "Actually, we never finished the contest. We were each supposed to get three tries. We'd each taken our first turn, when our father caught us."

"What happened?"

"We thought we were really in for it, but he surprised us. He said since we thought chewing tobacco was so much fun, we should be allowed to do so."

Juan's eyes widened. *"Tu padre* said it was okay to chew *el tabaco?"*

"Yes, but he had his reasons. Insisting we continue with our contest, he made all of us—except Lucas who was too dizzy and weak from being sick—take another bite of tobacco. Before long, we realized why Papa had encouraged our mischief. Soon Sean, Brodie, and Trevor were all as sick as Lucas."

"Did you get sick, too?"

"No, I didn't." She chuckled. "Guess I didn't swallow enough of the tobacco juice, or maybe I just had a stronger stomach, I'm not sure. At any rate, Papa was astounded I had no ill effects from our little game.

"He took us back to the house and sent us to our rooms, while he thought about our punishment. He decided my brothers had learned their lesson by becoming violently ill, a sickness that lasted two days. As for me, Papa confined me to the house for the same length of time my brothers remained in their sick beds. He knew how much I loved the outdoors, and forcing me to stay inside was the perfect punishment.

"Needless to say, none of us tried chewing tobacco again. Although," she added with a smile, "we did try smoking cigars a few years later."

"Really?"

Looking down at Juan, she smiled. "Yes, really. I'll save that story for another night. Now you go to sleep." She rose from the chair and tucked the sheet around him. "Sleep well, Half-pint," she murmured, bending to place a kiss on his forehead.

Sassy left him to his dreams, then turned to Kitty. "We'll bring Domino by in a little while," she said in a low voice. "Ty and I are going to the American Saloon, to see if there's any word on Teddy."

The evening started out like a carbon copy of their other evenings in town: Kitty stayed in her room with Juan and Domino, content with her sewing to occupy her time, and Sassy and Ty headed for one of the saloons.

As they stepped out into the warm evening air, Ty was in a particularly chipper mood. He laughed and joked with Sassy on their walk to the American Saloon several blocks away.

Like other nights, he joined a game of poker, and after a few hands was enjoying a string of good luck. Then he looked up and saw Sassy talking to a handsome young Mexican at the bar.

That was the turning point of the evening. From then on, everything changed.

Twenty-two

At first, Ty hadn't thought much about Sassy spending so much time with the young Mexican. After all, she was personable and outgoing, and she often made friends in the saloons they visited—Kitty's presence in Laredo proved that. And, although Sassy also met and talked to men in those establishments, none of them looked like the young swain currently drooling over her.

Tall, slim, and well-built, in spite of looking to be no more than twenty, the man had a cocky sureness about him that set Ty's teeth on edge. The quicksilver smile he continually flashed Sassy made Ty want to break him in two.

When Sassy reached out to touch the man's hand, Ty's emotional turmoil heated his anger to a low simmer. Refusing to analyze his reaction to seeing her being courted by the handsome young Mexican, he tried to ignore them. Still, he couldn't keep his gaze from repeatedly straying to the bar. Seeing Sassy run her fingers over the man's arm in a subtle caress, Ty's anger became increasingly difficult to curb. Even harder to accept was how she flaunted her behavior so openly, as if he wouldn't view her actions as an insult.

When the man leaned over to place a kiss on Sassy's

cheek, Ty had seen enough. Shoving back his chair, he headed toward his wife. *Dammit, you're a married woman, Sassy Beaumont, and you'd better start acting like one.*

"Pardon me," he said, stepping between the couple, "I'd like a word with my wife." His emphasis on the last word had no visible effect on the man. Sending him a pointed glare, Ty added, "Alone."

Recognizing the look on her husband's face, Sassy wondered what she'd done to earn this flare of his temper. She turned to her companion. "Antonio, would you excuse us, please?"

"Certainly, *Señora* Beaumont," he replied in heavily accented English. With a flourishing bow, he kissed the back of her hand, earning a glare from the big *Americano*. He flashed Sassy a brief smile, then sauntered across the room.

Grasping her arm, Ty escorted her away from the bar. In a less noisy corner of the saloon, he stopped and swung her around to face him.

She looked up at him, her eyes burning with rage. Other men had probably scurried for cover when they'd received that look. Not Ty Beaumont. He was too filled with wrath to care.

Jerking her arm from his bruising fingers, she said, "What the hell's the matter with you?"

Ty's eyebrows shot up. "What's the matter with *me?*" he repeated, stupefied by her reaction. "The question is, what the hell's the matter with *you,* spending so much time with that . . . that slick-talking, oily-looking young pup?"

"I'll have you know Antonio Alver—"

"I don't give a goddamn what his name is," he

262

snapped. "You're asking for trouble, talking to the likes of him. I won't have it. Do you hear?"

She straightened her spine and lifted her chin a notch. *"You* hear this, you knothead, I'll talk to whomever I please, whenever I please."

"Oh, no, you won't, Sassy Beaumont. And don't call me names."

"Why not? You deserve them," she retorted.

Ignoring her barb, he continued, "Now, see here. You're my wife, and you'll do as I say—"

"On second thought," she said, interrupting him, "knothead isn't quite right. A more accurate name for you is ass—"

"That's enough," he roared, earning strange looks from the men sitting at a nearby table. Lowering his voice, he said, "As I was saying, you'll do as—"

Again she cut off his words, this time by turning on her heel and heading for the door.

"Hey, where are you going? I haven't finished talking to you."

"Anywhere but where you are," she said over her shoulder, wending her way through the crowd.

"The hell you are," he muttered under his breath, striding after her.

Catching up with her at the front entrance, he reached out to push open the double doors at the same time she did. The result sounded like an explosion—the doors bursting open with such force they slammed against the outside walls, vibrated on their hinges for a moment, then bounced back. Ty gave them another shove, this one nearly ripping them off the door frame.

Head held high, her shoulders rigid, Sassy marched down the boardwalk with long, purposeful strides. Ty followed, quickly catching up with her.

"Dammlt, Sassy, listen to me," he said, matching his strides to hers. "You shouldn't be talking to men in saloons, and especially not to men who look at you like you're the main course, and who—" He couldn't finish his sentence with what he'd started to say—*Who could take you away from me.*

"He's only a boy," she fumed, picking up her pace.

"A boy? No, darlin', I'd say he's definitely a man. A man who could toss you on your back and throw your skirts over your head before you could make a peep of protest." He gave her a quick, sidelong glance, then grumbled in a lower tone, "That is, if you wanted to protest."

"How dare you imply that I would welcome . . ." Her scathing retort drifted away, the reason for Ty's reaction hitting her with sudden insight. His anger stemmed from a source she hadn't considered until now. Halting her march, she turned to face him.

"My God, Ty, you're jealous!" she stated, her temper cooling under her revelation.

"Damn right," he replied before he could stop the words. *Nice going, Beaumont,* he silently chastised himself. *Now she has another weapon against me—as if she needed one to add to her full arsenal of sharp tongue and fiery temper.*

Until he'd admitted it aloud, he hadn't permitted himself to see the truth. Raw jealousy ate at his insides like a canker sore. He refused to dig into the reason for feeling an emotion he previously thought only for insecure milksops.

Seeing the confusion on his face, Sassy laid a hand on his forearm. "Ty, Antonio *is* a boy. He's only seventeen."

At his snort of disbelief, she said, "Okay, a well-developed seventeen, but it's true, I swear. Anyway, he was feeling homesick, and I thought if I spent some time with him, he'd feel better. We talked about his home and family down in Mexico. I asked him if he had a sweetheart." Ignoring Ty's derisive grunt, she continued, "He told me about the woman he's in love with, but she treats him like a brother. I gave him some ideas on how to gain her attention, nothing more. Honest."

Ty stared down at her, wishing he could see into her eyes to gauge the truth of her words. Although hampered by the darkness, an inner sense told him she hadn't lied. The hard knot of anger in his gut began to unravel.

Amazed at how easily she could rile his temper, then defuse it with as much ease, he took a deep breath. Exhaling slowly, he pulled her against his chest.

"Guess I acted like an idiot, didn't I?" Before she could reply, he said, "I overreacted, and I'm sorry."

Aware he hadn't admitted jealousy was the impetus that drove him to react so strongly, Sassy didn't mention it either. As she stood in his embrace for a minute, savoring their closeness, she heard music drifting toward them.

Ty heard it, too. Glancing around, he realized they had stormed out of the saloon and not paid attention to which direction they'd taken. In their anger, they'd ended up in an unfamiliar section of town.

Stepping away from him, she grabbed one of his hands. "Come on," she said, her voice bubbling with excitement. "Let's see where the music's coming from."

Ty let her pull him along, laughing at her spirit of adventure.

A Mexican cantina was the source of the music, where a lively celebration was under way. The cantina's doors stood open, revealing a crowded interior, the overflow of people spilling out onto the patio.

Ty insisted they stay in the shadows. Content to be close enough to listen, Sassy did not argue. The sultry Latin music affected her like a drug, melting into her body until every part of her sang with the rhythmic strum of the guitars. Completely absorbed in the music, she didn't hear a man approach until he spoke.

"Señora, Señor, you would like to join our celebration, *sí?* I am Manuel Carrillo. This is my daughter's wedding fiesta. You are most welcome to join us."

"Señor Carrillo," Sassy replied, "you are most kind, but we don't want to impose."

"You like the Spanish guitars, *sí?"*

"Yes, their music is beautiful."

"Then I insist you join us. Come with me," he added when the couple hesitated.

Sassy glanced up at Ty, tilting her head in question. He smiled in response. Turning back to Mr. Carrillo, she said, *"Gracias. Señor* Carrillo, we'd be pleased to join the fiesta."

Leaving the shadows, Ty looped Sassy's arm through his and followed their host into the cantina.

After Sassy and Ty congratulated the newly married couple and met some of the other guests, the Carrillos offered them food and wine. Seeing Sassy's fascination with the dancing, *Señora* Carrillo handed her a pair of castanets, encouraging her to join the dancers.

At first she refused Ty's invitation to dance, uncertain if she could execute the unfamiliar steps. Yet, the music continued to call to her, plucking at her nerve endings, setting her senses afire. Her body thrumming like the strings of the guitars, she could no longer resist their pull. When the musicians began a new song, she led Ty onto the section of the patio reserved for dancing.

Arms raised over her head, castanets on her fingers, Sassy began moving in the pattern of the fandango. His jacket removed, Ty took his place next to her. Their movements started slowly, then increased in tempo as the guitars played faster and faster.

Clicking the castanets with one hand, Sassy lifted her skirt with the other. Head thrown back and eyes closed, she twirled round and round. As the vibrant music warmed her soul, the night air cooled the heated flesh of her exposed legs. She opened her eyes and met Ty's penetrating stare. The unmistakable glitter of desire burned in his dark eyes.

As if speaking only to them, the guitars continued their arousing melody. Swaying and twisting, she could feel his gaze touch her face, then move lower. A blazing fire of need stole over her body, as if he'd reached out and touched her. She had the sudden sensation that they were making love fully clothed, while dancing the fandango.

The surely sinful but definitely exciting idea of making love to Ty on the dance floor in front of several dozen witnesses, sent a rush of exhilaration through her.

He looked down into her flushed face and saw his own banked desire reflected in her eyes. Everything around him began to fade away, the music growing fainter, the other guests disappearing. There was only Sassy and the need to do more than dance, the need to do what the Latin rhythms suggested. With a start, he realized the song had ended.

Grasping Sassy's hand, he ushered her toward their hosts. After thanking them for a wonderful time and pressing some coins into the hand of the new bridegroom, Ty and Sassy hurried from the cantina.

Though the walk back to the Rio Grande Hotel was a long one, their desire didn't abate. Ty kept it primed and near-to-exploding by stopping every block or so to taste Sassy's luscious mouth. In spite of knowing he should hurry so he could appease his hunger, he couldn't resist the temptation of her lips.

Inside the privacy of their hotel room, Ty turned to face his wife. He could still hear the music of the fandango playing in his head, making his body throb and his pulse increase. Seeing the fire in her eyes, he knew she also heard the guitars, and shared his feverish desire to finish what they'd started on the dance floor.

He slowly raised one hand and reached out to cup her cheek. When she turned her face and placed a kiss on the sensitive skin of his palm, he sucked in a sharp breath, his arousal growing more acute.

"You're so beautiful," he murmured in a raspy voice.

"So are you," she responded, reaching up to caress his chest through his ruffled shirtfront.

In a matter of moments, they tore off their clothes and stretched out on the bed.

As his hands skimmed over her, she groaned in pleasure, arching and twisting to give him access to more of her aching flesh. When he lowered his head and brushed her mouth in a fleeting kiss, she whimpered in protest. Grasping his hair in frustration, she pulled him back down.

He teased the seam of her lips with the tip of his tongue until she opened her mouth, allowing him to explore the inside. His hands did some exploring of their own, touching and massaging sensitive spots and eliciting moans of pleasure and whispered words of encouragement.

Cupping her breasts, he shifted his mouth to his newest

target. As Ty first kissed, then suckled each nipple in turn, they puckered into tight rosettes under his ministrations. Anxious to continue exploring, he left the silky mounds to trail his tongue down over her ribs and onto the flat plane of her belly. He buried his nose in the dark triangle of curls, inhaling deeply, filling his lungs with her heady scent. Fighting the urge to fall atop her and drive into her moist center, a groan vibrated in his chest. He opened the folds of her secret place with his fingers, exposing the pink nub nestled there. His tongue flicked out to lave the swollen bud.

She cried out, jerking in reaction to the first rasp of his tongue. As he continued stroking her most sensitive place, the fire roaring through her veins burned hotter. Her breathing becoming labored, she opened her thighs, unashamedly offering herself.

Ty eagerly accepted her invitation, kissing the petals of her flesh, then licking the same spot with exaggerated slowness.

"Ty, please," she moaned, her hips lifting, seeking relief.

"Soon, darlin', soon," he crooned, his mustache brushing the inside of her thighs.

When his tongue touched her again, slowly teasing her inflamed senses, she gripped the sheet on either side of her. "Ty!" she pleaded again, frantic for the delicious torment to end.

"God, you're so sweet," he whispered, unwilling to hurry, even though he was painfully aroused and she was nearly hysterical with need. He opened his mouth on her succulent flesh, then tugged on the tender bud with his lips.

Sassy gasped with surprise, arching urgently against him. Her release came almost immediately, the intense pleasure ripping a scream from her throat. Her hips bucked against his mouth, another scream piercing the air. Calling out his name in a strangled cry, she rode the waves of her climax to the crest, tumbled down the smaller swells on the other side, and finally glided into the calm sea of total fulfillment.

Ty kept his mouth pressed to the opened petals of her feminine center, until the last, tiniest spasm passed. He nuzzled her gently with his lips, his tongue darting out to sample the dew of her release. Taking another deep breath of her woman's scent, he raised his head.

"You're wonderful," he murmured.

Sassy didn't reply. She could barely breathe, let alone speak. Although not the first time Ty had made love to her with his mouth, it was by far the most intense climax she'd ever experienced. Words couldn't begin to describe how she felt. When he shifted positions and slipped inside her, all efforts to regain her powers of speech fled.

Wrapping her legs around his waist, Ty braced himself on his forearms and pushed forward. Buried as deeply as possible in her silky depths, he gritted his teeth and threw back his head. He forced himself to remain absolutely still. One move, and it would end much too soon.

When he gained control over his overwrought body, he began rocking forward, then back. Sassy lifted her hips each time he thrust into her, her inner muscles clenching around his shaft. He set a slow rhythm that soon accelerated, his heart pounding in his ears, his breathing a rasping wheeze.

No longer was he concerned about the young Mexican she had talked to, no longer did jealousy roil inside him, no longer did his temper threaten to boil over. He could only feel the pressure build, the friction increasing between their joined bodies. He tried to slow the tempo, but found his efforts wasted. His hips continued to move faster and faster.

Then it began. His engorged flesh swelled even more, pressing closer to her womb. He thrust one last time. Although he held himself perfectly still, he continued throbbing inside her. Spent and weak from the intensity of his release, he collapsed atop her with a groan.

When his strength returned, he rolled to his side. He sighed, then fell into an immediate sleep.

Although she would have liked to cuddle next to him, then fall asleep in each others' arms, Sassy wasn't peeved that her hopes wouldn't be realized. Ty still had bouts with insomnia, so he needed a good night's sleep.

She brushed a lock of hair from his face, and smiled. "I love you," she whispered. What a relief to say the words aloud. Then her smile faded. *If only I could tell him when he's awake.*

Moving to the other side of the bed, she curled into a ball. Against her will, her thoughts drifted to Teddy. *Why can't I be the most important person in his life?* She closed her eyes, afraid insomnia would have a new victim that night.

Twenty-three

Bright Sky ran his hand over the neck of his horse, murmuring softly in Comanche. "I will return soon, *Cona*." Leaving the small lean-to, he turned toward the east and started running. A deerskin pouch slung over his shoulder, his moccasin-covered feet made only a whisper of sound on the hard ground.

When he reached a stream, Bright Sky stopped and stripped off his clothes. He stepped into the water and quickly bathed. Not bothering to dry himself, he donned only a breechclout and the moccasins, stuffed his other clothes into the deerskin pouch, and took off at a lope.

The slight breeze chilled his damp body, but he ignored the discomfort. He had a long way to go, and running would soon warm him. His long braids slapping silently against his back, the eagle feather tied in one plait brushing his shoulder, his legs quickly took him closer to his destination.

After several miles, he stopped. He sat down on the ground, then withdrew a bone pipe and a small bag of tobacco from his pouch. He lit the pipe and inhaled deeply. Looking up at the sun still high in the sky, Bright Sky prayed to his guardian spirit to give him power.

When the tobacco was gone, he replaced the pipe in the deerskin pouch, then continued his eastward run.

He repeated the routine three more times, stopping to smoke his pipe and pray for power. It was dusk when he reached the spot he'd selected, the south side of a small hill with a clear view to the west and east. Sitting cross-legged, Bright Sky began the final part of his religious ceremony.

When the Comanche—who called themselves The People—had been forced onto reservations, many in Bright Sky's band believed the power-giving spirits had forsaken them. Some turned to another form of religion, peyotism. Peyote did not solve the problems of adjusting to life on a reservation, but it did help ease their suffering. Having adhered fiercely to old tribal ways, Bright Sky could not give them up so easily. As a compromise, he'd created his own religion—a combination of the old and new—to seek his *puha,* power.

After building a fire, he withdrew a piece of dried *wokowi,* peyote, from his deerskin pouch. He chewed the *wokowi* into a pulp, spewed it into his hand, made four circular motions toward the fire, then swallowed the mashed cactus. Bright Sky sang a song, then prayed to his personal guardian spirit.

Through the night, he ate more *wokowi* and prayed for his spirit to come to him, to talk to him as it had in the past.

Near dawn, Bright Sky's sharp hearing detected a far-away sound—the howl of a wolf. He smiled, grateful for the sign his guardian spirit, the wolf, was near.

Closing his eyes to the brush-covered plains, the vision came to him. He saw the scene clearly, as if Father-Sun

273

had shed his light and driven away the darkness of night. Bright Sky saw a man, a man with yellow hair like his own, a man with skin as pale as his had once been, a man with a heart filled with hatred . . . just like his own. Two women and a boy were with the man as he made some sort of quest—a quest which had to be successful, or he would face terrible danger.

Before the danger facing the man could be revealed, Bright Sky's vision ended, the scene behind his closed eyelids fading back to the blackness of night.

Arms raised to the heavens, he opened his eyes and sent his silent prayer skyward. *Oh, Great Spirit of the wolf, hear me. Show Bright Sky what he is to do with the vision you have given him.*

From out of the darkness, a voice came to him, a voice only he could hear. "You must find this man. Look for him in the town called Laredo. Find him, Bright Sky. Protect him, for one day he will be your brother."

May fifteenth came and went. Then two more days dragged by, and still no Teddy. There were several new faces in town— professional gamblers unless Ty missed his guess—but Teddy was not one of them.

Since arriving in Laredo, Ty had finally learned the game was to have been hosted by Ricardo Gonzales, owner of one of the largest spreads in the area. Although a successful rancher, Gonzales had a penchant for high-stakes poker. His games, legendary among gamblers, drew high rollers from all across the state and beyond. For some reason, the game scheduled for May fifteenth hadn't materialized.

The situation frustrated Ty beyond belief. If not for

Sassy and the balm of her passion, he'd surely be a viable candidate for an insane asylum.

Then, on the afternoon of the eighteenth, Ty overheard some men in the American Saloon discussing *Señor* Gonzales. His wife had been ill for several weeks, and when she'd taken a turn for the worse, he'd canceled the game. While the man's love for his wife and concern about her health were admirable traits, his canceling the game Teddy was to attend put another crimp in Ty's plans.

Gonzales had sent telegrams to notify those invited of the change in plans. Some of the expected participants, already en route to Laredo, showed up only to learn that they'd made the trip for nothing. Unfortunately, Teddy must have received her telegram in time to stay put— wherever that was.

"Damn, now what?" Ty muttered under his breath, leaving the saloon in disgust. Relieved to know why the game had been cancelled, the knowledge didn't stop the familiar, helpless frustration from swamping him.

After sending a telegram to Josh in Austin to report his latest setback, he headed for the hotel. Thinking about having to tell Sassy they'd lost another round, he slowed his pace. Another delay like this, and he'd have no choice but to divorce her. The prospect brought a lump to his throat. As painful as the thought was, he couldn't keep her with him, if he continued to be a wanted man. Sooner or later someone would recognize him, and he couldn't bear the thought of Sassy suffering the humiliation of her husband's arrest. Swallowing that bitter pill of truth, he entered the Rio Grande Hotel.

After an unbearably hot and humid afternoon, Sassy and Ty left their hotel to head for the American Saloon.

Hoping he might hear more about the gamblers invited to Gonzales's game, Ty decided to maintain their previous routine.

Waving a fan in front of her face to coax some cool air her way, Sassy said, "Damn, it's hot. I swear, if somebody poked a fork in me, they'd find me well done."

Ty flashed her a crooked smile. No matter how grim his mood, she could always lift his flagging spirits. "I know what you mean," he replied, running a finger inside the collar of his shirt to ease the chafing of the stiff material on his neck. Glancing up at the sky, he added, "Can't see the stars, and the wind's picking up. Maybe a storm will blow in and cool things off."

Sassy nodded absently, too uncomfortable from the heat to reply.

The doors of the American Saloon stood open to take advantage of even the smallest breeze. The air inside was hot and stale. Smoke hung in thick clouds, smarting the eyes and making breathing difficult. The uncomfortable temperature made everyone jumpy and thirstier than usual.

Observing the other patrons of the saloon, Ty didn't envy the bouncer. One man could never keep the peace if the hot spell didn't break soon. The combination of heavy drinking and hair-trigger tempers wasn't a good omen.

Selecting a poker game to join, Ty took his seat. He immediately realized that the man sitting directly across from him, a man called Farley, had already had too much to drink. Determined to make the best of it, Ty tried to ignore him.

When Sassy approached a few minutes later, Farley's eyes lit up. "Say, does that piece a' fine-looking woman belong to you, Beauregard?"

Ty nodded. "Gentlemen, this is my wife." After making the introductions, he slipped one arm around Sassy's hips. He purposely leveled a cool stare at each man to assess his reaction.

After playing a few hands, and watching Farley give Sassy bold, appraising looks, Ty knew he had to do something. Whispering to Sassy to find some other way to spend her time, he hoped the man's interest would wane once she was out of his sight.

"She's right pretty for a saloon gal," Farley said, dashing Ty's hopes. "Must be ya ain't lent her out much."

Ty's hands tightened on his cards; a muscle twitched in his jaw. "That's right, I haven't," he replied blandly.

The men played a few more hands, and Ty began to think Farley had forgotten about Sassy. The man's next statement proved him wrong again.

"How 'bout letting me try her out?"

"I don't think so."

"I'll pay ya real good," Farley said, trying to focus on Sassy across the room. Too much whiskey and too much smoke made seeing anything difficult.

Ty gritted his teeth, then murmured, "I said no."

Downing another shot of whiskey, Farley squinted across the table at him. "Ya know what I think? I think you're not man enough for that wife o' yorn. What she needs is a real man, a man like me to—"

"You're out of line, Farley," Ty interrupted. "I suggest you keep your opinions to yourself."

Ignoring Ty, he waved one hand toward the bar, where Sassy stood talking to a group of men. "Look at her, twitching her tail like a mare in season, in front o' all those randy stallions. Must be ya ain't taking care of that little filly. Why else would she—"

"I've heard enough," Ty said, reaching for his chips.

He nodded to the others, then pushed his chair away from the table. "Gentlemen, if you'll excuse me."

"What are ya, some kinda coward?" Farley said. Shoving back his chair, he rose unsteadily to his feet.

Ty turned an icy stare toward the other man. "No. I'm just fed up with your insults."

Farley swayed on his feet, his face mottled with rage. When he regained his balance, he moved around the table and stopped in front of Ty. "Well, here's one more insult for ya." Doubling up his fist, he drew back his arm.

As Farley's swing started toward Ty's jaw, another man stepped between them. "Hold on there, Farley, you—" His words stopped abruptly when Farley's fist clipped him on the cheek. "Goll darn it, Farley, have you lost what little sense you had?"

"Dammit, Calvin, what ya doing sticking yer nose in where it ain't got no business," Farley said, keeping his blurry gaze on his original target and drawing back to take another swing.

Before Ty could do anything to stop his premonition from becoming reality, all hell broke loose around him. A third man joined the fracas, receiving Farley's punch on the side of his head. Faces twisted with fury, the two men grabbed for each other. Locked in a bear hug, they toppled to the floor, each cursing soundly while trying to gain an advantage.

Another pair of men squared off. And then another. In a matter of seconds, the entire area around the poker tables became an arena for an assortment of fisticuffs and wrestling matches.

Deciding that making his exit would be the wise choice, Ty turned to leave, only to find an opponent who took exception to his decision. Whether he wanted to or not, Ty joined the fray. Taking a defensive stance and holding his fists in front of his chin, he circled the man, looking for a weakness. As drunk as Farley, the man was glassy-eyed, his mouth distorted by a snarl. Ty faked a right, then struck with a quick left to the jaw. A surprised look on his florid face, the man staggered backward, fell over a chair, and landed on the floor with a grunt. He didn't get up.

Ty's next opponent wasn't drunk, catching him off guard and landing a right hook to his chin before he could react. His head snapped back from the force of the blow, forcing him to take a step backwards. He would have taken a second punch, if his head hadn't cleared in time for him to raise his arm to block it.

His nostrils flaring with the scent of battle, Ty brought his fists up, growling for his opponent to make his move. Strong as a bull, the man landed several solid fists to Ty's midsection, before he could retaliate. Ty peppered him with jab after jab until the man rocked back on his heels, his arms swinging wildly, his punches going wide of their mark. Smelling victory, Ty maneuvered for the final blow.

Kit Dancer watched the growing brawl from his position near the door of the saloon. Thinking this might be the opportunity he'd been waiting for, he drew his gun and moved across the barroom. He was almost at Ty's side, when he heard a woman scream, "Ty, watch out!"

Recognizing Sassy's voice, Ty sent his newest opponent sprawling with a hard right, then looked up to scan the area. What had she tried to warn him about? The metallic glint of a gun barrel gave him his answer. He tried to move out of the way, but surrounded by men embroiled in the fight, pushing and shoving against him, there was no escape.

Everything suddenly went dim, the sounds of chairs

scraping, punches landing, men grunting, faded away. Ty had the sensation of being in a tunnel. Coming toward him, he could see the gunman, silhouetted against the light at the opposite end of the tunnel's dark length. Was this how it was to end?

As if seeing it in slow motion, Ty watched a chair appear from the blackness of the tunnel to crash down on the man's head. The impact splintered the chair and caused the gun to slip from his fingers. He took one more step, then sank to his knees, and slowly slid to the floor.

Staring at the motionless man, Ty shook his head. The noises and brightness of the barroom returned in a rush. Lifting his gaze to his benefactor, he blinked with surprise. Sassy held what was left of the chair, a broad grin creasing her face.

Shaking his head again as she approached him, he murmured, "If that don't beat all."

Grasping her hand, he found an opening between the remaining combatants and pulled her toward the door. "Let's get the hell out of here, before the law shows up."

When they were well away from the saloon, Sassy said, "What was that about?"

"Farley and I didn't agree about something."

"About what?"

Ty frowned, then finally said, "You."

"Me? I don't even know the man. What could you disagree about?"

"Farley wanted to—" He cleared his throat, then muttered, "He . . . um . . . he wanted to try you out."

Sassy gave him a wide-eyed stare. "Try me out? But you introduced me as your wife, so why—" Her eyes got even bigger. "Oh, my God, do some married men actually do that?"

A brief smile curved his lips at her outrage. "Yes, unfortunately they do."

"Why would they let their wives be with other men?"

"Greed, I reckon. When a man becomes obsessed with money, he'll stop at nothing to get it. And if he doesn't care about his wife, I suppose the choice becomes easier."

Doesn't care about his wife. The words echoed in her head. Dear God, would he consider doing that with her? She shivered at the thought. She didn't know which would be worse: Ty divorcing her, or staying married so she could whore for him. Even knowing that Ty had refused Farley's rude suggestion, her spirits didn't lift. They had to get this whole mess straightened out. She couldn't stand being pulled in a half-dozen directions at once. Life had been so much simpler before Ty.

Falling in love and learning how to be a lady had changed her in more ways than she could have imagined. She just wasn't sure the changes were for the better—not when they brought her so much pain. Glancing at the man walking beside her, she felt foolish for thinking such drivel. She loved Ty, no amount of self-pity would change that. She'd help him clear his name, and then, Teddy be damned, she would make him fall in love with her.

Kit Dancer awoke slowly, keeping his eyes closed against the throbbing in his head. When the pain eased, he carefully lifted his eyelids. He blinked several times against the sunlight streaming across his face, trying to figure out where he was.

Sitting up took every bit of strength he could muster. As his surroundings registered and he realized where he was, he sucked in a surprised breath. "How the hell did I end up in a jail cell?" he wondered aloud.

A voice to his left answered his question. "Y'all got arrested for fighting at the American Saloon."

"Fighting?" Kit said, gingerly rubbing the back of his head. A knot the size of a large egg was tender to the touch. "Ow," he grumbled when he pushed on the lump too hard.

The man in the next cell chuckled. "Doc looked at ya, 'fore they threwed ya in that there cell. Said ya had a hard head and would be right as rain come mornin'."

Kit turned to look at his talkative fellow prisoner, an old man with a white shock of hair and a scraggly beard. "Were you in the fight, too?"

He chuckled again. "Nope, not me. I'm too old for that kinda stuff. I had me too much to drink, and the sheriff brought me here to sober up." The man rubbed his head, then added, " 'Course, I don't know if the headache I got is any better than the one yer nursing from having a chair busted over the back of yer head."

Kit closed his eyes again, trying to put together the pieces from the night before: A fight at the American Saloon, getting hit over the head with a chair. Of course! Now he remembered. He'd been watching Ty play poker, when one of the other men at his table picked a fight with Ty. And when he'd tried to make use of the distraction, everything had suddenly gone black. Kit silently cursed his own stupidity. *That's what I get for being so set on getting Beaumont. I was so intent on finally ending this job, I never saw the other man coming at me.*

He rubbed his head again and groaned.

"That musta been one strong woman, hefting a chair and knocking y'all out cold."

His eyes snapped open. "Woman?" Kit murmured to himself. He could only remember one woman in the sa-

282

loon. He groaned again. Sassy Beaumont was proving to be more of a hindrance than he'd imagined.

"So, when do I get out of here?"

The old man shifted on his cot, turning his back to Kit. "Don't rightly know. Y'all'll have to talk to the Sheriff. It'll be a couple o' hours anyway. He never comes in 'fore ten. Y'all should do like me, and use the time to get some sleep."

Before Kit could reply, snores drifted to him from the other cell.

"Helluva note," he muttered, getting to his feet. He doubled over with the sudden nausea gripping his middle. Willing his stomach to stay put, he walked back and forth in the small cell. He had to look like he'd suffered no ill effects from the fight, otherwise the sheriff might not let him go. If that happened, who knew what the Beaumonts might be up to.

Kit had made a foolish mistake in his pursuit of Ty Beaumont, a mistake he wouldn't make again.

Twenty-four

Thankfully, Ty didn't have long to stew over Teddy not coming to Laredo. He received a telegram from Josh the morning after the saloon brawl. He couldn't believe his eyes, reading the message again to make sure he hadn't wished the words onto the paper. "Teddy in Galveston . . . Stop . . . Been there several weeks . . . Stop . . . Sources say she plans to stay . . . Stop . . . Advise your plans . . . Stop . . . JM."

Cramming the telegram into his pocket, Ty detoured to the train station before heading back to the hotel.

"Pack our bags, darlin', we're heading for Galveston on the morning train," he told Sassy jubilantly.

"Galveston?"

"Yup. I got a telegram from Josh. He says Teddy's been there for several weeks and plans to stay. We have to get there, before she changes her mind. Come on, getta a move on, let's get packed."

"What about Juan?"

"Juan?" Ty had momentarily forgotten about their young charge. "Juan," he repeated dumbly, slumping onto a chair.

He knew what Sassy would say if he asked her what

she thought, so he kept silent. Contemplating what they should do, he realized that his feelings for Juan had changed yet again. Not only had he come to accept the boy's Comanche blood, he now genuinely cared about him.

Glancing up at Sassy and seeing the anxiety on her face, he said, "Juan's too young to be on his own. He'll go with us."

Smiling at Sassy's squeal of joy, he quickly sobered. As if he didn't have enough to worry about, he'd been unable to kick his irritating new habit, collecting people—and animals, he amended, remembering Domino. He rose from his chair, grabbed one of their carpetbags and threw it onto the bed. As he pulled his clothes from the dresser and stuffed them into the bag, he tried not to think about the additional responsibility he'd just added to his ever-increasing list.

"Go tell Kitty to get Juan and herself packed and ready to leave by morning. We're taking the eight o'clock train for the coast."

Sitting on the train heading east out of Laredo toward the Gulf of Mexico, Ty had plenty of time to contemplate the tremendous burden of keeping not only himself but two women, a dog, and now, a boy, safe. It was a heavy load, and one he wasn't sure he could handle. Especially since he continued to have the uneasy feeling he was still being followed, a constant nagging by a sixth sense that someone watched his every move. He'd experienced the strange, prickly sensation most of the time during their stay in Laredo, but it had been strongest when he and Sassy were at the saloon. He hated the frustrating, helpless feeling. Now that he had so many others to watch out for, he was even more concerned about the danger posed by the unknown person following him.

Listening to Sassy's happy chatter with Kitty and Juan, and the boy's excitement over his first train ride, Ty tried to catch their light mood. It didn't work. His mind continued to poke and prod into parts of his psyche he would have preferred not to disturb.

Unable to control the direction of his thoughts, Ty finally gave in and let his brain have free rein. The brawl at the saloon immediately came to mind. The corners of his mouth lifted with amusement. He hadn't been in a rip-roarer like that since before he'd become a Texas Ranger. Rubbing his chin, he winced when his fingers touched a sensitive spot.

"Does it still hurt?" Sassy asked, gently placing her fingers on the discoloration on his jaw and momentarily pulling him from his thoughts.

"Not much," he replied, meeting her gaze. Seeing the same tender concern he'd heard in her voice also shining brightly in the depths of her eyes, brought Ty to a startling discovery. Somewhere along the way, he'd shed his skepticism of Sassy and had actually begun to trust her. He thought back, trying to pinpoint exactly when his distrust had reversed itself. Unable to find a particular incident, he concluded the change had been gradual, brought on by a series of events. That's why he hadn't realized his metamorphosis until now.

Turning his face, he gave her fingertips a nibbling kiss, then said, "Did I thank you for helping me the other night in the saloon?"

Sassy's cheeks grew hot. "Yes," she murmured, the color of her face deepening with the memory of what he'd done to thank her.

Ty chuckled. "I take it my thanks was sufficient?"

She gave him a playful punch, then whispered, "Yes, more than sufficient."

When she turned her attention to Juan, Ty's thoughts dwelled on her. His gaze traced her profile, down her smooth forehead, over her slightly upturned nose, across her full lips. Sucking in a surprised breath, he had the sensation of being back in the saloon brawl. His head snapped back, as if from another punch to the chin. Only the culprit wasn't a fist, but the feelings hit him with as much force, feelings he could no longer deny. He'd continually shoved the truth to the back of his mind for weeks, refusing to deal with what he conveniently called lust. Now the truth demanded to be heard.

He loved Sassy.

As the seriousness of his latest discovery settled over him, he stared out the train window in grim silence. How had he fallen in love, and not even been aware of it?

He'd always figured he'd fall in love with a docile, quiet woman, then settle down on his ranch and raise horses and a couple of kids. Instead, he'd fallen in love with Sassy, anything but docile and quiet. She was fiery-tempered, infuriating, stubborn—the list went on—certainly not the type of woman he'd pictured himself living with for the rest of his life.

Idly stroking his mustache with thumb and forefinger, he thought back to the first time he'd laid eyes on Sassy. Stiff-backed, eyes shooting fire while pointing her rifle at him, she'd accused him of horse stealing. She even threatened to do him bodily harm, if he moved. His mouth twitched at the memory. Boy, she'd sure been something!

He now realized something else about that day. In spite of her accusations and sharp tongue, that's when his love for her had begun to put down roots. Now firmly entrenched in the deepest regions of his heart, his love for her could never be routed out.

How he could love a woman who knew as many curse words as he did, challenged him at every turn, provoked his temper as no one ever had, went completely beyond his understanding! Yet, there was no doubt in his mind. He loved Sassy, and in spite of her unorthodox ways, he wouldn't want to change anything about her.

Damn, now what do I do? He sighed heavily, his troubled thoughts continuing. *I can't tell her how I feel. I can't give her false hope of a future for us. If I don't find Teddy, or can't get her to change her story, I'll still go ahead and divorce Sassy. It wouldn't be fair to tell her how I feel, then slap her in the face by ending our marriage.*

It was bad enough, he decided bitterly, finally facing his feelings and admitting to himself that he loved Sassy. Now he had to keep his newly recognized love to himself. God, what a mess!

Closing his eyes, he leaned back against the seat. He had to stop thinking about what he'd just uncovered—a task he found nearly impossible to accomplish with the woman he loved sitting so close, her soft curves tantalizing his body, her scent teasing his nose, her voice tickling his ears.

You've done it now, Beaumont, he chastised himself. *You fall in love. then have to live with the guilt of not being able to tell her how you feel.* He finally drifted into a restless sleep, only to have the woman filling his conscious thoughts reappear in his dreams. It was small consolation, but at least in his dreams he could say aloud, *I love you, Sassy.*

* * *

Bright Sky looked out the window of the passenger car, his stomach lurching from the strange, rocking motion. He had seen the white man's train since leaving the reservation, but he had never ridden on one. He preferred traveling as his Comanche fathers had—on horseback. And just like his Comanche fathers, he couldn't disobey his guardian spirit. To do so would bring him bad medicine. The spirit of the wolf had seen him through many trials, and Bright Sky knew his guardian would continue to protect him.

After traveling to Laredo in search of the man his guardian spirit had bid him to find, Bright Sky had seen the yellow-haired man with two women and a boy, just as his vision had foretold. He had secretly watched the man from a distance for several days, unable to determine what danger the *tivo* faced, or what part he would play in preventing it. When Bright Sky realized the man meant to leave town, he saw no alternative except to buy a ticket and board the same train. His spirit told him he must help the man, and Bright Sky could not disobey.

He squirmed restlessly on the seat, uncomfortable in the white man's clothes and having to keep his hair tucked under a hat. Hating the restrictions of the tight pants and boots, he longed for his well-worn buckskins and moccasins. Wise enough to know that dressing the way he preferred might have kept him off the train, Bright Sky suffered in silence. Now he wished he'd stayed in the stock car with *Cona*. His horse hadn't liked boarding the train any more than he had. If he'd remained with *Cona,* his presence might have calmed the horse. Plus, by staying in the stock car, he could have stretched out on the straw-covered floor and found some measure of comfort.

As he stared out at the passing plains, he raised one

hand to his chest. He touched the necklace of wolves' teeth beneath his shirt, symbol of his powerful medicine. Fingering the familiar amulet, his anxiety eased, his thoughts drifting again to his most recent vision, similar to the ones plaguing him for months.

Bright Sky had been taught how important visions were to the Comanche. They were an integral part of their lives, beginning with a young boy's first vision quest as part of his initiation into manhood. Not to be confused with ordinary dreams, visions came only under certain circumstances, and only when sought for one of the traditional recurring reasons: mourning, successful hunts or raids, revenge, or curing disease.

Mourning had been the reason for seeking the solace of his guardian spirit, when he experienced his first vision of the yellow-haired man. Still on the reservation near Fort Sill, Bright Sky had sought guidance from the wolf spirit to ease his grief. Instead of soothing words, his guardian spirit chose to ignore his pain. The wolf spirit spoke only of a yellow-haired *tivo;* a man he said Bright Sky would meet one day.

Bright Sky had dismissed that vision, blaming himself for making a poor attempt to summon his spirit, because of his grief. He also dismissed his next several visions as merely recurring dreams. But when the yellow-haired man continued to appear time and again, Bright Sky realized his guardian spirit had something important to tell him.

After he left the reservation and returned to Texas, the visions came more frequently, and often without his seeking them. Then several months ago, the spirit of the wolf spoke louder than any previous time. He told Bright Sky to ride a horse with a red skin, and go toward the river far to the south.

Bright Sky captured and broke a red-skinned horse he named *Cona,* fire, then headed south. He'd set up camp just north of Laredo, when the latest vision instructed him to find the yellow-haired man in town. The wolf spirit told him something new in that vision as well. He had said, "Protect him, for one day he will be your brother."

Pulling his brows together in concentration, Bright Sky tried to figure out what his guardian spirit had meant. *I am Comanche. The man in my visions is a tivo. A white man can never be my brother!* Although not born to The People, he became Comanche. Adopted and raised by a childless couple, Bright Sky grew into one of the fiercest, bravest warriors in their band, leading successful raiding parties when he was only eighteen. *Bah, how can a white man be my brother?* Bright Sky scoffed silently.

He closed his eyes, trying to ease the queasiness in his stomach and hoping to change the direction of his thoughts. Instead, memories long buried by his hatred of the *tivo* sprang unbidden into his mind.

He saw a dark-haired young woman, singing softly to a baby cradled in her arms. Shaking his head, Bright Sky chased the memories back into their hiding place, but his distressing thoughts did not end.

His people had suffered greatly at the hands of the *tivo*. Not content with nearly annihilating the Comanche through war, his hated enemy resorted to starvation to force them like a herd of cattle onto a reservation.

The lying white fathers didn't care that reneging on their promises of food would cause the deaths of many of The People, especially the old, the children, and women like Singing Wind. If only he had known more of the white man's tongue when he first went to the reservation. Perhaps he could have talked to the agents and done something to save his people, to save Singing Wind.

Bright Sky's hands clenched into tight fists on his thighs, his heart aching for revenge. He would never forgive the *tivo* for killing Singing Wind. Never.

Kit Dancer stepped through the doors of the Laredo jail, his hand flexing on the butt of his revolver in frustration. He'd spent forty-eight hours locked up—the sentence for disturbing the peace—and had just gained his freedom.

Though he needed a bath and a shave, his appearance would have to wait. First, he had to find the Beaumonts. After checking with the desk clerk at the Rio Grande Hotel, Kit left the hotel cursing soundly, his mood decidedly surly. He rubbed his bristled jaw, then tugged his hat lower, grimacing when it grazed the still-tender lump on his head. He hadn't had this much trouble since he'd taken up bounty hunting.

Within an hour he'd learned that the Beaumonts, the woman named Kitty, and the boy they'd taken in, had left on the eastbound morning train. Grateful the ticket agent had been willing to talk for the ten-dollar gold piece he flashed as an incentive, Kit headed back to his hotel.

Since the next train to Galveston wasn't until the following morning, he'd have to spend another night in town. His stomach rumbled loudly. One side of his mouth lifted in a smile. Maybe the delay wouldn't be so bad, he decided. A much-needed bath and shave would be first on his agenda, then he'd find the thickest steak in Laredo. Afterward, maybe a woman. On second thought, he would forgo the female company. His head still hurt like the devil, and he hadn't slept well on the narrow jail cot.

He'd just take it easy, then tomorrow head for Galveston. It was time to quit pussyfooting around and get the matter of Mr. Ty Beaumont's fleeing from the law settled, and the matter of the man's reward in his own pocket.

Twenty-five

Galveston. As the train crossed the bridge spanning Galveston Bay and moved onto the island city, Ty felt both relief and anticipation at reaching their destination. Relief to be ending a long, tiring trip from Laredo, one that required changing trains several times—an ordeal with a child, a dog, and two horses to transfer—and anticipation about finally confronting Teddy face-to-face.

Looking at the modern buildings and bustling activity of Galveston, he realized that he should have considered coming here sooner. As the most sophisticated and advanced city in Texas, it was the kind of place Teddy would enjoy.

"Sassy, will you see to the unloading of the horses?" he asked, helping her down the railcar steps. "I'll see about finding a carriage."

Nodding her agreement, she left Juan and Kitty to wait with their luggage near the depot, then headed for the stock cars.

In a few minutes, Ty and his entourage pulled away from the train depot in a rented hack. A wagon carrying their baggage, their horses tied to the back, followed behind.

"Our driver recommended the Old Chicago House Hotel," Ty told his companions. "He assured me it's comfortable and in a respectable part of town."

Sassy chuckled, then whispered, "He probably gets paid to deliver customers there."

Ty's laughter joined hers. "I hadn't thought of that. Well, regardless of what it's like, we'll stay there tonight. We all need the rest, and I don't feel like looking for another place. If the hotel isn't all the man claims, we'll look for another one tomorrow."

When their carriage arrived at the Old Chicago House on the Strand, Ty jumped down, then assisted Sassy, Kitty, and Juan to the brick sidewalk. While the driver saw to the baggage, Ty glanced at the outside of the hotel, pleased with its well-kept appearance. The lobby proved to be most impressive as well.

After registering, he turned to Sassy. "Go on up to our room," he said, pressing the key into her hand. "I'll find a stable for the horses, then join you."

"Fine, I'm going to bathe and take a nap," Sassy answered wearily. Not even the lecherous smile Ty flashed at the mention of the bed they'd share for the first time in several days, raised her flagging spirits. Being in the same town as Teddy filled Sassy with a strange mixture of emotions. While happy for Ty and his hope of clearing his name, depression and sadness pressed down on her. This could well be the last place she would ever see him. If he couldn't convince Teddy to tell the truth and clear his name, he might end their marriage in Galveston and send her home. *If only I could be more of a lady,* she railed silently. *Then maybe I'd know how to keep him.*

After eating supper at a restaurant several blocks away, Ty walked the two women and Juan back to their hotel. At the front door, Kitty pleaded exhaustion, then took an equally sleepy Juan up to their room. Turning to Sassy, Ty said, "Would you like to walk for a while?"

"Sure." She smiled up at him. "Where shall we go?"

"Let's go down by the channel."

As they strolled along Water Street, Sassy said, "Where are we going to look for Teddy?"

"I've been thinking about that. And I've decided it would be best, if I looked for her by myself."

Sassy stared up at him, wishing she could see his expression in the fast-encroaching darkness. "Why can't I help?"

"For one thing, you don't know what she looks like, on the off chance she isn't using her real name. And until I find out why she named me as Slater's killer, I don't want to give her any more ammunition by having her learn about you."

Though his explanation made sense, she had the suspicion that there was more to his not wanting her to meet Teddy than he'd admitted. Accusing him of hiding something would only make matters worse, so she accepted his plan.

"I'll start checking the hotels in the morning. Since Teddy likes the best, I asked the man at the livery which hotels are considered the fanciest. I also asked him where I could find some high-stakes poker. He told me gambling is illegal in Galveston, so—"

"Illegal?" Sassy interrupted. "If that's true, what's Teddy doing here?"

"The man said gambling is against the law, but tolerated," Ty explained. "Unless there's trouble, the police ignore private games. The problem is, most of those games are behind closed doors, either in a saloon's back room or upstairs parlor, and most often by invitation only. If I don't find out where Teddy's staying, I'll have to start checking saloons and gambling halls. It may take some time, but I'll find her."

"Galveston is a big city. Did the man at the stable know where you should look for those private games?"

"Not for sure," Ty sighed. "Unfortunately, the man isn't a gambler, but he did tell me most saloons in town are in a four-block area between Market and Post Office Streets."

"What about Josh? He didn't send another telegram telling you where Teddy was staying?"

"No. I haven't heard from Josh since the telegram in Laredo. He didn't say if Teddy came to Galveston to gamble, or just enjoy the gulf air. Whatever brought her here, I'm sure she's still gambling. Like I told you before, that's how she makes her living." He sighed again. "I'll just have to keep looking until I find her."

Ty began checking hotels the next morning. After inquiring at several he considered elegant enough for Teddy's taste, he found one whose guest list included a Theodora Fitzsimmons.

Taking a deep breath, he asked the desk clerk if the lady was in. At the man's affirmative answer, Ty headed for her room, anger and apprehension warring inside him. As he lifted his hand and knocked on her door, anger began to pull ahead in the race for domination.

"Who is it?"

Although muffled by the door, he recognized the voice, instantly adding fuel to his already unstable temper. He knew if he lost control and lit into her, such behavior would only make matters worse. Taking several deep breaths, he tried to calm himself. His efforts did little good. "Open the door, Teddy."

After a long hesitation, the door swung inward, giving him his first view of Teddy Fitzsimmons in over four months. Although undeniably an attractive woman, he saw her full-blown figure, elaborate hairstyle, rouged cheeks and lips and kohl-darkened eyes in a new light. He'd once found such overpowering femininity strongly appealing. Not any longer. He now preferred more lithesome female curves, unbound hair, and natural beauty that didn't need artificial paint.

Shaking his head to clear his distracting thoughts, he met Teddy's gaze. Dilated slightly, her eyes proved he'd taken her by surprise. Other than that, she displayed no outward emotions at finding him at her door. He felt a stab of disappointment. He'd wanted her to show some sign of regret.

She looked him over slowly, moving her gaze down to his boots, then back up to his face. "You're looking good, Ty. And I like the mustache. What are you doing here? You're the last person I expected to see in Galveston."

"I bet you did," he said, brushing past her to enter the room. He closed the door behind him, then grabbed her by the arm. "Come on," he growled, pulling her into the sitting room. "You have some explaining to do."

"I'm not one of the local doxies, so stop manhandling me," she snapped, jerking free of his grasp.

Ty blew out an exasperated breath, then ran a hand through his hair. "Look, I have to talk to you, Teddy. I swear I won't touch you again, if you'll just tell me why you did it."

Teddy glided over to a settee and sat down. Waving him to a chair opposite her, she said, "I had no other choice."

Ty's brows pulled together in a frown. "What the hell

do you mean? You didn't see me kill Slater, so the only choice you could possibly have made was to tell the truth."

"I had no choice, because I had to protect the man who really killed Benjamin Slater."

"Protect him! Why would you need to protect him?"

"Because he has my grandmother's brooch. He cheated me out of it, and I mean to get it back."

"You named me as a murderer, because of a piece of jewelry?"

"I couldn't very well get it back if the man got sent to prison, now could I? I had to come up with a name when I told the sheriff I saw who killed Slater, and yours was the first one to pop into my head."

Ty stared at her long and hard. "And just why would my name be the first one you thought of? We hadn't seen each other for a long time."

A flush appeared on her exposed bosom, then crept up her neck and cheeks. "A long time!" she declared indignantly. "It was only two weeks, two weeks to the day you refused my proposal."

He glared at her through squinted eyes. "Are you talking about the night you said you wanted to get married? Come on, Teddy, we both know you were just joking."

Her eyes flashed dangerously. "No, damn you, I wasn't joking."

Ty blinked in surprise. In all the time he'd known Teddy, he'd never heard her swear. "I don't get it. You always said you weren't the kind to settle down in one place, that marriage wasn't for you. I don't understand why you're sore at me for turning down your proposal."

"That's the problem with you, Ty. You didn't get a lot of things. You couldn't see what was right in front of your face. I used to think I wouldn't be happy settling down with one man. That changed after I met you." At his confused look, she added in a harsh whisper, "I loved you."

Pinching the bridge of his nose to ease the sudden pounding in his head, he took a deep breath. He dropped his hand and looked over at Teddy. "Listen, I didn't realize how you felt, or I wouldn't have treated your proposal so lightly. That still doesn't excuse what you did, dammit! *I'm* the one wanted for murder, but if you think you're the one who deserves an apology, then I'm sor—"

She lifted her hand to silence him. "Save your apologies, Ty. It's too late for them now."

"Fine," he snapped, then calmed himself before he said, "Will you tell me what happened that night?"

She stared at him in silence for several minutes, then finally nodded. In a low monotone, she told Ty about the night of Slater's death.

After she finished, Ty mulled over her story. Finally, he said, "What can I say to get you to tell the Waco sheriff the truth?"

Rising from the settee, she moved toward the door. "Nothing. I think it's time for you to leave."

The cold, sharp edge of fear settled in his stomach. "Are you telling me you won't change the statement you made?"

"That's exactly what I'm saying," she said, her voice rising in irritation. "I told you I'm determined to get my grandmother's brooch back, and I can't if the man who has it is behind bars." Waving him toward the door, she added, "Now, good day, Ty."

Swallowing the retort he would have liked to make, he rose and stalked to the door. As he passed Teddy, he said, "You haven't seen the last of me." Giving her a chilling smile, he left her suite of rooms.

Teddy flinched at the sound of the door slamming shut. Walking into the bedroom, she sank onto the chair in front of the dressing table. Her mouth puckered in a slight moue, she stared at her reflection. She'd wondered what it would be like to see Ty again. The meeting hadn't been exactly as she'd envisioned.

She'd expected to feel more of the pain she'd experienced when Ty rejected her marriage proposal. There was no heartache, no great need to throw herself into his arms and beg him to change his mind. Strange, he no longer affected her the way he had in the past.

Absently pushing the hairpins back into the coils of her upswept hair, she realized she might have overreacted in Waco. If she hadn't learned that young couple outside Slater's room were newlyweds, or seen how solicitous the man was to his bride after she'd suffered the shock of seeing a dead man, perhaps Teddy would have handled things differently. The love and happiness reflected on their faces made her think of Ty. *It could have been my honeymoon,* she thought, envious of the closeness they shared. Remembering the pain and humiliation of his turning down her proposal, then laughing about it, had been too much to bear on top of an already trying evening.

When the sheriff asked if she'd seen anyone in Slater's room, she knew she couldn't tell him the truth, or she'd never see her brooch again. She could have agreed with the others who hadn't seen anyone, but the argument she'd overheard between Ty and the dead man—coupled with her envy and anger—propelled her to say Ty's name.

Studying herself in the mirror, Teddy knew her anger and pain had faded, but she wasn't ready to forgive Ty. His rejection still rankled. Besides, her other reason for not telling the truth hadn't been resolved: recovering her brooch. That was about to change; the man who'd cheated her out of the pin, Foster Gorman, was in Galveston. As soon as she came up with a foolproof plan, her grandmother's brooch would be back in her jewel box.

Arriving back at the Old Chicago House Hotel, Ty found Sassy eating lunch in the dining room. He slipped his arm around her waist and leaned close. "If you're finished, let's get out of here," he murmured.

"Ty, what is it?" she asked when they were outside the hotel. "Did you see Teddy? What did she say?"

"I'll tell you everything, but first I want to get away from here. Let's go to the beach."

He remained quiet during the ride across the island. When the streetcar stopped at the Beach Hotel, Ty jumped out, then turned to help Sassy.

After walking along the shore of the gulf side of Galveston for a few minutes, Sassy could stand the silence no longer. "Are you going to talk to me?" she demanded softly.

Lifting his face to the moist breeze coming from the thunderheads gathering to the west, he acted as if he hadn't heard her. "There's a storm brewing. Could be a bad one."

"Dammit, Ty. I don't want to hear about the weather. Tell me what happened."

In spite of his somber mood, Ty smiled at her sudden display of temper. Remembering his conversation with Teddy, his amusement fled. He stopped and turned to face Sassy.

"I found Teddy, and I talked to her."

"And?"

Ty cleared his throat. "I told you about the time she proposed to me, didn't I?"

"Yes."

"Well, it seems I took her wrong. I thought she was kidding, but Teddy really——"

"Wanted to marry you," Sassy said, cutting him off.

Ty nodded. "I thought I knew her better than that."

"Is that why she said you killed that man, because you didn't take her proposal seriously?"

Staring out over the choppy ocean, he exhaled wearily. "That was part of it. Teddy had an emerald brooch that belonged to her grandmother. She called it her good luck charm, and never sat down at a gambling table without it. That night in Waco, I didn't know it, but she was in the saloon when I confronted Slater. All I could think about was telling him to stay off the Circle B. I never noticed her at one of the other tables.

"Anyway, Teddy had been playing poker and lost her brooch to one of the other players. She found out later she'd been cheated, and went looking for the man to demand he return her brooch. As it turned out he was staying in the same hotel as Slater, and when Teddy arrived at the man's room, she heard voices raised in anger across the hall. The door was ajar enough to see inside. Two men, one of them the man she'd come to see, were exchanging some heated words. Hiding in the shadows, she heard a thud and then only silence. Before she could react, the door flew open, and the man with her brooch raced from the room. After a minute or two, she moved to the open doorway. The second man lay stretched out on the floor in a pool of blood."

"Slater?" Sassy asked, pushing a wisp of windblown hair off her face.

"Yeah. Seeing a dead man momentarily shocked her. She didn't realize she was no longer alone in the hallway, until she heard a woman scream. Teddy came to her senses and found a man trying to comfort his very distraught wife. Then the hall filled with more people, drawn by the scream. While they waited for the sheriff, Teddy realized that everyone else had arrived on the scene *after* the man who killed Slater fled from the room."

"If no one else saw the real killer, why didn't she tell the sheriff she hadn't seen anyone either?"

Ty shrugged. "I can't say for sure. She mumbled something about finding out the woman who screamed and her husband were on their honeymoon. I'm not sure what that had to do with anything, but she said they made her think of me."

"You spurned her proposal," Sassy whispered.

He gave her a confused look. "What?"

She swallowed the sudden lump in her throat. She knew how Teddy must have felt, seeing someone else living the life she wanted. "Naming you as the killer was a way to get even for your turning her down."

After a long pause, he nodded, then said, "You're probably right, but there was more to it than revenge against me. She also wanted to make sure the real killer stayed out of jail. Teddy has a good head on her shoulders, and she had it all figured out. She knew there were other witnesses to the argument I'd had with Slater. With such a perfect motive, I became the prime suspect. And besides, if the sheriff had an eyewitness to the crime, he wouldn't bother looking any further. Which means, as long as Teddy continued to say I killed Slater, she could go after the real killer, and not worry about having the law snatch him away before she got her brooch back."

Seeing the despair on his face, Sassy said, "You can't give up, Ty. Maybe if you let her think about it for a while, then go see her again, she'll change her mind."

He gave her a weak smile, silently wishing he could keep such a positive attitude. He didn't believe giving Teddy time to think about the situation would change anything. She was nearly as tenacious as Sassy when it came to doing what she wanted. Wrapping his arm around Sassy's shoulders, he pulled her against him. Not wanting her to know the depth of his dejection, he smiled again and said, "Maybe she will."

Twenty-six

On the second morning after his visit to Teddy's hotel room, Ty made a decision. He would take Sassy's suggestion and see Teddy again. This time he'd offer to help her get her brooch back. Knowing how much she valued the emerald pin, he hoped she'd accept so he'd have something to keep him busy. Sitting around waiting to see if she had a change of heart would drive him mad. He headed for Teddy's hotel, hoping he could convince her to let him help.

Teddy opened the door to him, a slight frown marring her otherwise smooth face. "What is it this time, Ty?"

Ignoring her petulant tone, he strode purposefully into the room. "I came to offer my help in retrieving your grandmother's brooch."

Eyeing him suspiciously, she said, "Why?"

"Since I'm involved in this up to my neck—if you get my drift—I think I should be allowed to help save it."

One thin, reddish gold eyebrow arched. "You think that, do you?"

He flashed her a perturbed look, then said, "You know I'm good at tracking people down. That was my job for seven years."

"Hmm," she replied, sitting down on the settee. "Yes, you were good. I just don't know if . . ."

Ty ran a hand impatiently through his hair. "Come on, Teddy, I *can* help you. Admit it. Once I return your brooch to you, there'll be no need for you to continue protecting the bastard who cheated you, and you can clear my name."

"I should have known," she said, her annoyance growing, "you'd have your own selfish reasons for offering to help."

"Selfish? I wouldn't call saving my own skin selfish. Look at this from my perspective. If you were wanted for a murder you didn't commit, wouldn't you be willing to do whatever was necessary to clear your name?"

She tapped her fingers thoughtfully against one arm of the settee. "I suppose you're right. Just let me think about it for a minute." While Ty nervously paced, Teddy silently considered his request. Foster Gorman was the reason she'd come to Galveston, so she had no need of Ty's skills at hunting people down. And as for her brooch, she didn't need his help with that either. *I'm quite capable of getting it back on my own,* she thought irritably. *If he continues to hang around, constantly nagging at me to let him help, he'll only get in my way.* She wished he would go away and let her get on—Say! Maybe he could help after all.

Glancing up at him, she smiled brightly. "All right, Ty, I've decided to accept your offer."

He hurried over to where she sat. "Great." Sitting down opposite her, he leaned forward in anticipation. "Now, who is this man? What does he look like? What kind of—"

Teddy held up one hand to stop the questions he rattled off. "I'll get to all of that in a minute. First of all, you'll

307

need to leave Galveston. I want you to look for him in Houston."

"I want you to take Kitty and Juan, and go to your father's ranch," Ty said over his shoulder, while stuffing some clothes into a carpetbag.

"What? What are you talking about?" Sassy replied, her brow furrowed with confusion.

"I want you to go to San Antonio as soon as possible. Teddy agreed to let me help her find the man who has her brooch. I'm leaving for Houston tonight."

"Houston? Ty, you're not making any sense."

Straightening from his packing, he turned to face her. "Teddy thinks the man is in Houston, so I'm going there to check it out. I'll be gone for a couple of days, maybe longer. I don't like the idea of leaving you, Kitty, and Juan here alone, so you're taking them to the Star. I'll rest easier, knowing you're all safe." The idea of being separated from Sassy hit him like a fist in the pit of his stomach, the breath nearly knocked from him. He pulled her into his arms and held her close. He wished she could stay, but he knew sending her home was the best choice. "You'll leave Galveston on the first available train."

"I want to stay," she said, her voice muffled against his chest.

"No, you're leaving." He inhaled the spicy scent of her hair, savoring the smell, committing it to memory, in case—No! He wouldn't consider that possibility.

Pushing away from him, Sassy looked into his face. She saw the determination hardening his jaw, but ignored it. "Don't tell me what to do, Ty Beaumont. I've been with you for almost two months, and I've taken care of myself just fine. I even saved your life in Laredo. I'm going to stay, and that's that."

"The hell you will," Ty roared, her contrary nature agitating his already strained nerves and priming his temper to near exploding. "You will do—"

"I'm not afraid to stay here," she interrupted, arms crossed under her bosom, chin lifted in defiance.

Inhaling a deep calming breath, he said, "I know you're not. That isn't the issue." When she started to open her mouth, he quickly added, "I know what you're going to say, but it won't change my mind. Sassy, I couldn't live with myself, if something happened to you." He wanted to convince her by saying he loved her, but couldn't bring himself to say the words. He clung to the notion that if she never knew how he felt, she wouldn't feel his loss so deeply if he divorced her.

She stared at him for several seconds, unsure what to make of his explanation. Something didn't ring true. Whatever it was, it stayed just beyond her grasp. She loved this man, in spite of his determination to send her away, and she wanted to stay and help. Back on the Dublin Star, she'd have no way of helping. She had to remain in Galveston.

Seeing the stubborn tilt of her chin lift even more, he said, "Sassy, I'm serious. I want you to take Kitty and Juan, and leave town as soon as possible."

When she saw the look on his face, her protest died. He'd never listen to her arguments. Still, she didn't want to leave. Wait! Maybe there was a way. "Okay, Ty," she finally said, "I'll see that Kitty and Juan get to my parents' ranch."

He blew out the breath he'd been holding in preparation for another volley of her attempts to change his mind. "Good. You can leave on tonight's train with me, that way we can ride together as far as Houston."

"No," she nearly shouted. "I mean, Kitty and I can't possibly be ready by tonight. We have a lot to pack. You go ahead and leave tonight. There's another train in the morning."

Relieved she'd accepted his decision with no further argument, he said, "Okay, if that's how you want it."

Standing on the railroad platform, Kitty looked at Sassy, still thinking her friend must have taken leave of her senses. "Are ya sure ya won't change yer mind? Ty will skin ya alive, if he finds out what y'all are doing."

Sassy smiled, but didn't comment on her friend's prediction. Instead, she said, "I know what I'm doing, Kitty. Quit worrying. Everything will be fine, you'll see."

"But what am I gonna say ta your papa and stepmama when Juan and I get ta their ranch? I ain't never met those folks, and they ain't gonna take kindly to a former saloon girl and an orphaned boy showing up on their doorstep."

"Kitty, you're all worked up for nothing," Sassy replied, handing her an envelope. "Here, take this. It's a letter I wrote to my father, explaining everything. Just give it to him, okay?"

As she watched Kitty tuck the letter into her handbag, a lump formed in her throat at having to say goodbye. Kitty had become a close friend, and she'd miss her. Swallowing the tears threatening to make her lose control, she said, "You best get on board."

Kitty nodded, her own eyes brimming with tears.

Turning to Juan, Sassy smiled at the boy who tugged on her maternal heartstrings. "You take good care of

Domino, hear?" At his solemn nod, she pulled him into her arms for a fierce hug. "You mind Kitty, and be a good boy."

He looked up at her and gave her a beaming smile. *"Sí,* I will be good, *Señora* Sassy. I will miss you and *Señor* Ty."

"I know you will, and we'll miss you, too," she said, ruffling his hair playfully. "I promise, we'll see you soon, Half-pint," she added, praying she wouldn't have to go back on her word.

"Come on, Juan," Kitty said in a choked whisper, reaching for his hand. "We'd best get on that train, 'fore it leaves without us."

Sassy gave each of them one last hug, then watched them step up into the passenger car.

After the train pulled away from the station, she waited until it disappeared across the bay bridge. Sighing heavily, she headed back to the hotel, unsure of how to fill her time until Ty returned. If only she could do something to help him. Since she'd never seen Teddy Fitzsimmons and Ty had never described what the woman looked like, Sassy didn't see much chance of finding a way to lend her assistance before he got back.

Kit Dancer followed Sassy at a distance, crossing Water Street, then up Twenty-fifth Street. He wondered what was going on. Ty left town the night before, and Sassy had just put Kitty and the boy on a train. *Now what?* he thought. *Do I go after Beaumont, or stay and see what the woman claiming to be his wife is up to?* What he should do, he realized, was forget about the reward on Beaumont's head. The money he'd get for taking the man in would barely cover what he'd already

311

shelled out in expenses. Plus, the case had already taken too much time. In a business where time meant money, Kit knew when to throw in the towel. Yet he found the whole situation much too intriguing to walk away from.

Deciding Sassy wouldn't remain in Galveston unless Ty planned to return, Kit made a decision to stay as well.

Bright Sky's second train ride wasn't as distressing as his first, but he still didn't like the white man's way of travel. He'd watched every move of the man who called himself James Beauregard since they'd left Laredo, and had yet to discover what danger the man faced. And when the man had boarded another train, Bright Sky was there to make the same ride.

Staring across the big water the *tivo* called the Gulf of Mexico, his thoughts continued to dwell on the man his visions had predicted he would meet. Bright Sky had followed him around Galveston, from one hotel to another, until the yellow-haired man found the one he sought. What did the woman with hair like the skin of *Cona* have to do with the one called Beauregard?

Bright Sky was certain the man and the raven-haired woman were married, at least they would be considered married by the Comanche, since they shared the same sleeping place. Perhaps the red-haired woman was another wife to the yellow-haired man. Comanche tradition allowed a man to have as many wives as he could buy and support. But he'd never seen the custom among the *tivo*.

And there was also the mystery of the *tao-yo*. The young boy obviously had mixed blood, likely not family to any of the three adults he traveled with. So, why would they take him along?

Bright Sky didn't have the answers to the relationships between these people, nor was finding the answers important. He knew his guardian spirit would reveal what he needed to know, when the time was right. He must practice the patience all Comanche were taught from a very early age. He had never had trouble following the teachings of the Great Spirits. Yet, for the first time, he felt impatience chafe at him: impatience to end his vision-induced mission, impatience to return to the simple life he cherished.

The morning after Teddy sent Ty to Houston under the pretext of helping her, she sat before her dressing table. Carefully scrutinizing her face, she checked for any new crowsfeet or tiny wrinkles that would require extra attention when she applied her makeup. At thirty she had to take special care with her appearance. She didn't want to look old before her time.

Finally satisfied with her daytime, nongambler look, she chose a pair of kidskin shoes and a jacket-bodice dress with long, close-fitting sleeves for her outing. Pinning a matching, decorated bonnet in her hair, she left her hotel, the waterfront her destination. The moist breeze would be good for her complexion, while her lace-trimmed parasol would shield her face from the harsh sun.

Teddy strolled down to Galveston Bay, walking out onto one of the less-busy wharves sticking out into the water. The cries of sea gulls and the groans of ships rubbing against the docks holding them fast made Teddy think of New Orleans. She'd spent a lot of time there. Perhaps she should go back. To do what? She still had family in Louisiana, but they didn't approve of her gambling, so there was no point in going.

When she'd first become a professional gambler, she thought it was an exciting way to make a living, until a man came along who would marry her and carry her away from the hoopla of saloons and gaming rooms. *Hah!* she scoffed silently. *What a starry-eyed fool I was.*

After a while, she'd realized gambling was in her blood, and she couldn't give it up for any reason, even a man. And no man wanted a professional gambler for a wife. Then she'd met Ty, and began to think perhaps she could have everything she wanted. Ty was different; her gambling didn't bother him, and she thought he truly cared for her. She'd even swallowed her pride and proposed to him. It would have been perfect, except he'd turned her down flat.

Realizing the sting of his rejection hurt more than her broken heart, Teddy knew she'd only tried to convince herself that she was in love with Ty, because of her silly pipe dream. Oh, she cared for Ty, perhaps even loved him a little, which had been easy to do since he'd treated her better than most men she met. *That's in the past,* she silently scolded herself. *Foster Gorman is who I have to think about.*

Teddy contemplated how to get her brooch away from Gorman. She could just walk up to him and demand he return it, but she had no way to prove the brooch belonged to her. *I could offer to pay him for it, but that goes against my principles. Besides, there's no guarantee he'll accept,* she thought miserably. She doubted he'd let her sit in on a game where he was one of the players, eliminating the possibility of winning the brooch back fair and square. That left only one option: she'd have to come up with a plan as devious as his cheating her. Having sent Ty off to Houston under the delusion of helping her, she had to come up with a plan quickly. Ideas swirling in her head, she turned to leave the wharf.

Suddenly famished from the walk and stimulating gulf air, Teddy headed up Twenty-fifth Street. She'd find a place to eat, then return to her hotel room for a nap. An afternoon nap always refreshed her before going out for the evening. Remembering she hadn't gone out since arriving in Galveston so as not to scare Gorman away, she slowed her pace. *I must come up with a plan to get my brooch away from that low-down cheat.*

She selected the Bon-Ton Restaurant on Market Street for her noon meal. Stepping through the door, she hesitated. She hated to eat alone. A young woman in the same circumstance caught Teddy's attention. Moving through the restaurant, she stopped next to the woman's table. "Would you mind if I joined you?"

A voice jarred Sassy from her thoughts. She looked up to find a woman, older than herself, elegantly dressed, with flaming red hair and the greenest eyes she'd ever seen. Grateful for the diversion from her thoughts of how to help Ty, she smiled. "I'd like that very much. My name is Sassy." She waved to the chair opposite her. "Please, have a seat."

"Thank you, Sassy." After settling her skirts around her, the woman returned the smile, then said, "Call me Dora." Although a gambler by night, her good breeding brought out a different persona during the day, one the name Teddy didn't suit. Wanting something more in keeping with a cultured, mature lady, she'd chosen the name her father had always called her. Teddy thought it appropriate for her daytime activities, and used it on those occasions.

"Nice to meet you, Dora," Sassy replied, unable to stop staring at the woman's lovely face. "Do you live in Galveston?" she asked at last.

"No, I'm just visiting. What about you?"

"Me, too." Sassy fell silent. She'd never been any good at small talk, especially with such a refined lady. Before she could think of anything else to say, their waiter came to the table. Grateful for the interruption, she studied Dora while the woman gave the man her order. Sassy had never seen such smooth skin nor such radiant hair. Old feelings of inadequacy as a woman flooded back. She wondered if she'd ever get over feeling like a draggle-tailed scullion when facing the genuine article.

Noticing the look on Sassy's face, Dora gave her an encouraging smile. "Are you enjoying your stay here?"

Dora's openness soon made Sassy forget how intimidated she felt by the woman's beautiful looks and impeccable manners. By the time they finished dessert, they were chatting like old friends.

"Have you seen the Beach Hotel?" Sassy asked.

"Yes, I took a streetcar over to see it yesterday. It's quite impressive."

As they prepared to leave the restaurant, Sassy didn't feel like going back to an empty hotel room. "Dora, can we do something together this afternoon?"

"I'd like that. How about if I pick you up at three? Where are you staying?"

"My husband and I are at the Old Chicago House Hotel. Well, actually, I'm the only one there now. James, my husband, had to go out of town for a few days."

Hiding her surprise at learning Sassy was married,

something she hadn't mentioned until now, Dora said, "The Old Chicago House is on the Strand, isn't it?"

Sassy nodded absently.

Dora gave her a quick sidelong glance, sensing the reason for her sudden preoccupation. "How long have you been married?"

"Since March."

"March? Why, you're still newlyweds," Dora said, a slight catch in her voice. "How could your husband go off and leave you so soon after your wedding?"

"He had some very important business to take care of," she replied with a sigh.

Something in her tone of voice touched Dora's heart, a longing for the man she loved. Not wanting to embarrass her new friend, or patronize her by saying 'I know how you feel,' instead she said, "You love him a lot, don't you?"

"Yes. I just wish . . ."

"You wish what?"

"Never mind. What shall we do this afternoon?"

"I don't know, what would you like to do?"

"I saw some people on Broadway yesterday riding bicycles. They looked like they were having a great time. I'd really like to try bicycling."

"Bicycling? I don't—"

"Oh, come on, Dora, where's your sense of adventure? Say you'll go. It'll be fun."

Dora threw back her head and laughed. "All right, Sassy. I may live to regret it, but I'm game to try."

Twenty-seven

Sassy lounged on an upholstered chair in Dora's sitting room, casually swinging one leg back and forth from its position over a chair arm. A small satchel sat on the floor beside the chair. "How are you feeling today, Dora?"

"Don't ask," she replied, entering the sitting room. "I soaked in a hot bath for over an hour, otherwise I might not be able to move." She stopped in front of Sassy's chair. A frown of irritation moved fleetingly across her face. Having known Sassy for less than twenty-four hours, Dora had begun to see the depth of the unreserved, carefree nature this woman possessed. Strangely, she liked Sassy all the more for it, so she made no comment on her unladylike pose. "How about you? How are you faring after our bicycling outing yesterday?"

Understanding the unspoken berating in Dora's expression, Sassy's cheeks warmed. "I'm fine," she said, removing her leg from the chair arm and smoothing her skirt. "Must be you don't ride horses. If you did, your muscles wouldn't be so sore."

Dora stared across the room thoughtfully. "No, I don't ride. In fact, I don't really like horses very much. If riding a horse is like the pounding I took yesterday, I'm

glad I don't care for the beasts. My bum will never be the same," she said, gingerly rubbing the injured area.

Sitting down with great care, she nodded toward the satchel at Sassy's feet. "What do you have planned for today? Nothing too physical, I hope."

Sassy laughed. "It's physical all right, but not for you. I'll do all the work. You just have to sit, or stand," she added with a smile. "And watch."

Dora's eyebrows rose in question.

"I'm racing at Oleander Park today."

Her eyebrows lifting even higher, Dora said, "You're not serious?"

Sassy shrugged. "Why not? I've been riding since I was old enough to trade my tricornered pants for a pair of britches."

Dora chuckled. "You do have a unique way with words. So, what's in the satchel?"

Her cheeks flaming again at the rebuke she read into Dora's comment, she mumbled, "My Grunt clothes."

"I beg your pardon?"

"The clothes I wore when I went to the Gray Mule in San Antone with my brothers."

Dora's eyes sparked with interest. "The Gray Mule?"

"It's a saloon. I dressed like a man, so no one would know who I was. My brothers called me Grunt 'cause of the noise I made the first time I tried to talk like a man."

"Why did you have to dress like a man? Women are allowed in most saloons these days. I've spent a lot of time in both gambling halls and saloons, and believe me, I never had to dress like a man to get into any of them."

Sassy wanted to tell Dora that with her beauty and manners, it's no wonder she had no trouble. Instead she said, "Even before I went to the Gray Mule, I dressed like my brothers. I tried wearing a dress a time or two, but I hated it. So wearing britches to get into a saloon was natural. Besides, the place isn't anything fancy. It's just a place where the locals go to cut the dust from their throats, or play a friendly game of cards, or go upstairs with one of the——" She cleared her throat. "Anyway, I liked playing poker, and I wanted to know what went on in the Gray Mule. I wasn't about to dress like a harlot to——" Her gaze snapped to Dora's face. "I didn't mean to imply you're a . . . one of those women because you go into saloons."

"I know you didn't," Dora said, smiling her encouragement for Sassy to continue her story.

"Besides, my brothers wouldn't have taken me to the saloon, unless I went as Grunt. They got a real hoot out of me fooling their friends."

"Your family approved of such behavior?"

"No one knew except my brothers. I did everything with them, so they'd never squeal to our father. I'm sure he would have had a thing or two to say if he'd found out. Thankfully, he never did."

"So you plan to wear this Grunt character's costume and ride at Oleander Park?"

"You bet!"

"Then you have a horse lined up to ride?"

"Yes. The owner of the livery where Blarney and Joker——" Seeing a strange look settle on Dora's face, she said, "Blarney is my horse; Joker belongs to my husband. The owner told me about a man who needs someone to ride his horse in today's race. The man's regular rider took a fall a couple days ago and broke his arm."

"And you volunteered to take his place," Dora managed to say, hoping Sassy would forget about her reaction to hearing about a horse named Joker. Surely other people had chosen that name for their mounts.

"Sort of. I told the man I knew someone who could replace the injured rider, but I didn't tell him that someone is me."

"Don't you think the owner might be angry when he finds out you're a woman?"

"He won't. I don't plan to tell him." Not explaining that she couldn't risk having Ty find out about her exploits when he returned, Sassy simply said, "Not even after I win."

Dora smiled. "You're pretty confident."

"The livery owner said the horse was the race favorite. This morning I went to see for myself. He's a long-legged beauty named O'Shaughnessy's Luck. As soon as I heard his name, I knew we couldn't lose. Like Papa always said, there's no better combination than Irish blood running through the veins of both horse and rider. After I took him out for a run, I was even more convinced. His feet barely touched the ground. Shaughnessy can't lose. So, are you going to come?"

Seeing the confidence shining in Sassy's eyes and the determined set of her chin, Dora saw no point in trying to dissuade her. She smiled, then said, "You bet."

Sassy returned the smile, pleased her friend wasn't going to argue. She could ride as well as most men, and with a horse like Shaughnessy beneath her, she intended to prove it.

"I told you I'd win," Sassy said triumphantly, her face and clothes spattered with mud from the wet track.

"I never doubted you for a minute," Dora said. "Follow me. I have a carriage waiting."

After settling in the covered carriage, Dora smiled at the energy radiating from her friend, amazed that even covered with grime Sassy looked lovely. "We have to celebrate," she announced, "Let's go out to dinner. You'll be my guest, of course."

Sassy's brow furrowed slightly. "I can't allow you to spend your money on me."

"Don't be silly. I won rather handsomely by betting on you and Shaughnessy. Since no one else wanted to put their money on an unknown rider, I got unbelievably good odds. If it weren't for you, I wouldn't have the money. So it's only right we both reap the benefits."

"Okay, if you insist," Sassy said.

"Yes, I insist."

Dora's talk about betting on her at Oleander Park made Sassy's thoughts stray from her successful debut as a jockey to something Dora had said earlier. "Do you gamble a lot?"

Meeting Sassy's ingenuous gaze, Dora said, "Yes, that's how I support myself. Does that shock you?"

"No," Sassy said, then quickly added, "Just because it didn't shock me, doesn't mean I think your being a gambler makes you any less of a lady or . . . uh . . . a loose woman. Hells' bells, I'm not saying this very well."

Chuckling at Sassy's obvious frustration, she said, "You said it just fine. I'm a lady who happens to make a living as a professional gambler."

The carriage gave a lurch, then pulled to a stop in front of Dora's hotel. After stepping from the vehicle, Dora turned back to Sassy. "Why don't you come up to my suite for a bath, then we can go out for dinner. It'll save you the trouble of going to your hotel and having to come back later."

Sassy nodded, grateful for the change in topic. While

soaking in the tub in Dora's sumptuous private bath, she thought about what Dora had revealed. She'd never considered female professional gamblers to be true ladies, yet Dora seemed to buck that tradition. Sassy had never met a more beautiful, finer dressed, better mannered woman—the epitome of being a lady. Yet, Dora's chosen profession of gambler was completely at odds with Sassy's perception of how Ty would define a lady.

She rested her head against the back of the tub and sighed. Trying to be a lady was so confusing. She wanted to be like Dora, but didn't want to disappoint Ty—which she surely would, if he knew she'd patterned herself after a professional lady gambler.

When the water cooled, Sassy forced herself out of the tub. While dressing, she made a decision. Becoming a gambler was not something she aspired to, but asking Dora questions about her lifestyle certainly wouldn't be out of line. And if she picked up some ladylike behavior alone the way, so much the better.

Entering the sitting room, she found Dora looking at an issue of *Godey's Lady's Book*. "Can I ask you some questions?" she asked, taking a seat in the opposite chair.

"You certainly may."

"How long have you been a gambler?"

Putting the magazine aside, Dora settled more comfortably in her chair. "I started when I was fifteen, but I didn't become what you would call a professional, until I was eighteen. I started as a monte dealer on a Mississippi riverboat. Then after a few years, I quit the riverboats and set out on my own. I've been traveling around, playing poker ever since."

"It must be an exciting life."

"Yes, sometimes, but it can also be lonely. Different towns, different hotel rooms, different gambling halls,

323

they're all so much alike, you lose track of where you are from one day to the next."

"There must be excitement, though," Sassy insisted. "Doesn't that make all the other worth it?"

Smiling at Sassy's thirst for adventure, she said, "Yes, there's excitement: feeling Lady Luck shine down on me, anticipating the turn of the next card, the thrill of being dealt a winning hand, the exhilaration of coming away with a fat purse."

"Poker's your specialty?"

"Sometimes I try my hand at keno, or the roulette wheel, but yes, as you put it, poker is my specialty."

"Is that why you're in Galveston?" Before Dora could answer, she said, "Gambling's illegal here."

"Yes, I know. Although there are games to be found, if you know where to look," she answered, deftly side-stepping Sassy's original question. "How do you know gambling's illegal in Galveston?"

"Ty told me when we first got here."

Dora's breath caught in her throat. "Ty?" she finally managed to ask.

"My husband, Ty," Sassy replied glumly, silently chastising herself. *Dammit, why can't I control what comes out of my mouth?*

"I thought you said his name was James," Dora said carefully. Hoping her voice didn't betray the turmoil inside her, she silently wondered if it could be possible.

"I did. Um, James Beauregard is the name my husband uses while he gambles. He . . . um . . . doesn't want his family to know he's . . . um . . . gambling, so he uses a fake name." Hoping her explanation didn't sound as lame as she knew it to be, she kept her face averted while waiting for Dora's response.

After studying Sassy for several seconds, she said,

"Why don't you tell me about your husband?" For a moment, Dora thought the younger woman wasn't going to answer, then she lifted her head and began speaking.

"We met on my family's ranch near San Antone. I'd never met a man like Ty. I treated him like a squashed lizard at first, but then, I felt this kinda pull toward him. It wasn't something I wanted to feel. But it was there all the same, and I couldn't make it go away. I finally figured out it was—" Her face flaming, Sassy fell silent.

"Love?" Dora suggested softly.

"Yes. When I realized I loved Ty, I wanted to prove to him that we should be together. He wasn't very cooperative."

"How's that?"

"He went out of his way to avoid me. And when he couldn't do that, he always made up some reason to excuse himself, so he wouldn't have to be in the same room with me. Then, when I found out my friend Greta's parents planned to have a party, I knew it was the only chance I might get."

"What did you do?"

"I . . . um . . . took Ty into the barn and asked him to—" Sassy jumped to her feet, unable to admit the rest. Moving across the room, she murmured, "A priest married us the next day."

"Ah, I see."

"I don't care how our marriage came about, we're man and wife, and I love my husband," Sassy declared, her back ramrod stiff.

"I can see you do," Dora replied. "Doesn't he love you?"

Sassy's shoulders slumped forward. "I'm not sure. Sometimes I think he must, or he wouldn't—" She hastily cleared her throat. "He's never told me how he feels."

325

"You have to be patient with men, Sassy. They don't always recognize how they feel, or else aren't willing to admit it, until long after those feelings began."

Sassy looked over at Dora, her eyes wide with hope. "You've had so much more experience with men than me, do you really think so?"

Although she should have been peeved at Sassy's inadvertent insult regarding their age difference, Dora gave her a gentle smile. "Yes, I think so. Of course, I can't say for sure in your case, but for men in general, that's true."

Sassy nodded her understanding, her mood lightening. "I hope you're right about Ty. He told me about his ranch, the Circle B, and how much he looked forward to quitting the life he'd led before we met, and settling down on the ranch. He wants to raise horses, and I want so much to help him. I want to make a home for us, and to start a family," she finished quietly.

"I thought you said he was a gambler?"

Realizing she was going to have to tell at least part of the truth, Sassy moved to the sitting room window. She pushed back the lace curtain and looked out. "Dora, I'm going to tell you something that I shouldn't be telling you, but I feel I can trust you. Do you promise to keep it just between us?" Glancing over her shoulder, she waited for Dora's response. At her nod of agreement, Sassy shifted her gaze back out the window. "My husband is only posing as a gambler. Ty is really a Ranger. He's looking for someone, a gambler who's supposedly here in Galveston." Thinking perhaps Dora's being a gambler might prove useful, she decided to take a chance and reveal one more piece of information. "Perhaps you know the person Ty's looking for—a woman named Teddy?"

Dora said nothing; she couldn't. What she'd suspected was true.

When Dora didn't respond, Sassy dropped the curtain and turned from the window. She sucked in a surprised breath. Although Dora's skin was very pale, she had blanched even more. Her rouge looked startlingly dark on her cheeks. "Dora, what is it?"

"Nothing," she said in a raspy voice, "Just a little indigestion. I guess something I ate didn't agree with me. If you'll excuse me, I'm going to lie down for a few minutes." Rising onto quaking legs, Dora somehow managed to make it to her bedroom.

She dropped onto the edge of the mattress, her head reeling with disbelief. Ty Beaumont was married!

Stretching out on the bed, she grappled with what she'd just learned. How could he, she ranted silently. *How could you turn me down, then marry the little chit sitting in the next room a few months later?* She wondered if he'd known Sassy while he had been seeing her. Dora didn't think so. Still, her pride wouldn't let her overlook the possibility.

She expected to feel jealousy or anger at learning Ty had taken someone else as his wife. She even tried to summon a hatred for Sassy. Her efforts failed. At the very least, she should want to boil the woman in oil for securing the position she had once coveted. Surprisingly, she felt no inclination to do so.

In spite of the shock she'd just received, she truly liked Sassy. And Dora could also see what must have attracted Ty to the spirited woman. He always did enjoy a challenge, and likely Sassy challenged him at every turn. Dora smiled at the thought, pleased with the idea of someone not kowtowing to Ty.

Her forehead furrowed slightly. Then, of course,

Sassy's age was another consideration, something else Ty no doubt found attractive. Rather than a woman three years his senior, he'd hitched himself to a younger, more vibrant female. Who could blame him for that?

After wrestling with her thoughts and recalling the soul-searching she'd done on the wharf several days earlier, Dora came to the same conclusion about Ty. At one time she'd loved him, or thought she did, and he'd turned her down. In retrospect, she was glad he had. Sassy was welcome to him and the—what was the name she'd used, oh yes—the Circle B. She could never live on a ranch, for heaven's sake. Nothing appealed to her any less than living around smelly horses. Her nose twitched at the thought.

She would never have considered proposing to Ty if she'd thought there was even an outside chance they would settle on a horse ranch. Her visions of their married live had always placed them in an elegant town house in Austin, or one of the other cities she visited on her travels. She also hadn't known he was about to retire from the Rangers and planned to take up ranching, when she proposed. If she had, she would have kept her mouth shut, letting their relationship continue the same course.

Swinging her feet off the bed, Dora sat up. As she set her hair to rights, she knew the time had come to be honest with Sassy *Beaumont*.

When she entered the sitting room, Sassy asked, "Are you feeling better?"

"Yes, much better, thank you. Are you ready for our celebration dinner?"

"Are you sure you're up to it? We don't have to go out."

"Nonsense. I feel fine. It's not every day a woman wins her first horse race," she said, thinking, *or learns that her dinner companion is the woman her husband is looking for.*

Twenty-eight

Dora remained unusually quiet during dinner. Even the bottle of wine she'd ordered for their celebration didn't put her in a festive mood, nor did it relax the tension surrounding her.

Sensing something amiss, Sassy took Dora's cue and said very little, the thrill of her victorious horse race fading under the somber cloud hanging over them.

When the waiter appeared to clear the last of their dishes, the clatter of china snapped Dora out of her lethargy. She clasped her hands tightly on the table in front of her, then said, "Sassy, there's something I have to tell you."

Her eyes wide with curiosity, Sassy waited for an explanation.

"On the day we met, I introduced myself as Dora. However, I neglected to tell you my given name. It's Theodora. Theodora Fitzsimmons. I'm also known as——"

"Teddy," Sassy murmured in a stunned whisper, before Dora could say the name.

"Yes. Teddy. The gambling world knows me as Teddy, and since I met Ty in a gambling hall, that's what he always called me."

Sassy stared at her dinner companion long and hard,

the expression on her face slowly changing from astonished disbelief to impish amusement. "Well, if that don't beat all," she said softly. "I wanted to meet you, but Ty wouldn't hear of it. As it turns out, I found you on my own and didn't even know it."

Dora smiled for the first time since leaving her hotel suite. "Yes, it appears fate has thrown us together. Though to what end, I don't know."

After a moment of silent contemplation, Sassy said, "I think I know why. We're supposed to work together to get your brooch back."

Her eyebrows arching, Dora replied, "What else did Ty tell you?"

A blush crept across Sassy's cheeks. "He said you lost your brooch to the cheating son of a—" She caught the warning look on Dora's face in time to change it to, "Biscuit who killed Benjamin Slater. He also told me you had several reasons for naming him as Slater's killer. One was to protect the real murderer, so you could get your brooch back, and the other was because . . ."

"The other was because . . . what?"

Sassy swallowed, then said in a torture-filled voice, "Because you wanted revenge for his turning down your marriage proposal."

Dora leaned back against her chair, tapping her fingers on the table. "That's true. His refusal really bruised my pride. I now realize a marriage between us would never have worked, but at the time, I saw accusing Ty as just revenge. Plus it was a way to give me the time I needed to retrieve my brooch. To be perfectly frank, Sassy, I never thought it would take this long. Foster Gorman has been a hard man to track down."

"I thought Ty said the man's name is Perkins."

Dora chuckled. "That's what I told Ty, to get him out

of my hair for a few days. Though it was kind of him to offer, I didn't need his help. I also knew he wouldn't take no for an answer, so I made up the story about a man named Perkins."

Sassy's eyes twinkled with mirth. "I take it the man being in Houston was another of your stories."

"I had to get Ty out of town. I didn't want him underfoot, perhaps accidentally doing something to scare off Gorman."

Sassy laughed, then quickly sobered. "You realize, of course, he's going to be madder than the devil himself when he gets back and finds out you lied."

"That's an understatement, I'm sure, but one I'm willing to face," Dora said with a smile. "The important thing is to get my brooch away from Gorman, before Ty returns."

"That doesn't give us much time."

Dora cocked her head to one side. "Us?"

"You said fate brought us together. So I'm going to help you," Sassy stated matter-of-factly.

Eyeing her carefully, Dora said, "Are you sure you want to help a woman who knew your husband intimately, and once thought she was in love with him?"

Her chin jutting forward, Sassy met her gaze. "You're the reason I met Ty. I admit knowing the two of you were involved is like being gut-shot. But if it weren't for your involvement, I wouldn't be married to him now. To my way of thinking, I owe you."

After a fit of hysterical laughter, Dora wiped her eyes, then smiled across the table at Sassy. "You're a treasure, Sassy, a real treasure. I wonder how many wives would say 'I owe you' to the woman who caused their husbands the anxiety and anger I've given Ty. Probably none, which makes you the rare exception. I hope Ty appreciates you."

Seeing the distress flash in Sassy's eyes, Dora reached across the table and squeezed one of her hands. "Give him time. Ty is a stubborn, infuriating man. But he'll come to recognize his feelings. He loves you, Sassy, I'm sure of it."

Sassy's lips curved in a thin smile. "I hope you're right."

Dora released her hand and gave it an encouraging pat. "Ty Beaumont would never have married you, if he hadn't already begun to care for you, believe me. I've known him for a long time, and nothing in this world could have made him take the wedding vows if he hadn't wanted to."

Silently praying Dora was correct, Sassy nodded. "What do you have planned for this Gorman?"

Dora poured more wine for each of them before answering. "I'm having a bit of a problem coming up with a plan. He knows me, so I have to be careful how I approach this. I've learned one thing about him that could be useful. Gorman isn't like most gamblers, who like to blend in with their surroundings. He dresses like a dandy, always preening and strutting like a peacock in front of a peahen. He considers himself a real lady-killer." She gave a huff of disgust. "That pompous popinjay is no more a ladies' man than I'm the Queen of Siam."

"So how do we get this piss-poor excuse for a man to cough up your brooch?"

Nearly choking on a sip of wine, Dora cleared her throat, then said, "He'll never allow me to sit in a poker game with him. As soon as he sees me, he'll know what I want, so winning my brooch back fairly is out of the question. Which leaves cheating or stealing as my only other options." Taking another sip of wine, she looked at Sassy to gauge her reaction to her next statement. "I've never resorted to cheating in my life. Everything I won has been because of my skill—or luck, if you will—but I never resorted to cheating. And I don't intend to start now. Not even for Grandmother's brooch."

Sassy's eyes widened at the implication of Dora's words. "You're going to steal it! This is getting even more exciting."

"Provided we don't get caught," she replied, realizing at some point she'd unconsciously accepted Sassy's offer to help.

Sassy waved one hand dismissively. "We won't. So tell me, what have you come up with so far, Dora? Or do you want me to call you Teddy?"

"Whichever you prefer."

Sassy chewed on her bottom lip, while giving Dora a thoughtful look. "I think I like Teddy better. Why do you use two different names anyway?"

Dora lifted her shoulders in a shrug. "I wanted a different image for when I wasn't gambling. And I didn't think Teddy sounded very ladylike."

"That's ridiculous. You're a lady no matter what name you go by."

Dora actually flushed at Sassy's praise. "Although there are many who would disagree with you, I thank you for that, Sassy. Now, let's get back to Gorman. I think the best way to approach him is to use his vanity to our advantage. He believes no woman can resist him. I want to play on that. The problem is the poor helpless female, who must appear to fall under his spell. I can't play the part unless I disguise myself. Even then I'm not sure it would work. Gorman is extremely shrewd, and would likely recognize me. The only other alternative is to have someone else take the role. Unfortunately, I don't know anyone in Galveston, who might be willing to star in my little production."

"I do. I'll do it."

Meeting Sassy's unflinching gaze, Teddy smiled. "Are you sure you know what you'd be getting yourself into? And what would Ty say if he found out?"

"I know perfectly well what I'm getting into, Teddy. By helping you, I'll be helping my husband, which is worth any price. And as for what he would say, I know he'd be angry, but," she flashed a devilish grin, "I'd make sure he got over it."

Draining her wine glass, Teddy said, "Drink up, we have plans to make."

Back at Teddy's hotel, Sassy listened carefully to her description of Foster Gorman. "He's tall and slim, probably in his late twenties, and wears his hair slicked back with pomade. He always wears a black broadcloth suit with tailored frock coat, ruffled white shirt, stiff wing collar, and a black bow tie. Every time I've seen him, he wore one of those brightly colored hand-painted vests, usually one with a gaudy hunting scene. That reminds me, if he reaches into his vest pocket, watch out. He carries a derringer, and from what I've heard, he isn't bashful about using it.

Sassy nodded, then said, "Ty said Slater died from a stab wound. Does Gorman carry a bowie knife with him, too?"

"If he does, it must be strapped to his calf or in his boot. Whenever Foster Gorman joins a poker game, he goes through the same routine. Like most of us gamblers, he's very superstitious. He makes a big production of taking off his coat and hanging it on the back of his

334

chair before taking his seat, which is how I know he doesn't carry a knife on his belt. Then, after he sits down, he lays his cigar case on the table to his left, stacks his poker chips in front of him, and finally adjusts his cuff-links, making sure they're aligned exactly the way he wants them."

"What a sissified ass," Sassy commented, bringing a chuckle from Teddy.

"Once he gets through with all his rigmarole and actually plays cards, how do I get him to leave the game?"

"Gorman loves poker, but I'm banking on his high opinion of himself and his reputation as a rake making him forget about gambling. I think once you show interest in a private liaison, he'll not hesitate to leave the poker table. He'll be too anxious to add another young pigeon to his list of conquests."

Sassy's brow wrinkled. "I'm not sure I know how to persuade him that I'm interested."

Teddy started to make a humorous remark, then realized Sassy was serious. Remembering her admission of how she'd trapped Ty into a compromising situation, Teddy said, "Surely something you did to attract Ty worked."

"I tried flirting, but like I told you, he went out of his way to avoid me."

"Perhaps because he was *too* attracted to you. Have you considered that possibility?"

Sassy gave the idea a moment of thought, then shook her head. "I guess it's possible, but I don't think so. He never gave me any indication he felt anything toward me except anger after I accused him of horse stealing."

"Horse stealing?"

Her cheeks burning, she shrugged. "The first time I saw him, I thought he was stealing my horse, but that's another story. Anyway, I don't know what I should do to

335

make Gorman think I want him. I'm not very good at female stuff," she added in a low whisper.

"Don't sell yourself short, Sassy. You're a beautiful young woman, with an earthy sensuality no man could resist if you play him right." Seeing the look on Sassy's face, she raised her hand to stop what Sassy was about to say. "I won't listen to your denial. Perhaps your skills as a woman haven't been finely honed, but you know enough to stir Gorman's interest. Try flirting with him. Send him secretive glances from across the room. Lean over the table, and let him have a teasing peek at your bosom. Walk behind his chair, brush against him, then move away before he can touch you. Tantalize him, but keep him at arm's length. What's dangled in front of his nose just beyond his reach, will be more appealing than what's handed to him directly. Does that make sense?"

Teddy's description of flirting sounded very similar to the night in El Paso, when Sassy had played a teasing game with Ty in an effort to improve his mood. That night she'd wanted the results to be an intimate liaison, but it would be different this time.

Sassy nodded, then said, "It's sort of like the teasing board in the covering yard. The stallion picked for the job gets to sniff the mares as they're paraded on the other side of the teasing board. By his reaction, you know which mares are in season. He can look and sniff all he wants, but the poor randy fella doesn't get to cover any of them. I always thought it was a dirty trick to play on a stallion, but I see its benefit in Gorman's case."

Teddy blinked, a dull flush staining her cheeks. She'd never heard anyone discuss horse breeding techniques. The women in her family weren't privy to such information. When she was able to speak, she said, "Yes, well, I'm glad you agree. Now, after you've caught his attention and he's ready to leave the poker table behind, you'll have to suggest a place for your secret assignation. He's been finding private games down on Market Street, and I've learned he'll be in a game at the Imperial Saloon tomorrow night. That's when you'll make your move. We'll get a room for you at one of the hotels in that part of town in the morning."

"What if he doesn't have your brooch with him?"

"He will. I caught sight of him in one of the saloons one night, after I first arrived in town. The fool is wearing my brooch as a lapel pin."

"You'd better tell me what your brooch looks like."

"The setting is heavy ornate gold. It's oval shaped with a scalloped edge, and has a large emerald in the center surrounded by tiny diamonds. You should have no trouble recognizing it, since it's a rather distinctive piece of jewelry."

"Once I get him into the room, then what?"

Seeing the apprehension on Sassy's features, Teddy smiled gently. "Don't worry, you won't have to suffer his attentions, although you may have to allow him a kiss or two in order to get him to the hotel. I don't care how you do it, but you have to convince him to leave the poker game and go with you, okay?"

"Yes. I'll figure out a way."

"Good. Once you get him to the room, you'll pour yourselves a drink, slipping a sleeping potion into his. When he's out cold, you can take my brooch and leave. Can you do that?"

Sassy nodded.

"Let's see, what else? Oh yes, before you leave, pour the rest of the bourbon down the sink—I'll make sure I get a room with a private bath. Oh, and take some money from his wallet, too."

"Why should I take his money? I don't intend to do anything to earn it."

"Of course not, but it should help convince him you were what you appeared to be."

"I'm not sure I follow"

"He'll wake up with a roaring headache, see the empty bourbon bottle, and think he drank too much. Then he'll find his much lighter wallet, think he paid for a night of enjoying your charms, and he'll blame the liquor for wiping out his memory. With all of that on his mind, hopefully he won't notice my brooch is no longer on his lapel. Even if he does, it won't matter anyway, because I intend to have the police arrest him before he leaves that room. Do you understand now?"

Yes. I don't like the idea of touching the bastard's money, but I'll do it."

"Good. Now for your costuming. It must be a *pièce de résistance.*"

"Piece of what?" Biting the inside of her lip to hold in a giggle, Teddy said, *"Pièce de résistance.* It means outstanding. Do you have an evening dress with a low décolletage?"

"I have the ones Ty had made for me in El Paso, when we spent our evenings in saloons."

"Bring them over here in the morning, so I can see if they need any alterations. From what I've seen of Gorman, he likes low-cut dresses revealing plenty of cleavage."

Sassy made a sound of distress, drawing Teddy's attention. "What is it?"

"This might not work after all. I . . . I don't . . . I mean, I'm not . . . Dammit, Teddy, I don't have a big bosom. Maybe you'd better find someone else."

Teddy crossed the room and wrapped an arm around

Sassy's shoulders. "Oh, my poor, dear innocent. Many woman who look like they're ready to pop right out of their gowns, aren't naturally that way!"

At Sassy's surprised look, she said, "It's a feminine trick, knowing how to make ourselves appear like we're better endowed. Even a woman with a small bosom— which yours definitely is not—can look much fuller and more rounded with the help of a corset."

"Corset? I don't think I could wear one of those contraptions. Is it really necessary?" she asked, horrified at the prospect. She'd fought first with Sheena, then with the seamstress in El Paso, about the necessity of wearing all the ridiculous female underclothes. Thankfully, she'd won those battles. However, she wasn't as confident about the outcome of this one.

At Sassy's distress Teddy laughed aloud. "Not to worry, dear girl, a corset won't kill you, and it's only a temporary inconvenience." Swinging Sassy around to the door, she said in a low voice, "I believe that's enough for tonight. I've quite filled your head with plenty to think about. I'll send my carriage for you tomorrow morning at nine."

Sassy had trouble falling asleep that night, her mind filled with Teddy's numerous instructions and visions of a corset squeezing her to death. It was past midnight before sleep finally released her from her thoughts.

She awoke at eight, surprisingly refreshed, then quickly bathed and dressed to await Teddy's carriage. Her evening dresses draped over her arm, she entered Teddy's hotel suite a little after nine.

"Good morning, Sassy," Teddy said, sweeping into the sitting room in a long flowing peignoir. "Oh good, you

339

brought your dresses. Hand them here, and let's see what you have."

After examining the dresses, Teddy selected a red silk. "Red is a wonderful color for you, and should easily catch Gorman's eye. I'll just lower the neckline, and it will be fine."

They spent the rest of the day going over their plans, until Teddy was satisfied Sassy knew them perfectly.

Finally it was time for Sassy to dress for the evening. Having no idea how to put on the corset Teddy insisted she wear, she accepted Teddy's offer to help.

Wrapping the boned and busked corset around the young woman, Teddy said, "Take a deep breath, Sassy. Good. Hold it, while I fasten the hooks down the back. No! Don't exhale yet. There, all done. Now turn around, so I can see how you look."

Sassy turned toward Teddy very carefully. It hurt to breathe, let alone move. "This corset's as tight as a bull's ass when the flies are biting," she muttered.

Teddy gave a peal of laughter. "You'll get used to it, I promise. Let's get your dress on, then you can look in the mirror."

Once the red silk was dropped over Sassy's head and smoothed into place, she walked to the full-length mirror. Her eyes widened in shock. Pushed up by the corset stays, her bosom looked round and plump, nearly spilling out of the lowered neckline of her dress. "My God, Teddy, is that really me?"

"Most assuredly. Ty's never seen you like this?" When Sassy shook her head, she murmured, "When he does, he'll never let you out of his sight."

"What?"

"Nothing. Come on, let's finish getting you ready."

Sassy sat carefully perched on the stool in front of

Teddy's dressing table, while Teddy arranged her hair, then applied her makeup.

"Do you know anything else about Gorman?" Sassy asked.

Her brow furrowed slightly with concentration as she outlined Sassy's eyes with kohl, Teddy said, "He's from somewhere in Georgia. Atlanta, I think. Other than that, I've told you all I know."

"Did you know him before the time he cheated you?"

"I'd seen him a time or two, since we share the same line of work. But, no, I didn't know him." Stepping back, she said, "There. Now turn towards me." Examining her work critically, Teddy announced, "Perfect."

Glancing at the clock, she took a deep breath. "It's time to go. Are you going to be all right?"

Sassy nodded, unable to get a word through her tight throat.

In their carriage on the way to the Imperial Saloon, Teddy went over everything one last time, then said, "Do you have the key I gave you to the room at the Atlantic Hotel?"

Sassy nodded.

"Remember, I'll be waiting in the adjoining room. If something goes wrong once you get there, just call out."

Sassy nodded again.

"Do you have the sleeping potion I gave you? Don't forget it takes a few minutes to work, so make sure you slip it into his drink as soon as you get to the hotel room. I'll make sure there's a full bottle of bourbon on the dresser."

"Yes, I remember."

Now that the time was at hand, a knot of nervous fright formed in Sassy's stomach. The closer the carriage got to the Imperial Saloon, the tighter the knot became. She knew she had to get a grip on herself, or she would fail Teddy. More importantly, she would fail Ty. That thought gave her the strength to give Teddy a bright smile, when they stopped in front of their destination.

"Next time I see you, I'll have your brooch," she murmured as she and Teddy hugged.

She smiled at the man who opened the carriage door and accepted his hand. Stepping lightly onto the sidewalk, she lifted her head and glided regally through the saloon doors.

Twenty-nine

Keeping Teddy's description of Foster Gorman in mind, Sassy had no trouble picking him out of the crowd in the private gaming room. "He looks like a damn banty rooster, all decked out in his finery, looking for a hen dumb enough to fall for him," she muttered under her breath.

She selected a place near Gorman's table, but out of his line of vision, to get a feel for her surroundings and observe her costar in the upcoming drama. Watching how he looked at the women passing near him—undressing them with his eyes, then flashing each a confident, knowing smile—Sassy wanted to retch. Someone should make mincemeat out of the oily bastard, she groused silently, her fingers itching to do the job herself.

Determined to pull off her charade successfully and knock Gorman's overinflated ego down a peg in the process, she moved closer.

She knew the exact moment he saw her. It was as if a hot burst of air had touched her, so heated was his gaze. She could actually feel his dark eyes moving over her in a thorough, almost intimate inspection. Her skin crawled with revulsion. Resisting the urge to cover her exposed bosom, she stopped across the table from Gorman and turned toward him. With chin held high she allowed him to finish his rude perusal, although she longed to slap the insolent grin off his face.

When his gaze finally rose above her cleavage, she forced her lips into a smile. She was thankful a table separated them, otherwise she might have given in to the urge to stuff her fist down his throat.

Trying to ignore Gorman's dark, penetrating stare, she watched several hands of poker, then slipped away from the table. Certain his gaze followed her, she glanced over her shoulder and flashed him a coquettish smile.

A few minutes later she returned. She circled the other players, watching her prey through partially lowered lashes. He kept his hooded eyes riveted on her face, until she stood next to him, then once again dropped his gaze to her bosom.

His indecent ogling made her feel soiled and cheap, stirring her already simmering temper. She hid her reaction, knowing her future with Ty depended on the successful conclusion of her performance.

"Good evening, my lovely," Gorman drawled, pulling Sassy from her thoughts.

She tipped her head in response, stepping back when he reached out to touch her arm. Making her way to the keno tables across the room, she tried to twitch her backside, as she'd seen other women do. Apparently, she'd done a credible job, since his gaze continually found her wherever she went.

After more of the ridiculous cat-and-mouse game, doing what Teddy suggested, remaining just out of his reach while taunting and teasing him to increase his interest, Sassy could take no more. She wanted to get this whole business done and over with.

Sidling up to him, she ran her fingers lightly across his shoulders and down one arm. "I saw how you looked at me. You are interested in more than poker, yes?" she purred near his ear.

His eyes burning with desire, he lifted her hand from his forearm and kissed her wrist. As he withdrew his mouth, he ran his tongue over her fingertips. "Yes, very interested."

Her eyes burning with a fire having nothing to do with desire, she managed to keep her voice low. "I have a place where we can be alone, if you're willing to leave your poker game."

"Absolutely, my lovely."

"Call me Camille." Stepping away from the table, she gave him a look she hoped passed for an invitation to follow, then moved toward the door. When he shoved away from the table, grabbed his coat off the back of the chair, and started after her, she breathed a silent sigh of relief.

On the sidewalk, he grasped her elbow and fell in step beside her. "My name is Foster. Foster Gorman. Where are we going?"

"To my hotel room," she replied, waving toward the building just ahead. She leaned toward him, allowing her breast to brush his chest. "You have no objections, do you, Foster?" She purposely lowered her voice to a raspy whisper when she said his name.

"No, none," he responded, his voice cracking at her sultry tone. Clearing his throat, he said, "As long as I'm with you, Camille, I'll go anywhere."

Sassy wanted to gag, but kept her lips tightly pressed together. She remained silent for the rest of the walk to the hotel. Gorman also said nothing, but she frequently felt his gaze move over her. His fingers burned her arm, where they held her fast.

The door had barely closed behind them, when Sassy found herself in his embrace. Slipping out of his arms, she laughed softly, "Not so fast, Foster. There's no need to rush, is there? After all, we have all night." She batted her eyelashes playfully. "Let's have a drink."

Gorman chuckled lightly, then tugged his gaudy vest back into place. "You're right. There's no rush. The longer we wait, the more the anticipation builds, thus the consummation of our amourette will be heightened. Don't you agree, my sweet?"

"Of course," she replied, grateful he was so malleable. Pointing toward the bed, she said, "Why don't you make yourself comfortable while I pour us a drink?"

While she opened the bourbon and poured the whiskey into two glasses, Sassy could hear the swish of fabric as Gorman removed his jacket, then the squawk of the bed springs when he sat down on the mattress. Working quickly, she pulled the packet Teddy had given her from her handbag, dumped its contents into one glass, and swirled it around.

Hoping she had done nothing to rouse his suspicions, she plastered a smile on her face and turned toward the bed. She exhaled the breath she'd been holding when her gaze found Gorman. Her brows pulled together in irritation. She wished she could tell him what he could do with his rudeness, but kept her thoughts to herself. *You were staring at my ass, you jackanapes. I should throw this drink in your face, but I'd hate to waste good bourbon on the likes of you.*

By the time his gaze moved lazily up to her face, Sassy had forced another smile. Unable to speak for fear she'd say what she'd been thinking, she silently handed him the doctored bourbon.

He accepted the drink, capturing her hand between his and the glass. Giving her a lustful smile, he made no objection when she pulled her fingers free.

She lifted her glass in silent salute, then took a sip of bourbon. The liquor burned her throat, but had an instant calming effect on her temper. Warning herself to stay in control, she watched him carefully as he took a drink. When he noticed nothing amiss, she hid a smile behind her glass. Teddy was right. He was so full of himself, he'd never suspect anything. She took another sip of her drink, thinking she might enjoy this after all.

He patted the bed next to him, where he lounged against the headboard. "Come, sit," he whispered, flashing another smile.

Finding no alternative, she eased onto the mattress, staying as far from him as she dared. He downed his drink in several quick swallows, but Sassy deliberately took more time. If she followed his example— She shuddered at what she would do, if he tried to do more than touch her. Her plans did not include suffering more of his attentions than were absolutely necessary.

"You're very beautiful," he murmured, running his forefinger up her arm and across the neckline of her dress. Gooseflesh appeared instantly where he touched. "So you want me, too," he said with smug satisfaction.

Wanting to tell him her reaction wasn't from desire, but revulsion, she forced herself to meet his gaze. "Of course, I do," she whispered, hoping he wouldn't guess the reason for the huskiness in her voice had nothing to do with lust.

She set her glass on the nightstand, then reached toward his chest. "Here, let me make you more comfortable." She silently cursed the trembling in her fingers, as she loosened his tie. Sneaking a peek at his face, his expression told her he thought the tremble of her hands was the natural reaction to his presence. She clenched her hands into tight fists, then relaxed them, and reached for the buttons of his vest.

When the last button slipped free, her heart sank. Although his eyes were overbright and his face had taken on a ruddy hue, the drug had not taken effect.

"Let me return the favor," he said with some difficulty, pushing himself to a sitting position. When he tried to turn her around, so he could get at the hooks on the back of her dress, she pulled away.

"No, not yet. I want to see all of you first." Apparently pleased by her announcement, he stretched out flat on the bed, his hands at his sides.

"How about a kiss, to tide me over until the main course?" He didn't appear to notice how he'd slurred the words. "Come on, Camille, give me a little taste of your sweet kisses."

She bit her lip with indecision. When she'd unbuttoned his vest, her fingers had felt the derringer Teddy warned her about. Unwilling to risk his reaction by refusing, she finally scooted closer. The pungent combination of pomade and cologne stung her nostrils, and made her stomach roil.

Just as she was ready to concede this round and kiss him, his body suddenly went limp, a heavy sigh rushing from his slack mouth.

She eased off the mattress and stood next to the bed. Staring at his relaxed features and his chest rising and falling in the cadence of drug-induced sleep for several seconds, she closed her eyes and whispered a prayer of thanks. Satisfied the sleeping potion had done its job, she snatched his jacket from where he'd folded it across the footboard. She carefully examined the brooch pinned on the lapel, checking it against the description Teddy gave her. Ornate gold, oval-shaped, large emerald, tiny diamonds.

Certain it was Teddy's, she freed it from the lapel, then pulled his wallet from the jacket's inside breast pocket. Momentarily shocked by the amount of money it held, she finally took all but a few bills, replaced the wallet, and carefully refolded the jacket. She hoped Teddy was right in thinking he might not discover the loss of the brooch, when he found how much she'd *charged*.

After tucking the money and brooch in her handbag, she returned to the bed. She shook his arm, but his only response was a loud snore. Biting her lip to hold in a fit of giggles, she set about the task of undressing him. When she finished the task, she threw a sheet over him, then hurried to the small desk in the corner of the room, and pulled a piece of paper from one of the drawers. As she mulled over what she wanted to say, she tapped the pen against her pursed lips. She smiled, then quickly scrawled: "You were sleeping so soundly that I hated to wake you. Hope you don't mind, but I helped myself to my fee. You were absolutely wonderful, Foster. Thank you for a night I shall never forget. Camille."

Rereading the note, her smile widened. *That should stroke that damn male ego of yours.* Remembering to empty the bourbon bottle down the sink and switch his glass with another, so he wouldn't find traces of the sleeping powder, Sassy glanced around one more time. Satisfied, she slipped from the room, hoping her efforts would buy enough time for the law to catch up with him.

Heady with her success, her feet barely touched the hallway carpet as she walked to the next room.

Teddy answered her knock instantly. "Oh, thank God! Waiting was about to drive me mad. How did it go? Are you all right?"

"Everything went like we planned, and I'm fine." Opening her handbag, she handed Teddy her brooch. "I believe this belongs to you. And look what was in Gorman's wallet. There must be a thousand dollars here! I bet I'm the most expensive pigeon he's ever done business with."

Teddy chuckled, pushing the money away when Sassy tried to give it to her. "You keep it. You deserve it for what you did tonight."

"I didn't do anything a person wouldn't do for a friend. Here, you take it."

"No, Sassy. I insist you keep the money. Now, let's get out of here."

Shoving the wad of bills back inside her handbag, Sassy followed Teddy down the hall.

Once they were inside her carriage, Teddy said, "I'd rather you didn't tell Ty what happened tonight. I'd like to be the one to tell him I got my brooch back."

"I promise, I won't tell him anything," Sassy replied, not adding that she had never intended to tell Ty. After all the times he'd harped at her to avoid strangers and stay out of trouble, there was no way she would tell him she'd met and befriended Teddy while he was in Houston. Telling him how she'd gotten Teddy's brooch back was also out of the question. He'd have a hissy fit for sure.

Ty stepped down off the train, exhausted and more than a little miffed with Teddy Fitzsimmons. He'd scoured Houston for a gambler named Perkins, with no luck. No one had seen or even heard of the man he described. Finally, Ty realized the truth. Teddy had concocted a story to let him think he was helping, when in fact she only wanted him out of Galveston. Like a greenhorn, he'd swallowed everything she'd told him. Being played for a fool didn't sit well.

He looked up at the pink-hued sky, then checked his watch to verify the time. "Almost seven," he muttered, rubbing the back of his neck to ease the tense muscles. Too tired and frustrated to confront Teddy for the truth at such an early hour when he knew she never rose before ten, he headed for the Old Chicago House, grateful he had a comfortable bed awaiting him.

He entered the sitting room of his suite, locked the door behind him, then threw his carpetbag onto the sofa. He glanced at the decanter of whiskey on the sideboard, but decided against it. Having been up all night, sleep sounded more inviting than a drink.

Inside the bedroom, he pulled off his boots, then slipped out of his jacket and shirt, and tossed them onto a chair. His hands on the top button of his pants, a noise across the room brought his head up with a snap. Through narrowed eyes he stared toward the bed. He could make out the shape of someone beneath the sheet. Silently cursing the hotel for renting out his room after he'd paid to keep it during his absence, he reached for his boots.

The bedclothes rustled, and a sleepy voice drifted to him. "Who's there?"

Ty froze. Then, as the voice registered in his tired brain, he swung around to face the bed. On stocking feet, he moved toward the side of the bed.

"I said, who's there?" The voice was louder this time. "I have a gun. Now who are you?"

Seeing the glint of metal, he stopped, blinking with surprise. "Dammit, Sassy, it's me."

A moment of silence answered him, then a hopeful, "Ty?"

Taking advantage of her hesitation, he reached the bed in one stride. "Yes, Ty." Snatching the gun from her hands, he snapped, "Where the hell did you get this? And what are you doing here? I thought you agreed to go home."

When she didn't immediately answer, he went to the window and jerked open the draperies. Shifting his gaze back to the bed, his breath stuck in his throat. The picture Sassy presented in the soft glow of the morning light sent a burst of desire racing through him.

She sat naked in the center of the bed, her hair a tousled mess, tumbling over her shoulders and allowing her breasts to play peek-a-boo through the thick waves. There was a wild sensuality about her, making him forget his weariness. His lips tingled with the need to taste her soft mouth. His manhood swelled painfully, aching to find release in her sweet depths. His entire body screamed for him to take her right then, hard and fast.

Ignoring his discomfort, he laid the gun on the nightstand, then sat down on the edge of the bed. "Are you going to answer me?" he asked softly.

"I bought the gun for protection," she said, then seeing the fear leap into his eyes, she added, "No, nothing happened. I wanted a gun just in case I needed it. I'm here because I belong with you. And, if you'll recall, I said I would see that Kitty and Juan got to the Star. I didn't say I would go with them."

Ty shook his head with disbelief, realizing he might never completely know his wife. He should have guessed she'd find a way to get around his wishes without directly disobeying him.

Staring at his wife's face, he chuckled. "Come here, you little minx."

With a glad cry, Sassy rose up on her knees and threw herself against him.

He caught her in his arms and held her tight. "I should be mad as hell at you, but I'm not," he whispered against her hair. Inhaling her spicy scent, he pushed her away from his chest and held her at arm's length. "I'm glad you're here."

"Me, too," she murmured as he lowered her to the bed. He quickly shed his pants, then dropped down next to her. When he took her mouth in a searing kiss, a deep groan rumbled in his chest.

Ty kissed and caressed her soft curves, until their breathing became ragged. "Please, Ty, I can't wait any longer," she said in a raspy voice. "Love me."

He wanted to yell 'I do love you,' but bit back the words. He still didn't know the outcome of the murder charge hanging over him. If he couldn't convince Teddy to tell the truth, there was no hope for his marriage. He was determined to try once more to get Teddy to change her mind, but if he wasn't successful, he'd have no choice except to leave again. Only this time, he wouldn't return.

The only bright spot in his painful thoughts was the woman in his arms. Finding her still in Galveston and in his bed was truly a godsend. He'd expected to have the bed all to himself. Now he intended to make the most of having it filled with his wife.

He made love to her throughout the morning, his insatiable desire fed by the fear that if he couldn't settle things with Teddy, his time with Sassy would quickly come to a permanent close.

Every time she started to drift off to sleep, his insistent mouth and fingers pulled her from the darkness of slumber, branding her body with the taste, the smell, the feel of him.

The sun had reached its highest point in the sky, when Ty joined their bodies yet again. The room took on a warm golden glow, as he thrust gently into Sassy's dewy center, moving in a rhythm as old as mankind. Her legs locked securely around his waist, she arched up to meet each downward stroke of his hips.

In a swift movement, he rolled onto his back, never letting his body become separated from hers. With her sitting astride him, he grasped her waist with his hands and urged her to continue the rhythmic pattern he'd started when their positions were reversed.

When his hands moved to her breasts, her eyes closed in rapture. His fingers brushed the pebbled tips in a circular motion, until they hardened even more. Continuing to tease her nipples with one hand, he lowered the other to the dark triangle pressed against his pelvis. When his fingers found and rubbed the swollen nubbin, a gasp of delight escaped her lips.

He studied her face carefully. He wanted to see her climax, watch the pleasure he gave her reflected in her features—a memory he would tuck away in his heart to cherish forever, if he was forced to leave her.

Her hips grinding against him in a frenzy, his fingers continued to rub her slick flesh, bringing her masterfully to the crest of her pleasure. As she neared the peak, she moaned deep in her throat, her senses swirling into mindless oblivion. The fullness in her loins continued to build, until she could stand no more. As the first spasm racked her, she shouted with joy. Her breathing a harsh pant, her body bucked against his fingers.

With a second piercing scream, she gave in to the pulsing of her release, letting it take her on its magical journey. In the dim corners of her mind, she heard Ty's groan of pleasure.

He thrust faster and faster, then pushed up into her one last time. His body taut, he dug his heels into the mattress and shouted, "Yes. Oh, God, yes!" Another groan vibrating in his chest, he went still. Buried deep inside her, his manhood throbbed in climax, then, too, went still.

Her muscles suddenly too weak to support her, Sassy fell forward onto his chest. "I love you, Ty," she murmured against his neck, unable to hold the words in any longer.

Feeling the unfamiliar closing of his throat, he swallowed hard, then managed to say, "I know you do, darlin'."

She rolled off him, then snuggled close, tucking her head between his shoulder and neck.

He stroked her hair, smiling against the silky waves at her soft snores. Exhaling heavily, he wondered if he should have told her how he felt. He continued to think it would be better if she didn't know his feelings, in case he couldn't clear his name. Still, the idea of telling her stayed in his mind. How would she react, if things worked out and he could tell her he loved her? She'd probably throw herself in his arms and kiss him senseless, he decided. Grinning at the mental picture he'd created, he fell asleep with his wife cradled in his arms.

Thirty

Ty rose from bed and stretched his arms lazily over his head. The stiffness of his muscles brought a smile to his face. Glancing at his still-sleeping wife, his smile broadened. How many times had they made love? He didn't know the exact number, but it was no wonder his body was pleasantly sore.

He moved quietly to the window and pushed the lace curtain to one side. Leaning a shoulder against the window frame, he stared down onto the Strand, idly stroking his mustache. So much for visiting Teddy on the day he'd arrived back from Houston. After his lengthy reunion with Sassy, he'd slept clear through to the following morning. With some time to fill before making the trip to Teddy's hotel, he decided to bathe and shave.

Taking care to be quiet so he didn't awaken Sassy, he crossed the room to the dresser. Rifling through a drawer for clean hose, shirt and underdrawers, he moved Sassy's underwear. Something tucked between the silky garments fell back into the drawer, stopping his hand in midair. "What the hell?" he murmured, staring in disbelief at the roll of money.

Tossing his clothes aside, he picked up the wad of

money. He unrolled the bills and whistled softly as he made a quick calculation of their total.

"Ty?"

His brows pulled together in a fierce scowl, he swung around to the bed.

Sassy sat in the center of the bed much as she had the morning before, still as beautiful, although she now wore a thoroughly loved look. Ignoring her naked curves and kiss-swollen lips, Ty stalked over to the bed and glared down at her.

Rubbing her eyes, Sassy yawned. "Why are you up so early?"

"I have a more important question," he said in a deceptively soft voice.

Her sleepiness fled at his severe tone. Wondering what he held behind his back, she stared at him with confusion. "What question?"

Bringing his hand in front of him with an angry jerk, he threw the roll of money onto the bed. "Where the hell did *that* come from? I left you some money in case you needed it before you got to the Dublin Star, but it damn sure wasn't that much!"

Sassy looked at the wad of bills and licked her suddenly dry lips. She knew she should have hidden her booty in a better spot. Since the excitement from her exploits of the previous night had left her exhausted, and it had been well after two in the morning when she returned to her hotel, she'd stuck the money in one of the dresser drawers and went to bed. Then, after Ty's surprise return, she'd had neither the time nor even a thought of moving the money to a more secure place.

Now she had to try to explain where it came from, without telling him about Teddy. Deciding to tell as much of the truth as possible, she took a deep breath and said,

"I . . . uh . . . went out last night. To a saloon that had a private gaming room and—"

"You did *what?*" His eyes narrowed; a muscle jumped in his clenched jaw. "Don't tell me you pulled that Grunt routine, and tried to pass yourself off as a man?"

Sassy's mouth twitched at the picture he made. Hands fisted on his hips, legs widespread, he stood next to the bed like a golden Viking warrior—minus his clothes. When a giggle bubbled up in her throat, she coughed to cover her amusement, then said, "No, I didn't dress like a man. I wore a dress."

"You wore a dr—Jesus Christ, that's even worse! Do you have any idea what you look like in a dress?" Not allowing her to answer, he continued, "I told you once, if you put on a dress, you'd turn every male head in San Antonio. But I miscalculated. You look better in a dress than even I imagined. You do more than turn men's heads; you make them want to do a helluva lot more than look."

In spite of his fury, she flushed with pleasure at the compliment mixed up in the middle of his tirade. "I don't understand you. If I'd gone to the saloon dressed like a man, you would have been sore as hell. I went wearing a dress, and you're *still* angry!"

Flustered at having his illogical reaction thrown back at him, he finally said, "Going to a saloon by yourself was a stupid thing to do."

Since his temper seemed to be cooling and he didn't know the truth about her visit to the saloon, she didn't take offense at being called stupid. She'd let him win that one point. Dropping her head, she whispered, "I won't do it again."

Mollified by her contrite words and posture, Ty relaxed his stiff pose. "What did you play to win that much money?"

Since saying "a prostitute" was out of the question, she settled for, "You know how much I like poker. My opponent for the evening was a professional gambler."

Shaking his head, he said, "You won that much from a professional gambler! Maybe you should have been sitting at the poker table all those weeks while we were searching for Teddy." Mentioning the name of the woman who he must visit later, he fell silent, lost in his thoughts.

Silently congratulating herself on getting out of a tight spot, Sassy hid a smile behind an expansive yawn. Seeing the clothes Ty had pulled from the dresser, she said, "What were you planning on doing?"

"What? Oh, I was getting some clean clothes. I planned to take a bath."

Her eyes sparkling, she tossed the sheet to the foot of the bed, then slid off the mattress. "Sounds wonderful. Would you care for some company?"

Throwing back his head, Ty laughed heartily. "Only if you'll wash my back."

She ran her hand across his hair-covered chest, down over his flat stomach, then lower. "Oh, I'll wash your back, all right. In fact, I'll wash anything you want me to," she said in a silky whisper, her fingers giving his flaccid manhood a playful tweak.

His body responded instantly, his sore muscles forgotten. Sweeping her into his arms, he carried her into the bathroom, the money lying on the bed a quickly fading memory.

After scrubbing each other amid giggles of delight, rumbles of laughter, and wildly sloshing water, Ty and Sassy spent nearly an hour in very playful lovemaking. By the time he brought his wife to completion, then gave in to his own release, the bathroom floor was soaking wet.

Stepping out of the tub and wrapping a towel around his waist, he helped Sassy from the tub. "Watch the floor, darlin', it's slippery."

She smiled up at him. "Guess we made a mess, didn't we?"

"Do you regret it?" he asked, his eyes alight with mischief.

"Absolutely not."

"I didn't think so," he responded, giving her bottom a gentle swat as she moved past him. "Hurry and get dressed. I want to get some breakfast, then I have an extremely important call to make. I have to see Teddy as soon as possible.

She grabbed a towel and left him in the bathroom to shave. After drying herself, she started pulling on her clothes, wondering how he could think of another woman so soon after they'd made love.

It was just past noon by the time Ty arrived at Teddy's hotel suite. He knocked on the door several times, but she didn't answer. Going down to the front desk, the clerk on duty told him Miss Fitzsimmons had gone out, and he didn't know when she would return. Ty waited in the lobby for over an hour, then finally left a note to send word when she returned and he'd come immediately.

By the following afternoon, he still hadn't received any kind of message from Teddy. Unable to stand the strain of waiting, he told Sassy he was going out for a while, and headed for the beach.

Sitting in the sand, watching the waves race onto the shore, then retreat down the beach to rejoin the water of the gulf, he mulled over his options. Unfortunately, he didn't have many. He could continue to wait until Teddy summoned him—which appeared to be less and less likely—he could hunt her down and demand she clear his name—definitely not a wise idea since there were no guarantees she'd carry through on his demands—or he could pack up and leave—the most painful choice.

Although none of the alternatives appealed to him, he finally decided he'd go to Teddy's hotel again and leave another message. If she didn't respond, he'd have to face the fact that she had no intention of clearing his name. A shudder rippled over his shoulders. He didn't want to think about that possibility.

Teddy felt a pang of guilt for not returning the messages Ty left at her hotel, but she had her reasons. Until she took care of some important business, she didn't want to talk to him. Besides, letting him stew in his own juice a little longer would serve to make him all the more grateful when they finally met.

Early that afternoon she'd finally received word the business had been successfully concluded, so she sat down to write a note to summon Ty.

An hour later she let him into her suite.

"Teddy," he said in greeting, walking past her into the sitting room.

"Ty. I'm glad you were able to come right away."

"And what else would I be doing? Still looking for a man named Perkins, perhaps?" Though antagonizing her with his sarcasm might hurt his chances to gain her co-operation, he couldn't stop his frustration from surfacing. "You've had plenty of time to conjure up another story to feed me. Is that why you sent for me, to send me on another of your contrived missions?"

A faint smile appearing on her face, she said, "I don't blame you for being put out."

"Put out! I don't think put out even begins to describe how I feel."

Ignoring his snide tone, she continued, "I had to make sure you wouldn't interfere in my plans. And, no, I don't want you to go on another mission, as you called it."

He shot her an angry glare, but said nothing.

"I sent for you because I wanted to tell you I've been to the police about the charge against you."

"Ah, I see. They're going to come busting through the door any minute. That's why you wanted me here, so you could gloat when they arrest me."

"Don't be ridiculous. If having you arrested was my goal, I wouldn't have cared whether it was accomplished in my presence. I'd simply have told the police where to find you, and be done with it."

Other than his eyebrows lifting slightly, he showed no reaction.

"Now, are you going to let me explain?"

At his curt nod, she settled in one of the chairs. "Like I started to say, I went to the police here in Galveston yesterday, and told them I wanted to clear your name of a murder charge."

Ty took a seat opposite her, but remained silent.

"I explained that I had wrongly charged you with the crime, and I wanted to make it right. I insisted they send a telegram to the Waco sheriff. This afternoon the Galveston chief of police notified me that he'd received a response. You are no longer wanted for murder."

"Are you sure?" he asked dubiously.

"I went to see Chief Jordan, and he showed me the telegram. The Waco sheriff said the charges against you have been dropped."

After a long pause, Ty said, "What made you change your mind?"

Teddy chuckled. "Your wife."

Taken aback by her answer, he finally said, "My wife?" Wondering about her reaction at learning he'd married someone else after refusing her proposal, he couldn't stop a self-conscious flush from creeping up his neck and cheeks.

"Right after you left for Houston, I met this wonderfully fresh, thoroughly enjoyable young woman. We had such fun together, bicycling, going to Oleander Park. It wasn't until a day or two later, that I learned her real name was Sassy Beaumont, Mrs. Ty Beaumont." When he started to interrupt, she held up her hand to stop him. "Let me finish. Needless to say, Sassy was equally shocked to learn I'm the woman you've been looking for. You see, I'd introduced myself to her as Dora."

At his confused look, she said, "I go by the name Dora when I'm not gambling."

"I never knew."

"No, you didn't. There are a lot of things you don't know about me." She sighed, lost in her thoughts for a moment.

Ty's restless shifting brought her back to the present. "Anyway, Sassy asked to help retrieve my brooch when I explained the situation. In fact, she's the one who got it back. So you see, now that grandmother's brooch has been returned to me, I no longer need to protect the man who killed Slater. Both the Waco sheriff and Chief Jordan were most interested in learning his name, and where they could find him. I believe he's now in the city jail."

Ty sat in stunned silence, trying to comprehend everything Teddy had told him. He couldn't believe Sassy and Teddy knew each other. Yet, he saw no reason for her to lie. Then he remembered something else. When he'd first returned from Houston and found out Sassy hadn't left town, she never asked him about his trip. He knew first-hand about his wife's curious nature. She should have peppered him with questions. The only reason she hadn't asked had to be because she already knew the answers.

"Tell me how Sassy retrieved your brooch. She didn't do anything illegal, did she?"

"She might have bent the law a little, but she definitely didn't break it," Teddy replied with a laugh. "I'll tell you how she did it, if you give me your word you won't be angry with her."

"Tell me," Ty said, his hands gripping the chair arms.

"Not until I have your word."

He forced his hands to relax. "All right, dammit, you have it."

"The man with my brooch, Foster Gorman, has a well-known reputation as a roué. So we decided the logical choice was to have Sassy pose as a *fille de joie.*"

"Dear Lord, she played a prostitute?" he asked in a strangled whisper.

"We had to make sure Gorman would leave the saloon and go with her, so that seemed the best idea."

Teddy then went on to explain the rest of the plan she and Sassy had come up with. Seeing the anger spark in his eyes, she warned him he'd given his word, then said, "Sassy will have to tell you the details of how she carried out our plan, that is, if she wants to, but I can tell you what I do know."

After she repeated what Sassy told her about how she'd slipped the sleeping potion into Gorman's drink, took the brooch and some money from his wallet as her fee, then left him in a drugged sleep, Ty slumped in his chair, momentarily speechless.

Snapping out of his shock, he murmured, "That's where the money came from."

"You knew about the money?"

"Yes. No! Well, I found the money, but I didn't know where it came from. Sassy said she won it from a professional gambler in a poker game."

"She said she played poker with Gorman?"

"She didn't tell me his name, but she—" Ty stopped abruptly, trying to remember Sassy's exact words. "She said she went to a saloon where there was a private gaming room, that I knew how much she liked poker, and she got the money from a professional gambler."

Teddy burst out laughing. "She's a clever one. What she told you was true." When he didn't look convinced, she added, "Think about it, Ty. You just assumed by what she said that she'd played poker and won the money."

His mouth thinned to a severe line. He didn't like being duped by Sassy's word games.

"I'll remind you again, you gave me your word. You should be proud of your wife, not angry with her."

Ty thought about that for a minute, then nodded. "What about my refusing your proposal?" he asked carefully. "Are you still mad about that?"

"No, although I admit I haven't entirely forgiven you for having the gall to laugh when I proposed. That was a very painful blow to my pride. But I've decided you've already been given a fitting sentence for your faux pas."

At his expectant look, she said, "I think being married to a spitfire like Sassy—who will keep you continually off balance and on your toes—is just punishment."

He stared at her for several seconds, then burst out laughing. "I think you're absolutely right." Then, in a lower voice, he added, "It's a punishment I gladly accept."

"So, I was right. You do love her."

"Yes," Ty answered softly, his cheeks growing warm again.

"Do yourself a favor and tell Sassy."

At his surprised look, she said, "The poor girl thinks you don't care for her. She loves you a great deal, Ty. I never thought I'd say this to you, but you're a lucky man to have a woman like her. Tell her how you feel, all right?"

"I've already imagined her reaction," he said with a smile. "I have every intention of telling her, so I can reap the benefit."

Although Teddy's story was too preposterous not to be true, Ty still planned to find out if his name had in fact been cleared. Going to the Galveston police could be disastrous if she'd lied, but he had to take the chance. First, he wanted to share his news with Sassy.

As he hailed a carriage and climbed in, he thought about Sassy's part in Teddy's decision to clear his name. He couldn't decide whether to admire Sassy's gutsy achievement, or be mad as hell for putting herself in another dangerous position. When the latter started to win his inner battle, he forced himself to take a deep breath. As the rest of his conversation with Teddy replayed in his mind, his rising irritation disintegrated.

Teddy was right, he *was* a lucky man to have a woman like Sassy.

Smiling broadly, he paid the carriage driver, then entered the Old Chicago House. As he opened the hotel suite door, he called to his wife. There was no answer.

"Damn, where'd she go?" he mumbled sourly. She's probably off on another adventure, he decided. He wondered if he'd ever be able to keep her from doing such outrageous stunts, like the one she'd done for Teddy. He shook his head, still finding it hard to believe that she'd actually posed as a lady of the evening to help the woman who had once been his lover.

He waited for over an hour, but she didn't return. Anxious to get to the Galveston police to confirm Teddy's claim, he finally wrote Sassy a note and left the hotel.

Chief Jordan was busy when Ty arrived, so he took a seat to wait until the man could see him. It was well past dusk before the chief called Ty into his office.

Although Chief Jordan assured him that the murder charge against him had been dropped, Ty insisted on seeing the telegram from the Waco sheriff.

"Sorry if I sounded like I didn't believe you, Chief," Ty said. "I've been waiting for this day for a long time, and I had to be sure."

Offering his hand, Jordan said, "No need to apologize, Beaumont, I understand. I'd probably do the same thing."

Ty shook the police chief's hand, then stepped outside. He took a deep breath of the salty gulf air, feeling almost giddy with relief. After many months of continuous pressure, the weight bearing down on his shoulders had suddenly been lifted.

Too exhilarated to sit in a carriage for the ride back to his hotel, he opted to walk the several blocks to burn off some of his abundant energy.

His long strides took him toward the wharf and past several dark alleys. He whistled softly, his soaring spirits making him only vaguely aware of the clomp of someone running on the sidewalk behind him. The back of his neck prickled in warning, jerking him out of his joyous stupor. He continued walking, his ears straining for every sound.

When the footsteps behind him stopped, he started to breathe easier. Then he heard the swish of something rubbing against leather, followed by a metallic click. Before he could duck into a doorway or down an alley, a voice rang out.

"Hold it right there, Beaumont."

Thirty-one

Resting her elbows on the window sill, Sassy placed her chin in her palms and stared out into the deepening twilight.

Unable to bear simply sitting around and waiting for Ty to return from seeing Teddy, she'd spent the afternoon visiting O'Shaughnessy's Luck. Being around the horse was a balm to her flagging spirits, and kept her thoughts off her husband. She'd returned from her outing over an hour ago, expecting to find him waiting.

What she found was the note he'd left, making her wish she hadn't gone out. If she'd been there when he returned from Teddy's, he would have told her everything, and she would have been able to discern his mood. Instead, he'd written a note that gave her no clue to what he was feeling.

In his obviously quickly penned message, he'd said that Teddy had cleared his name of murder. While Sassy was overjoyed at that bit of news, there was still one piece of unfinished business he had to tend to, one that overshadowed her happiness for him. His decision on that final issue set her insides quivering with fear.

Now that Ty could go on with a normal life, would he want her beside him?

As she recalled more of his message, her heavy heart pounded even harder, thudding in trepidation. "I know what you did. We'll talk about it later," he'd written. She chewed on her lip, wondering if he did know everything she'd done, and what he would say about it. Was he angry, embarrassed, or did he even care about her enough to feel anything?

"Dammit, Ty, where the hell are you?" she murmured, scanning the street below for some sign of him. His note said he was going to the police. It shouldn't take this long to make sure his name had been cleared. Although she tried to think about something else, her mind continued to pick at the subject, like a tongue continually worrying a sore tooth. *Maybe he went back to Teddy. No, I know Teddy no longer wants Ty so he wouldn't go there. Maybe he's so disgusted with me for what I did, that he doesn't want to face me. But he'll have to face me sooner or later, especially if he's decided to make good his threats and file for divorce.*

"Oh, God," she groaned aloud, closing her eyes against the sharp pain squeezing her chest. *Maybe he already has. Maybe he's already signed the papers. I wouldn't blame him for not wanting to stay married to me, a woman who brings him nothing but trouble, a woman who knows next to nothing about being a lady. Teddy was wrong; he doesn't love me.*

She gulped down the lump in her throat, wishing she could go somewhere or do something to help pass the time. Not wanting to risk missing him again, and in spite of the painful thoughts her mind conjured up, she knew she had to wait in the hotel suite for his return. After all, she wasn't a coward. Even if it meant her fears would become reality, she had to know his decision about their marriage.

Bright Sky stood frozen in shock. Beaumont. The name rang over and over in his head. He must have misunderstood. The man he'd been following—the man in his visions—was known as Beauregard. Why then did the other *tivo* call him Beaumont?

After spotting the *tivo* dressed in black, also following the yellow-haired man, Bright Sky had crossed the street, sprinted silently up the opposite side, then recrossed to hide in an alley ahead of the man his guardian spirit told him to protect. From his hiding place he watched the man in black pull his gun from his holster, then heard him call out to the one he knew as Beauregard. Except he'd called him Beaumont.

Bright Sky remained still, trying to listen to the words the two men exchanged. Hearing the name Beaumont made it impossible to concentrate. Unbidden memories flooded his mind, sealing out all surrounding sound. He saw two yellow-haired boys playing in a river, then a yellow-haired woman standing on the porch of a ranch house. As if she stood next to him, he heard her call to the boys. "Ty and Dayne. It's time to come in."

Shaking his head, Bright Sky forced the unwanted memories back to their hiding place. He'd seen that scene and similar ones in his mind before, but he'd refused to acknowledge their meaning. His inability to prevent unwanted thoughts shamed him. As a Comanche, he should be in complete control of his body and his mind at all times.

He touched the necklace encircling his throat, fingering the wolves' teeth to regain his composure. His mind once again free of distractions, he took a step toward the street. His senses alert, he waited for the chance to fulfill his guardian spirit's prophecy.

Silently cursing his stupidity, Ty took a deep breath, then turned around slowly. A man holding a drawn pistol stood perhaps twenty feet behind him.

"What do you want? Money?" Slowly raising his arm, he said, "If you want my wallet, here, take it."

"Put your arm down, Beaumont. I don't want your damn money."

Recalling the man had used his real name when he'd ordered him to stop, Ty strained to see his face. The man stood outside the circle of light cast by the nearest street lamp. Even if he'd been directly beneath it, he wore his hat pulled so low, Ty could have seen no more than his chin. "Do I know you?"

"We met once a long time ago, but that doesn't matter. The only thing that matters is, after all these months, my trailing you has finally come to an end. I don't know what game you've been playing: calling yourself Beauregard, posing as a gambler and hauling that woman who claims to be your wife around with you. I gave up trying to figure it out. Since I found you not hiding behind the skirts of your chair-swinging protector, I'm taking advantage of it."

More to himself, Ty commented, "Damn, I forgot I was being followed." Then louder, he said, "So you're the one Sassy clobbered in Laredo. Who are you?"

"My name isn't important. What's important is your real name. Ranger Tyler Beaumont, wanted in Waco for murder. I'm taking you in to stand trial."

Ty shifted uneasily. "What are you? Lawman? Pinkerton? Bounty hunter?"

"Not that it matters any, but you guessed it. The name's Dancer. Kit Dancer, bounty hunter. That's enough talk. You're coming with me."

Ty's brow furrowed at hearing the man's name, but couldn't place him. "That won't be necessary. I'm no longer wanted for murder."

"You really think I'm going to fall for that? I'm not a snot-nose kid trying to collect my first bounty."

"Dammit, man, it's true. I just came from the Galveston police. Chief Jordan showed me a telegram from the Waco sheriff; the charges against me have been dropped."

Dancer chuckled dryly. "I have to hand it to you, Beaumont. You do sound convincing. But I'm not buying it. Turn around and get a move on, we're leaving town tonight."

"I'm not going with you, Dancer." He inched forward, hoping he could slip into the alley he'd passed before Dancer's shout had stopped him.

Seeing his intent, Kit also moved forward, slowly closing the distance between them. "Don't try anything, Beaumont. I have a wanted poster with your name on it, and I intend to claim the money on your head. I'm not against using my gun to get what I want." He took another step forward. "The fact is, maybe you'd be a whole lot easier to manage if I *did* put a hole in you."

"My wanted poster has been revoked. Better check it out, otherwise I'll—"

"Otherwise you'll what?" Dancer interrupted. "You'll sic that woman on me again? She isn't going to get a second chance, 'cause we'll be long gone before she finds out what happened."

"Don't be so sure, Dancer," Ty said coolly. "She knows where I am, and if I don't miss my guess, she may already be tailing me. In fact, she could be behind you right now."

Dancer hesitated, giving Ty the opening he'd been looking for. Taking two long strides, he headed for the alley. Just as he ducked into the welcoming darkness, someone hidden in its depths jumped in front of him.

"Damn you, Beaumont." The crack of Dancer's pistol echoed down the alley.

The man who'd shielded Ty sucked in a hissing breath, and went down on one knee.

Unwilling to risk killing his prey, Dancer held his fire, but pulled the hammer back on his pistol again just in case. Before he could react, the blade of a knife flashed in the streetlight, swishing through the air and hitting its target with a soft thump.

Dancer grunted with pain, dropping his gun to grasp his shoulder where the blade had pierced his flesh. He slumped against a building, then slid to a sitting position on the brick sidewalk.

Jarred from his momentary shock over the fast chain of events, Ty hurried over to pick up Dancer's gun, then returned to the alley and the man stretched out on the ground.

It was too dark to see how seriously the man had been injured, but he could see the dark stain of blood on the side of his face. Putting his fingers to the man's throat, he was relieved to feel a strong pulse. He had no idea why anyone would throw himself in front of a bullet meant for him, but he sure hoped the man survived so he could thank him.

Drawn by the gunfire, the street filled with people.

Wagons were summoned to take Dancer and Ty's unknown savior to the city hospital.

After arriving on the scene and completing his initial investigation, Chief Jordan returned to Ty's side. "You're good at getting yourself out of one scrape and right into another one, aren't you, Beaumont?" he asked with a smile.

Chuckling in response, Ty said, "Yeah, guess you're right, although this wasn't my doing. After I left your office, someone yelled at me. I turned around, and there's Dancer with his gun drawn, telling me he's taking me in. He had no way of knowing my name had been cleared."

Jordan nodded. "Who's the other man, the one Dancer shot?"

"I have no idea. I was hoping you could tell me."

"I've never seen him before." Jordan eyed him strangely. "You didn't get a good look at him, did you?"

Ty's brow furrowed. "No, it was too dark in the alley. Why do you ask?"

"It's just—never mind. You gonna go see how he's doing?"

Ty nodded. "He probably saved my life. The least I can do is thank him."

"I'm going over to the hospital to talk to Dancer, if you wanna come along."

"Much obliged. I want to make sure he learns I'm no longer a wanted man," Ty replied, falling into step with the police chief. "I've been thinking about what happened tonight, and I can't figure out why Dancer fired his gun. I don't think he intended to kill me, since I had to be alive for him to collect the reward. But in that dark alley, a bullet meant to nick me could easily have been fatal."

"When we get to the hospital, you can ask him about that," the chief said.

"I'd just as soon not see the son of a bitch, 'cause I might be tempted to give him more than a knife wound. If it's okay with you, I'll let you talk to him alone."

"Sure, if that's what you want."

At St. Mary's Infirmary, Ty waited just outside Dancer's room, so he could hear the conversation between Chief Jordan and the bounty hunter.

After explaining the situation to Dancer, the chief added, "I don't like having innocent people shot up in my city. So I'd appreciate your leaving Galveston, as soon as you're fit."

"Don't worry," Kit replied. "Since the man I've been following for months no longer has a price on his head, I don't plan to stick around for one minute more than I have to. I'll be out of your town as soon as the doc says it's okay."

"Fair enough."

After Chief Jordan left Dancer's room, Ty went to find the other man. A doctor stepped from the room as he arrived.

"How is he?"

"The bullet grazed the side of his head. He lost a lot of blood, but with rest he should be just fine."

"May I see him?"

"He's still unconscious, but you can go in if you like. Don't stay too long, we just finished dressing his wound and still have to get him settled for the night."

Ty moved quietly into the room, stopping just inside the door. The man lay on his back, wearing only a pair of buckskin pants and moccasins. Ty scowled.

His gaze moved upward, across the broad, muscular chest, stopping at the necklace around the man's throat. His brows pulled together in puzzlement. What the hell is that, he wondered, moving to the foot of the bed. It looked like some kind of animal teeth, strung on a piece of rawhide. His gaze shifted from the necklace. Although the man's hair was light-colored, it had been woven into braids, an eagle feather dangling from one plait. His scowl deepened and his back stiffened. Long-felt hatred cramped his gut.

In spite of the urge to rush from the room, Ty forced himself to move his gaze higher, prepared to see the visage of a savage. What he saw was not what he expected. Staring at the man's face, relaxed by sleep and partially covered by a bandage, Ty blinked, thinking his imagination had played a trick. Glancing at the man again, he grabbed the footboard, gripping so hard his knuckles turned white. "My God, can it be true?" he murmured, studying the face he'd never thought to see again.

Although many years had passed while the boy he remembered had grown into a man, there was no mistaking the jawline, the nose, the blond hair. No wonder Chief Jordan acted strangely when he asked if he'd seen this man. The resemblance between them was uncanny.

The sudden joy filling his chest left in a rush, his thoughts a tangle of conflicting emotions. *He's dressed like a savage! But he's Dayne, my brother. No, he can't be, he's a thieving Indian, just like the bastards who killed Dad and burned our ranch. Yet, there's no denying he has the stamp of a Beaumont.*

It was all too much for him to absorb—his brother miraculously returned to him, only to realize he'd apparently been living as one of the people Ty had spent his entire life hating.

The man on the bed stirred, snapping Ty from his painful stupor. Turning on his heel, he hurried from the room.

Sassy still sat at the window, when she saw Ty coming down the Strand. Watching him move under the streetlights toward the hotel, her worry for his safety eased, but did nothing to lessen her concern for their future. She rose and rushed to the mirror to check her appearance. There were dark circles from worry and lack of sleep under her eyes, and the wet washcloth she held to her face did little to help. After running a brush through her tangled hair, she returned to the sitting room.

As she waited, she could feel every beat of her heart pounding against her ribs. "Hurry up," she whispered, not sure if she intended to cosh him over the head, or throw herself into his arms when he came through the door.

Ty turned the key in the lock carefully, not wanting to disturb Sassy. As soon as he pushed the door open, he realized his efforts were unnecessary. She stood across the room, the soft glow of a single lamp casting most of her in shadow.

"I thought you'd be asleep," he said, closing the door and moving to the sideboard.

She watched him splash some whiskey in a glass, noting the tenseness of his shoulders, the slight shaking of his hand as he lifted the glass to his lips. Moving closer, she said, "Are you all right?"

"Yeah." Keeping his back to her, he took a healthy swallow of whiskey, then gritted his teeth against the burning in his throat and stomach.

"What did the police say? Did Teddy clear your name?"

"Yeah," he said again, taking another sip of his drink. "Dammit, Ty. Talk to me."

He swung around to look at her, his brows pulling together at the dark smudges beneath her eyes. Realizing she'd waited up for him, he knew he had to tell her what happened. "Sit down."

When she'd taken a seat on one end of the sofa, he eased down on the opposite end. After taking another fortifying drink, he began speaking in a low voice. He told her about going to the Galveston police, and his conversation with Chief Jordan. "I was so relieved to know I could get on with my life that I did a very stupid thing. I decided to walk back here, and let myself fall right into the hands of a bounty hunter."

"Bounty hunter?"

"Remember I told you I thought someone was following me? His name is Kit Dancer."

Something in his expression made her ask, "Do you know him?"

"I thought I did, at least the name sounded familiar. He said we met once, but I still don't remember where or when. Anyway, I made the mistake of not watching my back, and he got the jump on me."

"What happened?"

Ty told her about his confrontation with Dancer, and how another man leaped in front of him when Dancer fired his gun.

"Why would a stranger step in front of you like that?"

"I wondered the same thing, so I went to the hospital to ask him." Ty shook his head slowly. "I still can't believe it."

"Can't believe what?"

Ty downed the rest of his drink in one gulp, then said,

"The man who took the bullet Dancer meant for me is my brother."

Sassy's forehead furrowed. "I thought you said your brother was killed by Comanches after they raided your ranch."

"I thought so, too. I don't know why we were never able to find out my brother didn't die like we believed, but it's true. I saw him tonight."

"Did you talk to him?"

"No." His voice turned hard. "The bullet grazed the side of his head. He's still unconscious."

"You're going back to see him when he wakes up, aren't you?"

Ty rose and went to the sideboard for another glass of whiskey. He sipped the drink, refusing to speak.

"Well, aren't you?"

He shrugged.

"Ty, he's your brother!"

"Yeah, he's my brother—my brother turned savage."

"What are you talking about?"

"I went into his room, so I could see the man who'd willingly risked his life for me. I found a man wearing moccasins, an animal tooth necklace—probably some sort of savage hocus-pocus—and shoulder-length braids. Except for his blond hair, he looked like a damn Comanche."

Sassy sat back, stunned. After a long silence, she said, "You have to talk to him. Maybe he had no choice. He was taken captive by the Comanche, and maybe he had to become one of them to survive."

Ty swung around to glare at her, his eyes filled with venom. "No choice!" he nearly shouted. "He's almost thirty years old, for Christ's sake." He took a deep breath, then said in a lower tone, "I agree he might not have had a choice when he was first taken from the Circle B, but that was over twenty years ago! He's had plenty of time to refuse the life forced on him, and start living and dressing like a white man."

"Maybe he doesn't want to be a white man," she said softly.

Her words stopped his hand halfway to his mouth. "Sweet Jesus, I hope not."

He downed the rest of his drink in one gulp. "This has been one helluva day," he muttered. "I nearly get shot by a damn bounty hunter, then I learn my brother is not only alive, but thinks he's a Comanche." Setting the glass down on the sideboard, he turned toward the bedroom. "And if that's not bad enough, I found out my wife pretended to be a goddamn whore."

"Ty, wait, I can explain." Sassy jumped up and hurried after him.

"I don't want to talk about it," he said, shrugging out of his jacket.

"I know you're probably angry with me, but if you'll just let me—"

"Not now, Sassy. I know you did it for me, and I appreciate it. But that doesn't mean I approve. I'm too tired to discuss your behavior, so drop it, okay?"

Seeing the hard set of his jaw, Sassy swallowed the words she wanted to say. She watched in silence as he stripped off the rest of his clothes, then got into bed.

She undressed and tentatively slid in next to him. When he pulled her into his arms, relief rushed through her. He couldn't be too angry, otherwise he wouldn't want to touch her.

Although she wanted to make love to him and perhaps ease his mind for a little while, she knew they were both too exhausted. Instead, she cuddled close to him, molding her body tightly against his, one hand resting on his chest, one knee thrown across his thighs. She knew he'd fallen asleep, when the tension left his muscles and his breathing became slow and even.

As sleep pulled her deeper into its web, she realized she still didn't know whether Ty wanted her in his future.

Thirty-two

Bright Sky was hot. His skin burned like he'd been staked out in the merciless, summer Texas sun for days. He tossed his head from side to side, seeking relief from his torment.

He stilled at the sound of a soft voice, then something wet and cool touched his forehead. A trickle of water from the cloth ran down his cheek, and pooled at the corner of his mouth. He licked his dry, cracked lips, welcoming the moisture on his tongue, wishing for more to soothe his parched throat.

The damp rag moved over his face, then down onto his neck and across his chest. He sighed with pleasure, then slipped back into the darkness of sleep and dreams of another time and place—dreams he did not want to have, but could not stop in his feverish sleep. Long-buried memories continued to haunt his dreams in one scene after another.

He saw two yellow-haired boys running across a field of wildflowers, fishing poles clutched in their hands. The biggest of the boys could run faster, and soon was well ahead of the younger boy. "Hey, Dayne, wait up," the smaller boy called.

That scene faded and another came into focus.

"Come on, son. It's time to get up," a large man with dark hair and eyes said, shaking the boy's shoulder. He moaned and pulled the covers over his head. The man chuckled, then pulled playfully on the blankets. "I know you want to sleep. We're going into town today, remember, and we need to get an early start. Come on, Dayne, hurry it up. Your mother has breakfast waiting."

A voice near his ear ended the scene, and pulled Bright Sky from dream-filled sleep. He tried to open his eyes, but his eyelids were too heavy. He lay perfectly still, trying to identify his surroundings by the sounds and the smells. His sharp senses picked up only the strong scent of soap, some sort of medicinal smell, and a hint of flowers. Unable to decipher those clues, his brow furrowed. He grimaced with the intense throbbing on the left side of his head, then raised a hand to find the source of the pain.

"No, you mustn't touch it." The same soft voice he remembered from earlier brought his eyes open slowly. He turned his head slightly, his gaze finding the source of the voice. A young woman wearing a starched white apron, holding a basin of water, and smelling of flowers, looked down at him with wary eyes.

"Where am I?" he whispered in a raspy voice.

"You're at St. Mary's Infirmary. You were shot. Don't you remember?"

After a moment, he replied, "I remember." He started to sit up, then clamped his lips shut against a groan brought on by the pounding in his head.

Setting the basin on the table next to the bed, the woman placed a hand on his chest and gently pushed. "You're not supposed to get up. You're much too ill. Lie

384

back down, and I'll give you another sponge bath. You still have a fever."

Bright Sky eased his head back onto the pillow, his gaze riveted on the woman. A deep green, her eyes reminded him of lush buffalo grass. Her hair, dark brown with streaks of gold, was gathered into a net snood at the base of her neck. He longed to reach up and free her hair, to run his fingers through the silky strands.

He quickly banished such thoughts, yet he couldn't make himself look away. As he continued his silent perusal, a dull flush spread across her high cheekbones. "Were you the one who bathed me?"

The flush deepened. "Yes. My Papa said it was important to keep you cool, so your fever would break."

"Your papa?"

"My father is a doctor. We came to Galveston so he could teach at the Texas Medical College. He also works in the hospital, when he isn't teaching. He's the one who treated you."

"Are you a nurse?"

"No." Her chin lifted with pride. "I'm studying to be a doctor. Part of my training is working here at St. Mary's."

"How long have I been here?"

"Since the night before last."

Bright Sky didn't reply, but silently let her bathe his face, chest, and arms. In spite of the cool relief her ministrations gave his skin, her touch caused another heat to build, a heat he hadn't experienced in a very long time. Not since Singing Wind had he felt the stirring of desire, and definitely never before for a white woman.

Forcing his mind away from his body's reaction to her touch, he said, "What's your name?"

"Lily."

385

"Lily," he repeated in a low whisper. He gritted his teeth against the flash of pleasure produced by saying her name.

"What's your name?"

"Bright Sky."

Her hand stilled briefly, then continued wiping his warm, smooth skin with the wet cloth. "That's an Indian name. Don't you have a white name?"

"No," he snapped.

"Papa says you're a squaw man. Is that true?"

His jaw clenched in fury. He'd been called the name before, when he'd had to deal with the white man, buying food or ammunition. Many had looked at how he dressed and his braided hair, and called him a squaw man, or worse.

"I am Comanche," he said in a harsh voice. "When a man of the People takes a wife from his tribe, he is not a squaw man."

Lily jerked her hand away from his chest. Her eyes wide with shock, she said, "You have an Indian wife?"

Remembering his beautiful Singing Wind, Bright Sky's heart ached with the loss of his wife. "She's dead." He turned an accusing glare up at Lily. "She died from one of your white man's diseases."

Her tongue peeked out to wet her lips, sending another stab of desire slicing through him. "I . . . I'm sorry," she murmured.

After a few moments of awkward silence while she finished his bath, he said, "Leave me."

Gathering up the cloth and basin of water, Lily couldn't bring herself to meet his hard gaze. "Your fever has come down. I'll tell Papa you're awake." With that she turned and hurried from the room.

Bright Sky watched her leave, feeling another lick of

unwanted heat in his loins at the sight of her firm little bottom disappearing through the door. He sighed and closed his eyes. Even his disturbing dreams were better than the feelings Lily stirred.

On the morning after the shooting, Ty sent a telegram to Josh to notify him about Teddy clearing his name, then went back to the hospital. There he learned that Dayne had taken a fever, and the doctor forbade visitors.

Since he had no other alternative, Ty left, returning several times later that day and again in the evening. Each time he was turned away.

Finally on the second morning he learned Dayne had improved, no longer plagued by fever. Although Dayne was asleep, Ty was allowed in his brother's room. He pulled a chair close to the bed and sat down.

Ty watched his brother sleep, wondering at his restlessness and the pained look on his face. It was as if something tortured Dayne's dreams, just as his own mind overflowed with tortuous thoughts.

A groan from the bed brought Ty out of his chair. Dayne groaned again, lifting one hand to his head. When he started to pull at the bandage, Ty grabbed his arm. "No, leave it, Dayne."

Feeling the sudden tightness in his brother's arm, Ty's gaze shifted to Dayne's face. Blue eyes, the exact color of their mother's, stared back at him.

"How are you feeling, Dayne?"

"My name is Bright Sky," he answered in a hoarse whisper. "Dayne is no more."

"No more? What are you talking about? You're Dayne Beaumont. Is that why you dress like a savage and wear

387

your hair in braids, because you don't remember who you are?"

"No!" he shouted, then grabbed his head with both hands. "I am Bright Sky. I am of the People, the Comanche," he said more softly.

Ty's back stiffened, his jaw hardening with anger. "Do you deny you were born Dayne Alexander Beaumont?"

"That was my birth name. When I was adopted by the People, I was given the name Bright Sky."

"Dammit, you're still Dayne Beaumont. And I'm your brother, Tyler—Ty." When Dayne didn't react, he lowered his voice to say, "Our mother will be so happy to see you."

"She lives?"

"Yes. She's on the Circle B. She still wanted to live on the ranch, even though it was burned to the ground when Dad was killed and you were taken."

Bright Sky's eyes clouded for a moment, then closed while he regained his composure. "My Comanche parents told me my white family had all been killed."

"Momma and I hid in the storm cellar. Thank God those damn savages didn't find us, otherwise we would have been killed." Ty took a deep breath. "We tried to find you. When the searches turned up nothing, we thought they'd killed you, too. Can you tell me about that day?"

At first he wasn't going to answer, but seeing the look on the man's face, Bright Sky began speaking in a low, expressionless voice. "Father and I returned from town, and found the house and barns burning. He told me to hide; he would look for you and Mother. We did not know those who set the fires were still near. They started shooting when he ran toward the house. He was shot in the leg, then in the back. He still tried to get to you. Another shot hit him. He did not move after that. I tried to go to him, but I was grabbed from behind and pulled onto a horse's back."

"Where did they take you? Momma sent out two different search parties, but they weren't able to find out what happened to you."

"I do not remember where they took me. It was like my mind was at another place. When I became aware of what had happened, I fought the warriors who took me with all my strength. They hit me in the head, and everything went black. When I woke up I was in a large camp in the mountains, but I do not know where it was."

"Well, it doesn't matter now," Ty said, squeezing his shoulder. "Momma will be beside herself when she sees you. 'Course we'll have to see about getting that hair of yours cut, and some decent clothes, before we head for the Circle B. She'd have a fit, if she saw you dressed like a savage."

Bright Sky's eyes turned cold. "I will not cut my hair, it would bring bad medicine."

"Bad medicine?" Ty scowled. "What the devil are you talking about?"

"Comanche braves all have long hair. We do not cut it, except as a sign of grief."

"Well, you're not a Comanche anymore, so you can—"

"I am Bright Sky, Comanche warrior," he insisted, cutting of Ty's words.

"The hell you are! Those heathen bastards killed our father, and took you captive. You had to become one of them to survive, I understand that, but not any longer. You're a white man, and it's time you dressed like one."

Bright Sky glared at him in stony denial. Closing his eyes, he said, "Leave me, I am tired."

His hands clenched in impotent fists, Ty stared at his brother for several seconds. He finally spun around and left the room, silently giving vent to his temper. *Damn him, damn him to hell. When's he going to realize he's not a Comanche?*

Ty hesitated outside the door to the hospital room, wishing he hadn't let Sassy talk him into coming back. After that morning's fiasco, he wasn't altogether sure he could face his brother again. Though he knew Sassy was right—he and Dayne were brothers and had to settle their differences—shedding twenty years of hate wouldn't be easy, and accepting the fact that Dayne considered himself a Comanche seemed damn near impossible.

"Come on, you promised," she said, grasping his arm and pushing him toward the door.

"You'll come with me?"

Hiding her smile at his childish tone, she said, "I told you I would. Now go on in. I'll be right behind you."

Ty opened the door and took a cautious step inside.

A young woman was helping his brother with a bowl of what looked like broth. "Should we come back?"

The woman turned her attention away from her patient, and smiled. "No, Bright Sky is finished."

Ty's back stiffened, but he held his tongue.

After the woman excused herself and left the room, Ty cleared his throat and approached the bed. "I'd like you to meet my wife." Pulling her alongside him, he said, "Sassy, this is my brother, Dayne." Seeing the look on his brother's face, he quickly added, "I mean Bright Sky." Saying the Comanche name really rubbed him the wrong way, but if it meant a possible reconciliation with his brother he would use it—this once.

Approaching the bed, Sassy's eyes widened at her first view of the man lying on the bed. Other than his much longer hair and blue eyes, the similarity in looks between the Beaumont brothers was remarkable. Smiling, she held out her hand. "Pleased to meet you, Bright Sky. I hope you're feeling better."

He shook the hand of the white woman he'd seen with Ty so many times, surprised at her firm grip. "I am much better." In spite of his aversion to whites, he found himself returning the lavender-eyed woman's smile. Before he could halt the words, he said, "You have eyes the color of wildflowers. Bluebonnets, I think your people call them."

Sassy's smile widened. "Thank you, that's very kind." Unsure of how she could help heal the breach between Ty and Bright Sky, she tried to keep the conversation on safe ground. When the topic of the Comanche came up, she decided it would be best to clear the air. "Have you lived with the Comanche ever since you were taken from the Circle B?"

"Yes, until five years ago, when I left the reservation."

"Why did you leave?"

"Because they are my people, I went with the others in my band when the white man forced us onto a reservation, even though I did not believe the promises we were given. Living conditions were not fit for the lowest of creatures. We kept asking for what was promised us, but it did no good. Once again the white man lied to the People. We were supposed to have plenty of food and medicine, yet many went to bed with empty stomachs or sick with diseases we did not know how to cure. Even when my people started dying from hunger and sickness, nothing was done to help us. When my parents and my wife became ill with one of the white man's diseases, I actually begged for someone to save my family. They spit in my face."

Bright Sky took a deep shuddering breath, and slowly unclenched his fists. "They died because of the white man's lies. I could not stand being near the place where I buried Singing Wind, so I left the reservation."

"If you hate us white men so much," Ty said, "why did you risk your life to jump in front of me?"

Bright Sky shifted uneasily on the bed. To the Comanche, visions were very personal and rarely discussed. But since this was the man his guardian spirit had instructed him to find and protect, and the vision had already come true, he saw no harm in revealing the truth. "Even before I left the reservation, I started having visions about helping a man."

"Visions?" Sassy asked. "Do you mean dreams?"

"No, not dreams. Visions come to me while I'm awake, after I prepare myself and call to my guardian spirit, the wolf. I kept having the same vision: I was to help a man, a white man, who my guardian spirit said would one day be my brother."

"My God," Sassy whispered. "It came true."

"Of course," Bright Sky declared reverently. "All visions, even those which do not return over and over, come true in one way or another. Comanche guardian spirits do not speak false."

"How did you know where to find me?" Ty asked.

"The Wolf Spirit knew where to look. The last vision I had told me to go to Laredo. I found you and followed you here."

"Let me get this straight. The only reason you looked for me, your real brother, was because a spirit told you to?"

"I did not know I had a white brother. It was as I told you, my Comanche parents told me I had no white family."

Laying her hand on Ty's arm, Sassy tried to defuse the

anger she sensed stirring inside him. "Why would he believe any differently? You told me how he saw your ranch destroyed and your father killed. That's reason enough to think no one survived that day. If you'd been in his place, would you have believed otherwise?"

After a moment he grudgingly said, "No, I guess not."

"Good. I'll leave you two alone for a few minutes, so you can talk." At Ty's panicked look, she whispered, "You'll be fine. I won't be gone long."

Sassy left Bright Sky's room and immediately went in search of Kit Dancer. She found him struggling to pull on a shirt, his progress impeded by the heavy bandage on the upper left side of his chest.

"Can I help?"

Kit's head snapped up, the empty shirtsleeve dangling behind him. His eyes narrowed when Sassy Beaumont entered the room. "What do you want? A chance to put another lump on my head?"

Sassy started at his words. What was he talking about? Her eyes widened when she realized he was the one she'd whacked over the head with a chair in Laredo. Moving toward him, she said, "No, I—" Her words died when she got a close look at Kit Dancer. He wasn't at all what she expected. When Ty said the man who'd tried to shoot him was a bounty hunter, she'd pictured an ill-kempt, homely-as-a-hedgehog reprobate. This man didn't fit her preconceived image in the least.

Deep-set beneath thick brows, his very pale blue eyes were extremely striking against his dark complexion. Though his black hair was unfashionably long and his jaw shadowed with several days of stubble, he was a very handsome man. Even the scar on the right side of his face didn't detract from his good looks.

She cleared her throat, then said, "I came to tell you

393

to leave my husband alone. His name has been cleared, and I want you to stay away from him."

Kit's eyes crinkled with amusement. "You do, do you? And I'll bet you had a hand in getting his name cleared."

"Yes, as a matter of fact, I did. How Ty's name got cleared isn't important. I just want you to—"

He held up a hand to stop her. "Don't worry. The chief of police already told me the murder charge against your husband has been dropped. I have no reason to bother him any longer."

Sassy studied him silently for a moment, then said, "Ty said the two of you met once before?"

He sighed and laid back down on the bed. "Yeah. It was about five years ago. I was sheriff in a little town near Abilene, and Beaumont came through with a prisoner. He asked to leave the man in my jail, until he could send someone to pick him up. It's no wonder he didn't remember me." He ran the tip of a finger over the scar. "I've changed a lot since then."

Something in his voice made Sassy ask, "Why did you give up the law and become a bounty hunter?"

His eyes darkened with an intense inner pain. "Like a fool, I didn't pay attention to a man's threats, and it ended up costing me everything important in my life." He fell silent, lost in his memories. At last he said, "Anyway, I turned in my badge and took up bounty hunting."

Puzzled by his story, which left more unanswered questions than it explained, she sensed his reluctance to talk more on the subject. He blamed himself for a devastating incident in his past, had changed his profession to forget, but was obviously still haunted by whatever had caused his pain. The irritation she'd felt when she decided to confront Kit slipped away.

"Now that I know you won't be looking for Ty, I have to be going."

"No, ma'am, I won't be looking for him or anyone else with a price on their head. I'm sick of bounty hunting. It's time I changed my line of work." Pointing to his bandage, he flashed her a smile. "Something a little less dangerous." In a low voice he added, "I think I'll head back to El Paso."

Returning his smile, Sassy helped him with his shirt, then bid him good day, and left to collect her husband.

Relieved to see Ty and his brother hadn't harmed each other in her absence, she said, "Come on, Ty, we should leave Bright Sky to get some rest."

As they walked down Market Street after leaving St. Mary's, Ty remained silent, merely grunting in response to the conversation Sassy tried to carry on. At last she said, "I know it goes against your grain to care about someone who is what you hate most, but you can't let your hatred ruin the chance to reconcile with your brother. You've already lost twenty years. You may not get another chance to know Bright Sky."

Ty stopped abruptly and turned to face her. "His name is Dayne, not that damn Comanche mumbo jumbo."

"To you he's Dayne," she replied, jabbing his chest with one finger. "He thinks of himself as Bright Sky. Perhaps some day he'll take back the name your parents gave him, but in the meantime you should accept him for what he is, a man who thought he lost his white family, then years later his Comanche family as well. That's a lot of pain for any man to withstand. Remember how you first reacted to Juan, and I told you his mixed blood wasn't his fault?"

"Yes, I remember, and I agree Juan wasn't to blame. My brother is different. He doesn't have one drop of Indian blood in his veins," he answered curtly.

"That's true. He may not be Comanche by blood, but he believes he is, because of the life he had to live. Under the circumstances it isn't his fault he thinks that way, anymore than it's Juan's fault his grandfather was Comanche."

Ty drew in a deep breath, then exhaled slowly. "I know, but that won't make it any easier to accept the fact that my only brother believes he's an Indian." He was silent for a moment, then said, "What really sticks in my craw is Dayne actually choosing to continue living like a Comanche. He left the reservation five years ago, yet he still calls himself Bright Sky, wears his hair in braids, and practices some kind of nonsensical religion, where he says he has visions that predict the future."

"Give him time," she said softly. "He may never completely forget his Indian life, or never entirely give up some of their ways. But he's still your brother, and like I told you before, someday he may change his mind and choose to live like a white man."

Looping her arm through his, Sassy started walking again. "And you're right, it won't be easy, but if you want him in your life, you'll have to come to terms with it. Would you rather he just walked out of your life, never to be seen again?"

"No. It'll be damn hard, but I'll try to accept him, so he'll agree to come to the Circle B." A smile suddenly appeared on his stoic face. Momma would tan my britches, if she learned I found out her oldest son is alive and let him slip away before bringing him to the ranch."

Sassy chuckled. "I'd help her."

Ty looked down at his wife, his eyes no longer clouded

with uncertainty, but sparkling with mischief. "Would you now?"

She stuck her chin out in defiance. "You bet."

Laughing with delight, Ty planted a quick kiss on her mouth. "Let's find a restaurant and get something to eat. I'm starved, how about you?"

Looking up into his dark eyes and the face she loved so much, her pulse quickened, her belly tightened. Although referring to a very different kind of hunger, she whispered, "Yes, I'm hungry, too."

Thirty-three

After a leisurely lunch, Sassy and Ty strolled back to their hotel and entered the front door arm in arm.

As the Beaumonts crossed the lobby, Teddy rose to greet them. "Good afternoon, I was hoping you'd return before I had to leave. I'm taking the three o'clock train, and I didn't want to miss the chance to tell you goodbye."

Sassy blinked in surprise, then smiled. "I'm glad you waited." Giving her a fierce hug, she said, "Where are you headed?"

"I'm going back to New Orleans for a little while, then after that . . ." Teddy shrugged. "I want you to know it's been great fun getting to know you, Sassy. You keep this husband of yours in line," she said with a wink.

"Thanks, and I . . . um . . . I'll try," she murmured.

Wondering at the pained look on Sassy's face, Teddy's eyebrows pulled together. She shifted her gaze to Ty. Was he the reason for his wife's strange behavior? The flush creeping up his cheeks answered her unspoken question. Pressing her lips together in displeasure, she gave him a chastising scowl.

Running a finger inside his suddenly tight collar, he said, "Have a safe trip, Teddy."

"I will. Now give me a hug, I have to be leaving."

As Ty pulled her against him, Teddy whispered near his ear, "You better tell her, you rascal."

Setting her away from him, he whispered his response. "Count on it."

Teddy nodded with satisfaction, then straightened the jacket of her traveling suit.

"If you ever get back to Waco, you know where to find me. You're always welcome on the Circle B."

Teddy nodded again, then after another round of good-byes, she left the hotel.

Sassy watched Teddy until she disappeared through the hotel door, then sighed, a pensive look on her face.

Ty wondered at his wife's quiet mood, but didn't mention it as he escorted her to their room. Once inside the suite, he prowled the rooms restlessly. "I think I'll go back to the hospital. The doctor said Dayne might be able to leave by this evening, and I don't want to miss him."

"Do you want me to go with you?"

"No, I'd rather go by myself, if you don't mind."

"Of course not. You should have some time alone with him. Give him my best, will you? And tell him I hope to see him again soon."

Ty paced the infirmary hall impatiently. The doctor was in Dayne's room changing the dressing on his wound, so Ty had to wait to talk to his brother. He'd thought a lot about what Sassy said about Dayne during lunch, and on the trip back to St. Mary's. A smile played across his mouth. His wife sure was something. No matter the situation, she had the uncanny ability to know exactly what to say. Thinking of Sassy made him recall Teddy's words.

He *had* planned to tell Sassy he loved her, but the opportune moment hadn't presented itself, not with his near-miss with Kit Dancer, and the more shocking discovery of his brother.

When the doctor told him he could see the patient, Ty made himself two promises: he would try to square things with his brother, and he would make his feelings known to Sassy as soon as possible.

Satisfied with his decision, he pushed open the door to his brother's room.

Bright Sky sat on the edge of the bed, again dressed in his buckskin shirt and pants. As he bent over to pull on his moccasins, his long thick braids swung back and forth across his chest, the eagle feather tied in one of the plaits brushing his shoulder.

"Are you leaving?" Ty asked from the doorway.

Bright Sky's head snapped up, revealing only a small bandage on the left side of his head. He nodded, then went back to his task.

"I've been doing a lot of thinking, and I've decided I was wrong. I came back to apologize. I'm sorry about the things I said to you."

When Bright Sky remained silent, he said, "I know it doesn't make it right, but the hatred I've felt all these years toward Indians, especially the Comanche, came from the pain and helplessness of a six-year-old boy losing his brother and his dad. It isn't your fault you were taken from our ranch and thrust into an entirely different way of life. What's important now is the second chance we've been given to get to know each other, and hopefully be a family again."

Bright Sky stared at him coolly for several long minutes. He had also done a lot of thinking since this man's visit that morning. "You want to bury your hate of the

Comanche, because I did not die at their hands as you believed, is that not so?"

"I can't deny I'm happy you weren't killed. After our talk this morning, I've come to realize I had some pretty cockeyed notions about the Comanche, especially how they treated their captives. Although I still have a lot to learn, I want you to know my feelings toward the Comanche actually started changing before I found you. My wife and a little boy named Juan started chipping away at my hatred awhile back. They made me see how I'd misdirected my hate, wrongly blaming those who had nothing to do with what happened twenty years ago. I was also wrong for blaming you, and I'm sorry."

After another long silence, Bright Sky said, "I accept your apology. I, too, am sorry. We have both hated the other's people, because we lost members of our families. Now we must try to put those feelings aside."

Ty nodded, then said, "Where are you going?"

"Far to the north."

Although he wanted to ask for a more specific location, Ty resisted the urge for fear his brother would accuse him of prying. Instead he said, "You'd be welcome on the Circle B."

"You wouldn't care that I'm dressed like a savage?" In spite of the apology he'd just tendered, Bright Sky couldn't stop the bitter words.

Ty's cheeks burned at having his words thrown back at him. "No, I wouldn't care. You're my brother, and I want you to come home." Seeing the look on Bright Sky's face, he quickly added, "That wasn't meant as an order. And I didn't mean I expect you to come back to the ranch permanently. Of course, I'd like it if you did, but that isn't a condition of your coming to the Circle

B. You can visit for as long as you want, whenever you want. I'll never pressure you to stay on, I swear."

Bright Sky jumped off the bed, landing on his feet like a giant cat. "Our mother is in good health?"

"Yes, she's fine. She works too hard on the ranch, but she won't slow down for anyone. I'm hoping I can convince her to take it easy after Sassy and I get back, and take over running the place."

"The Circle B is on the Brazos, on a bend in the river upstream from Waco?"

"Yes," Ty responded, pleased he remembered the spot their father had selected for his ranch. When his brother said no more, he couldn't help prompting, "Will you visit us?"

"I have something to take care of first, then I will come."

Ty crossed the room, stopping in front of Bright Sky. "I'm not trying to pin you down, but I'd like to tell Momma when she might expect you."

"A few weeks, perhaps a month."

Realizing he wasn't going to get more of a commitment, Ty nodded. "Great, I'll tell her."

When his brother started to move past him, Ty said, "Bright Sky, I—I'm glad we found each other." He held out his hand, hoping this last overture to mend their differences would be accepted.

Bright Sky reached out and grasped the hand of his brother in the way of the white man.

Overcome by the moment, Ty pulled him into a fierce bear hug. When he stepped back, the depth of emotion clogging his throat and stinging his eyes surprised him.

"I will see you soon, my brother," Bright Sky said, then turned toward the door.

Ty swallowed hard. "Godspeed, Bright Sky," he whis-

402

pered in a husky voice. Although he wanted to follow
him, Ty forced himself to wait several minutes before
leaving. He didn't want to risk shattering the progress
they'd just made by letting Bright Sky think he didn't
trust him.

On the way back to the hotel, Ty had the carriage
driver stop at the train depot. There was no longer any
reason to stay in Galveston. A few minutes later, tickets
in his pocket, he ordered the driver to continue to the
Old Chicago House.

Sassy tried to keep busy during Ty's absence, but in a
rented hotel suite, there was little to occupy her time.
She opened a book and tried to read. After reading the
same paragraph four times, she finally threw the book
down in disgust. Playing solitaire ended when she
couldn't concentrate on the cards with any better results.
Since she lacked the usual female skill at sewing or em-
broidery, she finally settled for taking a nap to pass the
time.

Unfortunately, sleep didn't come, and having nothing
else to divert her mind's wanderings her thoughts were
fraught with all sorts of wild imaginings. When she heard
the door to the suite open, it was both a great relief and
a chilling moment of apprehension. She'd decided to let
him speak first, but if he didn't give her some answers,
she was determined to force them out of him if necessary.

"Hello, darlin'," he called from the sitting room.
"Sassy? Oh, there you are," he said, entering the bedroom. "Are you feeling all right?"

"Yes, I'm fine," she replied, sitting up and scooting
back against the headboard. "How did it go with Bright
Sky?"

A broad smile appeared on his face. "I think it went pretty well. Mind you, we still have a long ways to go, but we agreed to put aside the hate that's been eating at both of us all these years, and get on with our lives. The best news is he also agreed to come to the Circle B."

"That's wonderful. Your mother will be so glad to see him."

"I can't wait to tell her. Which reminds me, I went to the depot after I left the hospital, and bought two tickets to Waco."

Sassy's heart dropped to her toes. She closed her eyes against the sudden pain, dismal thoughts swirling in her head. *He bought two tickets, not three. He plans to take Bright Sky to the Circle B, not me. You should have known better than trying to be something you're not. You'll never be lady enough to keep a man.* Determined to get the painful scene over with as quickly as possible, she opened her eyes and slid off the mattress.

Noticing the lack of color in her face, Ty reached out to grab her arm. "Sassy, what is it? You're looking awful peaked."

Twisting out of his grasp, she moved across the room to the dresser. She jerked open a drawer and started pulling out her clothes. "I'll pack my bags and be out of here as soon as possible."

"Pack your—What the hell are you talking about?"

She kept her back to him, so he wouldn't see the depth of her pain. "I know you don't want me as your wife. You made that clear often enough on this trip. Now that your name has been cleared, there's no need to keep up the ruse of a happily married couple. So I'll save you the trouble of having to ask me to leave, by going on my own."

"Why would I ask you to leave? I love you."

Dropping the clothes back into the drawer, she turned to face him. "What did you say?"

"I said, why would—"

"No, not that. The last part."

"The part where I said I love you?"

"Yes, that part."

"I do, you know."

Sassy stared at him for several long moments, studying his face for some sort of trick. She saw nothing to indicate he was anything but sincere. Still, she wasn't convinced. "When did this happen?"

"Remember the first time you told me you loved me?"

Her brow furrowed with confusion, she nodded.

"Well, just like you told me, I fell in love with you the first day I saw you, too. Except I was so blinded with anger and frustration at Teddy, I didn't realize it for a while."

Her eyes squinting with suspicion, she said, "Are you telling me it was love at first sight?"

A broad grin on his face, he nodded.

Straightening her back and lifting her chin, she slowly moved closer. "To my recollection, the first time I said I loved you, you made fun of me when I said it was love at first sight."

With every step she took toward him, he retreated a step until the backs of his legs bumped into the side of the bed. "I know, and—"

"And now you have the balls to tell me the same damn thing." She gave his chest a hard nudge with her fingers. He lost his balance and sat down on the bed with a bouncing jolt. "If that ain't a case of the pot calling the kettle black, I sure don't know what is!"

Ty would have laughed at her scandalous outburst, but he saw the dangerous gleam in her eyes and thought better of stirring her temper any further. He stared up at her, thinking that her reaction to his declaration of love didn't resemble the scene he'd imagined in the slightest. He'd expected her to squeal with joy, not give him a tongue-lashing. On second thought, wasn't that one of the things he loved most about her, her unpredictability?

He cleared his throat to cover another laugh. "Look, darlin', I shouldn't have laughed at you."

She stared at him, her lips still pressed together in anger, her eyes shooting fire.

"The truth is, Sassy, I never did believe in love at first sight until I met you. Hell, before I met you, I'd never even been in love." At his confession, something flickered in her eyes, yet her posture remained stiff and unyielding. "Forgive me?"

When she didn't answer, he reached for her hands, hoping to erase the last of her anger. She shook off his grip. He sighed. "Now what?"

"How could you?" she ranted, turning away from the bed, her temper once more at full steam.

"How could I what?"

Pacing the bedroom, she said, "How could you go on letting me think you were going to divorce me if Teddy didn't clear your name, when all the time you loved me?"

In spite of her possible retaliation, he could no longer hold back his amusement. Chuckling, he said, "So that's what has you so riled up." At her furious glare, he held up a hand in submission. "Okay, okay. I did seriously consider divorce after I realized I loved you, but only because I thought you didn't deserve a wanted man for a husband."

"Not even when you knew I loved you?"

"I know it doesn't make any sense, but no, not even then. I had some twisted idea you'd be better off without

406

me. That was my plan, but I don't think I could have gone through with it." Grasping her hand when she passed near the bed, he pulled her down onto his lap. With one hand under her chin, he tilted her face up, forcing her to meet his gaze. "I couldn't have given you up. I love you too much, wildcat. I'm sorry I let you think otherwise."

He stared into her eyes, pleased to see the last remnants of anger and pain fade, as his words sank in. Yet, he saw a question there as well. "Is there something else bothering you?"

"You told Teddy 'you know where to find me,' not *us*. That doesn't sound like you wanted me with you."

"I plead guilty. We haven't been married all that long, and by force of habit I said me. I promise to do better. Is there anything else?"

"What about the tickets?"

"Tickets?"

"You said Bright Sky agreed to visit the Circle B, but you only bought two tickets."

"Guilty again. I didn't make myself clear. Bright Sky said he'd visit the ranch, but not right away. He has something he has to do first and will come to Waco in a few weeks. I'm sorry I didn't tell you the tickets are for us."

When she didn't say anything, he ran the tips of his fingers across one cheek, then along her jaw. "I said I was sorry, won't you forgive me?"

As his touch moved lower to glide down her neck, a shiver ran up her spine. Her flesh tingled with anticipation. "Well, I don't know," she whispered in an unsteady voice.

"Please, darlin'. How can I earn your forgiveness? I'm willing to do anything."

"Anything?"

"Yes. Just name it." His voice had taken on a raspy edge, the nearness of his wife bringing an instant arousal.

She leaned closer, her mouth hovering just above his. Her tongue darted out and touched the corner of his mouth, then gently lapped at his lips. "Kiss me," she murmured against his mouth.

With a soft growl he captured her lips with his, eager to do her bidding. As she opened her mouth and accepted his probing tongue, a groan vibrated in his chest. Wrapping his arms around her, he tried to pull her tighter against him.

Wrenching out of his embrace, she ended the kiss and slipped off his lap. She knelt in front of him and reached for the buttons of his shirt, a secret smile playing about her mouth. He cocked an eyebrow at her. "Now what, wildcat?"

"First we get undressed, then I'll show you," she answered in a silky whisper.

Trying to hide his grin, but not succeeding, his hands joined hers in a frenzied effort to remove their clothes.

Frustrated with the uncooperative buttons on his shirt, Sassy grabbed the fabric and gave it a fierce yank, sending the buttons flying. She pushed the shirt off his shoulders and sucked in her breath at the sight of his muscled, hair-covered chest. With a low moan, she leaned forward to touch her lips to the golden curls.

"I love you, Sassy," he murmured against the top of her head.

Rocking back on her heels, she met his gaze. "I love you, too." She shook a finger at him in gentle rebuke. "But don't think sweet words of love are going to put you back in my good graces. You still have to earn my forgiveness."

He bit the inside of his mouth to halt a chuckle. "I

would never be so presumptuous as to assume I could make you forget the matter at hand, by plying you with love—"

She pressed her fingers to his mouth. "Hush. That's enough talk. Better save your strength, because you're going to need it," she said in a throaty whisper. "You've got a lot more to do before I forgive you. A whole lot more."

Epilogue

Ty stilled his hand on the mare's neck.

"Uh, oh." There was no mistaking the sound of a shell being racked into a rifle's chamber.

"Move away from my horse, mister. And keep your hands where I can see them, unless you've got a real hankerin' to be gelded."

Ah, a woman! A smile teasing his lips, he dropped his hand from the pregnant belly of Blarney. She had been bred to his prize stallion, and was due to foal any day.

Moving slowly, Ty stepped away from the mare. "Take it easy, ma'am." He kept his voice calm, while gradually turning around. When his gaze met the woman holding a Winchester aimed at the floor, a full grin creased his face.

Standing just inside the door of the Circle B's main horse barn, legs widespread, dark hair tumbling around her shoulders in wild disarray, stood Sassy.

His physical reaction to her was as strong as the first time they'd played out this scene. Even the birth of their first child four months earlier hadn't diminished his desire for her. More rounded, a little fuller in the most

410

enjoyable places, she was still the most desirable woman he'd ever known.

His eyes twinkling with mirth, he gave her a bold wink. "Now, darlin', I really don't think you'd geld me. Not when it would mean you could no longer scream your pleasure, while I'm deep inside—"

"Hush," Sassy interrupted, moving closer. Her eyes alight with mischief, cheeks flushed with the truth of his words, she said, "You're right. I wouldn't cut off my *nose,* so to speak, to spite my face."

Ty's deep rumble of laughter filled the barn. "I'm glad you see it that way, wife."

Relieving her of the Winchester, he turned serious again. "We don't need this, darlin'. It'll just get in the way."

"In the way?" she asked, one brow arched in question.

"Yeah, since that brother of mine left yesterday, your family started for San Antonio this morning, and Kitty headed back to her dress shop in Waco an hour ago, that leaves just you and me to find something to do this afternoon."

"Your mother's still here," she murmured in a soft voice.

His gaze moved lovingly over her face, noticing how the color of her eyes had already deepened to purple, a sure sign her desire had flared to life.

"Yeah, I know, smarty pants. She lives here. Don't worry about Momma. You know how much she loves her grandson. She won't leave him alone. No more excuses. Now, come here."

As if a swath of silk had been pulled across her skin, his voice sent a ripple of pleasure racing up her spine. Stepping closer, she raised her gaze to met his intense stare. "I'm here, now what?" she asked in a husky whisper.

After giving her a quick, hard kiss, Ty grasped one o her hands and pulled her toward the ladder to the loft.

"Up ya go," he said, giving her a gentle push of encouragement.

As she glanced at her husband over her shoulder, her smile flashed white in the dim interior of the barn. "And what might we be doing in the hayloft in the full light o' day?" she asked in her best Irish accent.

He returned her smile, then gave her another shove "I want to make love to you in the hay. Just like the first time," he murmured next to her ear.

Climbing the ladder, her heart beat a little faster in anticipation. Since arriving on the Circle B fifteen months earlier, she'd found married life much to her liking. They still butted heads on occasion, since she couldn't always control her temper. By mutual agreement, when they did argue, they never stayed angry for long. Instead, they used the energy their heated exchanges generated for a much more enjoyable purpose making long, sweet love.

When she reached the top of the ladder, Sassy's smile widened. A blanket lay spread out on a pile of hay.

"How long have you been planning this?" she asked when he stepped off the ladder onto the loft.

"Ever since my brother, your family, and Kitty and her new beau all showed up here at once," he replied moving closer and drawing her against his chest. Although he'd enjoyed their house full of company, he was thankful to have his wife alone again at last.

"Didn't Kitty look happy?" she remarked, trying to ignore Ty's hands roaming up and down her back. "I told her she'd find a man who'd love her regardless of her past, and it's obvious Joe's crazy about her. Don't you agree?"

"Uh-huh," he murmured against her hair.

"Juan looks like he's grown a foot since the last time we saw him. I'm so glad Papa and Sheena brought him along. He seems real happy with Charlie Two Feathers, don't you think?"

"Hmm, you smell delicious." His tongue flicked out to explore the inside of her ear, making her shiver with pleasure.

"Has it really been six months since we went to Teddy's wedding?"

"Yup," he replied, his lips moving down the tender skin of her neck.

"Nathan nearly busted his buttons with pride when Teddy came down the aisle. She looked so beautiful." Her mouth puckered into a pout. "I was bigger than a cow. Seven months pregnant, and I couldn't get closer than an arm's length to you when we danced."

"You were beautiful, even if, to use your words, you were bigger than a cow," he whispered while his lips nibbled the sensitive spot where her shoulder and neck joined.

His compliment plus the moist heat of his mouth on her flesh turned her pout into a dazzling smile.

"I really like Brodie's new girlfriend, don't you?"

He didn't respond. He was too busy opening her dress and pushing it aside to reveal one creamy breast.

"Ty?"

"You talk too much, darlin'."

"Well, I wouldn't want you to take me for granted. You can't just spread a blanket in a hayloft, and expect me to fall at your feet." She tried to sound prim and proper and extremely put out. She failed miserably.

413

Laughter bubbled up in her throat before she could stop it, then escaped to ring off the barn's rafters.

He chuckled in response, thoroughly enjoying their lighthearted exchange. "I'd never take you for granted, wildcat. I just know what you like. Now hush, I've got some ideas on how to spend our time."

"Oh?"

"Yes. Get out of that dress, and I'll show you," he ordered in mock gruffness.

Her fingers clumsy with anticipation, she stripped off her clothes and stretched out on the blanket. Her oohs and ahs of delight soon followed.

It wasn't long before male sighs of pleasure joined hers, since she had an idea or two of her own on how to pass the afternoon.

WHAT'S LOVE GOT TO DO WITH IT?

Everything . . . Just ask Kathleen Drymon . . . and Zebra Books

CASTAWAY ANGEL	*(3569-1, $4.50/$5.50)*
GENTLE SAVAGE	*(3888-7, $4.50/$5.50)*
MIDNIGHT BRIDE	*(3265-X, $4.50/$5.50)*
VELVET SAVAGE	*(3886-0, $4.50/$5.50)*
TEXAS BLOSSOM	*(3887-9, $4.50/$5.50)*
WARRIOR OF THE SUN	*(3924-7, $4.99/$5.99)*

Available wherever paperbacks are sold, or order direct from the Publisher. Send cover price plus 50¢ per copy for mailing and handling to Penguin USA, P.O. Box 999, c/o Dept. 17109, Bergenfield, NJ 07621.Residents of New York and Tennessee must include sales tax. DO NOT SEND CASH.